LUCKY ENOUGH

LUCKY ENOUGH

LUCKY O'TOOLE VEGAS ADVENTURE: BOOK 11

DEBORAH COONTS

Chestnut
Street
Press

Published by Chestnut Street Press

eBook ISBN: 978-1-944831-02-8
Paperback ISBN: 978-1-944831-01-1
Hardcover ISBN: 978-1-944831-00-4
Audiobook ISBN: 978-1-944831-04-2
Large Print ISBN: 978-1-944831-03-5

Cover design by Streetlight Graphics
(www.streetlightgraphics.com)

Formatting by Kate Tilton's Author Services, LLC
(www.katetilton.com)

CHAPTER ONE

"*A*LMOST HOME, miss." The First Officer peeked his head through the open doorway of the small office off the largest bedroom in the back of the plane. "I'll need you up front and belted in for landing."

"Thank you." I shut down the computer and my efforts to try to catch up on what had been going on in Vegas while I'd been gone. My name is Lucky O'Toole and for the last two weeks or more I'd been ignoring my responsibilities as the vice president of customer relations for the Babylon Group, the owner of multiple properties in Vegas and one of the primo Strip properties. Not that a couple of hours over the Pacific would get me up to speed, but it might help me hit the ground running.

I reached to flip off the satellite television showing a live feed of the local news. The face on the screen stopped me. My best friend, Flash Gordon, newshound extraordinaire, reporting from a local party—not her usual beat. As the sun was out, it looked like the party was earlier this afternoon. I glanced at my watch.

Just after midnight.

In the feed, Flash interviewed another buddy of mine Jordan

Marsh, Hollywood heartthrob. They were promoting the Concours d'Elegance, a fancy car party starting soon, so I didn't bother with the sound. Next to Jordan, attempting to squeeze into a sliver of importance, bobbed a man I didn't know—tall, thin, graying temples and a smile that would have most smart men grabbing their wives and daughters. There was one in every crowd. I shook my head and snapped off the TV. That was Vegas right there: fancy cars, celebrity cachet, and a regular Joe soaking it up for the weekend, perhaps pretending an importance he didn't have.

The pilots pulled back power and started our descent as I buckled in.

The lights of Las Vegas spread across the valley below—thousands of pinpoints in the desert darkness. At ten thousand feet, the plane skimmed over the Sunrise Mountains then started the drop to final approach—the end of a very long trip. Along the way, I'd left broken hearts, numerous bodies, and perhaps some sanity in my wake.

It struck me that a few short weeks ago, I'd started out heading west and had kept going until I'd come full circle.

Home again.

Odd when the beginning can be the end. Sort of like that old joke: when do you leave home to get home? Guess my life resembled a game of baseball.

Hadn't struck out yet, but I couldn't shake the feeling that the damage I'd left behind wasn't going to stay in my rearview.

The plane that now carried me home, one of the Babylon's G650s, certainly had made a clean getaway all the easier. I thought I'd left each country with the approval and most likely the enthusiasm of the local constabularies, but I wasn't entirely sure. At some point it would be my luck to land on the wrong side of a modern-day Javert. Despite the body count, there'd been only one near fatality on the side of truth, justice and all of that—one of the fractured hearts was mine.

Thankfully, my body had survived. Most of the time I was grateful for that.

I pressed my nose to the window as the pilot banked the plane lining up on final approach. Landing to the north put the Strip on the left side of the plane. The lights beckoned with a false promise of fun. Oh, don't get me wrong; for most who came here, the city delivered.

But not for me.

As the Chief Problem Solver of the Babylon Group (my business card reads Vice President of Customer Relations, but let's be real), it was my job to keep the Vegas magic burning bright for all who stepped across the threshold of one of our properties. Consequently, I'd seen behind the curtain. And once you see the levers and gears, the magic isn't quite as…magical.

For me, Vegas was not a holiday, not one last toot with my BFFs before the impending stranglehold of marriage, nor did it provide even a simple weekend fantasy to offset the drag of real life.

No. Vegas *was* my real life.

My home.

And it was no fantasy.

Like everybody else, I lived with my problems lurking with the dust bunnies under the pieces of large furniture and whispering from the shadows. But unlike everyone else, I didn't have Vegas in which to offload them, not even for the weekend.

I leaned back in my seat and closed my eyes contemplating exactly where to begin my reentry, how to solve a few of the looming problems, but I hadn't a clue. I'd left a beautiful young girl killed on my watch in London, a broken engagement in Paris, and a slew of bodies and unanswered questions in Bordeaux. I'd delivered a Hong Kong financier on the run from some very scary Triad enforcers to Monte Carlo with only the slimmest chance to right a wrong and save his own hide. But those paled in the light of my worst problem. My father, the head and heart of the Babylon Group, still struggled to recover from a bullet to the chest. My mother couldn't...or wouldn't... tell me how sick he really was.

If he died it would change everything.

Between you and me, I found adulting to be a cruel hoax perpetrated on happy children. I once was a happy child...I think. But that little slice of Norman Rockwell (the *only* slice of Norman Rockwell in my childhood) was so far in my rearview it had vanished in the haze.

"Glad to be back?" A familiar voice knifed through my little bit of dirty laundry airing. Detective Romeo.

For a moment I'd forgotten about him—my personal Sir Galahad who had ridden to my rescue. (His take. I let him have the fantasy.) He'd arrived in Paris as I touched a match to the fuse and fireworks lit the sky. He'd stayed to help me pick up the pieces, then caught a ride home...via Monte Carlo.

While he was my secret weapon in the Las Vegas Metropolitan Police Department—Metro to us locals—he was just a kid. Although, tonight, he looked way more world-weary than his years would allow. In fact, he looked as tired as I felt, despite the now mashed lei around his neck, the white Plumeria blossoms starting to brown—we'd stopped for fuel in Hawaii and had done the whole customs and island thing. At the time, I'd resented the time it had taken but was grateful now we'd done it.

Romeo blinked at me, clearly expecting some kind of response—I couldn't remember to what. Dark circles underslung his red eyes. The hint of worry lines bracketed his mouth and radiated from the corners of his eyes. Somewhere over Indonesia he'd stopped worrying about straightening his tie or combing his hair. The flag of a cowlick sprung from the crown of his head.

I resisted the urge to brush it flat.

A hint of sympathy lit the blue of his eyes, faded by lack of sleep. "You left a lot of shit back there. Home must feel good." His attempt to make me feel better was appreciated but fell short of the mark. Not his fault. For some reason I wasn't feeling the homecoming joy.

Must home feel good? Did it? Jet lagged and heartbroken, and more than a little panicked, I didn't have an answer for him. In fact, I didn't have any answers period—heck of a place for a professional problem solver. The only answer I could give him was a shrug.

As the wheels kissed the runway, he turned to look at the Strip out the window that still held my nose print. "Pretty amazing, isn't it?" He was still young enough to be awestruck.

"One constant in a sea of change." Too tired to muster a grin at the irony—if Vegas stood for anything it was change, even if only for a weekend—I pulled my phone out of my bag and powered it up. A few seconds of silence, no more, and texts pinged like the ringing of a come-to-dinner bell but without eliciting the same salivating anticipation.

Romeo and I both looked at the offending device.

"Damn," he said. "You must be important." His smile told me he thought so.

I wasn't so sure. "Being the one who stops the proverbial buck makes me popular, but I'm not so sure about important."

Miss P, the head of customer relations for the Babylon Casino Hotel, our most exquisite, over-the-top Strip property and my right-hand man, caught me before I had a chance to begin to tackle the texts. I answered her call on the second ring. "Have you been bugging the FAA again?"

"I have a copy of your flight plan."

One more bit of proof that I could indeed run but not hide. "Along with a detailed transcript of my last visit to my therapist."

"You don't have a therapist."

"An oversight soon to be corrected."

"Riiiight." She knew me well. Whining was my go-to when pressure mounted. Sharing my innermost thoughts with a stranger didn't promise the same immediate gratification. "Can we talk now, without the whine?"

"Oh, if you insist." As the plane slowed to a taxi, Romeo pushed himself up and disappeared toward the back. I took his place at the window, working to draw energy from the wattage outside. I'd been told the Strip could be seen from a galaxy far, far, away. As I blinked against its brightness, I believed it. "Whatcha got?" The lure of a problem that perhaps I could actually solve tickled me. The old happy-to-be-home tingle shivered through me—a faint shiver, but there.

"I'm sorry to do this to you, but we've got a dead guy."

A dead guy! Oh yeah. Right in my wheelhouse. As I tucked the phone between my shoulder and ear and pushed up my sleeves, I resisted pondering what that said about my life. "How fresh?"

"Still warm."

"Where?"

"Delivery bay seven. Police are on their way. Jerry's pulling the security feed. You know the drill."

I did. Death was the flip side of the fun and frivolity in Vegas. Like all the properties, we had our share. But a dead guy in a delivery bay raised questions. He couldn't be explained away like a tapped-out gambler deciding to go out in a blaze of idiocy, or a panicked john shoving a roughed-up woman under a bed, or one of the millions of private negotiations that went on all over town going bad. "I've got Romeo with me."

"Paolo is on his way to get you."

"Thanks. Anything else I need to know?"

"Oh, we've got the full complement of crazy this weekend, but I can fill you in later." Miss P sounded tired. Little wonder—Vegas was a nonstop mischief shop and we were the proprietors. No doubt, my Paris respite with its lure of a normal life with a normal schedule had eroded my 24/7 skills. Although there had been the guy stuffed in a barrel of wine and then the shootout in Bordeaux. Maybe I wasn't as rusty as I feared. Besides, fire tempers steel and this one would be hot, even by Vegas standards.

"Did my father get home safely from the hospital?"

"Yes." Her tone turned guarded.

"I'm really surprised they discharged him so soon. A good sign, don't you think?"

A pause. "They didn't."

"They didn't what?" I asked, sitting up a bit straighter. This rat was stinking to high heaven.

"He left. They didn't discharge him."

"He just walked out of the hospital?" That sounded so much like my father.

"He said he had to talk to you. It's important."

"He's okay, right?"

"Resting comfortably according to your mother."

No one was ever comfortable in my mother's presence, least of all her family, but I took the words at face value for comfort. "Okay, dead guy first on the list, my father second."

I disconnected without waiting for a reply, then tossed my phone on the seat next to me. "Am I lucky or what?" I said to no one in particular.

Romeo plopped back down in the seat across from me looking all spit and polished, his eyes bright with anticipation. "People get shot for saying that in your presence." He watched me; his brows stitched together with worry.

I shot him a bit of slitty-eye. Unchastised, he grinned. Of course, he had a beautiful fiancée who would be very glad to see him—that could sure scrape away the travel grime. I hated to dim his wattage, but I needed his help. "Your homecoming will have to wait. We've got a bit of a problem."

I filled him in on the few details I had.

7

A puppy eyeing a bone, he perked up. If he had a damn tail... A look of grown-up competence replaced his slobberdog. Personally, I liked the slobberdog better. It reminded me of the aw-gee-whiz kid he'd been when we first met. Now he was Grasshopper all grown up and ready to snatch the stone from my hand. He pulled out his notepad and pencil, then shot me a half-smile. "A dead guy, you say? Welcome home."

Home. I took a deep breath. A dead guy in the delivery bay and all manner of craziness yet to be discovered and waiting to be dealt with.

Problems to solve, magic to preserve. The old sizzle burned stronger just under the surface.

Home.

Yes, it was good to be back.

As THE PLANE ROLLED TO A STOP AND THE PILOTS SHUT DOWN THE engines, Romeo jumped up to help the First Officer lower the stairs. Once the stairs had descended, they both stepped aside to let me go first.

"We'll call for your car, Ms. O'Toole. I believe one is waiting in the parking lot." The First Officer held out his hand. Fresh-faced, his cheeks devoid of stubble, his hair still wet from a recent combing—heck, even his shirt was pressed, and his pants still held a crease—he looked as if he could go around the globe again. Of course, he also looked like high school was still in his future. I wasn't sure when they allowed mere children to fly, but somehow, I'd missed it.

"Watch the first step, it's bigger than you think."

Even though the idea that he would think I needed help rankled, I put my hand in his. "Thank you," I said, surprising myself with the hint of sincerity. Romeo coughed behind me. "Manners, Grasshopper," I hissed over my shoulder.

The reference did a fly-by right past the First Officer as he continued without a hitch. "We'll grab your luggage," he said with the perfunctory tone of an order shaped like a suggestion. Jean-Charles had an irritating way of doing the same thing.

Jean-Charles.

"Are you French?" I asked the young officer as I paused at the top of the stairs.

Romeo sniggered behind me.

"No, ma'am. I'm from Idaho."

And cursed with a Y-chromosome, I thought. From the bland smile on his face, I hadn't given word to my thoughts for once in my life, for which I was profoundly grateful.

"I don't have time to wait for you to fetch my luggage. Would you send it later?" I charged down the steps, in too much of a hurry to wait for his answer. I folded a coat over my arm and took the stairs as quickly as I could with a tired, folded-up body and balky parts. Why was it so easy to sit but so hard to unbend and move again? Even my brain was having a hard time spooling up. The cold slap of wind provided the wake-up call I needed.

Late spring in Vegas was a mercurial thing. Clouds scudded low capturing the light and reflecting a multihued but mostly pink glow. The sting of a wind-driven pellet or two stung my cheeks. Water of any sort occupied a spot on the endangered species list here in the middle of the Mojave, so rain, or more precisely, corn snow, would likely cause citywide wonderment.

I welcomed anything that hinted of a season other than unblinking sunshine and skin-melting heat. Tonight snow, but tomorrow could be sunbathing weather. Nobody could forecast it, least of all the weathermen.

A low, dark limo with the Babylon logo scrawled in hot pink down the side stopped at the bottom of the stairs. The pink had been my idea. I still liked it. My father tolerated it but occasionally, when he thought I was out of earshot, did grudgingly admit it had a certain flair. We made a good team, father and daughter —cut from the same cloth but with a chromosomal orientation that differed yet complemented.

Paolo, the Babylon's head chauffeur, jumped out of the driver's side, smashing his chauffeur's hat on his head as he greeted me with a smile that hinted at his normal wattage but seemed dimmed, perhaps by the demands of a weekend already spooling at a high RPM. "Miss Lucky!" He opened the back door with a flourish. "Welcome home!" Paolo always spoke in exclamation points, something that used to bother me. Not tonight. Not anymore.

Life held precious few superlatives.

My lungs did a happy dance as I paused, breathing in the cold and damp. A few lungsful, then I dove inside.

"The Babylon. Step on it." I'd always wanted to say that, but tonight it didn't make me smile. Romeo barely had enough time to scramble in next to me before Paolo threw the car in gear and hit the gas.

The acceleration threw Romeo back against the seat. "Shit!" Apparently, he hadn't graduated to five letters from four as I'd been trying to do as I navigated my former fiancé's, Jean-Charles's, turf. French society frowned on such common vulgarity.

Turns out common was sorta where I lived. Growing up in a whorehouse didn't prepare one for navigating the halls of palaces filled with the intrigue, backstabbing, and head lopping —the whispers of kings and queens long dead. I pursed my lips as I pondered that. On second thought, maybe it did.

"My sentiments," I said, embracing Romeo's base assessment. As I watched the scenery race by and tried not to think about the number of tourists we endangered, I wondered just how much my parents and Miss P hadn't told me. I glanced at the rearview to catch Paolo's eyes bracketed by worry, taking quick peeks to check on me. "What is it, Paolo?" Surely, he wouldn't know any details about my father…or the dead guy—for me, a toss-up in importance. Duty or family—wasn't that a historical choice suffered by many through the annals? Just carve my name next to Gandhi, who gave up sex with his wife to best serve his people. Okay, not Gandhi. Maybe Richard the Lionheart or Alfred the Great.

"I picked up Mr. Teddie yesterday," Paolo said, his usual verve wilting to a whisper at the end.

Romeo swiveled a look as I absorbed the punch.

"See." I held my arms out wide, "all I have to do is think about sex and his name comes up." Obviously, my self-censor had taken a break. Of course, that presupposed I had any sort of filter. If I did, we weren't terribly well-acquainted.

That left Romeo struggling to keep up as red crept up his cheeks. "You were thinking about sex?"

"An odd thing, I know, all things considered. I won't explain how I got there. Besides they say men have a sexual thought every seven seconds. I'm merely trying to keep up."

"Lowering your personal expectations, I should think." Romeo coughed and straightened his tie, angling for a look in the side mirror—a thinly cloaked attempt to avoid my slitty-eye.

Paolo's eyes held the hint of the smile I could not see.

I eyed Romeo. Yes, the student had truly become the teacher. "Indeed. I will endeavor to up my game." What was it they said? Women who wanted to be equal to men weren't very ambitious. In a rare show of self-regulation, I kept that to myself.

"Mr. Teddie is here because of his show…" Paolo added. "He asked if you'd gotten home."

His show! Of course! I'd forgotten. My father, in a flagrant if rare break with family loyalty, had booked Teddie into the theater at the Babylon. In addition to being a super-hot, super-virile man whose voice would make the Pied Piper jealous—especially if he was interested in luring women instead of children—Teddie was also Vegas's foremost female impersonator.

Yes, the first man I'd given my heart to not only looked better in a dress than I did, but he also had daddy issues. I'd snatched my heart back…well, after he'd cut me loose…but I'd left a piece of it behind. Guess that's how it worked with love. If I were the great Poohbah of the Universe, I'd change that. That way the aftermath of a failed love affair would be a bit less devastating—not that there was any risk I'd ever assume that throne.

"And what did you tell him?" I asked Paolo, who was spending far too much time nervously glancing at my reflection rather than at the road in front of him.

Paolo slunk down a bit in his seat which made him all but disappear, not exactly comforting.

"I told him you'd be home tonight." He dropped even lower.

I inched toward the edge of the seat and leaned over the front. "I hope from down there you can see more than I can from back here." People and buildings, signs and cars passed by outside the window in an alarming blur.

"Not so much."

I reached over the seat and pulled him up by the shoulder of his jacket, reinstalling him to where I was pretty sure he could at least see through the steering wheel. "My whereabouts aren't a secret." Not that I wanted Teddie anywhere within eyesight until I figured out how to handle all my mixed emotions. Did I love him? Sure. Did I trust him? Not on your life. Could love exist without trust or did it become something else? Once broken could it ever be repaired, or was it forever lost? Could those questions even be answered?

"Terrific." I wondered if the show was the only reason he was here. Part of me wished it so. The other part wasn't so sure.

Romeo touched me on the arm. "It'll be okay."

Teddie and I had dodged bullets together in France. Bonding through bullets didn't sound like the glue to hold a relationship together. And there was still that bit where Teddie had thrown me over for some young songbird and the huge ego boost. Now he was back and singing a different tune. Still sounded a bit off-key to me.

"Okay?" I arched an eyebrow at the young detective who, to his merit, didn't wilt. "One way or the other." There was a tiny continuum between homicide and rekindled love. Where Teddie and I would fall was anybody's guess. "Come on kid, let's go solve some problems. Remember, no matter how shallow life gets, it's nice to be needed."

"Somehow, between you and me, I think we're looking for mental health in all the wrong places."

CHAPTER TWO

*T*HE YOUNG detective dogged my heels as I pushed through the glass double front doors of the Babylon into the lobby. Ten steps in, I stopped, then turned slowly in a circle as waves of energy from the milling crowd washed over me, lighting me up like juice from a wall socket.

Okay, now I was home.

The blown glass hummingbirds and butterflies still flew overhead. Skiers of all levels still shushed down the indoor ski slope behind a solid wall of plexiglass to my right. A tribe of scantily clad young men and women still laced through the crowd with trays of flutes filled with Champagne. At this time of night, the lines at Reception were shorter; however, each desk still had two or three patiently waiting as they sipped their libations. Sheets of multicolored cloth tented above the long reception desk, the colors matching the mosaic tiles inlaid in the marble floors. Wall sconces with flames under glass lent an air of desert mystery. On the far side of the lobby, the trees and shrubs lining the indoor meandering waterway I lovingly referred to as our very own Euphrates buffered the sounds of winners and losers from the casino beyond. Frank Sinatra crooned from the hidden speakers—a bit of old Vegas for my benefit, I had no doubt.

The excitement, the fun…the magic was palpable.

Home. I'd forgotten.

Vegas had always been my Shangri-La. Apparently, I didn't shrivel up and die if I left, but my mojo took a hit, that was for sure. Vegas was the only place I felt useful. I had no idea what that meant or how to fix it.

Miss P's voice pierced my reverie. "Lucky, there you are!" She hurried toward me—all spiked blonde hair, oversized glasses, pinched face, and perfect ensemble. "I'm sorry," she said, looking every bit like she meant it.

Before she could explain, a man shouldered her out of the way, drawing a scowl from me. "Ms. O'Toole?"

The man was unremarkable in every way—thin, with the pinched look of a former junkie, tats and long hair to match. At least his clothes were clean.

"Please, your manners?" I drew myself up to my full six feet. I had him by a couple of inches, which put a bit of steel in my backbone. "You may not treat my staff with such disregard."

"What?" He seemed genuinely confused—not a good sign. Finally, he glanced at Miss P who he had pushed aside. "Oh, sorry." He turned back to me looking so not sorry. "You see, I've traveled a long way to see you."

"Your lack of planning is not my problem. I've traveled halfway around the world, crossing so many times zones I don't know what day it is, much less what time. Make an appointment, preferably for day after tomorrow. By then I might be ready to deal with whatever has your knickers in a twist."

I turned to move past him. He stopped me with a hand on my arm and a growl in his voice. "You'll want to talk to me." Without letting go of me, he reached into his inside breast pocket, pulled out a black case and flipped it open, flashing a badge.

I gave it only a cursory glance and no appreciation, then I leveled a look at him and lowered my voice. "Take your hand off my arm."

"What?"

"You heard me." I hid a waver in my voice. He was a Fed; I could sniff a Fed from a mile away. Feds always scared me—no matter what, they had more power than me and could make my life miserable. I'd done enough miserable for a while.

He dropped his hand. A pink flush crept up his neck and colored his cheeks.

"I don't care who you are, or what agency sent you. Hell, you could be on a mission from God and I wouldn't care. If you want to arrest me, do it. Otherwise, get the hell out of my way."

Romeo stepped forward and flashed his own bit of metal. "You heard the lady." Somehow, he pulled that off. Even I was impressed.

Although several inches shorter, Romeo held his ground. Apparently, his show was enough to appease the other guy. He stepped aside and we left him in our wake. I didn't turn to see if he followed.

"You think that was somebody from…you know…across the pond?" Romeo asked, his voice hushed.

"They don't have any jurisdiction here," I said with a lot more confidence than I felt.

"Just think…you could be a fugitive from justice. That's so cool." Now he added a bit of reverence to his tone.

"I'm not even going to begin to dignify that with any meaningful response."

"You just did," Romeo said, his glee leaking out through tight lips. He looked all of twelve. He was acting like it as well.

Halfway through the lobby and on our way toward the back of the hotel, the hotel executive in me absorbed my surroundings. Excitement hummed. Even the guests waiting for their turn at reception looked happy. Most clutched a flute of bubbles and snuck wide-eyed glances at their fellow travelers and the over-the-top grandeur of the lobby. I winced as one of the foolhardy took a tumble on the indoor ski slope where the brave slipped and skidded, sometimes face-first, down the groomed hill. The whole thing was a carefully curated collection designed to inspire awe...and a desire to absorb it all. I felt a smile bloom. It seemed to be working. After my bit of gloat and prodded by Romeo's goading, I returned to the business at hand. "Who the hell was that?" I asked Miss P as I glanced at the agent's still visible back as he retreated toward the casino.

Of course, she'd been silent during Romeo's torture, letting me have my due. "DEA," she said with a shrug.

"DEA?" My feathers ruffled. If there's anything a hotel owner hated it was the Feds nosing around the property. "Damn. And he's loose in our hotel." I flipped a quick frown in her direction. "You know the Feds make the guests twitchy. And twitchy guests go to other properties to throw their money around."

"I didn't have a babysitter. We are maxed out."

I took her word for it. With my father's health gnawing at me, right now I couldn't process much more than a dead guy. I'm sure she was dealing with a similar overload.

"Any idea what he wanted?"

"Only to talk with you. Specifically, you. No one else. I tried foisting him off on our new Controlled Substances Concierge, but he would have nothing of that."

I skidded to a stop. "Our what?"

"Since the new law legalizing marijuana—"

"I know about that."

Color rose in her cheeks. "You told me I was in charge, and with everybody coming here now to get their toke on, so to speak, the concierge desk couldn't handle all those requests as well as the normal dining and show stuff." She wound to an

17

insecure stop, her eyes toward the ground, where she dug a toe into the mosaic.

"Good idea." I had no idea what qualifications would be necessary to execute that position, and frankly I didn't want to know. Not now anyway.

Miss P's head popped up. "You think so?"

"Yes, but really the only thing that matters is that *you* think so. You're the boss. I'm the titular figurehead staggering under corporate responsibilities who doesn't get to do anything fun anymore."

She didn't smile. I guessed she couldn't tell whether I was being funny or not. I didn't blame her; I couldn't tell either.

"Come on." I moved my little party of three forward. "Death awaits."

"You make it sound like so much fun." Romeo sounded happy, too. A dysfunctional duo if there ever was one. He fell in beside me as I charged across the lobby with Miss P on our heels.

At the end of the long reception desk we turned left, banging through a set of double doors and into the back of the house. Immediately the atmosphere changed. While the front of the house was about excitement, the back of the house was about quick, quiet efficiency. Here, thick carpet absorbed the footfalls of staff rushing to meet guests' needs, some pushing carts, some peeking from behind piles of fresh, crisp laundry, all of them men and women on a mission to please. Single file, we were careful not to interfere with the meticulously choreographed efficiency.

Having worked in every department in the hotel, I'd memorized these back hallways. They were the map of my young adulthood. They were the map that led me here, to the life that defined me. "We take a right at the next intersection," I said to my two colleagues trailing me, not that verbalizing directions was necessary. They'd follow wherever I led. After that, I didn't give them a running turn-by-turn. Within minutes, maybe less, we pushed through another set of double doors and found ourselves at the receiving dock—a broad cement platform at the exact height of the eighteen-wheeler containers when they would back in. That way, all the contents could be directly offloaded and taken into the building without lift devices needed, much like a large distribution center you'd find out in the middle of nowhere where major highways crossed.

When I worked in Procurement, I was astounded at the amount of product it took each day to supply a four-thousand-room hotel with five bars, two major nightclubs, a string of high-end shops, two theaters, an arena seating over twenty-five thousand, and a convention center rivaling the best and largest in the country, not to mention all the pools, sandwich bars, the spa...well, you get my drift.

This late at night, the place still swarmed with people and buzzed with activity. Trucks left, others came, a symphony of back-up beepers filling the night. The overhead argon bulbs sputtered and hissed but lit the place with midday brightness. Several bays down, lights strobed blue and red—the police were on the scene. Yellow crime scene tape cordoned off an area. Workers wielding dollies and pushcarts, forklift operators, and other personnel all with heads down, bent on a mission flowed, around the off-limits section like a school of fish avoiding a shipwreck.

Everyone glanced at us with limited curiosity when we burst through the doors. One of them, catching sight of me, peeled himself from a cluster of men after barking a few orders. "Ms. O'Toole. Good to see you, ma'am. I expect you're here about the fuss down the way." As he shrugged out of a gray hoodie, he tilted his head to indicate farther down the long row of bays. The hoodie he tossed in a garbage bin along with some booties he shucked off his shoes. "Getting down and dirty making inspections. Before that, I was getting down and dirty at my place. It's a new thing. We collect junk equipment, break them down, and let tourists pay us for the chance to beat them with sledgehammers. Folks got a ton of frustration, you know."

Jeff Morton had been one of my first hires—a stickler, as I recall. He'd risen through the ranks and now was one of the old-timers conducting the flow of essentials in and out of the hotel. His weathered face showed every second of his years outside in the desert sun. Of course, here in the Mojave, it was impossible to guess the actual age of the folks who worshiped the sun. In return, the sun sucked the youth right out of them, desiccating all who dared raise their face to soak up the rays. His Babylon shirt looked like it was an original issue, yellowed with age and frayed from use. His jeans were holdovers from a thinner time. They no longer circled his middle, so he'd adjusted them below his belly, like many men dealing with the same issue. I'd bet most women wondered as I did what kept those pants up, especially when the men's butts had diminished in proportion to the gains in their bellies. But the better part of self-preservation was not to ask. Some things were meant to remain a mystery.

"Apparently. Good to see you. I'm glad to have experience on the dock tonight, all things considered."

"Been a bit crazy, yes, ma'am." He had a hard time meeting my gaze as he shifted from foot to foot.

We all turned at a growl that raised goose bumps and a primal flight response. A forklift driver had speared a cage in which an agitated tiger paced and occasionally roared his displeasure.

"There's four of them," Jeff continued without a hitch. "Followed by a whole gaggle of geese."

"What could go wrong?" I said, not expecting an answer.

"I offload them. What happens next is your problem." He consulted a clipboard. "These are for some swimsuit and lingerie show."

I glanced at Miss P.

20

"As I said, a whole lot of crazy," she replied with her usual nonchalance.

Another crate went by filled with sleek furred animals. "What are those?" I couldn't help but feel a bit of panic. Animals among the guests—while it was part of the show, I could imagine all sorts of disasters. Actually, imagination wasn't required—I'd seen a lot of disasters, cleaned up most of them.

Jeff consulted his clipboard again, then shrugged. "Private party."

I resisted the urge to derail a murder investigation over a crateful of ferrets. "I'm sure you have it all under control." I lifted my chin toward the crime scene. "What can you tell me about that?"

"Truck was here when I got here. It was clocked in some time yesterday afternoon and had just been sitting here. This being a crazy weekend, we needed the bay…" He swallowed hard and ran a hand over his gray stubble. "Keys were in the ignition." He pulled them out of his front pocket and jangled them. "The driver was nowhere to be found. I took it upon myself to move the thing. We do that sometimes. The field across the way is a great place to park the empty rigs while the drivers are inside doing whatever."

"You moved it?"

"Yeah, I'd just inched it forward when the guys started shouting. The guy was under there; we just couldn't see him."

"What time was this?"

"Just after my shift started."

"So, after midnight?"

"Yeah. Like I said, it'd been here a while."

"His legs are sticking out the back. You didn't see him?"

"No, ma'am. It was busy. I was in a hurry and a bit pissed. Wasn't looking for no body."

Jeff looked a little pale. "You ran him over?" That would

almost be an open-and-shut case. I crossed my fingers behind my back where nobody could see them.

"I see that," Romeo leaned in and whispered in my ear.

"The secret to my superpowers," I whispered back.

"Secret's safe with me."

Yeah, until he needed blackmail, but I was good with that.

Jeff waited. "You done?" he asked with a tight smile.

"Sorry," I said but was so not sorry.

"You asked if the guy had been run over. Not so lucky." He paused for effect. I didn't give him the reaction he was looking for, so he continued. "Someone bashed his head in, then parked the truck to hide the body, I'm guessing."

"And he became my problem. God knows why."

He shrugged. We both knew why. As I'd said, I was the one who stopped the proverbial buck. My hotel, my problem. "You see anything that might be pertinent?"

"No, ma'am. It was all sorta strange, though." Although now he could meet my gaze, he couldn't hold it. Dead guys could spook anybody. With one hand he lifted the baseball cap that kept his mop of gray hair corralled, scratched his head, then replaced his cap, adjusting it until satisfied.

The truck was still there—an eighteen-wheeler that bore the logo of one of the national rental agencies. "What was in it?"

"That's what was strange. Just a car, ma'am."

"A car? Just one?" That truck could hold multiple cars.

"And we can't find the car anywhere in the hotel."

"Was it perhaps a Bugatti?" Miss P asked as she stepped in beside me.

His hands shook as Jeff double-checked his clipboard. "Yep, that's it. Never heard of one. Guess it's outta my price range." He gave a gap-toothed smile. "Just sounds like something fancy and worth more than I'll earn in a lifetime."

I raised an eyebrow in question at Miss P. "What's the link?"

Her turn to do the clipboard thing. "The car, more specifically an orange Veyron, camel interior with custom orange stitching—I have the VIN if you'd like it—is on the roof. It's registered to some fancy car outfit in Sonoma. It's on the list of things I planned to go over with you later. They had a helicopter waiting. They airlifted the car and put it on a platform over the pool at Babel."

Babel was our primo rooftop club and one of the hottest tables in town. The best place to see and be seen in Vegas as the *Review Journal*, our local rag, described it. We couldn't buy PR like that. And now we had a car in the middle of it. "They didn't pull any permits or get any permission from us?"

"Nope."

Normally, I could appreciate ingenuity, but when it crossed a few well-defined boundaries—like crashing my party—not so much. The least they could've done was give us a heads-up. Spinmeisters that we were, we could've done something fun with a fancy bit of iron on top of our hotel. Over-the-top was expected in this town where we all competed for the top prize. "You have time to research what joker did this?"

"On my list."

"The dead guy just pushed it to the top."

Miss P nodded—most of the time she was a jump ahead of me. That used to bug me, but I managed using the philosophy of surrounding myself with people way more competent than me, then letting them do their jobs. Worked so far. "What's going on at Babel that would warrant the trouble, not to mention the expense and the future legal fees, associated with dropping a car in the middle of it?"

"A private party for some of the NBA bigwigs and superstar players."

"When?"

"Tomorrow night."

I filed that away in the interesting-factoid-but-haven't-a-clue-as-to-the-connection mental file. "Jeff, you and your crew see anybody around that truck?"

"Like I said, it was here when we came on duty. Before they left, we asked the guys what the deal was. They didn't know either."

"Well, a ghost didn't back that rig in here, offload a car, then move it out and strap it to a helicopter. Better call the guys back in. Somebody had to see something."

Jeff's face reflected the lack of enthusiasm he would find when he rousted a tired crew from sweet slumber. Death had a way of making everyone miserable until the dead got their due. "They ain't going to like it, ma'am," he said, knowing I knew that and also that it didn't matter.

I turned to our young detective who, contrary to his normal operating procedure had stayed silent. "Detective, do you have anything?"

"Who found the body?" he asked. An obvious question that had flown right by me. The student had become the teacher. I was okay with that.

"Like I said, technically I did," Jeff allowed, surprising me. Why the heck hadn't he mentioned it? "Nobody knew nuthin' about the rig. Like I said, keys were in it. We needed the bay." At my look, he continued, "Yeah, they're going to find my prints all over that rig."

"Don't worry. You fess up to the cops, and I'm sure Jerry can confirm via one of the security videos." That didn't seem to make him feel better. "Can you tell me exactly what you did?"

"I went nosing around, trying to see who I might call to come get the thing."

I didn't point out the rental agency number was in twelve-inch letters down the side of the thing. Given we had a death to investigate, I was glad he hadn't found someone to take the rig. "And?"

"I was just pulling it out. Was gonna park it in the sand lot next door. The guys started yelling. That's when I got out and I seen him. Like I said…" He paused and took a deep breath. "His head… Blood…" He shivered.

I got the picture. We didn't have a death to investigate…we had a murder. "Detective, your show."

"Don't leave. I'll want a formal statement from you later," Romeo said to Jeff, who nodded. "And do your best to get the earlier crew in here. The truck was here when you got here at midnight?"

Jeff nodded.

"I got a report of the car and the helicopter from Security about nine in the evening," Miss P said.

"I wonder what happened in between?" Romeo asked, not really expecting an answer as he jotted down some notes.

Babel would have been closed. Like most of the clubs, it didn't even open until ten-thirty, and nothing interesting happened until the wee hours…well, except for the deposit of a car.

Next on my list would be a call to McCarran Approach, the air traffic guys and gals who controlled the airspace this close to the airport. Either the helicopter flew in without a clearance and the pilot was in FAA custody, which would be best-case for me, or somebody filed a flight plan and got permission to work this close to commercial traffic. Less ideal, but perhaps the plan could shed some light.

"Do you think you can try to find somebody who might've caught that car in mid-flight?" I asked Miss P. "A tourist, anybody. Scour the internet, see what you can find. I know it was dark outside at the time they supposedly airlifted that thing to the top of my hotel, but with all the lights around here, maybe someone caught something."

Miss P made a note. "I've also added a note for you to call TRACON," she said when she was done scribbling, restoring our normal balance of her being one step ahead.

25

Air Traffic Control might be my best bet at this point. "Thanks."

Romeo led the way down the platform, counting the bays, which wasn't necessary. Our target shone like a beacon, illuminated by multiple temporary lights. We stopped at the tape barrier.

"Forensics is here," I said unnecessarily. They were the only ones who needed a thousand candlepower to collect their microscopic specimens.

The coroner, dressed in white coveralls, his shoes secured in booties, crouched on his haunches behind the truck and tilted his head to peer underneath. With one hand on the truck to brace himself, the coroner leaned as far as he dared while avoiding the pool of blood, now a dark red with a light skin forming on it making it look slightly wrinkled. Much like the Wicked Witch of the East, two legs stuck out from under, not a house, but the trailer portion of the rig. They were clothed in what looked like warmups and ending in a pair of fairly righteous kicks—red and white with a thin line of black—probably a gift or an expensive aftermarket purchase.

"I wonder if he could be part of the NBA crowd filtering in," Miss P said from my shoulder.

"They're arriving already?" Somewhere in the dark recesses, I remembered the big tournament was starting this weekend. In an effort to woo a professional team to relocate to Vegas, the power brokers hosted a tournament featuring all the rookies, or at least the top prospects, during the All-Star break, to mix it up for the local fans. Most of the teams participated. The tournament was a good way to have their brand-new rookies get some court time at the professional level, which really helped the draw. The Rookie-fest had become one of our larger events.

Miss P glanced at her phone. The casino was such a timeless place that even for the employees one day stretched into another, then into another, until it was one unbreakable stream. "Tournament starts tomorrow."

My time and days were all mixed up, and I felt way behind. Circumnavigating the globe clearly jumbled what few active brain cells still pinged around my otherwise empty skull, complicating life reentry tremendously—nothing like a dead guy to jumpstart the synapses.

The police had set up a perimeter. Two cops manned the alley side. They glanced our way. Recognizing Romeo, they waved him into the crime scene. He stepped over the tape then moved around the perimeter careful not to add any of his own trace to the scene. Miss P and I waited for permission to enter as I stifled the urge to say, "Red rover, red rover, let Lucky come over." When faced with death, my brain often made odd associations and panic tended to override decorum, so I wasn't overly worried. At least for once I kept my juvenile urges to myself—a minor victory.

"Hey, Doc," I said to the coroner, perhaps a bit too loudly as he startled and banged his head on the undercarriage. I winced but resisted saying I was sorry. As a whole, women apologized way too much, and I'd resolved to do my part to stem that tide.

He rubbed the top of his head as he squinted our direction. "Hey, Lucky. What took you so long?"

"I've been tasked with letting the G650 stretch its legs. You got any idea how far that thing can go between fill-ups?"

"Just a tick over eight thousand miles," he said without pause. "I've been at this job a long time. The stuff you learn... But to be honest, I'm really glad you were out joyriding, and you weren't dealing with another one of these. I've got my hands full tonight." He glanced skyward even though he was under the overhang of the delivery bay. "Full moon."

I didn't ask. I didn't want to know.

"You got any idea what was in the back of this rig?"

I told him about the car.

"On the roof? I doubt you've got an elevator that would take a load that size and weight?"

"Not all the way to the roof and for sure not to the nightclub."

"So somebody airlifted it up there." He had the same thinking-out-loud habit I did.

"About 9 p.m. today," Miss P said. "We're on it."

"Do you need access to the car?" I asked.

"I'll send a team up to cordon it off. Once we're done here, we'll dust it, but it may not be worth it. Probably half the world has pawed on and drooled over the thing."

"Maybe not. It's on a platform in the middle of the pool." I glanced at Miss P who confirmed.

I patted my pockets looking for my phone. No joy. Where had I left it? I thought back. The airplane. I'd tossed it on the seat. "Damn."

Miss P knew the look—this wasn't the first time my phone had gone AWOL. Without being asked, she handed me hers. "Thanks." I punched up Jerry, our Head of Security and Tonto to my Lone Ranger in these sorts of messes.

"What's cookin', Sweet Cheeks?"

Momentarily at a loss, I struggled for the appropriate response. "You call Miss P sweet cheeks? I really don't think I needed to know that."

"Oh! Lucky! Sorry." Jerry's embarrassment blushed though the connection. "I didn't know you were back."

"And that makes it sooo much better. Why don't I have a nickname?"

"You're the boss. It wouldn't be right."

He hadn't caught the tease in my voice. Then again, I'm not sure I'd put any in there. "No, Miss P is the boss. I'm the corporate schmuck who circles in periodically to rattle cages."

"But…"

"No buts. She's the me I used to be. Treat her as such." I

wasn't sure I was doing her any favors equating her with me, but she was the boss. She'd earned it a million times over. Jerry knew better. Old habits died hard.

"Yes, ma'am."

"Ma'am" was a poor substitute for Sweet Cheeks. Okay, maybe not. Okay, not at all. "Have you been made aware of the...issue...in the dock area?"

"Yep, we pulled the tapes. You're not going to like it."

Closing one eye, I eyeballed the locations of the cameras filming the bay. "One of the dead zones?"

"Well, we usually don't film the middle of the bay. No reason to. A truck is usually there. Most of the time we're just interested in who's coming and going. First time we've ever had an issue."

"You've got a feed of the cab and one of the rear of the trailer, then?"

"Correct."

"And we're assuming somebody whacked the guy in the bay then pulled the truck over the body so they could make a getaway." That sounded farfetched even to me.

"It's a theory." Jerry sounded skeptical as well. "Yeah, we got a visual on the driver and then on the back of the truck. I'm sending you a snap of the driver. He backed the car out and took it to the alley. A chopper was waiting. Dropped a harness. Slick bit of work."

"Send the snaps to Miss P's phone, please."

"You lost yours again?"

I didn't need to confirm what he already knew. I stared into the darkness beyond the bay. They would have had to roll the car out and get it in the middle of the alleyway in order to lift it. Still, whoever did the flying did a masterful job. They'd done it before—big machines, heavy loads, tight spaces, disaster lurking only feet away on either side.

"We do have a quick shot of someone walking around the front of the truck, heading past the driver's door—"

"To where the guy was killed."

"Toward it, assuming that's where the guy was killed, yeah. But that's all we got. Just somebody in torn jeans and a gray hoodie, face obscured, hands in the front pouch of his sweatshirt."

"Time stamp all the photos including that one, and send them to Miss P's phone, and mine as well, in case I ever find it, please."

"It's at the airport."

"What is at the airport?"

"Your phone. Last time you lost the thing I had IT put that find-my-phone feature on it. Saves us all a bunch of trouble."

I didn't know whether to say thank you or accuse them of turning my work environment into a Big Brother State, monitoring all its citizens for deleterious activity—replacing my phone every month or so did hit the bottom line of our department's profit and loss. This was one of those if-the-shoe-fits cases that hit a bit too close to home. In keeping with the idea that anything I said could be used against me, I decided to shuck and jive. "And keep going over the tapes. You gave a copy to the police?"

"They've already been up here."

"Good. Maybe some of their video *wunderkind* can find something." We didn't have the same level of talent in our surveillance room. Most of the folks monitoring our monitors were felons, well versed in the ins and outs of cheating at all the gaming tables and machines—a whole different subset of criminal videography.

"Photos are on their way." Miss P's phone dinged their arrival before he finished. "We'll keep looking for anything unusual. Keep me posted."

I pressed the red button to end the call then pocketed the phone. Miss P didn't argue.

"Sweet Cheeks." I cocked an eyebrow at her.

"It's all just fun." Even she didn't sound like she believed that.

"You get the respect you demand." I needed not only to take my own advice but do some serious changing around here. Miss P would never step fully into the role if I was always a shout away to handle the difficult stuff.

I turned my attention back to the crime scene.

Doc eyed me. "You thinking what I'm thinking?" He loved to play this game.

"The helicopter?" He nodded. "Either military or construction."

"Yep." He nodded, seemingly pleased with me. "Doesn't really narrow it down."

"I got a bead on that." At least I hoped I did. It all depended on how many friends I had in air traffic control. "When are you going to move the body? I'd like to get a look at the guy's face, see if he's one of ours."

"It'll be awhile. I've sent you some photos—yes, to Miss P's phone. I heard the conversation, and she gave me the number while you were busy avoiding responsibility for losing company property." He grinned like he thought the whole thing was funny. "This place isn't exactly the cleanest," he continued, circling back to my original question. "It'll take some time to get a handle on the trace. And things aren't lining up right." As he pushed himself to his feet, one of his knees popped loud enough for all of us to hear it. "Never should've done all that running back in the day."

"Exactly why I steer clear." Physical activity wasn't even in the top ten of things I'd turn to for stress relief or self-betterment. And, as excuses go, it was way better than anything I could come up with on my own. "How do you mean not lining up?"

Doc started to run a gloved hand through his hair, then remembered where those hands had been and what he was doing. "First of all, if the guy was killed here, there's not enough blood for that kind of wound." He looked at Miss P. "The car was unloaded and lifted around nine, you say?"

She nodded.

"Yeah, the timeframe seems a bit off. The rigor is more advanced. I'll figure it out when I do a workup."

Romeo retraced his steps back to us. "What're you thinking?" he asked me.

"Thinking is beyond my capabilities at the moment. What I've learned is we don't have any video of the murder, so this isn't going to be a cakewalk. Photographer is getting me a few pics of the dead guy. I need to see if he belongs to me." The thought made my blood boil. My people were my family—sometimes even way better than my family, but that's for another day. "Do you want to call Air Traffic, or do you want me to?"

"Might be better if you do. You speak their lingo. Once a pilot, always a pilot, right?" Romeo referred to my limited piloting skills.

"I'll do it." I pulled in a deep, steadying breath, then took a gander at the photos Jerry had sent. They were just as he indicated—not particularly helpful. Other photos started pinging their arrival—the photos Doc had referred to. I winced but forced myself to look through them. Not pretty, but I hadn't expected them to be. While I'd been told death could be peaceful, welcome even, I had yet to experience that side. All of the exits I'd seen had been ugly. This one was no exception. I blinked away the images as I focused on Romeo. "I'll shoot you some copies. I'm sure you'll get the full set with Doc's report."

"Which will be a while," Doc said, his voice muffled as he peered under the trailer, then motioned a tech over. He pointed to something and she fell to work. "Full moon, remember?" His voice strengthened as he reappeared. "And this one isn't even close to the most bizarre exit tonight. I got six lined up in front of this one." At the look on my face, he paused. "Okay, for you, I'll move him up the order. Should have something to you late day tomorrow."

"Today?"

He glanced at his watch. "Yeah, later today."

"I'll buy you dinner at Tigris. Say eight o'clock?" My way of setting a firm timeline.

"That's bribing a public official." I gave him an innocent look. "See you then. I can fill your head full of death and dismemberment over succulent mussels."

My stomach turned. I understood using the macabre to deal with death, but combining it with food struck me as nauseating. I nodded anyway and then turned to Romeo. "You going to take the rental agency? We need to find out who rented that rig," I said unnecessarily.

Romeo was used to my think-out-loud method. "Yep." At my look, he said, "Don't worry, I'll do it myself." He was well aware of my low opinion of the Metro police department, present company excluded, of course. "Would you like to bribe this public official with perhaps a mixture of weird and wonderful healing waters at Delilah's?"

"Later. If I don't let you get home to Brandy, my office is not going to be a happy place." Brandy was now Miss P's right-hand man; the position Miss P had occupied with reference to me before I got booted up the corporate ladder. That whole bit of ascension had been my bright idea. Yes, I was rethinking it. I belonged in the trenches, not corralling a bunch of suits with sticks up their asses.

He glanced at his watch. "She's just getting off. Perfect timing." I watched him lope off, leaving the crime scene to the doc and the night to Miss P and me.

I steeled myself and took another gander at the photos Doc had sent, inviting Miss P to look over my shoulder.

"Jesus," she whispered.

"Not sure what this poor soul did to piss off the Almighty, but damn..." I'd been right about the warmups, but I was surprised about the gray hair and receding hairline. Not one of the players, for which I was grateful. People being taken out of the life game early hit me the hardest. The guy looked like medium everything—build, age, height, looks. The looks part was hard to tell, though. One side of his head had been bashed in and blood had run down the side of his face. I looked up. Doc was still there. "Any idea as to the murder weapon?"

"I'm guessing something heavy, a torque wrench, maybe? Speculating, of course. Won't know more until I get some measurements on the fracture. But there's nothing just lying around with blood and fingerprints on it, if that's what you're hoping for."

"One can hope, can't they?" No matter how many of these sorts of cases I stumbled across, I'd yet to have a Perry Mason, aha moment where things just fell into place and the murder weapon dropped out of the sky. Still, hope springs eternal. "You got any ID on the body?"

He tossed a questioning glance at the closest tech, who shook her head. "I've taken prints, but it'll take me a bit to run them. I'll let you know if we get a hit."

"I'll pass the photo around. Maybe somebody around here, perhaps one of the NBA-types will be able to give us a name." A long shot if there ever was one. He was probably just a hapless hopeful nosing around for access to somebody famous but who stumbled on something he shouldn't have seen instead. I turned to Miss P. "They are still arriving, yes?"

"The tournament starts Saturday, like I said." At my caught-in-the-headlights expression, she clarified. "That would be tomorrow."

I looked back at the poor guy in the basketball gear who wouldn't get to see a game. Not fair but thank God he wasn't one of mine.

But who the hell was he? And what did he do that inspired someone to bash his head in?

"Lucky, have you seen your father?" Miss P's voice trembled slightly, or maybe I imagined it in my fear.

That served as the cattle prod I needed to jolt me back. "Not yet. You grabbed me when I hit the front door."

Her face pinched with fear as she stepped away so I could see her fully. "You need to go."

"It's late. He'll be asleep."

"No, no, he won't. He's waiting for you."

CHAPTER THREE

"*L*UCKY! COME in. Come in!" As I stepped out of the private elevator that deposited me in the main room of my parents' apartment, my mother rushed to greet me, chiffon swirling around her in a cloud of peach. With her cheeks pink, her brown eyes bright, her hair piled on her head in a haphazard chignon caught with a tortoiseshell spike, and tendrils tickling her cheeks, she looked half my age.

Family time, at least my family time, came at a price.

While family typically provided a safe haven where one could lick the wounds inflicted by life, my family was…well, not that. At least, my mother, Mona, was not that.

She grabbed my arm, ushering me into the great room of the apartment she shared with my father, Albert Rothstein, otherwise known as the Big Boss. Over her shoulder I scanned the room—no signs of life. No sound emanated from the kitchen to my right. Lights had been dimmed.

"Where are the girls?" My mother, apparently having learned nothing while running a whorehouse for most of her adult life, miraculously found herself with child recently. Of course, at her age, which I guessed to be somewhere just south of fifty if I had the family story chronology right, most women were past the fertile part. Not Mona.

Of course, not Mona.

But Mona also played fast and loose with the truth, so only one fact had been established beyond a reasonable doubt—I had two sisters. Yes, twins. Mona never did anything half-assed.

"Frankie and Sammy are asleep. It's late."

"Somewhere in the world it's an acceptable hour to be awake. My body seems to be stuck there." I was thankful the girls had been corralled. I needed my father to myself.

With the conviction of a woman on a mission, Mona propelled me past the lesser works of the Masters that graced the walls. Perfectly lit, they looked a bit dour tonight, which increased my unease. We dodged the silk carpets on which nested tidy clusters of overstuffed furniture made from the hides of various beasts. The moveable fireplace my father always insisted on lighting, especially this time of year, was dark, devoid of the dance of flames. She didn't turn left toward the hall that led to the private areas. Instead she kept pulling more toward the couch facing the far wall of floor-to-ceiling windows.

"Mother." I peeled her fingers from my arm. "I need to see Father."

Her wattage dimmed and her lip quivered. It had taken a lot of effort to put on a brave front. My heart fell.

"He's where he always is when you come visit. You both love the windows."

"I'd hoped he'd be in bed. According to Miss P, that's exactly where he should be with doctors hovering. What is this about him checking himself out?"

Mona lowered her voice and darted a glance toward the windows at the far end of the room. "You know your father."

"Yes, but he's not going to help anyone if he's dead." I didn't bother with lowering my voice. In fact, I may have raised it a touch, hoping it would reach him. "He could have waited for me in the hospital."

"He said the walls have ears there."

That had the desired effect of stopping my bluster. This was so not good. Much more serious than I thought. "What could possibly be that important?"

The pallor my mother had tried to hide under a thicker-than-normal layer of powder crept through. "He wouldn't tell me."

I couldn't tell if she was relieved not to be shouldering the weight or feeling a bit left out. Frankly, I'd be fine if he left me out of the loop, since I was currently handling what life had dished out so well and all.

When my father and I were together, my mother often felt like a spare part, or so she told me often enough that I should be more cognizant. "I'm sorry." I patted her hand and put it back on my arm. "If it's any consolation, I'm as terrified as you are."

"Hardly comforting," she said, but I could tell just having me to take the load had lightened her exponentially.

Somehow, I felt okay with that although I could tell she still wanted to be a part of it all.

She led me toward the lights of the Strip framed in the wall of windows on the far side of the room. The view of the Strip unrolling at my feet filled me with awe every time, no matter how many times I'd seen it. Tonight was no different, although the worry muted the magic.

Someone had told me the lights shone so bright, they could be identified from the space station. As I blinked against them, I had no doubt. Turning my face to their sunlight, I closed my eyes and drew all the energy I could pull from them.

"Magic isn't it?" My father's voice, but a weaker facsimile.

"For over sixty years I've drunk them in. Not necessarily from this vantage point, but I never get tired of them."

"I know." I didn't turn. If I looked at him, I'd see the man I heard in his voice. For a moment I wanted to remember him as he always was. Short in stature but bigger than life, Albert Rothstein owned every room he walked into...and probably most of the people in them. With jet-black hair that had faded to salt and pepper through the years, a chiseled jaw that had taken many a blow but had never lost its knife edge, and a ferocity only slightly muted by his ever-ready smile, he'd been one of the figures often touted as one of the influential founders of Las Vegas.

Along with that came the implication he'd been mobbed up. I'd never asked. And I'd never seen anything that would give weight to the rumors. Of course, when I'd met him—I'd been fifteen when Mona had sent me away from her whorehouse to study under his tutelage—he was a big part of the new corporate Vegas that had filled the vacuum when the Family had been all but exterminated.

At the time, I hadn't known he was my father. That little factoid came to light not too long ago. My parents had kept the secret all these thirty-some-odd years. For good reason, yes. But the not knowing still had left a scar on a rootless kid. Time muted the pain, but it still throbbed when I took a long trip down memory lane.

After hearing his voice, I took my time before I looked at him. Tonight it would be him drawing strength from me and not the usual reverse. Something had shifted, something big. Friends had warned me of the eventual change in roles between aging parents and fully-fledged children, but I wasn't ready for it. I guess, like death, it comes regardless, and we all have to scramble to catch up. But he'd been my rock, the person I clung to in a storm, to whom I looked to ease my fears and focus my thoughts. He could always pull logic out of my emotional chaos.

Clouds of self-doubt obscured the path forward without him.

Funny how the specter of loss could vaporize the hurt.

I sucked in a ragged breath, then let it out in a slow, steady stream as I fought to find courage. All I really wanted to do was crawl into his lap and let him hold me.

Fathers and daughters. President and vice president. Mentor and mentee. The normal balance of the universe.

From the trajectory of his voice, I could tell he was sitting at the far end of the couch. Turning from the light and momentarily blinded in the relative darkness of the room, I felt for the couch, then eased onto the end closest to me while my eyes adjusted.

As things came into focus, a lump at the far end of the couch shifted. A head lifted. Gray hair, gray skin, a weak smile. He sucked in air then let it out in short bursts, fighting pain.

My father.

I almost didn't recognize him. How long had I been away? Three weeks? No, no more than two.

He'd lost years.

"Father!" I found his hand under the blanket covering him and squeezed it. His skin was cold, thin, a crepey vessel barely sufficient to hold his spirit.

"Lucky." He breathed the word like the whisper of a dream. "I'm glad you're home."

The effort to speak, to express, drew the energy from him. My petty problems with men...no, my problems with petty men fled. My father had been my rock.

Forceful, powerful, able to stare down the Family back in the day and not end up a pile of bones bleaching in the Mojave. Yes, my story and I was so sticking to it. Every girl needs a father who's a hero, no matter how late in life she gets him.

Maybe his absence during my adolescence had something to

do with my complete ineptitude with men. Not shifting blame —that was all mine—but an interesting theory for another day.

When I looked deep into his eyes, now a watercolor wash of their former vibrancy, I caught only the barest hint of the man I'd always known. Fear exploded inside me in an icy rush. I shivered and worked my features into what I hoped was a warm smile.

Be it until you are it. The Rothstein version of fake it until you make it.

All the years of practice saved me now as I mustered a smile. However, shock still tightened my words until they fairly twanged.

"Good work in London. Thank you." He squeezed back.

After he'd strong-armed me into going, I'd maneuvered a delicate situation at one of our properties there. My grudge evaporated. To be honest, the whole thing had been in my wheelhouse. I'd been the right choice. And I was strong enough to take the fallout.

My father always knew the right puppet to make dance.

What would I do when he wasn't here to make them anymore?

Mona fussed with his blanket, tucking it in. "Can I bring you anything, Albert?"

A smile lifted the corner of his mouth.

Mona tsked. "The doctor said no Wild Turkey." She glanced at me and softened. "But a little won't hurt...with Lucky." She disappeared in a swirl of fabric. How she did that, I'd never know. Surely, I'd step on a hem and fall on my face. No, I didn't have her grace. I didn't have her looks. I didn't have her magnetism. I didn't have her femininity.

But I had me. I was beginning to appreciate that.

"Mother, maybe bring the fireplace over." I raised my voice as she retreated into the darkness. "It's a bit cold here by the window."

"Good idea." Her voice tinkled…yes, it really tinkled…back to me. Like I said, Mona never did anything half-assed, not even her self-appointed role as the perpetual sunshine fairy, although Mona's ego tended toward goddesses rather than fairies.

"Sorry about Jean-Charles," my father said as he shifted his gaze to drink in the lights, most likely looking to draw energy from them as I had.

We were more alike than I was comfortable with. But I'd come to appreciate that, too.

Jean-Charles.

Hearing his name constricted my heart. Had I done the right thing? Emotion had Swiss cheesed my memory, but I was pretty sure I'd thrown his ring at him. Was hurling an engagement ring a forgivable offense? Did I care? To the world, Jean-Charles Bouclet, world-renowned chef, widower, and father to the most adorable five-year-old, Christophe, was the definition of a "great catch." Up close, he wasn't quite so perfect: he suffered from a superiority complex, that Y-chromosome nuance that led men to think their lives, hopes, and dreams were more important than those of the woman in their life.

So not true.

I once had a man tell me that when I'd agreed to date him, I'd agreed to live life as he imagined it.

He was lucky I let him live. Of course, I wasn't sure he wanted to after I rather forcefully disabused him of his notion. A bit of an exaggeration, but not much.

But I'd cut Jean-Charles some slack—he was French after all.

In my darkest moments, I often wondered what it would be like to be a white male in a world built by and for white males. No matter from where they came, or from what station in life, they all had that same air. Some only a whiff, but they all had it…until a good woman grabbed them by the short hairs.

In the long run, that whole French thing, and the cooking amazing food thing (have I mentioned I love to eat), and the great-in-bed thing, and the fiery-intellect thing hadn't made him any more tolerable. Hence, the hurling a ten-carat diamond at his head. To be honest, he hadn't been all bad. Really only a little bit irritating, which was probably the most one could ask of another.

And I had hardly been at my best.

Here, with my father, and with my mother out of earshot, I could be the authentic me. Maybe that was the best gift of all he'd given me. "I'm so tired of staring at my navel, trying to fix me."

My father laughed—not his normal booming guffaw, but it was a laugh. I took that as a hopeful sign. "Lucky, just *be* you."

"I'm too stupid to keep up the pretense of being someone I'm not."

"No, way too smart." He shifted, drawing the blanket higher. "Have you ever thought that maybe, sometimes, you didn't do anything wrong other than point out where someone was letting you down? It's your God-given right to demand what you need. If the friend, parent, lover, whatever, is who they should be and they care about you as they should, then they will be grateful to know what you need. Nobody can read your mind."

I shuddered at the thought. "If they could, I'd either be institutionalized or an Instagram sensation."

That lit a quick smile, and I saw the hint of my father still inside a shell that must be driving him crazy with its weakness. Then, he sobered. "I'm serious. You have to ask, honey, or you can't be disappointed if you don't get it."

"But it's not anybody's obligation to live up to my expectations, only their own."

"If they want to be in your life, they should put you first."

"And vice versa. What is it you tell me? That it works best when each thinks they are giving one hundred percent?"

"True. So if you choose unwisely..." He used that phrase-

43

ology on purpose—he took it directly from one of my favorite scenes from *Indiana Jones and the Last Crusade*.

"My head melts?"

"Only your heart."

"Yeah." I leaned back and turned my attention to the lights. "Totally sucks."

By his own admission, the only woman he'd ever loved was my mother, so he wouldn't know the broken heart feeling. But for my benefit, he pretended to. Of course, they'd been separated most of their lives, checking on each other from afar but unable to live together. That had to come with its own heartbreak.

Mona returned with libations—three fingers of amber liquid and one ice cube in crystal tumblers. The ice clinked happily as she first handed one to her husband, waiting until he'd secured it in both hands, then one to me. My father's hands were steady as he raised his glass and then drank like he'd crawled through the desert to an oasis, which I guessed he sorta had, metaphorically speaking. Even with a private room and staff to do his bidding, I'm sure the hospital had been less than comfortable. And I knew full well it hadn't come with a fully stocked bar.

I took a long pull myself. I'd recently promised myself I'd drink only when celebrating something—a hollow promise as I'd come to realize. Each day held plenty of small moments to celebrate, and sometimes even big ones. And with my life, sometimes just making it through the day could be cause for celebration. I'd have to rethink. The key would be to find a resolution that would make me feel proud but not be too onerous to semi-stick to.

Yes, clearly I remained a bit uncommitted.

In my experience, change involved pain, and I'd had enough of that for a bit. Maybe now wasn't a good time to whittle my habits into some form of respectability. I sidelined my guilt and took another sip. My father was here. My mother hadn't set the world on fire, and then asked the impossible of me to put it out as she usually did. I'd survived—a bit unsteady, uncertain, and fractured, but all wounds time could heal. So modest celebrations were in order.

Mona pushed over the fireplace. "Lucky, can you do the honors? Every time I try it, I singe my eyebrows."

I bent over the thing, hit the igniter, then turned on the gas. Reasonable flames flared; no hair was sacrificed. I pushed it as close to my father as I dared. His blankets draped to the floor. The last thing I wanted to do was immolate him.

Mona watched me. "That's what I do wrong. I turn on the gas first, then the whole thing goes *kablooey* and I find myself on my ass trying to get out of the way."

"I should've let you light it." I retook my position on the couch. Father hid a smile.

"Albert, are you hungry?" Mona turned back into Miss Fairy Sunshine. "Could I fix you a cold plate? I have some nice cheeses Teddie brought by." She paused, punctuating the Teddie bit with an innocent look tossed my direction. I'd never been able to decide whether Mona actually rooted for Teddie or whether she switched her allegiance to whoever was the odd man out. Knowing Mona and her penchant for championing the underdog, her strategy followed her heart and not any desired outcome. Not that it mattered. I'd long since become impervious.

She harrumphed, then continued. "I have some kielbasa to go with it and some of that grainy mustard you like."

"That would be great, dear. Thank you."

"Let me freshen your drink first."

We both waited while Mona topped off his glass and added a splash to mine.

"I'll be a bit. You two talk." Mona ceded the floor a bit too easily, piquing my already overactive worry. She usually wanted no part of serious. So it looked like serious was what I was going to get.

Both my father and I knew our cue. I eased back into the corner of the couch, angling so I could see him. I cradled my glass in both hands. "What's this I hear about you checking yourself out of the hospital?" I said as Mona disappeared through the swinging doors to the kitchen.

"You better have something bigger than a stick to slay that dragon." Mona's words filtered back before the doors stopped swinging.

My father shifted his focus to stare into the fire. He set his glass on the side table, then warmed his hands, but he didn't look at me. The classic Rothstein avoidance tactic. We only used it with big problems or big emotions.

Damn. Of course, after Miss P's warning I'd expected as much, but irrational hope sticks with me until the last possible moment. Its extinguishment left a nothingness, a cold ball of dread deep inside.

"They'd fixed what they went in for." He shifted, then winced.

"I don't think so. They were chasing a bleeder. You hadn't been there long enough for them to know they got what they were after and that you'd stabilized."

"They have their opinions; I have mine." He plucked at a ball of fuzz on his blanket, then rearranged the folds more tightly around his legs. He reminded me of the old people you see dotting the lawns in their wheelchairs on a pretty spring day. I stomped on that visual until it evaporated.

"Father, cracking open your chest is a big deal. The sutures inside haven't had time to do their job. I'd be willing to bet most of what I have that you still have those awful staples in your chest."

"You'd be right." He shifted again, clearly agitated. This time

I could see the muscles bunch in his cheek as he fought the wince. "I've got a big problem." He darted a look toward the kitchen. "Your mother doesn't know. In fact, nobody knows." He swiveled a side-eye at me and rocked his head back and forth. "Although anybody could figure it out if they thought to look."

Beating around the bush was so not like him. "I haven't a clue what you are talking about, which, come to think of it, stands to reason since nobody knows." I tended to blather when stressed. Now was no exception.

"Years ago, all the property we now consider the Strip was owned by the Mormons."

"A lot of it still is, as far as I know." I always loved that. They'd own the property and rent to sinners. Somehow reaping the rewards of debauchery didn't throw them off the Highway to Heaven. My smile evaporated. "I think I know this punch line. The Babylon?"

"I acquired this property back when I didn't have a dime and I pinched pennies so hard Lincoln screamed. Of course, I didn't have the green or the connections at the time to buy the land outright, so I leased it. Long term."

"Most of the property out here was initially acquired that way. I'm sure the buyout will be excessive, but we can pay excessive." I took a sip of my drink, trying to steady my hands. So far, I didn't see too much of a problem, or at least I didn't see any problems that a pile of cash wouldn't solve. "All the leases I've seen had a buyout provision."

A tick worked in my father's cheek. "I was the first lease out here."

On its next trip toward my mouth, my hand stalled. A bit of Wild Turkey sloshed out. I ignored the cold hit on my pants. "And you didn't pay a lawyer to help you."

"I didn't have anything to pay them with." A weak excuse. If anything, my father was and had always been resourceful and persuasive. He'd also had a hardheaded ego issue. Time had tempered that, but that wouldn't help us now. "There was a clause in the lease that I overlooked. Never even saw it. This was a long time ago. I was so green. Nothing was out here, not really. All the action was still downtown. This was a bit of silliness in far rural Clark County. Hell, it wasn't even in the city."

"Still isn't."

"Yeah, a curious bit of local arcana. The Flamingo was out here, but a few miles south. Everybody thought my play was a boondoggle. Oh, there were a few other properties, fleabags mostly, long gone, long forgotten."

"Not forgotten. But I will agree with you. Nobody foresaw all of this." I swept my arm toward the view.

"I had a glimmer. That's why I sold my car to lease a chunk of desert. Took me a long time to get the money to build this place."

He'd done it too, built up other properties, sold them, built more, until he had the stake for his own place. He'd made it grander through the years until it was one of the landmarks where everybody had to come, and more importantly, had to gamble.

"I figured I'd renew, at an exorbitant price, I'm sure. I banked on building a property that could afford it." He gave me his old full-wattage smile. "I did."

"Yes, you did. Legacy of a lifetime." Instead of puffing up, he wilted.

"What?" For the life of me, I couldn't see a downside so huge he'd put his life on the line to be here to tell me about it.

"They could take it all."

"What?" I could barely eke out the word.

"The lease is written in such a way that they can choose to renew. If they don't want to, I forfeit anything built on the property. Oh, it's written much more cleverly, but that's what

I've been told. Of course, we can litigate, but I might not live to see the end of that."

The fact that he'd lived with this and it hadn't killed him gave me hope. "At least that would buy us time." The enormity of the problem hit me, leaving me numb. The Babylon was my life, my home, even more so for my parents. The employees were our family.

"How long have you known about this?"

"A few months. A shady legal frontman out of Shanghai came calling, briefcase in hand. Some rich guy had bought out the lease. He's one of the big players in Macau now."

"And he's looking to upgrade to a primo Vegas property and all the face that comes with that." We both fell silent, each wrestling with our own thoughts. I needed to even the playing field. We needed a savvy, ruthless, and a bit sketchy player familiar with the power brokers in Macau. Someone willing to push the bounds of fair play…and sometimes ignore them altogether. This was life and death. A smile lifted one corner of my mouth.

My father must have seen it. "You've got something. I knew I could count on you." His relief was almost palpable.

"Not so fast. I've got a friend who knows the back alleys of Macau and is conversant in high finance, but he may be dead." Oddly, the thought made me sad.

"Dead? Who?" My father was clearly taken aback.

"Yes, you never want to know everyone your progeny hangs out with, trust me. He's a Hong Kong financier and weekend pirate. He'd run afoul of the Triad." I waved his concern away. "It was part of the Paris mess. Anyway, we got things sort of tidied up and I offered him a ride to Monaco to try to settle with the big bosses." I used the term specifically, not sure why. I really wished my father would stop thinking of himself as a Big Boss. That term invited all kinds of stupid behavior.

"Where is he now?"

"I have no idea."

"But you can find him?"

"Yes, once I have my phone back...if he managed to survive without my help, which I put at 50/50. The better question is whether I can outmaneuver him. He's a challenge." He'd tried to set me up for the theft of a bunch of expensive watches. I'd returned the favor. Then he'd tried again in Bordeaux, but I'd been a step ahead of him. I wish I could say I was that clever, but in truth, I was that lucky.

"Really?"

Something in the way my father said the word made me glance at him. "Yes, I like a challenge, but I have this trust issue thing, you know." I held up my hand, redirecting the conversation. "Tell me about the guy in Macau. He's not the same guy who put a bullet in your chest?"

"No, not related, at least not that we can discern."

"We?"

"Me and the only lawyer I trust." His gaze skittered away.

"Who?" I asked, but I knew.

"Squash Trenton."

Some days I hated being right. This wasn't one of them, not really. Squash was as clever as a junkyard dog and about as vicious in protecting those he cared about. He and my parents were tight, very tight. I blew the bangs that tickled my eyes, lifting them off my forehead. Squash and I had solved a problem or two together—a few big ones, several smaller ones. I liked him, perhaps a bit too much, which made him dangerous.

"You two work well together." My father said it as if he knew of the chemistry that sizzled between us. And it wasn't just sexual, although there was that. I couldn't explain it, but it was definitely a thing.

My father squirmed under my long stare.

Squash Trenton. If things weren't so dire, I'd say this reeked of a setup. I hated being maneuvered—my father knew that. But he was doing it anyway. That reeked of desperation. "Yes, but if Squash can't solve it with legal razzle-dazzle—"

"We could use your guy in Macau if he's not six feet under."

"And if they can't wiggle us out of this, what do you expect me to do?"

My father leveled a serious gaze. "Fix it."

CHAPTER FOUR

"FIX IT?" I mouthed the words since panic squeezed all sound into silence.

The look he gave me contained the depth of his past, the demons, too. I was my father's daughter—I knew what "fix it" meant.

Finally finding my voice, I managed a whisper, afraid the Fates would hear his suggestion and not react kindly. "Father...Dad...Vegas is no longer a place where swinging a baseball bat at someone's kneecaps will take care of a problem. We've moved on."

"Bullshit. The bat might be different, but the philosophy is the same. You know what to do. I've been paying you well to do it for years."

"Not exactly."

He shrugged. He'd never been a man interested in nuance. But he gave me silence and relief from his stare to process...or at least find my footing. What exactly did he expect me to do? To him, his life would be a small price to pay to save the Babylon.

For me? The stakes were different.

He'd made a mistake—a young, foolish mistake. He'd probably gotten a sweet deal, too. An irresistible carrot for a young man hellbent on making something of himself. And as a wet-behind-the-ears male riding high, he'd have thought it was a vote for his brilliance. Fool's gold is exactly that. Only in the passing of the years did we finally learn that nobody gave you something for nothing. And when it seemed like that's what they were doing, you'd better read the fine print.

His mistake. How did that translate into my problem?

Oh right. Problems were my thing. A sucker is born every minute, at least according to P.T. Barnum—this particular sucker several decades ago. I should know better by now, but if there was a windmill near, I'd be grabbing a jousting lance and sword and searching for my Sancho.

Besides, problems for me were a lot like food—cutting back was almost impossible since I couldn't eliminate them altogether. An explanation not an excuse, I know.

Surely, I had a limit…some sort of limit. Lately, I'd been plumbing the depths and I'd found some resilience, even when it came to those whom I loved beyond measure…and often beyond hope. My backbone at least now resembled a twig instead of a limp noodle.

But not with my father.

With my courage flagging and give-up and give-in overriding not only common sense but also my excessive self-preservation instinct, I opened my mouth to capitulate.

Before the words tumbled out on a wave of self-loathing, Mona breezed in, stealing my stage. In fact, her timing was so impeccable I'd be willing to bet she'd been waiting in the wings for an appropriate cue.

"Look what I have for you two." She held an immense plate which she deposited on the coffee table with pride as if she'd aged the cheese and stuffed the sausage herself. That'd be the day. What Mona knew about a kitchen involved speed dial and credit card. And what she knew about sausage allowed her to still eat it.

My hunger suddenly kicking up to the famished mode, I inched toward the edge of the couch, surveying the options. "Wow, Mother, this is amazing." Several different kinds of sausage, even more cheese selections, crackers, several slices of baguette, cornichons, and a nice smear of grainy mustard. She hadn't missed a beat. Impressive. I wasn't really sure what to do with the capers scattered over and around everything, but I knew better than to ask—she'd included two sharp knives to round out her presentation. Feeling a bit panicked as I was, I steered clear of the sharp knives—totally no upside there.

"Wow!" I tried to temper my incredulity.

"That's lovely, dear, thank you." My father pushed himself higher.

With a hand under his arm, Mona provided more leverage. Once settled, she tucked pillows around him and rearranged his blankets. "You need more than liquid calories to regain your strength, Albert." She settled herself between us and set about making him the perfect bite. "Dig in, Lucky, don't be shy. You must be starving for some American food."

Whatever game she was playing, I liked it. This was the first time in perhaps forever, but for sure in recent memory, that the three of us—Mona, me, and food—had occupied the same space and she hadn't skewered me with a remark about my weight. At six feet plus without shoes, I started the weight race way behind my mother. While I felt my weight was appropriate for my height, Mona had a different metric.

I did as she said and piled my own perfect bite on a cracker. A few more and I started to feel more like myself.

She fed my father, who accepted each offering like a baby bird, then followed it with a slug from his glass. I did the same, but without the vigor. Nothing like offloading a huge problem to put a bit of spring back.

Nothing more was said about *fixing* anything. But my father's expectations and willingness to see me in front of a firing squad hung over me like a pall.

Mona broke the companionable silence. "Oh, Lucky, I've been meaning to tell you! I have an idea!" She turned to face me, her eyes alight.

I resisted the urge to run.

There was nothing more terrifying than Mona with an idea.

Between you and me, my parents were scary as hell.

I had no idea what to say, so I sat there with my mouth open.

Mona gave me a sardonic grin, then gently closed my mouth with one finger under my chin. "It's not that bad."

Whoa. Self-awareness and introspection—Mona had been working on her heretofore rather limited personal skill set. The lights below painted her enthusiasm in a rainbow of colors making her look like a scary clown. Or maybe that was my imagination. Either way, it creeped me out.

"Really, you'll like it."

A bit optimistic. I hadn't liked one of her "ideas" yet. And she was so overselling—I could see it in her fake smile. Neither bred confidence nor calm.

Drawing energy from the lights of the Strip, I sucked it up… then took a few bracing pulls on my drink, almost draining the glass and delaying the inevitable. I gasped as the fire burned down to my belly, where it exploded. All that wine and fancy Champagne in Paris had made me a lightweight. Tomorrow I would fix that…*if* I survived Mona's…whatever. I took a deep breath, then painted on a smile to match hers. "Hit me with it."

"You know my political campaign?" With her hands on both knees, she smoothed her chiffon. I guessed it was a caftan, but she'd kill me if I said so. To her it was some fashion statement that a style Luddite like me would miss.

Her political campaign. I shook my head.

Despite all efforts, Mona had failed to understand that the

position she wanted on the Paradise Advisory Board was appointed by the Clark County Commission. No campaign needed—well, at least not a formal, public one. She'd have to use every erg of charm she had to convince the board to appoint a former madam married to the most influential player in town to a board overseeing the bit of desert that contained not only his main property, but also mega-resorts owned by his competitors. The whole thing reeked of conflict of interest, but I couldn't fault Mona for her do-gooder impulses. Of course, that streak had always run wide in her—that's why we all allowed her to live.

"Yup."

She picked at a ball of lint on one of the pillows. "And you know how I want to do something for the city and my people here?"

Her people? I didn't dare risk a peek at my father. "Yup."

"Well,"–she clapped both hands on her knees and pushed herself up as tall as possible—"I've figured out my platform."

"Is 'great' the appropriate response here?" My father choked back what sounded like a chuckle, then sucked in air against the price he paid.

"Lucky!" The word held a tinge of hurt, feigned of course— this was all a game, one we played over and over until I wore out. Mona turned back to her husband. "Albert, are you okay?"

"Yes, dear."

"I expected your support, of all people. You're my husband."

He looked around her, affixing me with a smile. "*She's* your flesh and blood."

Mona whirled back around as I shot daggers at my father, not that they would faze him. "That's *right!*"

I wiped the smile from my face and worked for earnest. Hey, it was the best I could do in my slightly fortified but still supremely jet-lagged state. "Okay, tell me. What are you going to do for the fair city of Las Vegas?" I know, not technically correct—this was the township of Paradise—but she knew what I meant.

"I intend to make it fur-free."

My synapses had a total sizzle-out. I don't remember what happened after that until Mona hurried up, holding the doors of the elevator before they closed, and I would be ushered down to the world where the sane people played. She leaned in, her voice a whisper. "Don't mind your father. He's still processing. Tomorrow, perhaps, he'll get his feet under him."

From her demeanor, I surmised I hadn't killed either of them nor done anything that would be written in indelible ink in the Book of Family Transgressions, but the night was young.

"Processing?" I was at a loss.

She reached in. I took her hand. "He doesn't mean for you to step outside the lines to solve a problem of his making."

So much for nobody knowing. I wondered how far and wide my mother had spread the ugly truth.

"What?" This was so not like my mother. Up until now she'd been the first to sacrifice me on the altar of Albert Rothstein, not that I blamed her. He'd been her everything for more years than I'd been here.

"He really wouldn't want you to do anything...rash." She glanced into the darkness where my father waited.

"Maybe, maybe not, but he'd be out there busting kneecaps, or worse, on his own if he could."

She didn't confirm or deny. Mona had always been my father's best defense against the world. I was too much like him. That had always pleased me since being like Mona was the other genetic option, but now I wasn't secure in my prejudices. I felt the weight of his past pressing heavily. You know that tidy bit of dirty laundry I'd been airing? Those pesky problems I'd been whining about that now paled in comparison to the new ones my father had dumped on me? Well, I should know better. The Powers That Be had never resisted showing me what a weenie I was. Clearly, they had no intention of easing up now. In fact, they were tightening the screw. Maybe one day I'd learn.

I looked past her to where my father sat in the reflected joy of his city. "How is he really?"

For a brief millisecond, Mona's mask slipped, then she brightened. "Don't worry about him. That's my job. You have more than enough on your plate."

"It's not that easy." While I was adept at compartmentalizing, when it came to family all boundaries crumbled.

"I know." Mona knew my weaknesses even better than I did. "What are you going to do now?"

"I'm oddly wired. I slept and showered and all of that on the plane." I should have known better than to do that as well. All that did was keep me in the time zone I left. "I left Miss P downstairs circling the wagons. Perhaps it might be good to get a download before I jump in tomorrow."

"Right. Good plan. We'll be okay." She gave me a long look then, apparently satisfied I wasn't hovering on the precipice, she let the doors slide shut. I patted my pockets for my phone.

For half the ride down, I stared at my reflection. *What had just happened?* That was so not like my mother. And who exactly did she include in "we"? If I died, she and father could go on? Is that what she meant? Knowing her as I did, that was the likeliest interpretation. However, she had been acting anything but normal during this whole little bit of joyous family time.

Try as I might, I couldn't figure her angle. In time, all would be made clear, even when it came to Mona. But especially when it came to Mona, getting a jump on her would ensure I at least had a fighting chance.

The whole family thing had me off-kilter. A seismic shift in my world was coming. I couldn't lose my father, I just couldn't.

Then Mona would be my problem once again. Having her otherwise occupied had been so nice. And the girls! Oh, I so didn't want them to have a fatherless childhood like I'd had.

Fuck.

I blinked at myself. Yes, a seismic shift rumbled, building strength, but I still looked oddly like me. Light brown hair that touched my shoulders. Big blue eyes and good cheekbones—my only redeeming physical trait, according to my mother. I pinched my cheeks to add pink to the pale. Tired lurked in the creases next to my eyes. I grimaced, checking my teeth. Then, satisfied, I plumped my hair and let it all be what it would be. I'd never be a drop-dead beauty, but I could live with the gifts I'd been given.

A hint of self-acceptance. Either that or my give-a-damn had shorted out. Either way, a new thing for me.

Time to get up to speed and back in the game.

I patted my pockets for my phone again. The one I found wasn't mine. Oh yeah, I'd lost another phone. This one I needed to find if I had any plans to summon help—and boy was I going to need some heavy hitters on my side to pull my father out of this mess.

I had no idea how many I'd lost lately, but I'm sure Miss P would let me know at some point. But she'd resisted going all corporate on me and had been a good sport about giving me hers. However, if I had her phone, I couldn't very well call her, could I? I glanced up at the security cameras tucked in between the panels lining the ceiling. Every now and again, being watched had an upside. I popped the call button, but I didn't press hard enough to trigger an alarm, only enough to get someone's attention.

"Yes, Ms. O'Toole? Do you have a problem?" The voice was sweet, young, and so welcome. This hotel was my home. These were my people. No way would I let anyone mess with the magic we'd created.

Apparently, overselling was a family trait.

"A problem? Many, but only one I could use your help with." I felt myself expanding, growing back into myself. "I seem to have misplaced my phone. I have Miss P's, so I can't reach her. Will you do the honors?"

"How—"

"I don't know. You see everything. Please figure it out and ask her to meet me in Delilah's."

"Yes, ma'am."

"Oh, and tell her if the DEA guy is still hanging around, ditch him before she meets me."

A pause, then another, "Yes, ma'am."

"Thank you." As the elevator slowed, music and the sound of revelry filtered in through the closed doors. Yep, this place was indeed my Shangri-La. If I'd die when I left, then what was the big deal in dying while trying to save it?

Clearly, jet lag induced melodrama. I'd have to find another way.

But could I really trust Sinjin Smythe-Gordon with everything and everyone I held dear?

CHAPTER FIVE

*D*ELILAH'S WAS our main bar and as such, the centerpiece of the casino. Out of the elevator and still vibrating with fear from family time, I hung a right. The crowds had thickened. Before I left on my around-the-world bit of craziness, I used to be pretty good at guessing the time by the age and size of the crowd. At the apex of one of the bridges crossing the Euphrates, I paused to drink it all in. The stream babbled below me, the ferns had curled, and the waterfowl had tucked in for the night. The reeds draping over the water looked the same, but I couldn't recall them ever changing. Young couples—the women dressed beyond the edge of propriety, the men clothed in distressed designer jeans and nonchalance— touched and darted in the age-old game of who was going to get laid tonight and by whom. Vegas, where a threesome was almost an expectation.

Personally, I was a one-guy gal. The only issue was, which guy? But, seriously, leave it to me to be the only one looking for deep in a sea of shallow.

On the other side of the bridge, the mosaic tiles gave way to lush carpet in equally brightly hued patterns. The walls were a deep purple. Wall sconces, glass around flame, provided the only light other than subtle chandeliers over the tables. Patrons three-deep circled most of the popular games. A few ladies holding their heels by the straps sat at the stools in front of their chosen slot machine. In light of the upcoming NBA tournament, the sportsbook was a raucous party with young men elbowing each other as they surveyed the odds on the big board that took up the entire wall, rising from a height of ten feet to over twenty-four. Every sort of sporting event worldwide had some sort of play.

Only a few stragglers in the crowd looked to be over sixty.

I'd say the day was long gone and the night had to be working its way to the wee hours. Twoish, maybe?

Another day.

Did I still have my magic? A silly game to calm the nerves. There was no need to look for a clock—there weren't any. From where I stood, it was impossible to tell whether it was day or night, early or late, all by design. Once captured in our cage, we didn't want anybody willing to wager to escape. So why remind them it was getting late, or it was too early to grab a drink or two and capture a position at one of the tables?

I checked Miss P's phone for the time. Yep, 2:05 on what was now Friday morning. If it's Friday, it must be Vegas? Who knew? That only worked in the movies and apparently on Tuesdays and in Belgium. Good to know I hadn't lost my touch by being out of touch.

Delilah's sat on a raised platform in the middle of the casino, also by design. While we didn't want anybody gambling while completely blotto, something the Gaming Commission took a very dim view of, a little…happy…was fine for the house. So we made sure some joy juice was never beyond a raised hand or a nod. Feeling oddly energized, I trotted up the three steps, studiously avoiding the white baby grand that sat neglected off to the side.

About this time of night, Teddie used to pull out that bench to do some winding down tickling of the ivories after his show. To finish the day off right, he used to say. His repertoire included some of my favorite old ballads, the kind of songs made famous by the Rat Pack and those who came before. I'd do my best to join him, not that I could add anything other than appreciation. I missed those days. I missed having him as my best friend. That was so much more important to me than having him as a lover. I couldn't tell whether he understood that or was hurt by it, or if he even knew.

But the choice to cut the ties that bind had been his.

In Paris he'd asked me if I could learn to trust him again. That was way beyond my capabilities at that time. With the wound still raw, homicide had still looked like a viable solution. But I was learning to step back from that.

To test myself, I slipped onto the bench and tucked my feet next to the pedals. How many times had I done that? Closing my eyes, I could feel Teddie's hip against mine, his shoulder giving mine a nudge; the remembered scent of his Old Spice embraced me with the warmth of a memory.

I languished in it for a moment, needing his touch, needing the connection, needing the joy that leaked into all the cracks and crevasses, needing the caress of his voice, needing the before…

But now it was the after. After the innocence. After the unbridled joy. After the trust was shattered.

So Humpty Dumpty really was an allegory about love.

Fuck.

Life and love were so tenuous, so fragile.

I opened my eyes and lifted the keyboard cover. Slowly, I stroked the keys that Teddie's fingers had coaxed into beautiful melodies.

They were cold, lifeless.

But I was okay. Not perfect. And only a little bit better. But I saw the hints of the old me in the hurt inside.

Don't leave the key to your happiness in someone else's pocket.

Yeah, well, I was never very good with keys or phones or anything capable of being lost, including hearts.

Miss P had beaten me to the bar. When my gaze slid over her spot, she waved in her own understated way. I almost missed it. She'd selected a nice round-top in the corner slightly raised above the flow of people as they milled around looking for the perfect game or the perfect target.

Thursday rolling into Friday, the night where everyone in town was trolling for a companion for the weekend. I never got that. Of course, I had enough of a hard time finding someone to commit to lunch. The whole weekend would clearly be pushing it. But just once, couldn't life hold more substance than a roll in the hay for forty-eight hours? A risky idea for someone in charge of the fantasy. Vegas wasn't in the business of selling commitment.

"Hey." I plopped down into the club chair across from Miss P's. She'd picked the chair that put her back to the crowd, leaving me to face it. People-watching was a favorite pastime. Thoughtful of her. "Thanks."

She nodded. "Champagne is on the way."

Wild Turkey with my parents. *Liquor then wine, I'll be fine.* "Great." As if she'd been waiting for a sign or something, the cocktail server appeared, popped the cork, then filled two flutes with perfectly pink bubbles, after which she magically disappeared. I held my flute to the light, then took a sip. "Sublime."

Miss P got a distant look on her face, and then started talking.

"Who are you talking to?"

She ignored me until she'd finished barking some quiet orders and pressed her ear.

At first, I thought she'd lost it, but then I noticed a subtle earpiece. "What's that?"

"New internal communications system. IT's been working on it for a while. They're in beta. Since I don't have a phone, I thought I'd test it out."

Somehow, I'd been out of that memo loop. Or maybe I missed it, which wouldn't be surprising. When I left the continent, I entered a different universe. Nice in a way. Totally disconcerting in another. "And?"

"You were in the loop." She must've heard the FOMO in my voice. "You had a few more important things on your plate, so I didn't push it. Anyway, they're cool."

"How do you reach who you wish?"

"You just talk. Here, watch." She composed herself, then said, "Customer Relations. Miss P."

Her phone jangled in my pocket. "Alarming."

She smiled like I was an...alarmist.

"So it's always listening?"

"Yep. Pretty cool, huh? No lost phones." She waggled her eyebrows at me, oblivious as to my point.

I looked more closely at the earpiece. "That tiny thing? Oh, I could lose it."

"No, we'd staple it to your head."

"You've thought about this?" I angled a look at her.

She puffed up a bit.

"I have one question: you know all the...delicate...things we handle around here? All the conversations that should remain private?" Her puff deflated. "If that thing is always listening, what about those?"

Her grump returned. "I hadn't thought about that. The whole system makes it so easy to get in touch with people all over the property, hands-free."

"You can do hands-free with your phone. And it's not prone to eavesdropping—at least, not yet."

"I'll talk to IT and give them our feedback."

I squelched a smile. "Good plan. Just have them insert a

command to turn the thing on like 'Hey Siri.'"

Miss P left her flute untouched. She looked all competent and perhaps a bit less confident, but underneath it all burbled that thing I'd heard in her voice before. Anger? A gazillion time zones had stretched between us for the last week or so. How could she be mad at me? Pissing people off was a skill, for sure. But usually, I had to try or at least be in close proximity.

"What's going on?"

"Nothing." She sighed. "Everything."

"I liked 'nothing' better."

She shot me a look that contained more pain than the contemplation of bodily harm, so I sipped and settled back. Her internal war marched across her face. It was interesting and alarming to watch. Not much rocked Miss P off-center. "Is everything okay at home?" A casual question. A shot in the dark.

"We'll get to that later." She clipped the words.

Bullseye. Damn. I usually tried to eliminate the worst-case scenarios first. Not this time.

She chose to divert the conversation and leave me hanging. "Did you find out anything from Air Traffic Control?"

"Not yet. The controller handling low flight along the Strip this afternoon went home at midnight. They tried to get him on the phone, but he must have Do Not Disturb on or something. Anyway, I'll track him down tomorrow. Only thing I do know is nobody filed a flight plan. I'm assuming they were just talking on the radio."

"What makes you think that?" Miss P avoided making eye contact, focusing instead on something over my right shoulder.

"If they weren't, the FAA would've been all over it. The air over us is Class Bravo airspace. To come play in here aircraft need a discreet squawk and permission from the controllers. Vegas is on the list of likely terrorist targets, so the Feds take all these rules very seriously."

"I see." She consulted her notes on the pad in front of her.

"Your mechanic called. Your roadster is ready for the show and will be delivered on time, but you need to be there."

The Concours d'Elegance! I'd forgotten. How I had let myself get roped in to showing my roadster in what amounted to a car show for the well-heeled, I didn't know. Well, actually, Jordan Marsh, an old friend, Hollywood heartthrob, and pal of the organizer exploited my weak spot for excessive horsepower hidden within fabulous design.

"Shoot. What day is it? It's Friday, right?" I'd lost track of the time zones we'd traversed, and somehow I had the impression that somewhere around Hawaii, today had become yesterday. Hadn't I confirmed that? I couldn't remember.

Miss P stared at me as if I'd grown a second head. "Shoot? Did you just use the word shoot? Could golly-gee be next? What did you do with the Lucky I know and love?" She looked slightly amused, which I took as a good sign.

"She traded up—five letters seem so much classier than four. Besides, I've learned that if you use those expressive words all the time, they lose their impact. You know me, always shooting for a high impact."

I didn't even get a chuckle.

Clearly, Miss P wasn't in an appreciative mood. "It's Friday, but just barely. You're in time."

In time. I hoped so.

And true to form, *just* in time. "Did you get any info on the helicopter used to lift the Bugatti? Getting a car like that to the top of a fifty-plus-story hotel—gotta be some machine. Did anybody give you a description? One rotor or two, that sort of thing?"

"No, not that I remember." She fingered the edge of the pad, ruffling the corners of the pages. "At that point, I didn't think it mattered. I've got requests out to my social media searchers. No report back yet on any videos surfacing."

"Understandable. But it had to be some serious helicopter.

I'm not sure, but I think the payload of a normal chopper wouldn't come close to touching the dead weight of a Bugatti... even the two-door version. And coming in that way, they'd avoid Security until the last minute—in and out, no muss, no fuss. But who the heck has that kind of stroke?"

"Is this important? You really think the car is related to the murder? The truck could've just been a convenient way to hide the body."

"The more we learn, the more we'll know."

She flicked a glance at me. "Yes, yes, of course."

"I'm counting on it being important to somebody when they want their car back. Maybe they can shed some light on the... incident...in delivery bay seven? The car is still on the roof, right?"

"Yes, as you said, it's going to take the Army Corps of Engineers to lift that thing out of there and I haven't had the time to make nice." She glanced at her notes. "Set up for the car show is tomorrow—well, technically later today." Miss P continued a dry recitation as if she was reading the dictionary. "How's your father? I assume you saw him?"

"Most of the texts on my phone before I lost it were from my mother. She must've started texting when I was somewhere over Hawaii asking me if I was home yet. I'm sure she was driving you crazy."

Miss P knew Mona almost as well as I did. I didn't have to explain that, when worried, my mother needed to reach someone, anyone, on the phone. It didn't matter whether they had the answer she was looking for, only that they were there and would keep answering. "No more than normal."

Mona could be that impossible-to-reach itch when she wanted to be. "You deserve above-and-beyond pay."

"I already have a great job and the perfect boss."

Maybe I wasn't the thing stuck in her craw. It'd be nice if she'd let me off the fence—damned uncomfortable. But history told me not to rush her. That usually ended up even more uncomfortable. "Well, there is that."

"While you were trading up, I'm glad you didn't trade hyperbole for false modesty."

"I know my limitations. Adopting affectations is way beyond my skill set."

"It's been one hell of a couple of weeks or so for you." Her voice softened, dropping the barb. "You okay?"

"No, not really. I haven't had a moment to process. I threw Jean-Charles's ring at his head and then turned and slapped Teddie telling him to grow up. Maybe I did Teddie first, then Jean-Charles. I can't quite remember the order."

"You did them both? One after another?" She could barely hide the smile that threatened to derail her grumpiness.

The idea elicited a snort. "I'm crazy but not cruel. And, like I said, I know my limitations. But I did dispatch them both with alarming efficiency."

"Really?" She gasped the word, drawing it in on an audible inhale. "A bit chummy, don't you think?"

"Would you quit? The single cylinder I'm running on is starting to cough."

"Well," she adopted a mothering tone. "It's about time you set them both straight. But seriously, they were there together?"

"Of course, they were. That's how my luck rolls, you know that. Especially when it comes to love. They both showed up independently of each other, but so close on each other's heels, it's amazing they didn't ride the elevator up together."

"I'm surprised they didn't kill each other."

"Alas, no blood mars the beautiful carpets at the Hotel Raphael. At least not that I'm responsible for. I slammed the door in their faces so whatever happened after that can't be pinned on me."

"I wouldn't say you were completely innocent." The smile broke into a wide grin.

"That argument would get me thrown in the slammer for perjury." Not that I was proud of it or anything, but I could own it.

Miss P flipped a page in her notes; she was a pencil-and-paper kind of gal. Her tone shifted back to business mode. "London has settled down—well, more or less. There's a bit of fallout over the high-speed chase through the heart of the city and the debris in the Thames from the helicopter that exploded." A question lurked in the high note at the end of the statement.

I had no idea what she expected as a response. "Let me guess, we don't have breaking-the-law-and-killing-people-by-blowing-up-helicopters insurance?"

She skewered me with a disapproving look. "You think this is funny?"

All this vacillation between humor and anger had me reaching for the bottle and a flute refill. "Inappropriate humor. My way of coping. You know that. And no, it's not funny at all. You know that, too. A girl died." And my father had just asked me to "fix" somebody. The shiver of his words and their implication raced through me. Should I tell her that, too? No, we weren't married so she could testify against me. But God knew I wanted desperately to tell somebody. The weight of my secret threatened to bury me alive. "I did make sure the girl's killer didn't get away." Yes, clutching at straws, but I needed something, anything to hang onto.

"Yes, well, a good thing too, but every police agency in the UK as well as a few international ones have some questions. I wouldn't be surprised if the Saudis sent a hit squad."

I may have imagined it but lurking between the words I caught a hint of wistfulness. I wondered what was eating her. Whatever it was, I was the bone she'd chosen to gnaw on.

Welcome home.

"Alert Security to the hit squad possibility. Refer everyone else to Legal. I gave my statement." I thought about throwing the U.S. agents who helped me onto the pyre but decided against it. Friends in unexpected places were priceless.

"And France…I'm not even sure where to begin." She once again consulted her notes.

"Then don't, please." I thought about it all—people being shot, getting shot at…Jean-Charles…his father—I didn't know if he was even alive or not. I'd left with him hanging in the balance. And Christophe, Jean-Charles's five-year-old son. How could I even consider bringing him into a life like this? Of course, that had been lurking under the surface in all my recent interactions with Jean-Charles, who'd left me with the indelible impression that I should give up my life to support his. As unpalatable as that sort of male entitlement was, he sorta had a point.

Would it be possible to give up the dead people and flying bullets part but keep the rest? That would be soooo awesome.

"Anything else?" I asked her after giving her a few moments to unruffle her feathers.

"You haven't forgotten about the basketball tournament?"

A rhetorical question I answered anyway.

"Of course not, but I wouldn't say it's been front and center. Once we get the ID on the dead guy from the coroner we can ask around, subtly, of course." We for sure couldn't pass around photos of the poor guy in his current state.

"The players are arriving, the press is circling, the entourages are keeping Jerry jumping—he's got most of the Security staff on twenty-four-hour rotations."

"Like I said, the normal feeding frenzy."

"Complicated by a murder. Frankly, it couldn't have come at a worse time."

This time it was my turn to skewer Miss P. "I'm sure the dead guy would agree. As much as I hate to say it, we've handled this before."

"Not quite. The politicos in town are driving us nuts trying to ensure we put on a good show for the NBA commissioners. Professional sports are good for the long-term growth of the city and all of that. And there's some potential owners' group from overseas that is working really hard behind the scenes."

"None of this sounds awful. Look at how the Knights grabbed the center stage nationwide." The Golden Knights were our NHL franchise—the first top-tier professional sports team sanctioned by its governing body with a permanent home in Vegas. Their first year they made it to the Stanley Cup Finals, and the town exploded. Always a bridesmaid, the two million-plus citizens of our fair city, relished finally getting a team...a real team...to act like idiots for.

"Yes, they've been amazing—such a rallying cry for the city. What everyone is worried about is another Marauders incident." The football franchise moving from San Antonio hadn't even officially arrived but had made headlines in a rather negative way. We'd buried it as soon as we could, but murder and other "misbehaving" tended to capture the limelight.

"Me, too." I recognized that Miss P, in her own inimitable way, was telling me I better hit the ground running—and bring my A-game while I was at it. "Brandy's on top of it?"

"Doing a bang-up job. But when things really get flying..."

"We'll need all hands on deck. Got it." On the long plane ride, I'd managed a bit of sleep. Now I was thankful for each and every Z.

Miss P finally leveled a long, steady gaze.

I knew that look. "What is it?"

"I can't shake the feeling something is going down with the NBA guys."

"What else is new? Something is always going down when the sports guys show up. Too much razzle-dazzle." I raised my eyebrows and grimaced, trying to elicit a smile. The footballers had snatched national headlines and not in a good way, which gave my Customer Relations Department a serious headache. It was our job to keep problems out of the papers, or at the very least, push them way down below the fold. I hoped the NBA guys would be a little less attention-grabbing than the NFL types.

My efforts went unappreciated. "That was only one bad player and an owner."

A few more were involved, but I didn't quibble. "Okay. What do you think is going down?"

"Don't know." She took a sip from her flute, flipping a glance at me over the lip of the glass. "I'm sure if Jeremy was here, he could sniff it out."

Ah, distract me and then circle back to the main issue. Clever.

Jeremy not being here surprised me. Miss P and her hubby, the Beautiful Jeremy Whitlock, Vegas's primo PI, were generally if not attached at the hip, at least on a short tether. Jeremy was fifteen years his wife's junior and the epitome of an Australian hunk. Miss P's confidence flagged sometimes—not often, and usually only with me to witness it. Frankly, I couldn't imagine always having to worry about sweet young things chasing my guy. Oh wait. I did know what that was like.

Teddie.

It sucked. But it came with the guy. So, choose the guy, choose the wondering. Trust issues had plagued me my whole life. I wasn't sure about Miss P. As a girl she'd been a Deadhead, following the Grateful Dead. To this day, she refused to confirm that she had, in fact, slept with Jerry Garcia. Had I been in that position, so to speak, I would've had kittens, or a cow, or some other barnyard animal that would have ruined the mood. I liked thinking Miss P had more moxie. Of course, she'd been raised on a farm in Iowa. I'd been nurtured in a whorehouse in Pahrump. The differences in our upbringings were staggering.

"Where'd he go?" I asked, trying to sound only casually interested and not concerned at all.

"He took some time off. A break, he said."

"Really?" I struggled for words. "A break?" I hesitated to ask from what. From his insane schedule? From his marriage?

"Yeah." Her lower lip quivered. "I don't know whether it's a break from life or a break from me."

"You didn't ask?"

"I never see him." She shot me a dagger or two as if somehow this was my fault. "Life was fine—well, I could keep it together—before you promoted me. Now, doing your job, I don't know how to be you."

So this *was* my fault. I was oddly relieved. Work problems I could solve; personal ones not so much. I could hold up my own personal life as testament.

"Thank God. Who the hell would want to be me?"

She blinked at me, then used a knuckle to tap at a tear that glinted in the corner of her eye. "I did."

"Well, I'm sure you quickly saw the error of your ways." I fortified myself with a long slug of bubbly. "Look, just do you. When you need personal time, take it. You have a great staff. Delegate. If we still can't find a balance, we'll adjust. Don't suffer the delusion that work is life. Work is just the thing that pays for your real life. People, relationships, that's life, or at least those are the only things that give meaning to our brief time on the spot of sand hurtling through the vastness of space."

She stared with her mouth open, then clamped it shut. "Profound."

"I might be developing some insight, but it's probably temporary, so don't go getting your hopes up."

"I feel like I'm not meeting expectations. Everything is going to shit." She poured the last drop into her flute.

I motioned to the cocktail waitress lurking nearby to bring another. "And now I feel like I'm not being a very good boss.

Clearly, we need to communicate. The way I did the job you now have was only possible because I had no personal life." Why had that not really been clear when I was mired in the sleepless nights and chaos? Tell me what you need, and we'll make it happen."

"I want Jeremy to stop chasing people with guns."

I laughed. "Okay, let me rephrase. Ask me for something that I can deliver."

That got a weak smile that tremored into a flat line. She waited while the waitress popped the cork and refilled our joy juice. While it wasn't delivering much joy, it was keeping me functioning. I couldn't tell with Miss P—she looked like life had knocked her off her rock. After bolting half the new portion, she leaned forward. "Murderers, drug dealers, desperate people. Lucky, what if…"

I found her hand and squeezed. "He's a big boy. He'll be okay." I wanted to assure her I had nothing to do with putting him in harm's way, but it really didn't matter. Besides, he'd gotten shot on my watch before, and we were still okay. He'd chosen his path, not that telling Miss P what she already knew would get me anywhere. "He's been doing this PI gig a long time. It's what makes his motor go. You knew that going in—he didn't hide it. You've got to find a way to deal with it. You can't expect someone to change for you."

She threw back the Champagne in her flute—a terrible waste of fantastic bubbles. "I'm enjoying your interpretation of a grown-up." She patted my hand. "You're right. How do you do it?"

"Do what? The job? I thought we'd already established I didn't do it well." Unattached and carefree, I didn't have anyone to worry about. For a trip of a second that made me sad. I needed the balance I offered Miss P. Maybe we could help each other.

"No. How do you dodge the bullets?"

Oh, yeah, I still had me to protect. "I've pissed off way too many angels. None of them want me to come play in their world, so they make sure I stay here."

That got the smile I wanted. "Are you and Jeremy okay? I mean really? You are, right?"

Miss P didn't brighten like I expected her to.

Great. If true love can't triumph, what can?

"Has he said anything? Made any demands? He went in eyes wide open as well. Same rules apply."

She rubbed a hand over her eyes, then leaned back in her chair. "Nothing. That's the problem. He hasn't said anything. It's me. It's this job."

I blew my bangs off my forehead and took her lead, leaning back as well. "We both need balance. Wanna start working through it?"

She tried for a lilt in her voice. "We don't really have the time." Irony. We both appreciated it. "It is what it is."

"A heart-eating soul suck that kills you from the inside." My words were out before I knew it. Where that bit of honesty came from, I didn't know, but it was someplace deep and real. "We're going to fix that."

"Top of my list. Well, after all of this." She riffled the pages of her notebook. Even from across the table, I could see each was filled with her tight scrawl on every line.

I wished I had the balls to put it at the top of mine. "Any idea why the DEA is looking up my skirt?" I'd sorta shelved this problem, the others being so much more terrifying. But if I knew what might be coming, I might be able to muster at least a thin defense.

"No, he insisted on speaking only with you."

"Great. Well maybe I can convince him to shut down the growing problem with smoke in the casino." With the advent of legalized pot in the state, folks seemed to think that our no-smoking signs didn't qualify as no-toking signs. Some guests objected. Some seemed confused. Others amused.

"Not sure how—"

"I'm kidding."

A smile tickled one corner of her mouth. She was pulling my chain, and damn good at it.

"I'd love to be able to give you more, but he showed up out of nowhere in a cloud of bluff and bluster right before you landed. No notice. No nothing. Since you've been gone, we've been dealing with the usual craziness—nothing that would attract the Feds."

That was good. Normal I could handle. To be honest, I could handle the DEA as well.

"Well, except for Mr. Ballantine."

She slid that knife in right between my ribs. "The cockroach guy?" Like water in a vacuum, my blood instantly boiled. I knew full well who he was, but I needed a moment to steady myself. The first time we'd met, he'd let loose a bazillion cockroaches in my hotel in an effort to blackmail us into a free room for life and a bunch of other perks. That try had ended rather ignominiously when I shoved him ass-over-teakettle out the front door, followed by his belongings, all landing in a heap on the sidewalk for all the world to laugh at. I'd enjoyed it. I'm shallow, what can I say, and totally not above getting a laugh at someone else's expense, especially when they so richly deserved it. But some-times—really most of the time—that bit of mirth usually came at a price. Mr. Ballantine returned sometime later with an anaconda. I should've shot him instead of the snake. Now I girded my loins for round three. "What's he back with this time?"

"He arrived a few hours ago. His reservation had been prepaid by some outfit out of California all about the ethical treatment of animals."

Caught in mid-sip, I snorted bubbles out my nose.

Miss P handed me a napkin.

"Thanks." I returned myself to acceptable. "There is a sort of delicious irony there, isn't there?"

"There's no way he could've reformed. I smell a rat."

"Or something worse." I couldn't resist. I felt the tension between us dissipate, the easy camaraderie return.

"There's a chilling thought. I searched every piece of his luggage and I couldn't find anything. That's what scares me."

"*Life* scares me." I wasn't lying.

"Yes, well, your recent history is enough to give one pause."

"And a lifetime of sitting in the corner rocking back and forth. What am I doing wrong?"

"I can't think of anything." She let me wiggle off the hook, for which I was grateful. "I'm sure, in time, Mr. Ballantine will give us good cause to shoot him. Do you know anything concrete about my father?"

"I thought you went to see him."

"I did, but Mona ran interference. You know the drill; life is all rainbows and butterflies."

Miss P shifted in her chair, clearly uncomfortable. "It's not good. That bullet did a bunch of soft tissue damage—I don't need to tell you that. They had to crack him open again to chase a bleeder. He came home today." She skirted the issue.

"I know he left on his own, probably in spite of the doctors."

She stopped her tap dance. "You know."

"You told me. Besides, my father has always done exactly as he pleased."

"He came home to talk to you." She didn't ask but I could tell she wanted to know.

"Trust me; you don't want this one."

"That bad?"

"Worse."

"I'm here to help if you need it." She didn't sound miffed at being left out, only sincere in her offer.

I knew his secret, and I'd been given my orders. A problem that made all the others look like child's play. No way would I bring anyone into this one unless absolutely necessary. "What is it with families?" I said, apropos of a secret I couldn't disclose.

"Everybody has one."

"Not like mine." Yes, a bit of a whine, but Miss P usually let me have my moment. Then she'd tell me to go kick some ass.

"You're the head of your family now," she said, surprising me.

"That was so not what I was expecting."

"Your father is not making good decisions—he doesn't have the energy to make the right ones, the hard ones. And Mona…"

I covered her hand with mine. "That may not have been what I was expecting, but it's exactly what I needed to hear. You have no idea."

She smiled as if she might.

"So tell me what you think is going on with the NBA crowd."

She opened her mouth to speak, but her cellphone cut her off with an incessant ring that sounded like sirens.

"Seriously?" I asked. "That'd have me jumping out of my skin."

"I'm rethinking." She looked at me, waiting. Then she snapped her fingers.

"Oh, right." I pulled her phone from my pocket and handed it to her.

She pressed the device to her ear. "Customer Relations, Miss P speaking."

Despite my exceptional sleuthing skills, I'd never discovered her first name—something she kept locked away, fueling fevered speculation. She'd even managed to seal her marriage license. To be honest, I hadn't the time or energy to dig deeper, like back in Iowa where she grew up. Secrets were personal things. I wasn't about to go traipsing around in her secret garden. Not my business.

"Yes, yes, she's home." Miss P covered the mouthpiece and angled a look to get my attention. "Do you have any idea where your phone is? I'm not going to spend my time taking calls for you."

"Neither of us would survive. Maybe we should tether the next one to me?" I thought back. "Last time I had it was on the plane. After talking with you, I tossed it on the seat next to me. Jerry confirmed it's still somewhere at the airport according to the find-my-phone thing."

She rolled her eyes and covered the microphone. "It's probably on its way to Bora Bora or somewhere, but maybe we can retrieve it." She uncovered the mike and raised her voice. "She's right here. No phone. Hang on." She thrust her phone at me—it was at least three models old. I hadn't noticed before. The woman never lost anything.

I bet I drove her crazy. A spark of appreciation warmed my heart, or maybe it was the Champagne. "Who is it? I'm not officially back."

"Rudy. And he sounds freaked."

Rudy Gillespie occupied the top spot in Jordan Marsh's heart. Yes, even though Jordan Marsh was a Hollywood heart-throb idolized by legions of women worldwide, he was gay. Through his early career, I'd been one of the gatekeepers of the secret. Hell, I'd even introduced him to Rudy. Recently, Jordan and Rudy had come out. Despite having broken many hearts with the revelation, their move hadn't dimmed Jordan's star in the slightest.

I took the phone. "Hey, Rudy, what's up?"

"Are you in the hotel?" His voice sounded stretched to the max.

"Yes."

"Oh, thank God! I need you to work some of your big problem voodoo."

CHAPTER SIX

"CAN IT wait?" I knew the answer from the tone of Rudy's voice, but I asked anyway.

"I'm sorry. I'm sure you're swamped. But I really need you...now."

"Is Jordan okay?"

"Other than driving too fast with his car buddies, he's fine."

"Where are you?"

"The Kasbah. Bungalow 10."

"On my way." I pocketed Miss P's phone. "Who's staying in Bungalow 10?"

Miss P consulted her notepad. "A Pearl Coleman."

"Well..." I took a moment to savor the last of my Champagne"...let's go find out what's going down with the NBA types."

She hurried to keep up with me as I strode toward the back of the casino and the hidden hallway that led to the Kasbah, our private and posh hotel-within-a-hotel reserved for celebrities and only the highest of the high rollers. "I'm taking it Mr. Coleman is with the NBA?"

"Check your list." Behind me she couldn't see my smile.

"According to many, he is the future of the NBA, the most sought after rookie. Rudy represents him. Jordan told me the whole thing has been brutal, a tightrope of a feeding frenzy. So many rules, so many willing to break them to bag their career-maker."

"If they don't land in jail." She followed me through the nondescript entrance half-hidden between two tall plants. I hung a right and motored down the long hallway. Wood-paneled walls and thick carpet muffled the energy and excitement of the casino that filtered in behind us.

"When was the last time you heard of that happening? The kids get slammed; the agents slither away."

"Rudy landed a big one?" Miss P still spoke in a voice raised to be heard above the gamblers. Here it sounded like a shout.

"Indeed. He loves looking after the youngsters."

The guard behind the desk looked up, then smiled in recognition. "Ms. O'Toole. Welcome home. Some of us didn't think you were coming back."

That stopped me dead. "Really? I never had any intention of staying away."

"That's good news, real good news."

"Thank you. We'll be in Bungalow 10." I pulled Miss P along as I took a right and got quickly back up to speed.

"Yes, ma'am." His voice filtered after us.

"Why would they think that?" I asked Miss P as I slowed my pace. We stepped into the main atrium of the Kasbah.

Miss P tucked in at my shoulder. "Love triumphs." She'd modulated her voice to a reverent whisper, suitable for the rarified air of the Kasbah.

"Over what? A good job with pay sufficient to compensate for the 24/7 requirement? A way to be needed and make a difference? Do you have to choose?"

"Maybe." She looked crestfallen. Women were often asked to make impossible choices. I never understood why there wasn't a better solution, sort of a meet-in-the-middle thing. Of course, that would require the other side to step down from their thrones.

Once again, the Big Boss hit it out of the park with the design of the Kasbah. Clusters of individual bungalows nestled under the glass of a huge atrium. Some of the bungalows had individual dipping pools. Others came with a baby grand or almost anything else the guest desired...and they could desire the most alarming things. There was the guy who couldn't sleep without a set of knight's armor standing guard in the corner. The sword had been an issue. We'd substituted a plastic one and he was none the wiser. So many requested hooks for various sexual swings and whatnot that when we did the remodel of all the bungalows, we retrofitted all the units with them to save time. One wanted a lion in a cage. Another a French chef, female, a barely-there size two, to do his bidding. That was a bit tricky, but we managed to stay within the law and keep everyone happy. And those were just the ones that popped into my head without much thought. And they were some of the tamest. Someday I'd write a book.

A stream wound through the properties and tall reeds and palms provided atmosphere as well as privacy. The entrances were guarded and security tight. That's why when I caught a young woman with a mike in her hand skulking through the brush, my radar pinged. The fact that she was followed by a cameraman sealed the deal.

I tapped Miss P on the shoulder, then focused her attention on the twosome. I put a finger to my lips, and then motioned for her to follow me. We fell into trail behind the cameraman and reporter. "Let's see where they're heading," I hissed at her over my shoulder.

We snaked around through the brush along the stream. I hadn't really dressed for the wetlands, but these bozos could buy me a pair of shoes. After all, there should be a price to pay for ducking past serious security. Of course, I'd buy them a pair of shoes or dinner or whatever if they told me how they got in…more precisely, who let them in. Securing the entrances was easy. Hiring people who couldn't be bribed, not so much. But then, they didn't need to know I was in a bargaining frame of mind.

Reeds tugged at my pants. Water oozed into my shoes—one of the few vintage pairs of Loubous I had left after the bomb in my apartment vaporized everything I owned. The thought made me pissy, which I channeled into some semblance of seething badass. Badass would be good when I caught my prey. I took delight in the fact that the young woman in front of me also sported some high-end duds. I doubted her boss would pay the freight, which made me happy. I wondered what target made the sacrifices worthwhile.

Miss P kept her hand on my butt like an elephant in line, as we followed them. "I'm betting Bungalow 10," she whispered.

"A good bet. The young Mr. Coleman draws crowds wherever he goes. Our highest profile basketball star since Magic Johnson, or so I've read," I muttered between clenched teeth as mud oozed between my toes. "Comes with the territory, I guess." Magic Johnson would have enough experience to eat these two in front of us for lunch. Our newbie? Not so much. No wonder Rudy called in reinforcements.

I slithered Miss P's phone from my pocket. It was a standard-issue Babylon device, so I knew the speed dial for Security. Jerry answered on the first ring.

I started in without preamble. "Tell me, why am I following two idiots sneaking through the Kasbah, hoping to catch one of our guests in a compromising position?"

"What?" His voice had a husky, raspy sound I didn't like. Too many cigarettes despite his wife and me hounding him half to death.

"We're sneaking around Bungalow 8." I stopped, taking

advantage of some bushes to hide us. With my free arm, I parted the greenery slightly. I watched the two butts as they slithered on. "They're heading toward Bungalow 10, I'd bet. Get a bead on them and a security detail…no, come yourself. There's a camera involved." I thrust the phone back where it came from.

"Let's go." Fairly sure of our OK Corral, I took a shorter route around Bungalow 3.

Miss P and I were waiting at the back of Bungalow 10 when the talking head and her videographer slipped sideways through a gap in the privacy fence of mile-high bamboo reeds a foot thick. Heretofore I'd thought them impenetrable. Another lesson learned.

I hadn't yet gotten an eyeball on her face.

"You guys looking for someone in particular? Or just some ill-gotten juicy, career-ending bit of Vegas debauchery in general?" With our backs to the French door rear entrance to Bungalow 10 and the plantation shutters buttoned up tight behind us, Miss P and I, arms crossed, formed a rather impenetrable front. The reporter used the cameraman for cover like somehow, I wouldn't notice her there. "You come here."

When she did as I asked and gave me the full frontal, I gasped. "Flash! What the hell?"

For as long as I could remember, Flash Gordon had been my best friend, cohort in minor crimes and misdemeanors, and the one willing to bury the bodies and not ask any questions, which took a Herculean effort for an investigative reporter. And she was the best of all those in town in that line of work. Award-winning, irritating, and staring at me, her mouth open, her eyes wide. Today she'd decided to encase her lush figure capped by a set of double Ds in a white sheath that started so low most men would be willing her to take one big breath, just one, and ending barely below her choochilala. As sheer as it was, it was unmarred by the unsightly lines of any hint of an undergarment. She'd stripped the color from her normal red hair making it platinum. She changed the color so often I could never keep up. One day, all that lovely hair would finally give up and fall out, but it still clung to her with abandon. Today she'd pulled it into a ponytail on top of her head in a terrifying *I Dream of Jeannie* caricature.

Flash wiggled her dress down a few inches, which had me holding my breath for the top coverage. Nothing bounded loose, for which I was grateful. This was awkward enough. I hadn't any idea what to say.

Flash clamped her mouth shut, then opened it. "You're home."

"No, I died years ago and now they've taken my body on a hologram tour."

She rolled her eyes. "We're on a case."

My turn for the eye roll. "This is private property, by invitation only and you are here at my largesse or lack of it." Most folks considered the hotel public property where anyone could come or go on a whim. Legally, that wasn't the case. "You know that. Sneaking in here like a couple of gossip mongers looking for some juicy tidbit of celebrity bad behavior. You're better than that."

"Lucky, seriously." She glanced around as if the bushes had ears. "I can't talk here, but just let me get on with what I was doing, and I'll explain everything later. Although, you've like super blown my cover."

"Your cover?" I knew better than to let her roll with this. Once a storyteller got up to speed, they could flatten the truth and you'd never know it.

"I'm not supposed to be me," she hissed.

"Yeah, well, I'm not supposed to be me either. I'm sure there was some snafu at the hospital; switched babies were the thing back in the day. But here we are."

"I got your back, Lucky." Jerry's voice rose from the other side of the bamboo. "You good in there?" He pushed through to join the party. He stopped short when he spied Flash. "Should I get between you two?"

We ignored him.

I turned to Flash. "The way I see it, you two are guilty of trespassing. You snuck in here when all you had to do was ask."

"But you weren't here!" Flash's voice slipped into a slight whine.

"I was here," Miss P said.

"Yes, well, you're a bit less of a soft touch than our Fearless Leader here."

"Great," I said, not the least bit pleased at being steamrolled.

"How do you know we snuck in here?" Flash asked, blood finally getting through the cinch of her sheath and firing a few neurons.

"I don't. But I don't see any credentials." Each person in the Kasbah had to be cleared at one of the two entrances, and each would've been issued a badge personal to them, outlining the boundaries of their admission. I waited, resisting tapping my foot as a bit too maternal. After a few moments, I continued. "As I said, trespassing. We take security and the privacy of our guests very seriously. My bad trumps your lie. Do we really have to play this game?"

Flash wilted just a tad. I knew her well enough to know what was going through her head—she was desperately searching for an angle to get herself out of this. She settled on the truth—I knew her well enough to see that, too. "There's a girl in that room." She lifted a chin toward the bungalow behind me.

"I'm shocked," I said, which was my way of telling her to get on with it and make it quick and preferably believable. "A setup?"

"Yeah. Something is going down with the basketball players." Flash was known far and wide for her affinity for the NBA, okay, maybe not the NBA per se, but for sure the players. That's how she'd gotten her nickname Flash—an interesting evening that involved Flash and a busload of NBA-types. But I was sworn to secrecy.

Miss P gave me a nudge. "See? I told you."

"You did." I turned to Flash. "What exactly?"

"I don't know. That's why I'm here. I paid off the tawdry bit of reporter trash that would've broken whatever con we're going to find in that bungalow. Right now, I'm known as Sheila Rothbottom, cub reporter."

Miss P snickered. I managed to keep a straight face. "*Cub* reporter?" She looked like a tigress ready to eat her young.

"We all have our fantasies," Flash admitted in a rare acknowledgement of the years that had passed.

"Tell me about it." We both grinned wicked grins.

I decided to let her run with this. "Okay, how do you want to play it?"

"Just act like I'm Sheila Rothbottom and I've been caught trespassing, and let's see what happens." She turned to her cameraman. "You in?"

"Man, can I work with you all the time? Nothing like this ever happens to me."

She turned back to me. "We're in. Let's go see what we see."

I glanced behind me and saw three sets of peepers looking through slats in the plantation shutters—two high, one lower. I knew of two people in the bungalow. I wondered who the third one was. Definitely shorter than the other two. A female, as Flash said. Rudy hadn't mentioned a female. A female in the mix sweetened the pot and evaporated any semblance of goodwill I might muster. I pressed my lips together as I turned back to Flash and the cameraman.

"This is a set up."

"Didn't I say that already?" Flash asked, a bit put out. "I'm just trying to find out who's blackmailing these kids and what for."

"Blackmail?"

She nodded. "With some interesting twists that I don't understand."

"You better give me everything once this goes down. You got it?" That was usually how we rolled—she helped me; in return, I gave her the inside skinny. However, today the roles were reversed. Another little life jab—Flash was in control. Did I trust her? That would be a hell yes! But only because I could catch her if she ran.

I turned and grabbed the handle of the French doors and twisted. Time to get my thespian on. "Jerry, will you escort our guests inside? Time to quit playing games."

The plantation shutters snapped shut, and I felt the knob turn as someone opened the door from the inside. They stepped out of the way to let us file through.

"Lucky, thanks for coming." Rudy sounded harried and a bit at a loss.

The room was dark, the only light filtering in through the slits in the window coverings. When everyone was inside and the door secured, I flipped on a few of the lamps. "Jerry, will you?" I lifted my chin toward the camera. The cameraman relinquished it without a fight, which I pretended made me suspicious. Flash didn't have room in her outfit for a phone or other recording device, so no need to frisk her. Although that little bit of indignity was almost too tempting.

"Trespassing is taken very seriously around here," I admonished Flash, who tried her best to look cowed. I've never seen her even mildly standing down, so this was a new thing. I enjoyed it.

Afraid of her answer, I didn't give her the opening. Instead, I leveled my gaze at the cameraman who once again caved. He offered his phone to Jerry, who pocketed it. Then I turned to survey the others gathered.

I lingered on the other woman in the room, the one I didn't know. Dressed in a French maid's costume with all the essentials most assuredly not covered and wearing a wide sash over one shoulder that had "Happy Birthday" spelled in large hot-pink block letters on it, she kept her eyes lowered.

The young Mr. Coleman towered over all of us. In kitten heels I was about six-three. He had a good eight or nine inches and a hundred pounds, I was glad to see, on me. I often outweighed the tall, skinny ones who could match or beat my height. To be honest, I had a bit of a complex about it.

"I don't know this woman." He gestured to the French maid. "She knocked on the door and then barged right in here."

"I'm from the Ditty Dolls," she said, not at all convincingly.

"Ditty Dolls? That's like a thing?" First I'd heard of them. I raised an eyebrow at Miss P. She shrugged.

Flash covered her smile at my rising indignation. "Hey, it's better than the Belting Broads."

I wasn't so sure. With a name like that in a place like this, they never would've gotten off the ground. After counting to twenty, I'd pushed it out of my mind and refocused. "Where's your badge to get in here?" I asked the French maid.

She patted her chest, making sure all the men noticed. "I must've lost it." She smiled sweetly at Rudy.

I wasn't going to tell her she was wasting her time, but she sure as hell was wasting ours. "Bullshit. You aren't from some singing service. You've been paid to sneak in here, then wait until the camera and the sleazy reporter were in place. Then you were to get Mr. Coleman in a compromising position."

I narrowed my gaze. I knew her. The French maid outfit was new. I searched my mental depths—okay, more like shallows. She was there…a faint memory. I snapped my fingers, then pointed at her. I *did* know her! "The woman giving blow jobs in the bathroom!"

She ducked her head. "Yes, ma'am."

Ah, yes, there was the hint of the South in her voice. I remembered that better than her face. What was it they said about sound? It can often trigger a memory almost as well as smell. Boy, I knew the smell thing. Someone in the room was wearing Old Spice which ripped my heart open. Old Spice was Teddie's *Eau de Choix*.

A bit wide-eyed, Pearl Coleman looked scared. "A set up? Man, who are these people? And why would they want to do that to me? I got a kid and wife back home. She'll have my balls."

Rudy patted his dark curls into place and adjusted his tie. Impeccable as ever. "And, while his contract has been negotiated, it hasn't been inked. We can't afford all this…" He made a sweeping gesture that included the room.

I bored into the French Maid. "Seems to me I gave you a free pass that day on the proviso I'd never see you in my hotel again. Right?" I moved to loom over her. Size did have its advantages.

I hooked my thumb at Flash, who stood off to the side, drinking everything in. "You guys acquainted?" They glanced at each other, then shook their heads in unison. "I'll take that as a yes. Rudy, why don't you take Mr. Coleman into the other room and pour him a glass of something potent?"

"He's only twenty."

"Man, today's my birthday." The kid didn't sound too happy about it.

As if remembering her story, the French maid grew a half-inch of backbone. "That's right! That's why I was sent here. His birthday!"

I whirled on her. "Who sent you?"

"Umm. Umm. This guy…" She wilted again. Flash groaned.

"Quite the duo you are—seasoned criminals. Jerry…"

He grabbed the cameraman by the arm. "Come with me. You and I gotta talk." He escorted him toward the kitchen.

Once they were out of earshot, I turned to the girls. "Somebody is playing you. I want to know who, what they paid you, and what they're after." I pointed at Flash/Sheila Rothbottom. "And, after you guys tell me all that, your get-out-of-jail-free card is telling me how you guys skirted Security."

"What's in it for us?" Flash pulled herself to her full height and puffed out her chest in a show of defiance that sorely strained her bodice.

I lowered my head. "I let you live."

"She'll do it, too." The French maid supported my bluff. "I tell you, Sheila. I heard things." She lowered her voice to a stage whisper. "You know who her father is."

My father's reputation preceded me. Good to know.

Rudy didn't laugh and ruin everything. He did give me a hint of a wry smile and a wink. His tastes ran to fine tequila. I'd buy him some Don Julio 1942. That stuff was smooth as liquid smoke...just like Rudy.

I kept up the pressure on the French maid. "So, you do know each other?"

"By name only. I was told to call her."

"By whom?"

"I don't know," she wailed. "It was all done over the phone."

"That didn't make you suspicious?" The moment the words were out, I wanted to corral them. Everything in her life was not like mine. Her normal would raise every red flag I had.

"The money was epic. Seemed harmless enough."

"But it wasn't, was it?" I snapped my fingers at French Maid Girl. "Your purse."

She clutched the beaded bag to her ample chest.

"You don't have to hand it over," Flash said, getting into her part as skanky Sheila.

"Fine for you to say." Little Miss French Maid puffed up. "You're not from here. My family lives here. You stay, you'll learn quickly—you don't piss off the casino people. My grandmother died in a car bombing in the parking garage at one of the casinos back in the day. It's not here anymore, neither is my gran, but she always said Vegas people take care of their own."

I know my mouth hung open. The Vegas she described lived on only in the movies and apparently the heads of impressionable people. Now we were a city of suits and hedge funds and lawyers. But I wasn't above using her naiveté to my advantage. I snapped my fingers again. "Baseball bats and bones bleaching in the desert."

"Rumors." Flash laughed but her bravado slipped, revealing a hint of fear. We were friends, but my father scared her. That had always made me laugh. Now, I saw a different side. How he handled family…well, he had different rules for us and…them. When it came to my father, I'd never walked a mile in somebody else's shoes.

"Where there's rumor, there's truth." I shot a warning glance at Rudy. It was unnecessary. He'd adopted a serious expression and managed to keep it that way.

"Is she serious?" The ballplayer couldn't keep quiet.

Rudy motioned for the kid to follow him. "Come on, Pearl. Let's go find that drink. You don't want to witness how this goes down." He led the kid off toward the bar. To his credit, the basketball player went reluctantly—even though the women had set him up, he still felt like he needed to come to their rescue, at least a little bit. I liked him, which made me madder.

I turned back to the two women who watched the men leave then turned to me with a mixture of fear and sadness. All this time Miss P had remained steadfast at my side. I could practically feel her indignation.

"Look, this has all been fun. I'm not in the business of killing people, well, at least not in my own backyard." It was the truth. I ignored Miss P's wide bit of side-eye. "This is a straight-up game of you scratch mine, I'll scratch yours. First the purse. Then a name. Then the security thing. Then I let you both walk out of here. But I warn you, you do this sort of thing again—you try to ruin someone's reputation to enhance yours—there's no place you'll be able to hide."

French Maid handed me her purse with a huff. "She'll do what she says, both the good and the bad. I've been on the losing end of this game with her before."

"May I?" I proffered the purse before I opened it. Not sure why, but evidence procured with permission was unassailable, or so I'd been told. But was that just for the cops? I couldn't remember.

"Be my guest."

I popped open the latch and started pawing through the contents. I didn't have to dig far. "What have we here?" I pulled out a plastic bag filled with dried green buds.

"Hey! It's not a crime to have a bit of weed."

"Depends on where you got it." I pocketed the weed. "Are you sure it was purchased from a legal dispensary?"

"Nobody can tell that!" She bit her lip as her flash of defiance disappeared. "Can they?"

"They can." What I knew about testing narcotics, especially the new legal stuff, embarrassed even me, but I wasn't above fudging. However, the time had come to invest in a short course.

"I think I'll keep this and see where it came from," I said. Flash went all wiggly, wanting to argue, but she kept her mouth shut.

The French maid went all Valley girl. "Oh man, it helps with the inhibitions, you know?"

The first time I'd let Little Miss French Maid go she'd been giving blow jobs, so I wasn't clear on any inhibitions the woman might have, not that I was dumb enough to ask. "You didn't buy this, did you?"

"No. It was part of my payment."

Now we were getting somewhere. "How was payment delivered?"

"Left in that car that ended up on the roof."

"Really?" Clearly, she didn't know about the dead guy or she wouldn't have put herself at the scene. "When did you go get it?"

"I didn't, one of the guys working the deliveries gave it to me —an envelope with my name on it."

And she was known to the guys in Delivery. "Which guy?"

"I don't want to get nobody in trouble." She kept looking at Flash for reassurance or guidance. Flash nodded her head.

"Okay, the head guy, Jeff. But he handles all my...transactions...down there. He takes a cut for looking the other way."

Calm proved elusive as I tried to focus. "You need to stop shading the truth here. You got paid alright, but not with the pot. What were you supposed to do with it?"

With one hand on her hip, she eyed me. "You sure you haven't spent time on my side of the street? You got a sixth sense on how these things go down."

"My mother..." I stopped and shook my head: her story, hers to tell. Besides, I refused to be drawn into a casual discussion with Little Miss Flout the Law.

"You were supposed to plant the stuff here where little Miss Rothbottom over there was supposed to find it. How close am I?"

"Spot on."

Her willingness indicated I'd earned her trust.

Pride and horror warred for my attention. "You do know a rookie being caught with weed would lose a serious bunch of green?"

Her eyes grew wide. She seemed genuinely shocked. Either she was a lot smarter than I knew her to be, or she really didn't know.

I pressed home my point. "Yeah, whoever paid you to come in here, maybe on the pretense of a birthday present for a friend? Well, he or she had an ulterior motive—to really hurt that kid bad."

"You can't know that." She looked like she was about to cry.

I liked her. God help me. "No, but why have you, clearly a hooker, bring the weed then hire a news crew to sneak in here and film it all?"

"I ain't no hooker." A tear slipped down her cheek. "My mother would be so disappointed."

I looked at Miss P. "How'm I doing?"

She winced. "A little rusty, but the theory is solid."

I returned to the now-empty purse. Tugging at the lining, I opened a slit in the bottom. I stuck two fingers through the hole and extracted a piece of paper. No, a business card. I held it up to the light and squinted.

Walker Preston
Fine Autos of Sonoma
Sales

There was an address and a number, but I needed context. "Tell me, who is Mr. Walker Preston, and why did you feel the need to hide his business card in the lining of your purse?" I couldn't shake the feeling that the name sounded familiar.

Flash inched closer as if she had the same question...or she knew the answer.

Maybe I could play this and get what I wanted. "I have always wanted a Karnac the Magnificent moment. Here it is!"

Miss P stifled a smile. The other two women looked lost.

What was it with kids these days? They had no appreciation for greatness. "Johnny Carson, only the best ever on late-night television?"

Still nothing but two white screens.

"I can see you both had a somewhat lacking childhood. Anyway, this is how we play. I give you an answer, and you give me the question." Not exactly as Johnny did it, but I was fresh out of envelopes. "Here's the first one. Who is a guy with a missing Bugatti?"

"Oh, Mr. Preston's car isn't missing," the French Maid said. God, I wished I knew her name. But actually, I really didn't want to know it—that would be a whole other level of intimacy that I had no desire to share with the woman. "It's on the roof."

"It's on the roof?" Flash couldn't hide her incredulity.

"Okay, that's not how we play. In this instance, you would answer, who is Walker Preston?"

"Huh?"

"Are you having fun?" Miss P asked, her voice as dry as the desert.

Apparently, I needed to add "playing along" to her job description. "Never mind." Games weren't fun unless everybody knew the rules.

"How do you know the car is on the roof?" I asked the French maid.

"Walker told me."

"When he bribed you to come plant some weed on the kid and get some nasty photos?"

Finally, a little bit of scared leaked into her presentation in the form of wider eyes and a tremor to her voice. "He said he was doing a favor for a friend. I swear." The clichéd hooker with a heart of gold or an opportunity in Hollywood missed? Hard to tell.

"Is he the one who paid you?"

"Like I said, the envelope was left in the car. He was the one who told me where it was, that's all." She sounded a bit sweet on Mr. Walker Preston.

"Did he happen to mention which friend?"

She looked surprised. "I assumed the basketball player."

Flash danced around like the smart girl waving her hand at the teacher. I thought I was a step ahead. "Any specific messages you were supposed to deliver? Other than happy birthday, of course?" I asked our French maid.

Out of the corner of my eye, I saw Flash deflate.

"Yeah." She nodded vigorously like she'd drawn a get-out-of-jail-free card. "I was supposed to tell him three strikes and you're out."

"Any idea what that meant?"

"Part of the game, I guess?"

She guessed better than she performed. "Any idea where Mr. Walker Preston is right now?"

Before answering, she looked up at the ceiling and to the left, a sure sign a lie was coming. "I'd never seen him before. Don't know him. Couldn't tell you."

Methinks the lady doth protest too much. Thank you, Mr. Shakespeare.

"Where'd you meet him?"

"Right here."

"In the Kasbah?"

"No, the loading docks. He said he didn't want us to be on camera together. I get that a lot. I showed him where the dead spot is in the video monitoring. A necessary skill if you get what I mean."

For a moment, she must've forgotten who she was talking to. While she was on a roll, I wasn't going to remind her. "The one in the bays?"

"Yeah, bay seven is the best."

"You go down there regularly?" I thought about all the security she'd have to avoid in order to do that, and I wondered how many she'd have to bribe.

"Like I said, necessary skill. Sometimes Jeff would let me in. He didn't see any harm, he said."

I tilted my head as a thought hit me. I tried to dodge it, but it was too good. "You want a job?"

Both Flash and the French Maid said, "What?" in unison.

"You want a chance at a safer life where you're not scared of johns or of being caught?"

Hope lit a fire that danced in her eyes, then they narrowed. "What do I have to do?"

"I'll let you talk to Jerry, the gentleman who was just in here, about that. He's our Head of Security."

"I know. I got all their names and faces down."

Flash hissed at me. "You wouldn't."

"She's perfect." I turned back to my future new hire. "You'll get all the benefits and a livable salary to start, and the opportunity to earn your way up the food chain. But you have to keep your nose clean. Can you do that?"

"I got a pimp who'll be pissed." Suddenly the ramifications of going straight hit her.

"I'll take care of him." I looked at the girl—and she was just that, a girl. The makeup and hard knocks added toughness that belied her age, but underneath she still was just a kid. "What's your name?" At her hesitation, I added, "I'll need the one that Social Security attaches to you."

"Chastity." She ducked her head waiting for the laugh that didn't come. Finally, she looked up. "Chastity Danielson. My father was a preacher. He had high hopes."

Preachers' kids, a cliché if there ever was one. "Not misplaced at all." Even I convinced myself of my sincerity.

Miss P cleared her throat, which meant I'd better stifle the rest of my do-gooder instincts. "Okay, back to the business at hand. Did Mr. Walker Preston put the car on my roof?"

"I don't think so," Flash said. "He doesn't have the stroke. He's a salesman, and a huckster if there ever was one."

Flash should know. I thought about that for a minute. "Good point. So, who does?"

"I don't know, but what about the owner of the dealership, Fine Autos of Sonoma?"

"Don't know how much stroke he has, but he's gotta have a ton of green. He trades in expensive iron."

"All the cars are on consignment."

"Really? Do we know who actually owns the Bugatti then?"

"It'll be titled under some obscure import company based in Hong Kong. Most of the Fine Autos of Sonoma inventory is."

"Hong Kong?" Man, I needed my phone! The more I learned, the more I needed Sinjin Smythe-Gordon. "I know buying expensive assets like cars and art, then exporting them to the U.S. is a great way to get money out of China, or anywhere else, I guess."

"Money laundering?" Flash asked.

"Maybe, but more likely just lifestyle smuggling. Anybody with eight hundred grand or so can buy a piece of property here and get a visa. Stupidest law ever, but there you have it. Or they can just get money out to play with. This is a town of excesses. How many Asian kids fly around this town in a different expensive car each day? They have to get the money somehow."

"A good theory." Flash pulled a pencil from between her breasts. I have no idea from where she pulled the notebook, but she flipped it open and started taking notes. "Might be interesting to dig some dirt on the owner?" She glanced up. At my nod, she bent to more scribbles. "I can handle that, but you can help. Something is going on with those cars. Don't know what. Don't know who. And I can't get cozy with toffs; I don't have the right cachet." She paused and gave me a tilted head look. "But *you* can."

CHAPTER SEVEN

*F*LASH ROUNDED up her cameraman and decamped, I hoped to put on more clothes.

Miss P and I walked back to the main section of the hotel from the Kasbah. We'd left Rudy giving his client a lecture about the sharks trolling for fresh meat like him.

Even in my hotel. "We need to debrief that girl, Chastity, on how she got in here."

"Level of priority?" Miss P, always the stickler for details.

"After murder, before anything else." If I couldn't keep my guests safe, then I'd fail at providing a haven for all who paid very top dollar for me to do so.

Jerry had been lukewarm about my hiring suggestion, but he'd taken the French maid with him. I'm sure I'd take the fallout later. One more call to make, then I could deal with my jet lag and worry by planting my face in a pillow...or drinking heavily. It was a toss-up.

Miss P's phone rang. I looked at the caller ID. "I'll take this one." I pressed it to my ear as I ignored the shake of her head. "Hey, Detective."

Romeo sounded tired and more than a bit defeated. "Have you solved our crime yet?"

"No, but I got an interesting angle." I told him what the French maid said about Jeff and the prostitution ring he was running in my delivery bays.

When I finished, Romeo waited a moment before speaking. "Man, this job is getting to me. I can't handle family doing shit to their own; even the little shit gets to me."

"Hurts worse when you don't see it coming. But the inside man is so ubiquitous he's a cliché."

"Like the butler did it." Romeo managed a laugh. "You think he had anything to do with the murder?"

The suggestion raised my hackles, but then I calmed down. "Well, a possibility, as much as I'd hate to consider it. But we haven't linked him to the dead guy or the car, so no motive. Without that…" But I was so going to bust his butt after all this was over. And there had to be someone else, someone with customer contact in on the deal. Another problem for another day. At least we could shut him down.

"I know, just barking up the nearest tree hoping to find the murderer so I can get some sleep. I know it's usually not the right place to look. But I'll put him on the hot seat about it, see if I can't open a can of worms that might be good bait."

"How about we tag-team him in the morning?" I was approaching *non compos mentis* and, despite his continuing facility with metaphors, Romeo had to be among the walking dead. "We both will be better with some shut-eye."

"Good plan. Your place or mine?"

"Yours is so much more incentivizing." Nobody liked the sterile environment of the interrogation rooms at the Detention Center. Much, much too real.

"Got it. I'll pull him in early, say around nine?"

"Sure. I got nothing else to do."

We both laughed. Up to our ass in alligators was standard

operating procedure for both of us. "Lucky, we got this covered." Romeo adopted a parental tone. "Now you wait while we do our jobs. Go get that sleep."

For once I thought I'd take his advice.

"By the way, the truck was rented by Walker Preston of Fine Autos of Sonoma. The company said they work with him all the time shipping cars all over."

"Thanks." I had no idea what to make of that…if anything. They weren't trying to hide, so that was something.

Life caught up to me in the lobby. Overwhelmed by fatigue, I sagged against Miss P. "I don't even know where home is anymore." My apartment was a construction zone. Besides, I felt sure the bomb hadn't incinerated all the memories of Teddie lurking in every corner.

Teddie had been using the smaller apartment next to my parents—the only other accommodation on the top floor. My owner's apartment at my own boutique hotel, Cielo, seemed to be the only option. But right now, Cielo's location at the southern end of the cool part of the Strip—far enough away, yet close enough for mischief—seemed like such a trek. "I don't even have my luggage. If the pilots tried to let me know where they sent it, they would be trying on my phone." I felt my brows bunch into a frown. "But don't they have my phone? Have I solved even one problem today? I don't think so. In my own inimitable way, I've collected more but not offloaded any, not even the ones I spend a lot of effort avoiding."

A smile fought against Miss P's all-business air.

"Happy?"

"Maybe not happy, but I am finding amusement in all this. Most folks who run away from problems usually leave town. You just change hotels."

"Another good theory that failed in the execution. Not only do I need balance, I also need a home, a real home."

Paolo rushed through the front door like my Saving Grace,

but with the energy of an Avenging Angel. I braced for impact. "Miss Lucky, I am here to take you home!"

"Do you know where it is?"

He laughed as if I was being funny. "Your suitcases…have been taken care of." He gave Miss P a curious look. "And…" he reached into his pocket, then handed me a phone with a flourish "…here's your phone."

"My phone!" I pressed it to my chest, then bestowed a kiss on his cheek. "Thank you! Did you happen to answer all the emails and delete the texts?"

He recoiled in horror. "I wouldn't dream of it."

"Too bad. You'd do a better job than me, I bet." I pocketed the phone and returned Miss P's to its rightful owner. I noticed she'd ditched the earpiece. "You need an upgrade, by the way."

"I hate upgrading my phone. I have to remember all the passwords."

And she had always upgraded/replaced mine without a whimper. "You get the phone, I'll do the upgrade."

"Dear God, no." Now she acted like I should be doing stand-up. Well, if the hotel thing finally ate my lunch, that could be an easy career move—same amount of criticism, shorter hours, open bar. Total win/win…win.

Hanging on Miss P's arm with Paolo ready to do the heavy lifting, I let myself absorb the fatigue. "Paolo, I am at your mercy."

"I think I'll ride with you," Miss P said. "Paolo, can you drop me at home after Lucky?"

"Yes, miss. Of course."

Miss P hooked her arm through mine. "Brandy's minding the store."

"Not my business. Your circus now." I didn't tell her I couldn't conjure even a modicum of interest. "I always forget that my body is super offended when I hurl it through the air in a small metal tube."

"Come on, let's get you home." She eased me toward the door.

I willingly let her lead. "Which home?" At Paolo's bemused expression, I waved my question away. "It doesn't matter. Surprise me."

Paolo held the limo door while I folded myself inside. Miss P climbed in next to me. I sagged back into the comfort of the seat, put my head back, and closed my eyes. I felt the car move, then stopped paying attention.

I must've dozed off, as the next thing I remember is the door next to me being flung open and an unexpected voice saying, "Welcome back, Miss Lucky."

I swiveled my head toward the voice and opened one eye. "Forrest?"

He stepped aside, then offered me a hand. "So nice to have you back."

"I don't understand." Forrest was the security guard at the Presidio, the tall glass tower that had housed my apartment on the second from the top floor. That apartment had been obliterated by a bomb.

"We're taking you home," Miss P said with a hand on my arm. She gave me a gentle squeeze. "Your apartment is ready."

"Ready? Ready for what?"

"You."

Paolo appeared beside Forrest. "We all worked on it, Miss Lucky. You need a home. And you do so much for us."

I tried to speak, but it felt like a stone sat on my chest. Tears welled. I let Forrest lever me out of the car. As a former NFL lineman, he had the strength and the bulk to counterweigh mine. In stunned silence, I listened to my merry band chatter as they escorted me through the lobby and into the private elevator that served the top two floors.

Teddie had the top floor.

I shut out that thought. He wasn't family—I still could

compartmentalize. Besides, I could close off access to my floor, both through the elevator and through the back staircase. At one point, Teddie and I had thought that a good idea, living separately but together.

How had life gotten so far away from when it was good?

As we rode the elevator, I could feel the nervous energy. I couldn't believe what they'd done. And for me! The elevator slowed, and the doors eased open. Miss P stepped out, pulling me after her into what I expected would be the great room.

But that was before. Now it was a lovely foyer with Carrara marble, beige with a few speckles of gold. A crystal chandelier cascaded from the twelve-foot tray ceiling. Where the walls had been white, they now were a dusty color, warm and welcoming, but a neutral backdrop for the art on the walls. The art was still colorful, which I loved. Scenes of the Mojave, my home. I'd been told that no matter how far you went, you never really left home. I'd never understood that before. I could live anywhere, but the desert would always open its arms for me.

"If you walk straight through, you get to the entertaining areas of the house." Miss P still clung to my arm. Her voice burbled and bounced with excitement. "The kitchen is pretty much where it always was off to the right and the bedrooms to the left. We took a bit out of one of the guest rooms and made an office for you. Do you want to see?"

"You did all of this?"

"Not just me. It took a village." She urged me through the doorway to the left. The marble gave way to a lovely burnished wood. Runners that picked up the colors in the art muffled our steps. They were so thick I resisted the urge to take off my shoes and walk barefoot on them. Better than grass, I bet. A short hallway separated the bedrooms from the entrance. "Two guest suites over there." She tilted her head to our left. "This is your room." She dropped my arm and stepped out of the way.

I gasped when I stepped inside. The entire curved wall was

floor-to-ceiling windows that captured an expanse of the Strip. A bit more distant than my parents' view, but more spectacular in the width. I could lie in bed—and what an inviting bed it was —all fluff and plush begging me to dive in and drink in my town. The Babylon was just at the far right, Cielo, at the very far left. The whole of my world.

And the room, the décor, so grown-up, so calm and serene, so classy, and so…me…even though I never would've chosen it. Funny how every now and then life shows us how differently others see us than we see ourselves.

"We left the bathroom and the closet pretty much untouched. We knew how hard you'd worked on designing those spaces. We did change the color a bit, and we updated the hardware and such."

"Who is *we?*"

Paolo stepped up. "Miss P, she was the—how do you say it— the wizard?"

I looked around me. "That'll do."

"Everybody had a hand in it," Miss P said. "Even your mother. But mainly all the people in the office, everyone at the front desk. Housekeeping put it all together once the pieces were here. Chef Omer put together your kitchen. For a woman who doesn't cook, you have a kitchen that would make a gourmet cook drool." She pulled Forrest into the room. "And Forrest. We couldn't have done it without him. He was our man on site. He managed everything from construction to deliveries."

"It's amazing. I'm stunned. Just stunned. I don't know what to say." I took them all in, lingering on each face. "I am so grateful for each of you. Thank you. They say home is where the heart is. You all are my heart. And now you are in every detail of my home."

"You have a home then," Paolo said, cutting to the core of the matter.

Yes, I was home.

"Come, come." Miss P rescued me from awkwardness. Expressing emotions always left me a bit befuddled and stuttery. "There's more."

The main room was my bedroom on steroids, the windows so vast, the view so sweeping, it felt like the northern part of the Strip was in the room. There were huddles of chairs—talking pits, I liked to think of them. Someone had placed a wingback chair next to the window in the exact spot my previous one had occupied. My place to curl up and heal from the barks and bites. They'd even put an extra pillow and a throw—fortifications for emotional emergencies.

Where the room had been simply a large open space before, demarcated with couches, now the curved wall between the foyer made it more intimate. And it provided space for a lovely gas fireplace, which someone had turned on. Dancing flames on a dark cold night added just the right bit of cozy. The bar occupied a nook built into the wall, the shelves already full of primo hooch. The caged corks of Champagne bottles were lined up in rows on the shelves of a small wine fridge.

"You guys didn't miss a trick. This is fabulous. I feel at home already."

"We got what clothes you left at Cielo and put them in the closet. Paolo and Brandy unpacked your suitcase earlier," Forrest said, finding his voice. He sounded a bit choked up. "It's so good to be able to do this for you, Lucky. You do so much for all of us."

Throwing sensitivity training to the wind, I gave him a big hug, rising to my tiptoes to do so. "Thank you," I whispered in his ear.

"My son is going to be a lawyer, thanks to you. Only one year left."

When I stepped back, I gave him a wide eye. "I don't know what you're talking about. He's doing it all on his own." And he had. He'd gotten into school. I'd found the money to pay for it, but I hadn't made it public knowledge. Of course, Vegas, despite its size, was still a small town. Info traveled quickly, and then, there was that whole what-happened-in-Vegas thing.

"We know you're tired," Paolo said, rounding up Forrest and ushering him toward the foyer. "You sleep."

Miss P hung back a little. "I'll be right there." As the others moved away, she leaned in and lowered her voice. "Rudy and Jordan designed and stocked the bar. Teddie picked out every color, every piece of furniture, all of it. He said he knew you best of anybody."

All that surrounded me told me he was right.

With that, she followed the others out, leaving me alone.

I shucked my clothes, leaving a trail back to the bedroom. Someone had laid out some silk PJs—not sure who that would've been. It was either throw them on the floor or shrug into them. I chose the latter. Once settled in down comfiness, I reached for my phone that I'd deposited on the nightstand.

In evidence of the Fates' meddling, Sinjin's number popped right up.

I offered up a wish and thank you, then pressed the green button.

That odd hollow foreign sound buzzed and buzzed until I'd lost count.

He never picked up.

LIGHT STREAMED THROUGH THE WINDOWS WHEN I OPENED MY eyes.

A figure stood by my bed. "What do you think?"

"Shit!" I bolted to a sitting position, looking around wildly for a weapon or something. Where the hell was I? Oh yeah, home. The voice. I knew the voice. With my heartbeat dialed to staccato mode, I fell back into the pillows and squeezed my eyes shut. If I didn't look, maybe he wouldn't be real. I waited.

"It won't work."

I squeezed my eyes shut harder. "What?"

"Willing me not to be here."

Damn! The guy was clairvoyant. "Teddie, what are you doing here?"

"I thought maybe if we went back to the moment where things started to go wrong, we could choose a different path."

"Like one of those alternate-ending stories?" Not a bad thought, I just wasn't ready for it. I opened my eyes. He'd shimmied into the body-hugging silver off-the-shoulder-gown just like before, but without the bleary eyes of a hangover. Today they were their usual robin's-egg blue dancing with some joke or the other, most likely at my expense. "Still channeling Cher?"

"She's one of my faves. I couldn't possibly leave her out of the new show." He still had the hot bod, the spiky blonde hair, the heartbreaking smile and the melted chocolate smooth voice. If only the inside could match the outside. I'd seen too much of the inside, the ego, the ability to... I shut that thought down. Only hurt down that road.

I pushed myself up then leaned back on fluffed-up pillows, trying to make sense of a Tilt-A-Whirl morning. "How'd that dress survive the fire?" Everything I owned had been turned to ashes. Teddie's apartment above mine had been gutted as well—collateral damage I still felt a pang of guilt for. The only saving grace was neither of us had been home. Then I'd been given the chance to dispatch the man who'd tried to kill us both—multiple times—brushing up against the intoxicating sweetness of revenge. An addictive rush I didn't want to risk again.

"I'd taken it to the theater along with your Manolos."

I leaned over on my elbow to stare at his feet. "My shoes!" A talisman to the me I used to be, or at least to my former life when things had seemed simpler. Then I was just the Head of

Customer Relations and Teddie was a singer and we were in love. Turned out not to be so simple. I became vice president of the hotel group and Teddie let his asshole show. Knowing that sooner rather than later should make me feel good, but it didn't, not really. I'd rather not have had to learn that side of him at all. In fact, I'd rather he didn't have that side at all.

How could someone so thoughtful, someone who had done everything I saw around me, someone who had clearly paid attention and cared, be so careless with my heart?

Starting at his feet, my gaze traveled up the thigh-high split, the zero-body-fat waist, the broad shoulder sticking out.

Same dress.

Different Teddie.

And different me.

When my gaze had traveled high enough, it met his and held. For the first time ever, I didn't feel like throwing myself in his arms and kissing him. I took that as a healing sign. "I'm not sure how I feel about you being here."

"That's an improvement over the last time I saw you. Come on." He extended a hand, which I ignored. Skin on skin, in my bedroom, dressed as we were, might be asking a bit too much of my nascent recovery. Although normally I wasn't super turned on by men in dresses, which I also considered a good sign. But Teddie was different. I knew what he was like out of the dress. And no way was I touching that. He dropped his hand, but not his smile. "Coffee awaits. The day is running off without you." He nodded toward my phone on the nightstand. "There are some messages I think you'll want to see."

I pushed myself up straighter. "You read my texts?"

"Don't get your back up. They've been dinging ever since I got here." With that, he turned on my heels and sashayed out of my bedroom. I always envied that sashay. His butt wasn't bad either.

He hadn't said he hadn't read them. There was a part of

Teddie that lived between the lines, playing with the truth, that somehow I'd missed.

Last night, I'd managed to skinny into a pair of PJs for which I was grateful. So unlike me, but life had been a bit off-center as well, so precautions were necessary. For once, I'd listened to my gut.

Teddie hadn't offered me a bathrobe and he knew I often slept in the altogether, proving that chivalry wasn't making as big a comeback as hoped. As I followed his swaying ass through the great room and into the kitchen, I glanced at the messages. A dozen from Mother, of course. I tried not to panic. If something bad had happened, she would've called. Two from Miss P. One from Dane. And the last one from Romeo. I stopped and dropped into the wingback chair by the window. "I'll be a minute," I said to Teddie's back as he disappeared through the swinging door to the kitchen.

"Right-o. But the day's getting away."

"No shit, Sherlock," I grumbled to myself as I hit Romeo's speed dial.

"I was wondering when you might surface," he said without preliminaries.

"It was a late night. When did you get up?"

"I'm still up. Helped Doc bag the body, then followed him to the morgue. Since it was for you, he stayed and did the autopsy, so I hung around."

True love indeed, or a slavish devotion. Either way, I was touched. Romeo was known for a less-than-strong stomach. "How'd he figure it was for me?"

"I told him it would be a personal favor, so you owe him. Besides, he didn't complain much. I think he's sweet on you."

Now there's an angle I'd never considered. At a loss, I chose to ignore it. But dinner… Hadn't I invited Doc to dinner at Tigris? Was that tonight? I thought so. That could be awkward if Romeo were right. I had to think about that. "You're getting pretty good at making promises for me."

"I thought it was important. Hope you don't mind." His standard response.

I let it go—my standard reaction. "All will be forgiven if you tell me you have an ID and a murder weapon. Some fingerprints on the murder weapon will grant you unlimited promises on my behalf." The sun glinted off the glass of the Babylon, painting the world in a golden glow. The cold front yesterday left behind a vivid blue sky. I had no doubt the air would be as soft as cashmere. And amid all this beauty, we talked about murder. For just one moment, would it be possible to experience the yin without the yang or the yang without the yin—whichever meant the healing without the horror?

"No actual weapon, but Doc says it does look like a big wrench or something like that. Heavy with a flat edge on one side, slightly rounded."

"Good to know. Wrenches like that are everywhere. Please tell me you have an ID."

"Working on it. Fingerprints didn't get a hit in any of the databases. Facial recognition might work, but with a side of his head bashed in, it could take a while if it even works. He did have a license on him. Says he was from Illinois. Name on the license is Shiloh Detering. Odd thing was, we found it stuck to the bottom of his foot inside his sock. Doc's checking the database in Illinois. I should hear anytime."

"Shiloh? That sounds a bit too Angelina Jolie for an older guy from the Midwest." I regretted the words the minute I'd said them. This thinking out loud thing had to stop.

"Profiling?" Romeo asked with a laugh. "So not like you."

"Sorry. Letting my uncaffeinated brain run my mouth. The stupid, offensive stuff doesn't get filtered."

"Well, I agree, for what it's worth—an odd name worthy of

doubt. If it's any consolation, I had the same thought. It just doesn't hit me right."

"Yeah, compounded by the weirdness of finding the license in his shoe? Guess he didn't want to lose it?"

"Or have anyone find it?" Romeo suggested.

"I like that better. Wonder who he was scared of?"

"We figure that out, and we're on our way."

"You wouldn't have any answers, would you?"

Romeo sighed. I could picture him running a hand over tired eyes. "Doc should be calling with the prelim and the ID soon."

"Those would go a long way toward me finding my smile."

"My primary goal."

"Ah, Grasshopper, do not be seduced by the dark side of snark." Lured by the aroma of fresh coffee, I levered myself out of the chair. "I'm pulling myself together and then heading to the hotel." The DEA would be waiting. There was Sinjin to track down, assuming he hadn't been dismembered and fed to the fishes. Then there was Squash Trenton to tackle. Neb's seemed like a port in a storm—a port with sustenance to fight the battles.

But first coffee.

As I pushed through the doors into the kitchen, Teddie handed me a mug of steaming brew, then poured himself one. "Don Francisco's Vanilla Nut, your favorite."

I inhaled the heavenly aroma. "I think smells are more powerful memory triggers than anything else."

"Science proves you right, I think." Teddie cradled his mug.

I held mine to the light. White with a gold rim that wouldn't survive the dishwasher wouldn't have been my choice. "I don't recognize anything."

"There's a reason for that." His eyes turned a moody blue. "The mugs are dishwasher safe, by the way."

Shit! He really did know me better than anyone, including me, but I wasn't about to tell him so. That was evident in all of the choices he'd made that surrounded me now, apparently, including the mug. But to be honest, I'd known it from the beginning. That begged the question: If he could see into my soul, then why did he break my heart? And why couldn't I find a way to slip him off the thin blade of my hellish hurt? Two questions, I know, but both parts of the same devastation.

"I understand most of the finishing touches are yours?" The kitchen enveloping us felt familiar yet new. New I could do.

"Do you like them?" The look on his face told me he knew the answer.

Just like a man to want to be fawned over. But he had gone to a lot of work, so he deserved a bit of fawning. "It's absolutely amazing."

"I thought you'd like it. Your old place reflected who you used to be. This one is more sophisticated, more assured, like the woman you've become."

And there it was, that inside-outside disconnect, but I'd take it. Where had this version of Teddie run off to? I guess we all could grow up and, in the process, make forgivable mistakes. Forgiveness I could do. Trust? With my heart? Not so much.

However, if he saw me as assured and sophisticated, I could at least put on a good show while the inner me caught up. "Thank you. I appreciate the time and effort and, dare I say it, love, that went into this."

"You are most welcome. I enjoyed it far more than I thought I would. There was something cathartic about trying to figure out what you would like now versus what you liked...before."

He'd done more of my introspection than I had. Somehow, that felt a bit invasive, but the intent was noble, so I let it go. A solid wall covered the spot where the doorway to the back staircase had once stood open. "How'd you get in here?"

Teddie pushed a key across the counter. "The elevator key. I used it while construction was ongoing. This is the only copy, so guard it."

He knew me well. I left it on the counter between us—if I didn't move it, I couldn't lose it.

"From your clothes strewn on the floor, I take it you didn't get to savor the bathroom?"

"Things are a bit blurry, but I seem to recall that once everybody left, I pretty much dove into bed."

"Why don't you give it a whirl? It'll be rejuvenating." He lifted his chin, indicating my phone. "I know duty has been calling, but there isn't a problem that can't wait for your attention. That's what you have staff for."

I thought about that whole delegation thing and letting Miss P run Customer Relations the way she wanted to.

"I'll leave you to it." Teddie took my mug and my shoes with him.

I left my phone on the counter, then went in search of that bath. Feeling a new sense of power in if not cutting the cord, then elongating it, I didn't check my messages and texts until I was fortified and fully ready. If there was anything more restorative than a long, lingering bath in a jetted tub, I'd yet to find it. I'd filled the tub, lounged until the water cooled, then refilled it, repeating the process. Time had passed. I hadn't a clue as to how much, nor did I care. As I rode down in the elevator, I scrolled through the messages. The new message from Romeo stopped me.

We got a problem.

The message was forty-five minutes old.

I hit his speed dial. He answered on the first ring. "Man, where you been? I thought you said you were pulling yourself together and headed this way. How long does it take to pull you together?"

"Longer with each passing day. The ravages of time, Grasshopper." So much for self-care. I wasn't about to tell him I'd been half-flirting with Teddie while still in my pajamas, then took a languid bath while sipping the Champagne he'd left on ice next to the tub. "You going to tell me what the problem is?"

"You know that air traffic dude you wanted to talk to?" Romeo didn't sound happy.

"Yeah?" I braced for impact.

"He's dead." Romeo's words were flat, lifeless, which stood to reason, I guess.

Blood drained from my head, leaving me a tad woozy. Now two dead. I hated it when this sort of nastiness escalated. One death could've been a crime of opportunity. Two deaths reeked of premeditation. "We've got a desperate murderer cleaning up his tracks."

"Thank you." Sarcasm punctuated each word.

I didn't blame him. My habit of thinking out loud often came across as condescending. Sometimes I meant it to. This wasn't one of those times. "When are we tag-teaming Jeff?"

"Already done. You needed sleep and I wasn't getting any. Caught him at the end of his shift, tired and not at his best to put up a good fight."

"Good thinking. Where are you?"

"In Neb's waiting for you to get your shit together."

I could've told him to stop waiting on that impossibility, but I'd save that for when I needed a better excuse. "I'll be right there."

After pocketing my phone, I checked my appearance in the long mirror leaning against the wall. As an afterthought, I also grabbed the small bag of pot I'd taken off the French maid. Somehow, I needed to trace its origins. If I could find out who bought it, then maybe I could start closing loops rather than keep chasing around in circles. Getting a bead on the elusive Walker Preston would be a great start.

I decided to hoof it. As I recalled, I didn't have a car—my antique Porsche had been immolated, and the Roadster was with my mechanic, hopefully being installed at the car show.

Besides my apartment was a short walk from the Babylon, so a walk was much quicker than calling for a car. Before the elevator doors opened, I double-checked my appearance in their mirrored surface. Not too shabby, but not what I hoped, not that it ever was. In the lobby, I nodded at the girl behind the desk—Forrest was nowhere to be seen. At least somebody was getting some personal time. I didn't begrudge him a nanosecond. The sunshine beckoned as I pushed through the doors into its warmth.

One thing Vegas had in spades was sunshine. I'd forgotten how many days per year we saw at least a bit of sun, but I think it was like 360 or something. For a brief second, I stopped, closed my eyes, and held my face to the sun, soaking in the rays. Sun in the early part of the day was supposed to be great for restoring circadian rhythms. Of course, with the sun already past its apex, I was pushing it. For sure, I needed that as my sleep/wake cycle was in another country altogether.

I'd picked an outfit of slacks, silk cami and a thick matching sweater, perfect for the warm sun and cool wind. Spring in Vegas came early and usually roared in with an attitude, teasing us with hints of sublime, then slapping us back with cold winds. But this season was the one thing that kept us all here and sustained us through the summers. I tightened the sweater's sash, then headed for the Babylon. I stayed to the roads, avoiding the empty sand-filled lot behind the Babylon—these Loubous with the kitten heels were the only half-comfortable good shoes I had left. Besides, Loubous should never be sacrificed in the name of expediency. It just wasn't done. Well, other than when one was called to tromp through wetlands after a friend gone rogue. Flash owed me big time.

Neb's, actually Nebuchadnezzar's, was our buffet restaurant. Located downstairs it was a veritable feast fit for a king. With the best cuisines from the far corners of the world, Neb's attracted guests from all the hotels, so it was always filled with patrons buzzing. Romeo wouldn't be easy to find, but I hadn't been smart enough to ask him which of the twenty thousand square feet he had claimed as his for the moment. I'd figure it out—if I couldn't, I had Security as my card up my sleeve. It had worked to find Miss P. Romeo might not be as easy, but he'd be findable. Of course, I could just call him now that I had my phone, but where was the fun in that?

Distracted as I strode through the lobby, the hand on my shoulder pulling me to a stop startled me. When I saw who it was, my startle changed to pissed-off. "Well, if it isn't Mr. DEA, back with his bad manners."

"I need to talk to you."

I slowed my breathing working on calming down. Unleashing anger on the Fed wouldn't get me anything other than a bigger headache. "Look, I'm not sure why you seem incredibly able to push every button I have, but if you stop touching me and stop acting as if all of us have nothing to do other than to talk to you whenever you feel like talking, I'll give you five minutes."

"Five?" He dropped his hand from my shoulder.

I glanced at my phone. "Five. And not right now. The police are taking precedence at the moment. I'll meet you in my office in twenty." I didn't wait for his agreement. Instead, I turned and motored on, taking the main staircase down, two steps at a time. My momentum almost hurled me ass over teakettle by the time I hit the lower floor. At the bottom, I staggered, then ran smack into a solid chest.

"Whoa there."

Two hands grabbed me, picked me up, and settled me on my feet.

Only one person who would use the word *whoa* and who could stop my bulk and pick me up. We'd done that dance before. "Hey, Dane. You back in town?" I stared up into Oz-green eyes that held no trace of the smile that curled his lips.

With a chiseled jaw, wavy brown hair begging to be mussed, and a body worthy of a Greek god, he could be a shoo-in for the next Marlboro man—assuming cigarettes ever came back in favor. His virility would be wasted on the e-cig craze.

"I've come to see a lady about a job."

He gave me an odd look that, in my low-blood-sugar light-headedness, I couldn't interpret. "Oh, that's great! What kind of job? Who are you talking to? Let me know and I'll put in a word for you." I didn't say a *good* word as I had no idea what I would say if pushed. If he could keep his ego in check, Dane would make anyone a great security person. With his ego...well, I'd be betting against it. "Aren't you working with Jeremy?" Yes, the one and the same Beautiful Jeremy Whitlock, Miss P's husband, and Vegas's best PI. In a fit of male loyalty, Jeremy *had* taken Dane in after Dane had gotten his wife, the wife he hadn't told me about, killed. Long story, lots of lies. Hell of a mess.

"Yeah, I was. Everything was okay, but I just felt I wasn't doing Jeremy any good. He didn't really need me. I don't much like taking charity, so I'm looking to stand in my own two boots now. I know I've messed up. I'll take the hit from that. A second chance is all I need."

"I see. Well, good you have your spiel down. I'm sure you'll make a good impression on your potential employer."

He gave me a long look. "Did I?"

I tried not to drown in the deep pools of green. "Did you what?" A sinking feeling dropped the pit of my stomach as the light dawned. Once again, my big mouth and a small brain landed me in hot water.

"Make a good impression." If he'd had a hat, this is the moment he would've swept it from his head. His voice turned earnest. "Give me a second chance, Lucky. I won't disappoint you."

"Me?" My voice cracked, and I cleared my throat. "*I'm* the woman you're seeing about a job?"

He knew a rhetorical question when he heard one, so he kept his mouth shut.

"Dane, I don't—"

"Think about it. That's all I ask."

How could I say no to a cowboy asking for a favor, and so earnestly? "Deal. I'll think it over. I'm assuming you want your old security position. That'd have to go through Jerry."

"Anything you have, I'll take it."

Anything? There was an opening I could do a lot of damage with. I wondered how he'd like to be a dishwasher or a busboy. I bit down on a smile. His arrogance had been his undoing. Starting again at the bottom of the heap would take a bit of starch out of him—but it might kill the rest of us. I needed to think, which, so far, seemed to be out of my reach.

"Let me sleep on it. Make an appointment sometime next week, and we'll talk. This weekend is insane." I scanned the area in front of Neb's, thinking maybe Romeo had given up on me and was lurking to catch me before I lost myself to the food. No joy, but my stomach grumbled at the thought of sustenance. It'd been many time zones ago that I'd had a solid meal. Despite being above and beyond, Mona's cracker, cheese, and weenies hadn't held the beast within for very long. And while I was pretty good at running on high-octane liquid refreshment, now would probably be a good time to feed that beast.

The DEA guy could cool his jets for a bit. Either that would soften him up or piss him off. Either way, I didn't much care.

CHAPTER EIGHT

URNS OUT Romeo was easy to find—he'd positioned himself by my favorite station, stacks and stacks of sliders with mouthwatering fries that were crispy and salty on the outside and creamy on the inside. I so planned on embarrassing myself with both of those.

He caught sight of me as I approached. "Pull up a plate. They just put a new batch out."

He didn't have to tell me twice. In a jiffy, I plopped down two full pates—one piled with sliders and one with fries—and took the seat across from him. "I don't like my food to touch," I said at his wide-eyed look.

He didn't look any better than the last time I'd seen him. In fact, he was living, breathing proof that "do not fold, spindle or mutilate" did not apply to cops.

"It's not that." He eyed my plate with more than a hint of longing. "If I had a death wish right now, I'd fight you for those plates."

"More where they came from." I pushed the plates toward the center of the table. "Help yourself." Without an ounce of shame, I eyed the thousands of calories I'd piled high. "I'm not the kind of eater the buffet managers are happy to see hit the line." I dove in. "Fill me in while I eat. I don't have much time. That DEA guy from last night is getting a case of red ass in my office. I don't want him abusing the staff."

"You catch more bees with honey."

I speared him with a look. "So you *do* have a death wish." Advice I didn't need. "Don't try to out-cliché the *meister*." I stuffed my face with the hot, crunchy fries and groaned. The French, okay, they stole them from the Belgians, but still, the French sure knew how to make a masterpiece with three ingredients: potato, salt, and fat—what wasn't to like? Of course, that's how they secretly conspired to conquer the world. We'd all get sick and fat from eating them, then the French would plant their flag. Personally, that'd be fine with me as long as they kept the fries coming.

"It's not a competition, Lucky. Just something my grandmother used to say."

"Coward," I said even though my mouth was full. "First, before we get into the nitty-gritty, you talked with Jeff but kept me out of it? What was your thinking?"

He looked a little sheepish, but not too much. "I made the call. Thought he'd be more forthcoming without his boss looking all homicidal at his perceived betrayal."

"The honey gambit? Good cop without the bad cop? I like it." Before he could answer, I shut him down with a raised finger. "I like it…in this case. What did he have to say?"

"Denied it all. Since it was a he-said, she-said, and lacking any real evidence of his complicity, I tabled it. You need somebody else to roll on him."

"I need a ton of things. What about Walker Preston?"

"Claimed he'd never seen him. Didn't know the guy. If we get more, we can bring it up later. I put Jerry onto looking at tapes. He said he had a new hire that could really help him key in on the timing." Romeo raised an eyebrow in question.

He'd taken that from my playbook. So Jerry had hired the girl. Or maybe he'd put her to good use and would make a determination later. Either way, his call.

"Glad Jerry's on it. Tell me what you know about the controller."

"I left Doc knee-deep in it, so what I have is really cursory stuff."

"Except that the guy is dead."

"Yeah, that." Romeo pulled out his pad. I managed two sliders and a handful of fries while I waited for him to stop scanning his notes. "Okay, the dude didn't show up for work today."

"Dude? You mean the air traffic controller?"

"Yeah, Joseph Adams. White male, thirty-two, recently divorced, living in an apartment over near Boulder Highway."

"Down on his luck. Okay, continue." I motioned to the empty spot in front of Romeo. "Did you get something to eat? It's on me." He wasn't eating any of mine, fueling a feeling of out-of-control gluttony.

"I did. I told them it was."

That made me feel better. Even though I felt a bit responsible for his decline, at least I could do something to bolster his reserves as well. He'd chosen his path; I'd just waxed it with Vaseline and given him a push. He'd been so fresh and young when we'd met.

I concentrated on eating and ceded the floor to the young detective.

"Like I said, the victim didn't show up for work today. His boss was unable to reach him and got worried as this was unusual. So he called Metro for a wellness check." Romeo reached for a fry.

I slapped his hand. "You've already eaten. Only one bite of this apple."

He yanked his hand back as if it'd been scorched. "You said—"

"I'm kidding." I gave the plates a push closer to him. "Take all you want before they get cold."

He snagged a few, but quickly as if he didn't trust me.

"Seriously, the guy didn't show up for work, and Metro actually did a wellness check?"

"Apparently, the guy had been taking his divorce really hard. Super depressed, that sort of thing." Romeo grabbed a few more fries, this time in a bit more unguarded way.

I pretended to slap at his hand, stopping short, then laughed at his hurt expression. "Simple mind, simple pleasure," I said as I stuffed my mouth with more fries. "Go on. I've had my jollies. I promise you may take as many as you want unmolested."

Romeo shook his head but refrained. "Here's the good part." He paused for effect.

Personally, I didn't think there were any good parts to murder, but I let him have his word choice. "He died from a blow to the head. Doc thinks it could be the same murder weapon. Similar wounds."

THE DEA GUY WAS PACING IN THE VESTIBULE OF MY OFFICE WHEN I pushed through the doors. Brandy's desk out front sat empty. Today, he let his hair flow free but had covered his tats with a sweater atop the same saggy jeans and sneakers. The agent fixed me with his best Fed frown. "You're late."

"Time waits for no one." That was the only axiom that came to mind. Another one about time and the dead hid among the synapses, so I went with what I had.

"You don't look like a Fed." What was it with me and profiling lately?

"Undercover."

"Okay." As explanations went, that one worked. "You've got five minutes."

At the sound of my voice, another one piped up. "Fuck you! Fuck you! Bad, bad girl!"

The agent whirled, startled and most likely a bit taken off-guard. "What the hell?"

"That's Newton. Don't mind him." I picked up a wedge of apple and pushed it through the slats over the birdcage, careful to keep my fingers on this side. The bird had taken a few chunks out of me before I learned. "Hey, pretty bird." Newton, a Macaw resplendent in his brightly hued feathers, actually preened.

He rewarded me with a perfectly inflected, "Asshole."

I laughed. "If Brandy were here, you wouldn't be so nice." Formerly my bird, Newton had taken a shine to my newest hire.

"Does he always talk that way?" the agent, still gathering himself, asked.

"No, only to me. I think at one point this job made me a very bad bird-mother. He's not forgiven me."

I breezed by the agent, turning left at the door to Miss P's office. Hunched over a stack of papers, she didn't look up. My office was finally habitable after months of the two-guys-with-one-hammer construction project. Oh, I still had a punch list, not that anyone was interested. I dropped into the chair behind my desk, which groaned in protest, then motioned to the DEA guy to take one of the two chairs across from me.

Instead, he decided to pace back and forth the length of my desk, which set my teeth on edge. "I need your help," he began. His tone indicated an order rather than a request.

"Are you always this twitchy?" I interrupted. His appearance and demeanor almost had me believing he'd crossed to the dark side.

"Comes with the territory."

No doubt pretending to be one of the bad guys and mingling with them came with a serious downside. I didn't have an answer and I was fresh out of platitudes. "You've got a funny way of trying to soften people up, don't you?"

He chased away my comment with a quick scowl. "You've got a car entered in the Concours, don't you?"

"This is about the car show?" I guessed my incredulity showed.

He stopped mid-stride, then planted his feet wide as he leaned down, placing both hands palms-down on my desk in front of me. "What else would it be about?"

Even though he seriously invaded my space, I resisted moving back. Instead, I leaned into him. "You called this little meeting. Why don't you tell me?" I could smell his aftershave—something cloyingly sweet.

He dropped into the chair behind him. First round to the home team. "What do you know about the state of the legal marijuana industry in California?"

For a moment I thought this might be a trick question; then I remembered pot possession was legal in Nevada as well. "Honestly, not much."

"It's under pressure. The state taxes the industry a great deal, the property costs are through the roof, not to mention the labor pool being fairly limited for that kind of work."

"The competition between the wine industry and the cannabis industry must be cutthroat."

"The upshot is that legal weed is way more expensive than the street product, which, while not legal, is still readily available."

"Okay, so the lawmakers didn't think this through. Not exactly the first time that's happened. They can fix it." I tried to cover my impatience. "What does this have to do with me?"

"We've gotten wind that many of the growers are smuggling their crop out of California to distribute it in other states. The pipeline goes through Vegas. You can get anywhere from here."

"True. I reiterate, what does this have to do with me?"

"Everybody tells me you've got your fingers on the pulse and your ear to the ground." He tented his fingers together and put them to his lips.

"Perhaps overstating. And if I did, that sounds like a rather precarious position."

"Maybe, but someone in your position might hear things."

His implication was clear. "So you want me to do your job?"

He flushed. "This is how we do our job."

"Point taken." I stood. "What does this have to do with the car show?"

"Maybe nothing." He raked his hand through his hair. I'd kill for that kind of wavy, shiny lushness. Why did the Fates always bestow gifts on those who wouldn't appreciate them? "We've checked the trucks, all the cars but *nada*. The people who put that bug in my ear have never steered me wrong. There's got to be something going down; I just don't know what."

"Well, I haven't heard anything, not even a whisper. Of course, I've been out of the country for a bit. I can ask around, keep my radar pinging, but I need something from you."

He looked put out. "What?"

"*Quid pro quo*, you know how the street works." I put the baggie of weed I'd scored off the French maid on the desk between us. "Can you test weed to see if it's legal or street?"

"Yeah, we keep a tight lid on who is growing what. Most plants authorized have a genetic key unique to that grower."

The guy was killing me with the puns. "Can you test this and tell me if it happens to be legally permitted by the state, then who grew it and who might be selling it here?"

He pocketed the baggie. "I should be able to tell you who grew it. Anything else?"

Other than being a bit creeped out at the ease with which it appeared Big Brother could track what, who, when and where? Most of us had signed away our right to privacy for the ever-elusive illusion of safety. We seriously needed to rethink.

I rose. "I'm sorry, I've got a murder on my property to deal with. A bit of pot flowing through my town will come second, but I'll make it a priority. If I hear anything, I'll let you know." I thought about following him out. Instead I escorted him to the door.

He followed my lead. "I'll do the same. Shouldn't take our lab long." He handed me his card. "Cell is best. I tend to move around."

I glanced at his card. "Agent Will Simon." A good name. And I was sure he was one of the good guys. Letting my bad humor bite him didn't make me feel proud—but I was used to crossing swords with the Feds, not having them climb in my back pocket.

I waited until I heard the outer door close, then tucked his card in my phone case and went in search of Miss P.

Miss P looked up when I took one of the chairs across the desk from her. "Have you had any luck tracking down video footage of the helicopter?" I knew it was a long shot, but in this Instagram-crazy world, surely someone would've thought a very expensive car dangling from a helicopter worthy of fifteen seconds. All I needed was a look at the thing—make and model, if you will. That should at least narrow my search.

Miss P peeled the top sheet from the pile of papers sitting at her elbow and pushed it across the desk, turning it so I could read it. "The first three lines are links to the videos I found. I put a clip of the helicopter through the database." She angled around so she could read her notes. "It's a Bell helicopter, medium load 412EP."

Okay, she was eighty-seven steps ahead of me. "Impressive. How many of those are in town?"

"According to the FAA, four are registered here. One is leased out to a firm from California. Two are in Arizona on a big highway project." Triumphant, but with no gloat, she leaned back. The chair, formerly my chair, groaned in protest as it had done with me. I took some comfort in that. "The other one, I'm not sure. When I called, they clammed up. I guess more people have seen that video than you would think."

"Could you see the tail numbers on any of the clips?"

"No, if there were any, and I assume there were since well, it's the law. Somebody covered them up."

"Curiouser and curiouser." I looked at her notes. "So, the first and the last are the helicopter operators with the appropriate machine and which are in-state?"

"The Bell 412EP. Yes."

"I'd be lost without you. Thank you. I need to get these to Romeo posthaste."

Miss P eyed me. "Did something happen I don't know about?"

"The air traffic controller was found dead this morning. Same MO Doc thinks it could be the same murder weapon." I let that sink in for a moment. "The pilot is the last loose end. And we haven't a clue as to who that might be. I've got one more thing of far less importance to run by you. Can you give me a minute to call Romeo and then a moment of your time?"

"Sure." She busied herself with paperwork—I didn't miss the endless office work of the job. I kept my seat—I didn't have anything to tell the young detective that Miss P couldn't be privy to.

Romeo picked up quickly. "You got something?"

I gave him the skinny.

"Miss P is a miracle worker," he said when I'd given him the pertinents. "You want to divide and conquer?"

"I think you're going to need to make it an official visit. Grab some warrants if you can find a judge, or bluff if you can't. The video of the car lift is on the internet. The helicopter owners clammed up when Miss P called them. I'm sorry, but they are circling the wagons."

"I got this. I'll report back. What are you going to do?" Romeo sounded better but still wrung out.

"I'm going to work on the car angle. Did Doc pull any prints from the Bugatti?"

"He didn't say. When I left him, he wasn't done, but he was confused by a couple of things. I'm sure he'll have more to report when you see him."

"Keep me in the loop." He sounded more and more like a world-weary cop that I didn't want him to be.

I once again addressed Miss P. "Did you happen to check the VIN on the Bugatti?"

She checked her notes. "Just like Flash said, some import/export company out of Hong Kong. I tried to get some information as to ownership, but the phone rolls to voicemail and you know the impenetrable paperwork over there." She fingered a pile of papers. "What about Sinjin? We could sure use his help. I know you guys didn't have the best of relationships…"

"As you know, it has long been my MO to have low people in high places."

"Not sure Sinjin qualifies. I really liked him."

"The noble Robin Hood, what's not to like? Until he tries to leave you holding the bag."

Miss P shrugged, unconvinced and unsympathetic. I couldn't blame her. Sinjin was the complete package—smart, charming, brilliant, and willing to break laws for the right reasons. I felt an affinity myself. A dangerous sign.

"I've been trying to reach him on another matter. I keep leaving messages, but so far nothing. Last time I saw him, I didn't have a lot of faith he could pull his *cojones* out of the fire, but I'll see if I can track him down…if there is anything left."

Miss P recoiled. "That's so awful."

"You know my motto; prepare for the worst."

"Then you can be pleasantly surprised." She finished it for

me. "I know. God knows I've heard it a million times. I just can't work myself up to always being so cynical."

"Not cynical, just realistic." I pocketed my phone and tried to switch gears. "Dane cornered me on the way here." Actually, I'd run into him, but I didn't know how to describe that. "He wants a job."

Miss P stared at me without blinking for so long that I started squirming. "I told him I'd think about it, which was a bit of a weasel. Not being totally spooled up, I didn't know what to say. He blindsided me. Should've seen it coming, but I walked right into it."

"Are you seriously considering it?" Miss P didn't show her hand one way or the other.

"I don't know." I picked up a paperweight from her desk and casually tossed it from hand to hand so I didn't have to make eye contact. A cockroach immortalized in Lucite. The paperweight had been a gift from my employees after my first run-in with Mr. Ballantine, who still was loose in my hotel. In the grand scheme, a small problem...maybe... but I didn't have the energy to deal with it right now. "I'm struggling with this whole concept of second chances." Recently life had been throwing me in front of the forgiveness train. So far, each time I'd been run over and left for dead. But in this *Groundhog Day* version of my life, each day presented a new challenge. Failure seemed to be my go-to, and I wasn't sure how to change that, or even if I should.

"If you decide to give him another chance, what job do you think he's perfect for?" A smile played about her lips.

"Am I that transparent?" I put the paperweight back, carefully positioning it on the corner, then met her gaze. "Okay, I am that transparent. How do you think he'd do as a busboy?"

"Anything customer-facing is going to require control and judgement."

"As long as I don't give him any power, perhaps he could behave." Ego and testosterone—the fuel of the fall of mankind.

Womankind would prevail. But was that really a victory? I didn't want to stand at the top of the heap surrounded only by women. Men added balance…and love…and heartache. All things that provided the depth to life.

Too antsy to sit any longer, I rose and strode to the window, raising the shade. The best part about my office was the wall of windows that overlooked the lobby below. My former office, the one I stood in now, and the front vestibule shared the window wall. Hundreds of people milled below, running on energy and joy. I pressed my palm to the glass, hoping to absorb some of the spark from below.

"Men, so disappointing. I don't know what I'm going to do with any of them." My father topped a long list.

"Tell me about it," Miss P sighed.

"Have you spoken with Jeremy?"

"He didn't answer."

"Do you know where he is?"

"Not really."

I turned and leaned against the glass, my back to the joy below. "What a pair we are."

"Men!" We said it in unison with a bit more vehemence than I'd thought I carried. A moment of silence, then we both burst into laughter.

"Asshole!" Newton sang out from the front office, which brought on another paroxysm.

When we were done, my sides hurt, and tears streaked down my face, but my heart was light.

I still didn't have any answers, but for the first time I felt like I might find some.

"Where are you going?" Miss P asked as I turned to go.

"To see a man about a car."

I reached for the knob of the outer door, but it turned and

the door flew open. A man stared at me—he was coming in as I was going out. Golden flecks in his eyes, and highlights to match in his hair. Broad where he should be and not where he shouldn't. I'd know him anywhere. "Hey Jeremy." I smiled.

He smiled back, looking happy and without a care and nothing like a man coming to do battle. My heart sang.

True love would triumph!

"She's in her office."

CHAPTER NINE

*T*HE CONCOURS d'Elegance covered the ninth and tenth fairways at the Golf Club of Las Vegas. Either the golfers were all car buffs, or they'd been outvoted. Of course, after the 2008 economic crash, many of the formerly private golf establishments could no longer cover the often-egregious expense of maintaining a world-class course in the desert. Through the years, they'd found increasingly creative ways to cover the shortfall. Many went to a daily fee structure, which really meant they opened their facilities to the unwashed masses. Others rented out their lush grounds for various events like this car show.

Fresh out of cars, I'd borrowed one from the dealership at the Babylon, the only Ferrari dealership in Nevada. They'd lent me a low-slung 360 Spyder in Ferrari red, sporting a cloth top that I'd retracted—the perfect entrée into this cool car pow-wow. I goosed the car up the short drive. It rewarded me with a growl that turned heads, including that of the young valet poised at his stand. He rushed to open my door, then practically drooled when I tossed him the key. I handed him a twenty. "Keep it close, please. I won't be long."

"Yes, miss."

A ten followed the twenty. It wasn't often anyone graced me with a "miss" anymore.

I strode up the steps, through the double wooden doors, and back in time. One of the original clubs in town, the Golf Club had hosted all the glitterati of days gone by. The members had done little to change the décor, preferring to keep it as an ode to the glamour of days gone by. I liked that—there was something calming about a place that had withstood the pressures of time. Of course, now most of the members also harkened back to a bygone era. I nodded at a few I recognized. Several asked about my father. They slowed me down a touch, but finally I reached the back doors that opened onto a wide patio, offering a sweeping view of the course. Cars lined the fairways snaking through the trees. Crowds of people clustered around the exotic cars, leaving only a fleeting glimpse of the treasures. Some rubbed their arms in the cool evening air. With no humidity, the days warmth quickly followed the disappearance of the sun. A refreshing breather from summer, but one many visitors didn't anticipate, equating the desert with heat.

From a young age, I'd loved cars—low-slung, fast, sexy cars. The minute I walked down the staircase and filtered among them lust thrummed through me. Ferraris, Lambos, McLarens, and Maseratis glistened in the sun as they preened for the onlookers. With puffed chests, the owners buffed and polished the cars and fielded questions from the gallery transfixed by the adventure that reeked from the cars and not a little bit curious about the mostly men who could afford such luxuries.

The American Dream, right?

The crowd was gathering. I pulled out my phone. Four thirty. Some folks skipping out of work early, I bet.

I strolled past, trying not to drool. Even the Porsches didn't stop me., although the 550 Spyder did cause a hitch in my stride. I wondered if that was the one that had sold for six million. My Roadster, all buff and baby blue, squatted next to the sleeker machines. She looked amazing. Jean-Charles, in a moment of embarrassing kindness, had given her to me as a birthday present. Not having wheels and being a lover of all things Porsche—especially rare and vintage Porsches—I'd been bowled over. But practical was not an adjective that would ever be bestowed on my temperamental antique. I had no idea what to do with her—and showing her off made me uncomfortable. Jean-Charles had probably paid more for her than most families in the Valley paid for a house. Exaggerating, but owning something just for show made me twitchy. If I paid that much for a car, I better damn well be able to drive it all over everywhere. If I couldn't drive it, where was the fun?

A man I thought I recognized ran his fingers across the hood of my Roadster. He'd either missed the fact that this was a no-touch show—hard to do with a sign to that effect right in front of the car—or he flaunted it. He was tall and thin, gray at the temples, and casual in his elegance. He wore a gray hoodie, sporting a logo I couldn't read, to hold back the coming chill.

A shiver raced through me. Not a chill, though—something else. Like I was being watched. The hairs on my arms rose as I scanned the crowd. No one looked out of place. Nobody seemed to pay any attention to me, abnormal or otherwise.

I turned my attention back to the man. A friend of my father's? I couldn't place him. And I didn't see my mechanic, so I kept on going. I knew the really exotic stuff would be in the back—the lure to pull the crowds through the whole exhibit. Carrying an almost three-million-dollar price tag, the Bugatti sitting on my roof would qualify as exotic. In my haste, I almost stumbled over an original Shelby—one of my dream cars. The sign said Carol Shelby himself had owned this car. Man, if I had a few million I could get in so much trouble here.

"Lucky! Lucky!" a male voice shouted above the fray, a male voice I recognized. Jordan Marsh. Scanning the crowd, I watched him gently moving fans out of his path as he worked his way toward me. He bestowed a smile on each but didn't let them stop him—a well-honed ability of celebrities of his caliber, not that many reached his level of transcendence. A Hollywood institution for decades, he'd reached Cary Grant status and a commensurate level of adulation far and wide. His marriage to Rudy had done nothing to dim his star. Today he wore his dark hair back from his forehead, which accentuated features a camera would love. His smile exposed perfect teeth and, oddly, a genuine delight at seeing me. I braced for impact. Jordan treated hugging as a contact sport, not that anyone would mind, least of all me.

I let him squeeze the air out of me, then, on the verge of apoplexy, I stepped back. "So great to see you! How's the show going?" Jordan was one of the instigators of the Concours.

"Brilliant, my dear. Brilliant." He swept his arm toward my insignificant entry. "Your roadster is lovely. Thank you for participating." He hooked his arm through mine and dropped his voice to a conspiratorial whisper. "But you can't go tooling around town in it—she's much too much of a queen. And your other car, well, there's not much left of it." He graced me with an impish smile. "Let's go shopping, shall we?"

I let him pull me along. "Eager to spend my money, are we?"

While Jordan chattered away and ignored all the looks of recognition tossed his way, I admired the amazing collection of exotic iron. We strolled past a Koenigsegg CCXR Trevita—I'd never seen one before. With a set of wings, the machine could fly, or at least it looked that way—all streamlined and ready to launch itself like a big cat back on its haunches. The next car I didn't recognize: a Lykan. I'd come back to take in that one. Low and hunkered down, it looked less likely to fly but more inclined to haul ass and hold the curves.

Aston Martin clearly had some stroke with the organizers—

several models dotted the landscape, surrounded by flashier iron. We even doubled back and lingered with the Porsches.

Somehow, I exerted enough self-control to keep a lid on my pocketbook. They'd brought all the flashy stuff. My tastes ran to the understated. Just a nice 911 GTS Cabriolet would do nicely.

After the Porsches came the Bugattis, pearls before swine. I'd never understood the attraction. To me, the Veyron looked like the progeny of a Ferrari and a Rolls that got too personal. Their numbers were impressive, and their fans rabid, but I wasn't one of them. Gauging by the crowds circling each car, I was in the minority. Or maybe they found themselves being pulled in much like wanting to pat an ugly dog.

"Let's stop here for a minute." I patted Jordan's arm to draw his attention away from his chattering. As an actor, he always got caught up in the telling.

He glanced around as if just coming to. "I never would have taken you for a Bugatti gal."

"I'm not. I just need to talk with a man about a car that has found its way to the top of my hotel." I saw the questions forming, but he resisted asking, knowing there would be a better time to debrief.

I left Jordan to his fans, who had followed us while I went in search of information and one Walker Preston. I found someone who looked like he might be in the know standing by an orange Veyron. "Excuse me. Do you know Walker Preston?" It struck me I wouldn't be able to pick Mr. Preston out of the crowd if he was standing right next to me.

"Yeah." He gave me the once-over, then bared his teeth in a leer. In his suit and tie, he looked out of place and uncomfortable—a lout wearing gentlemen's clothes. "You buying or selling?" he asked my boobs.

I bent down to capture his gaze with mine and pull it higher. "Just kicking tires." No doubt I could kick some ass too, if a touch further provoked. "I'm looking for Mr. Preston."

"You'll have to deal with me. Preston called in reinforcements. He couldn't be here today."

He was another loose end! *Shit! Death comes in threes.*

"When did he call you in?"

The guy gave me a quizzical look. "He stand you up or something?"

I decided to play along. Maybe if I appeared wounded or available or some such nonsense, the guy would be more pliable. "Somehow, we got our signals crossed." I glanced at my phone, then pointed at the time. Damn, almost five o'clock. Sleeping half the day away could do that, but now I was under the gun. "I thought I was supposed to meet him here an hour ago, but I've looked everywhere, and I can't find him."

"He was here until about two."

"Did you see him?"

"No, I spoke to him. He called me around then, told me he had to take care of something important, and asked if I would I come over. I work at a car lot over near the courthouse, so it wasn't far. My boss wasn't pleased, but Preston gave me two C-notes. He had a roll of them. I gotta get a gig like his."

So Walker Preston had been alive at two, and something or someone had spooked him.

No car salesmen left an event like this where the commissions on a sale could be in serious five maybe even six figures. Not unless it was life or death.

"Which of these cars are now under your care?"

He pointed to all the Bugattis. "All for sale?"

"All I need to do is sell one to make my wad for the year." He gave me another glance. His expression shifted. "When this gig shuts down for the evening, you wouldn't want to help me spend some of Preston's dough he gave me, would you?"

A hand on my arm saved me from an awkward exit. "Lucky? Albert Rothstein's daughter?" a warm, masculine voice asked.

Recognition dawned in the salesman's eyes, and a look of defeat when the realization of overreaching hit home.

"Another time," I said, giving him a graceful exit. He moved off to find a more pliable target. I hoped he made his wad, as he said. Sometimes, all it took was a lucky roll of the dice.

I turned to come face-to-face with the man who'd stopped me and found myself staring into the eyes of the guy I'd seen caressing my car. "I'm Lucky O'Toole. Do I know you?"

He was even better-looking up close. A bit old for me, perhaps my father's age, but that didn't mean I couldn't admire his God-given gifts and his apparent care of them.

He chuckled, a low, throaty, seductive rumble. "No, not really. Last time I saw your mother was right before you were born."

"A long time ago. You knew my mother?" I sized him up with a more than superficial interest this time. He carried the thick gloss of money and casual privilege. I couldn't fathom how this man had crossed paths with my then fifteen-year-old mother, as she awaited the birth of an unplanned child. Then again, life was different then. Mona was different, and I'd be willing to bet this guy was, too.

The misty look of a memory curled his lips into a smile. "I wish you could've known her then. She was transcendent."

"And underage."

A practiced veneer erased the smile. "With eyes only for your father. How is she?"

My eyes turned slitty. "Married." I thought it interesting he didn't ask after my father, if they were buds and all back in the day.

He laughed. "So, I heard. I'm glad she's happy."

Happy? I doubted that. Not right now. Not with my father's condition. How was it that this man knew so much, but not that? "How did your path cross with my parents'?"

"Vegas was a small town. All us hustlers crossed swords at some time or another."

An interesting choice of words. "If you give me your name, I can remember you to my parents."

"My manners! I'm sorry." His smile was panty-melting. He extended a hand. "Rivers. Carson Rivers. Riverbank Winery in Calistoga."

He held my hand in a strong grip for a few ticks past comfortable. His sweaty palm made me want to wipe my hand on my pants, but decorum prevented me. I shivered. Again, that feeling of being watched. I rubbed my arms and did another casual review of the crowd. Nothing leaped out.

"You're cold," Mr. Rivers said. "Take this." He extended a gray sweatshirt. "We're giving them to some of the folks here, you know, the ones who could buy one of our cars."

"Thanks. I'm fine. You're a long way from California. I'm assuming you have a weakness for fancy cars."

Jordan parked himself at my shoulder. "Everything okay, Lucky?"

A friend indeed. "Yes, this is Carson Rivers, an old friend of my parents."

"Your mother's." Carson smiled a tight smile.

I started with the introductions, but Jordan cut me off. "We're acquainted."

The coolness of his tone surprised me.

"You guys know each other?" Mr. Rivers asked us.

"Old friends." I turned to Jordan. "Mr. Rivers was just going to tell me about his fascination with fancy cars."

"Oh, do tell." Jordan clearly had some issues with Carson Rivers, which I brushed off. Getting in the middle of a pissing match between these two wasn't on my schedule.

Carson looked over my shoulder and squinted into the sun, now hanging low just above the horizon. "I dabble in buying and selling some of the top cars. Ship them all over the world.

It's amusing, but my heart lies with the older models, the ones that reek of history. The ones where you slip behind the wheel and wonder who had the privilege before you. What was their story? Were they happy? Successful? Married to the woman who inhabited their soul, or left destined to pine away in solitude?" He shook his head as color climbed his cheeks. "Sorry. My wife tells me I'm a bit of a romantic. An old sap, she calls me."

"Jeez," Jordan muttered under his breath. I shut him down with a look.

Mr. Rivers was clearly not above performing when it suited him—but I kept that to myself. I still couldn't place him. "Many women would find that charming." Conflicting signals radiated from him. Prowling as he was, the mention of a wife struck me as incongruous. An enigma for sure. I had no idea what to make of him. Parts of him seemed super solid, others so thin I could poke a hole through if I jabbed him with a finger. Not too different from the other men I regularly dealt with. I guessed the key was to find one that had substance where it mattered most to you. "What brings you here?"

"Curiosity, mainly." He made a sweeping motion with his arm. "I mean, who could resist? This is a rare collection of some of the world's most expensive cars. The car thing is a side hustle for me, but a nice distraction. How about you?"

"The same." I lifted my chin toward the Bugattis. "You know anything about these particular cars?"

"As a matter of fact, I do. They are all mine. Most on consignment. All available for the right price. He brightened considerably at the thought of a future sale.

"I'm always interested," I lied. "You own Fine Autos of Sonoma?" A winery and fancy cars—he was a walking, talking rich playboy flaunting his...assets. A cliché of personal lack compensated for by outward show.

"Me and a few investors."

"Does Walker Preston work for you?" I watched him carefully for his reaction.

He seemed nonplussed at my mention of the name. "He's my top guy and, as such, he's in charge of the car operation, the logistics, all of it. I like to acquire our inventory. He likes to sell it."

"Match made in heaven."

"Works well," Carson said. If he felt any nervousness at all, he hid it well.

"Except he's not here."

"He said he had something to take care of. One of his friends is helping out." He put a hand on my arm, which made me shiver. "Don't worry, if Walker made the first contact and you end up buying the car, I'll give him the commission. Not a problem."

The way he said that left me with doubts. Something about him struck me as a feather-his-own-nest kind of guy. "Did he say what he needed to take care of?"

Carson again flashed that Hollywood smile. "No, just that it was personal. Why? You interested in a car?"

"I'm interested in a particular Bugatti. It's sitting on the top of my hotel. I'd like to know who put it there." I neglected to mention the dead guy. In the past, I'd found murder could have a stifling effect on truthful conversation.

"Really?" He sounded genuinely surprised. "Can you describe it?"

"An orange Veyron, camel interior, orange stitching." I reached for my phone. "I can get the VIN number if that would help."

"Sounds like a car we delivered yesterday."

The timing was right. "Who to?"

"To that new phenom in the NBA."

"Pearl Coleman?"

"Yeah, that's the guy."

"You delivered it?"

"Walker did."

"Any idea how it ended up on the top of my hotel?"

He shook his head as he scanned the crowd behind me, already looking for his next mark. "Great prank though, don't you think?"

I could tell he didn't think so. Neither did I.

Again, the feeling of being watched tickled down my spine. Again, I couldn't place it.

With nothing left to say, Jordan pulled me away after hasty goodbyes. Once out of earshot, I asked him, "What is it with you two?"

"He's all bullshit and arrogance—uses other people's money. Doesn't have any of his own."

"What about his winery?"

"You know what they say about how to make a small fortune with a winery?"

"Yeah, start with a big fortune."

"He's a con man in a cravat. Hate those types."

Finally, it hit me! "Wasn't he the guy trying to get a bit of PR by standing by you at the pre-Concours party?"

"Indeed. He followed me around the whole time. You know the type, horning in on somebody else's camera time. I don't mind really, just don't want anyone thinking we're friends or anything." Like all A-listers, Jordan carefully guarded his culti-vated public persona.

"I get that." The guy creeped me out. "I wonder why Rudy didn't mention the car?"

Jordan gave me a long look. "That kind of ride is not some-thing Rudy would let his young rookie buy. Not in a million years."

I'D GIVEN JORDAN A DRAMATIC KISS ON THE VERANDA. PLAYING TO the photographers below, he'd bent me backwards and dipped me low. Frankly, I was happy to have survived. As I made my way up the final steps, I couldn't shake that being-watched feeling. From this vantage point, I could see the whole of the car show.

There, off to the side. A man, half-hidden behind the trunk of a palm. Gray hoodie. Jeans. The white of his shoes catching the dying sunlight like a beacon.

I called to a waiter weaving through the crowd with libations.

"Red or white?" he asked.

"One of each." I grabbed the glasses.

Jordan was regaling his fans right where I'd left him. "Here." I thrust a glass at him. "I need your help. But act normal."

His thespian kicked in. He smiled, took the glass and asked out of the side of his mouth, "With what?"

"There's a man to your right half-hiding behind a tree. Don't look. I just want you to casually ease me in that direction."

"Sure, for what?"

"So I can wring the truth out of him."

Jordan perked up. "Bodily harm. Fun!"

"Hush." I looped my arm through his, and we strolled, laughing, sipping, enjoying like the old friends we were.

Finally, we'd worked around the right side of the gallery of cars. The man still lurked behind the tree.

"Here I go," I whispered to Jordan as I handed him my glass. "Wish me luck."

I counted to three, then whirled and ran straight for him. A moment's hesitation, then he turned and ran. The chase was on.

We bolted into a stand of trees lining one of the fairways. After that, we were out of sight of the throng and no one paid any attention. He dashed and darted, using trees, shrubs, anything to keep distance between us. He needn't have worried. With younger, stronger legs, he outpaced me.

But I could out-bulldog him.

I smiled through my gasps as he headed toward the back of the golf course. A high wire fence ringed the property, separating it from the road behind.

We bolted down fairways and across greens. On one, he grabbed a stick and hurled it behind him. Dodging it slowed me a bit, but probably less than it had slowed him.

I tucked my chin and dug deep. My breath tore at my throat.

Close now. I could hear the traffic beyond. I had him.

I could see the fence. I slowed. He was trapped!

He glanced behind. Then, he turned to the fence.

Without missing a stride, he leaped. He landed on the fence and stuck like Spiderman. Then, he scrambled to the top. The barbed wire at the top caught his jeans at the right knee. He tore it loose, slithered over, then dropped on the other side, landing softly.

I hit the fence, but there was no way I could pull that same high-wire act—not in these clothes, not in my condition.

On the other side of the fence, he tossed back his hoodie.

He struggled for air as he backed away. With a grin, he turned and ran.

CHAPTER TEN

*T*HE VALET must've seen me coming as he had my car ready and waiting, the door open. I thanked him and dove in. Jordan had been waiting, a bit concerned. Thankful I was in one piece, he made me promise I'd get together with him and Rudy later in the week.

Romeo rang me before I had a chance to call him. "I almost had him!" I said, shouting a bit above the wind that came whistling by through the open top as I shifted through the gears heading up Paradise toward the hotel. The sun had dropped out of sight and now painted the horizon in brilliant pinks and oranges, deepening the sky above to a dark turquoise. No place in the world had sunsets like the western deserts. With the warmth of the sun now a memory, the chill of a high-desert evening whipped around me. I cranked the heat to high.

"Who?"

"Walker Preston. I won't swear to it until I see a picture." I gave him the play-by-play.

"He taunted you?"

"I hadn't really thought about it, but yeah. He was watching me. Gave me the creeps."

"Watch your back."

When he said that I glanced in the rearview—nobody there. "Why'd you call?"

"The dead guy in delivery bay seven?" Romeo said. He loved to milk it when he had a nugget.

"Yeah?" I played along, but oddly, this time it didn't irritate me.

"He doesn't exist."

"He looked pretty real to me." I swerved to avoid a couple so caught up in themselves they stepped off the curb in front of me, scaring all of us. "Damn."

"What?" Romeo sounded concerned. "Kill someone?"

He was joking but closer to truth than he imagined. My heart had leaped into my throat, squeezing my voice to a squeak. "Almost turned a couple of tourists into a hood ornament. This town. So, what is this about the dead guy not being real?"

"Oh, he's real, alright. He was just riding on a fake ID, and we can't determine who he really is."

"Hang on." I pulled over to the curb and put the car in park but left the engine running. Using Safari, it didn't take me long to find the homepage of Fine Autos of Sonoma. There was no mention of Carson Rivers, but they had photos of the salesmen prominently displayed. My fear wasn't realized. I'd thought for a minute we'd been chasing the wrong ghost.

Walker Preston was young and florid, with pink cheeks and dark curls. He bore no resemblance to our John Doe. But a striking resemblance to the guy I'd chased, minus about fifty pounds.

I put Romeo on hold and dialed the salesman's number. He didn't answer, not that I expected him to. I switched back to Romeo. "You still there?"

"Of course. What?" Romeo's patience had worn thin.

I didn't blame him—no sleep and no answers would do that

to the best of them. And if not the very best, Romeo had to be damn close. "I was worried the dead guy might be a runaway Bugatti salesman I'm tracking, but he's not. The guy I almost caught looked a lot like him."

"I'd love to know who spooked him." Romeo's turn to voice the obvious. His voice turned deadly. "He's another loose end. We need to find him before the skull-basher does."

While I wasn't comfortable with the description, I agreed with the sentiment. "Can you put out a BOLO on him?"

"Sure. You got a visual?"

I took a screenshot with my phone, then messaged it to Romeo. "On its way, but he weighs a lot less now."

"I'll put it out. What I don't know is how and why the dead guy scored a fake ID," Romeo said, forcing me to switch tracks.

"I don't know about the why, but I think I can help you with the how, but it's going to have to wait until tomorrow. Offices are all closed by now, and I've got a dinner date with Doc."

"So, this is a legitimate business and not one of your shady leads?"

"A shady lead hoping a storefront lends legitimacy." I thought about my source, Freddy Morales. He was as legitimate as a fake papers kind of guy could be. He even officed with a lawyer turned bail bondsman. In thinking about that, I wasn't sure that enhanced Freddy's legitimacy.

"I want to be you. You get to hang out with all the cool kids." Romeo sounded like he meant it.

"Grass is greener, Grasshopper." If he only knew... Even though I really could use a shower before meeting Doc, I turned into the big curving drive leading to the front of the Babylon. On the sidewalk a small group huddled between the driveway and the Strip. Marching in a circle, they held signs and chanted. Even with the top down, I couldn't quite make out what they were saying. However, their signs had drawn quite the crowd. Dead animals, eviscerated critters, and photos of fur coats on various celebrities marked with big red Xs. They sort of reminded me of the photos I'd seen of slaughter-houses—horrible things that induced a bilious reaction...as they were designed to do. Not that we didn't have a ton to fix in our food supply but leaving me with those visuals only made me mad.

Much like tonight.

And why the Babylon? What had we done to offend the cruelty crowd?

Their signs ran the gamut of stomach-churning, anger-inducing ugliness.

Out in front, holding the biggest sign, was my mother.

Ah, understanding flashed across my synapses. This was a stunt—a typical Mona stunt, but a stunt just the same. Most of the time my mother had a noble cause which kept me from killing her. Tonight, though, reeked of self-serving interest. I'm sure, when I got my hands around her throat, all would be made clear.

She caught sight of me, and her mouth gaped, matching my reaction to seeing her there. I didn't stop. Somehow a confrontation with my mother when media lurked nearby seemed like a very bad idea. The odds were pretty good they'd catch at least an assault, if not a murder on tape.

Live on the ten o'clock news: hotel executive strangles mother. Might be a bit juicy for prime time, though. Of course, they'd never report that Mona had it coming. I made a note to research things that qualified as justifiable cause when accused of matri-cide, just in case I lost my iffy self-control. A lifetime of emotional turmoil should be enough, shouldn't it?

Abuzz with activity, the hotel was already ramped up for the night's festivities. Of course, the presence of the NBA enhanced the normal Vegas cachet by many multiples and had all us customer service types feeling lapped by the field.

Still holding the phone, with Romeo dangling at the end of

the line, I mustered some semblance of function. "Gotta go. So, first Doc, then I'm going to kill my mother."

"Don't do anything I wouldn't do." Romeo disconnected with a laugh.

∾

AT BARELY BEFORE EIGHT, I SLID INTO THE VESTIBULE OF OUR primo, multi-starred restaurant Tigris. All posh décor with subtle torches under glass, it demanded a decorum hard to muster in my frazzled murderer-on-the-prowl-want-to-kill-my-mother state. Somewhere in the hushed interior hung an original copy of Hammurabi's Code. Was it possible to have an original copy? Hell, Vegas was built on them so it must be. As I waited for the hostess to return from seating a couple who had walked in ahead of me, I grabbed my phone and called my mother.

Amazingly, she picked up. "Lucky, let me explain." Her tone was hushed, her words hurried.

I heard chanting in the background, oddly much clearer now than when I'd been in the car. "Babylon hosts killers. Fur lives matter."

"Fur lives matter? Are you KIDDING ME? THE BABYLON HOSTS KILLERS? JESUS, MOTHER!" At the stares of the patrons who waited behind me, I corralled my voice into a murderous growl. "You're picketing OUR OWN HOTEL!" I wasn't totally successful. "You are so lucky you're out there and I'm not!"

"Biting the hand that feeds me gives me legitimacy in my political campaign." Now she sounded all high and mighty. I could see her puffing up with misplaced righteous indignation. "It makes me appear unbiased and able to see all perspectives, not only my own."

Words fled, leaving me to huff and puff without a house to

blown down. She had a point—one which I wasn't about to give her right now. But at what cost? "You're gut-shooting Father. It's not like he doesn't have enough to deal with at the moment." He cared for the hotel like a firstborn child. God help anyone messing with it.

And his own wife!

"He won't know, not unless YOU tell him." She made it sound like a capital offense.

"WON'T KNOW? You're on the friggin' evening news for chrissake."

"I won't let him watch." She sounded so smug, so sure of her plan full of a million holes.

"And none of his friends, none of the staff, none of the TWO MILLION people living in Las Vegas will spill your little secret?"

The chanting came in loud and clear during what amounted to a long pause while my mother tried to regroup. "Okay, maybe I didn't think it through. But I want so much to be important, to make a difference. That's why I'm running for a place on the Advisory Board."

"You're making a difference all right. You're taking years off my life, and probably Father's, too." Okay, that was cruel…but true. She needed to hear the truth. "You are not running for office. How many times do I have to tell you?"

"I know that, Lucky." She adopted a tone used with a small child. Even then it would be considered condescending. "But I am running for legitimacy. I must convince the Clark County commissioners that I won't be a one-woman wrecking crew if they appoint me to the Advisory Board. I need them to know that I will support all the casinos in my jurisdiction, not just the Babylon—and that the Babylon won't be unduly favored."

What happened to my mother while I was gone? Aliens had abducted her and swapped out her brain; that was the only explanation. I took a deep breath, then another. Counting to twenty usually helped, but I didn't have the time. "Why don't you just talk to me? Tell me what you're feeling and what you want instead of springing these half-baked idiocies on me then expecting me to clean them up."

"Oh, we'll talk. You and I will find ourselves having this discussion more in the future. There are some things that need to be addressed around here."

I could handle my mother as a child but as an adult? All bets were off.

"We're on the same team, Mother." I preserved my ego by hanging up, proving each of us had our childish moments.

The hostess returned. With a smile, she escorted me to a table for four tucked into an alcove and protected from eavesdropping. A bottle of Champagne chilled in a bucket on a stand next to the table. Being predictable had its upside. Doc had yet to arrive, but I motioned for the waiter who hovered nearby. "Roham, so good to see you!"

"When I saw your reservation, I switched sections so I could serve you." He gestured to the bottle of bubbly. "May I?"

"Please." Anger at my mother and pressure to find a killer, not to mention a guy I thought might be his next victim unless I figured some of this out, all redlined my adrenaline. And I'd almost had one of them! That made it all worse. What if the killer killed him before I got a chance to? What if *he* was the killer?

A glass of bubbly would, if not solve the problems, mute my response.

A second glass did the trick. I glanced at my phone. Doc was late. At this rate, without food, I'd be nonfunctional if I swilled any more of the bubbles. But, oh, they called to me. Contemplating a third glass, I was startled when a young woman in a medical tech jumpsuit appeared at my side, out of breath and wide-eyed. "Ms. O'Toole?"

"Lucky, please. Yes, what's happened?"

"Doc sent me. Can you come with me?"

I dropped my napkin on the table and followed her out of the restaurant. "What's going on?" I asked, out of breath at trying to keep up with her youthful half-run.

"We've found something he wants you to see."

"I guess he's not going to join me for dinner."

She shot me a surprised look.

"Don't mind me. I have strange coping mechanisms."

"You're going to need them."

Her comment was oddly disturbing. "This way."

She led me toward the bays of express elevators. I ignored the startled expressions of the milling crowd. They parted like the Red Sea for Moses as we rushed through.

Another tech held the door to one of the express elevators to Babel. A large sign next to it announced the closure of the club for a private party.

The NBA! I'd forgotten. The party hadn't started and wouldn't for another couple of hours.

We jumped inside, and he stepped in after us. They both looked a little green around the gills.

"You found something in the car."

The young man averted his eyes. The girl nodded. Neither told me what, but I got the impression they both didn't want me to ask. I could take a hint. All three of us watched the numbers tick off as the elevator ascended.

The doors opened, and once again, like every time I took this ride, I felt like Dorothy opening the door of her house and seeing the Land of Oz. A huge rooftop deck with bistro lights strung everywhere and tinier lights winding through the trees that dotted the expanse, Babel oozed its own little bit of Oz magic—an oasis high above the fray. This being the tail end of winter and the days still being short, darkness surrounded us, enhancing the display. The bar to my left bustled with activity in preparation for the party. A pool in the middle of the deck sparkled as a light breeze ruffled the water, which shattered the reflected light in a dance of diamonds.

The yellow crime scene tape and the stomach-churning bustle of forensic investigators pealed the only sour note. And quite a sour note it was. Doc, his arms crossed and his expression anything but light, stood off to the side as a photographer bent over the boot of the car, which occupied a prominent position on a platform above the pool. A small staircase, hastily erected, provided the only access. The camera's light strobed with each frame captured. Other techs gathered around, awaiting their turn at whatever it was. My escorts joined them.

Doc, catching sight of me, waved me over. "You are so not going to like this," he said as I stepped over the tape perimeter, then hauled myself up the narrow, wobbly steps to join him.

"I hear that a lot."

"Before you take a look, I need to tell you about the John Doe from the delivery bay."

"I'm all ears." He shuddered. I wasn't sure why. "Yeah, well, he wasn't killed in the delivery bay. He'd been stuffed up in the undercarriage for a while—several hours, maybe more, and hauled around town during that time."

"Okay," I stammered, not knowing what to do with that.

"He was killed with a large wrench and he had odd splatters of motor oil and metal fragments—aluminum and steel alloys mainly."

"Something to do with cars?"

He shook his head. "Maybe. We're testing the truck now, but he could've gotten all of that from being stuffed around the axle like that."

"We're assuming it was the same truck."

"I'm confident saying it was."

"Okay, one less thing to search for." I turned to look at the car.

"You still have that iron stomach you're known for?" Doc asked me. I didn't like the veiled warning in his voice.

I didn't know I was known for it, but I could, and actually had, made it through several autopsies without...incident. So, I guess I had a strong stomach. "Depends, I guess."

"You're going to need it." He motioned to the trunk, which, if I remembered correctly was almost too tiny to fit even a few six-packs. I couldn't imagine what horror its tiny interior could hold. We waited until the photographer finished and stepped away. "Take a look. I need to know if you can identify...well, you'll see."

Tentatively, I stepped closer and leaned over. Immediately I recoiled. "Damn."

A face stared out at me. A severed head. Other body parts jammed in around it.

I fought the bile that rose in my throat.

"You know who that is?"

I nodded, working to find words. "Freddy Morales." My fake ID *wunderkind*...in pieces.

WITH A MURDERER ON THE LOOSE, POTENTIAL WITNESSES dropping like flies, and my father's problem gathering like a storm, I needed help. Once again, I borrowed the Ferrari. Thankfully, the valet hadn't put it away. Not wanting the temptation of running over my mother, I took the back entrance out of the hotel, which put me on Paradise. With thoughts racing, I worked to control my lead foot as I motored north.

I jogged through the neighborhoods as I worked my way toward downtown. Darkness was complete when I turned onto Squash Trenton's street and eased the Ferrari to the curb. Even though well-lit by streetlights, this neighborhood had a mix of good and not-so-good, so I took the time to raise the top and secure the car.

His house, a well-cared-for little Craftsman, looked like the unlikely lair of a bold and ruthless litigator. Although it did fit his persona—lure them into complacency or arrogance, then bite them in the ass and gnaw off a leg. I'd developed an appreciation for his shrewdness and, hopefully a resistance to his charm. To be honest, as much as I liked him, I found Squash Trenton to be hard work. But, like my father, I'd run to him when I had my ass in a crack—sorta like now.

"He isn't home." The voice made me jump as I stood on the sidewalk staring at the dark house and working on my story.

An older lady with one hand on her walker and the other one holding a pie aloft toddled in next to me. "You a friend of Squash's?"

An interesting question from the neighborhood Nosy Nellie. "Friend" might be a bit too casual, but "business associate" made me sound like I'd just made bail. "I think so. You must be Mrs. Buell." Squash had told me about her pies.

She didn't confirm or deny, and she didn't seem overly concerned that I knew her name. "He's not into ladies with fancy cars," she said as she took in the Ferrari, then turned up her nose. Only the ignorant turned up their noses at a Ferrari. Whether you were the showy type or tended toward understatement, it didn't matter—a Ferrari was a work of art.

"Really?" I said. "If he's not into fancy cars, what is he into?" I had no idea why I asked. The last thing I needed was another difficult man. And Squash Trenton was the Grand Poohbah of Really Difficult and Too Smart for My Own Good Men. "And for the record, the car isn't mine. I borrowed it." So, now I'm into winning over Nosy Nellie? Geez. *Get a grip!* Handling Squash Trenton required I be on my best game, not slathering in front of the neighbors.

"Well," the lady gave me a toothless grin, "I'd rework your strategy if I were you."

"Isn't it a bit late for you to be out? Bad things happen after dark." Although the neighborhood had been slightly brought back by those who took pride in their homes, it was surrounded by many streets filled with rental properties unloved and falling into ruin.

"I can take care of myself." She patted the deep pocket of her apron, which she still wore and which bore testament to the authenticity of the homemade pie. Nosy Nellie was packing? That idea filled me with horror and hope. Before I could dream up a rejoinder, she thrust the pie at me. "Give this to him, will you? I promised him an apple pie the next time I made some. It's still hot." She pulled out a knife and fork from her apron pocket. "You look like you could use a piece of pie. Tell Squash I told you that you could have it."

I took the pie and the culinary weapons, then watched her amble back down the street. Three houses down, she turned up the drive and disappeared into the house, leaving me alone with a pie—a very dangerous situation for both of us.

A cool wind tickled the back of my neck, sending shivers down my spine. Without the warmth of the sun, the temperature dropped quickly. Retreating to the doorway, I tucked myself up against the house, using the awnings and the pillars of the porch for protection. An improvement, but not much. I needed more than my sweater. In fact, I needed inside. When I pushed the button, the doorbell tinkled through the house, but no sound of movement greeted it. The house remained dark.

Nosy Nellie was right, Squash wasn't home. I balanced the pie with one hand as I scrolled through the contacts on my phone. I'd listed several numbers for Squash. At this time of day, I doubted he'd be in court. As far as I knew, he didn't have a paralegal or anyone else in his office. If he wasn't there, the calls rolled to a service. Considering the clientele, he often worked with, that was probably a good thing. I touched his cellphone number, then hit the speaker function.

"Well, if it isn't Lucky O'Toole." His warm, deep voice held a hint of familiarity, riding on an undercurrent of seriousness. They say all great litigators are frustrated actors. Squash was their leader. He played every angle. "I wish I could say I was surprised," he continued. "But, well, with things being what they are right now, I expected you to call."

"You're on speaker. I'm on your front porch. It's getting cold. So is the apple pie I'm holding."

"Thinking of a little breaking and entering?" His chuckle showed he didn't think I would consider it. He didn't know me as well as he thought he did, which was to my advantage.

"I know a good lawyer."

"Wait, you said apple pie?" He dropped the fun and games.

"A little slow on the uptake, Counselor." Yes, I was enjoying this, swine that I am. But hey, everyone kept telling me to play to my strengths.

"Like Mrs. Buell from down the street apple pie?"

I could almost hear him salivating. Yes, this was so much fun. Squash was one of the reasons that "the way to a man's heart is through his stomach" was a cliché. Knowing one of his weaknesses gave me the upper hand. "I'm hungry. She gave me a knife and fork. Told me to tell you she gave me permission."

"She gave you permission to eat my pie? See if I shovel her sidewalk again."

"It doesn't snow here."

"Details. Don't you eat my pie. I'll be there in a few, and we can arm wrestle for it."

While I could best some men at arm wrestling by catching them unawares, I wasn't fool enough to tangle with the lawyer. "I have the pie. Not much you can do about it."

"You want my help." Now he was playing dirty.

"There is that. Your neighbor also told me you don't go for women with fancy cars."

"Chided you for the Ferrari, did she?" Squash's laugh rumbled through the connection. He knew my penchant for borrowing the car and he'd guessed right. "Showy girls are gold diggers."

In my case, that was laughable, so I graced him with a snort.

"She's very protective," Squash insisted.

"She doesn't understand how easily you can be had. Her apple pies, Mrs. Morales' green chili." I blocked the image of her son in pieces. "I'm sure there are more."

"The Fifth Amendment is my shield." A door slammed. An engine jumped to life. "I'm in the car. Don't touch that pie. Ten minutes, at the most. Promise me you won't touch that pie."

I made a habit of trying not to promise what I couldn't deliver. "Pushing that piece of junk you drive could be dangerous." I ended the call, pocketed the phone, and broke out the knife and fork. He said ten minutes. That meant I had five.

Sitting on the front stoop, I'd just forked in the last bite of a smallish piece of the absolutely exquisite pie when headlights knifed through the darkness as a car took the turn onto the street a bit too quickly. I glanced at my phone—five minutes exactly. Squash hadn't over-promised when he'd told me before Mrs. Buell's pies were things of perfection: delicate pastry with perfectly gooey yet not-too-sweet fillings, and firm but not crunchy apples.

The car wheeled to the curb behind the Ferrari. It looked like an Audi. Squash had upgraded.

He bounded out of the car, leaving the lights on and the door open. "I knew you'd eat my pie!"

I dabbed at one corner of my mouth. "Just one tiny slice. A small price to pay for a man who keeps me waiting."

"I didn't know you were coming!" He stared down at me, his hair charmingly disheveled. His eyes sparkled with impishness…yes, that's what it was. Squash Trenton was an overgrown child playing a part in life. It hit me right between the eyes. I'd never figured that out before. A child in man-clothes. Not that that didn't describe most of the chronologically adult males of the species. In that moment, I realized that I was looking for someone who'd made the hard climb to adulting, not someone who wore the clothes but left the substance behind.

I patted a spot beside me. "Sit, let's talk turkey while you eat pie."

He plopped down beside me. He smelled of fear and fight with a dash of this morning's aftershave. His suit was rumpled, his tie abandoned. When he extended his legs, I could see he wore matching shoes, but one sock was black and the other blue.

What is it about men who need mothering that is so alluring?

Just another problem to solve. And there was my answer and my way out.

I resisted the urge to lean into him. If there was a guy I shouldn't be with, I'd be wildly attracted to him. Squash Trenton fit that bill. Barely my height, he made up for the height he lacked with a body laced with muscle and a personality that oozed out of every pore. "How much did you eat?"

"Only one small slice. I'm mean, but I'm not that mean." He reached for the pie. I pulled it back and leaned so he couldn't reach it. "Not so fast, Cowboy. Let's talk shop before you go all woozy on a sugar high."

"It's my pie." He leveled his gaze and tried for a serious tone.

"Possession is nine-tenths of the law, and all of that." I saw defeat in his eyes and handed him the pie. "Here. It's even better than billed. No more playing. Tell me, have you seen Freddy Morales lately?"

"What?" My question clearly wasn't what he'd been expecting. "Freddy Morales?"

"Yeah. I've got a dead guy in the loading bays at my hotel. He's sporting a fake ID hidden inside his sock and stuck to the bottom of his foot. I thought I might quiz Freddy about how such a thing might have come to pass." Freddy was known in town as the go-to guy when someone wanted a new identity for life or for the weekend. He operated out of a parking lot somewhere on North Rancho.

"Freddy's your guy."

Defeat weighed heavy. "There's only one problem. He's in pieces in the trunk of a Bugatti sitting on a platform above the pool at the Babel."

His hand paused halfway to his mouth; the fork poised to deliver a perfect bite of pie. Slowly, he set it down. "He didn't deserve that. He ran a nice, clean, illegitimate business. But he provided a good service. I never knew him to cheat anyone."

"Me neither. Do you happen to know if he kept any records?" Yeah, I was clutching at straws, but I could use a break.

"I don't. But I know who would."

"His mother." Mrs. Morales scared the bejesus out of me. I sure didn't want to be with her in an enclosed space when she found out about Freddy. "Someone needs to tell her. She should hear it from someone she likes, someone she trusts." That so let me out. We'd gotten off on the wrong foot and had stayed there. Mrs. Morales was the tough guy in the family, and God help anyone who messed with her Freddy as I was wont to do on occasion, twisting arms and making idle threats to elicit his help.

Squash let out a burst of breath. "Man, I don't know. I bet she's killed for less. And you know what happens to the messenger."

"I'll go with you." While I wasn't the best backup, I was motivated.

"That'll complicate things." At my smile, he caved.

"Tomorrow after court, say around eleven. Meet me at the office. You can drive. The cops will have settled her down by then."

"Or have her in jail. But, deal. Now to the meat of the matter. Tell me what kind of mess my father has gotten us into."

His shoulders slumped and he let out his breath in a whoosh. "Lucky, it's the very worst kind."

For some reason, I wasn't defeated. I wouldn't let the specter of failure in. "Sounds like we need fortification before tackling that problem." I helped him get his stuff out of the car, turn off the car lights and turn on the house lights. We settled in the kitchen, the pie between us, a set of cutlery for each of us.

"Okay, worst-case scenario, we lose the hotel." I dispensed with the knife and just started in on the pie with my fork.

Squash, after his initial wide-eyed surprise, did the same. "You got any ice cream?" I asked through a mouthful of apple explosion.

He plopped down a gallon-sized carton of Blue Bell French Vanilla next to the pie. "Blue Bell? Wow."

"I got sources." He forked out a bit of ice cream, then deftly swooped in to add a bite of apple pie.

"You also got skills." I tried the same but lost the pie halfway to my mouth.

"Right now, losing the hotel looks like the only scenario."

I used my fingers to corral the wayward bite and drop it into my open maw. "Yes, well. In my experience, these things are rarely at their core about money." I made my experience sound far more impressive than it was.

"You can't put a price tag on the Babylon." Squash held his fork poised, the ice cream dripping as he stared me down.

"Sure, everything has a price. Our job is to figure out what that figure is for the opposing party."

He slipped his fork out between pressed lips, then set it

down. "And therein lies the problem. We've got an ancient lease with pretty airtight language."

"That's been bought –or more correctly, assigned—to someone in Hong Kong, is that right?"

"Yeah." Even with his mouth full of pie and ice cream, Squash looked dejected.

"Was the original lease assignable?"

"Yep."

"What do you know about this Hong Kong buyer?"

"He's actually some high-ranking politico. Been working his ill-gotten gains out of China for decades. He's amassed quite a portfolio of high-priced real estate all up and down the West Coast. He's also a big player in Macau—loves the gaming business."

"Can he even get a gaming license in Nevada?"

"Doesn't have to. He can bury himself behind a bunch of corporate layers, at least enough to satisfy the Gaming Commission."

"What's the guy's name?"

"Wu Tang Fong. Goes by Johnny Wu. For such a high-profile guy, he keeps his mug out of the newspapers. The only photo I've found is ten years old and pretty grainy. It's at the office. I'll show it to you tomorrow."

"It'd be nice to recognize him if he came up behind me in a dark alley."

"He's a player but I haven't caught even a whiff of dirty deal-ings. But he did send a pack of cutthroat lawyers to give me the squeeze."

"Sounds like he's more well-connected than the Big Boss." I meant it as a joke.

Squash didn't laugh. Instead he cut another piece of pie and separated it from the dwindling amount left, then attacked it.

"I wish I had your metabolism." I eyed another slice but just couldn't handle what it would do to my thighs. Besides, I had precious few outfits as it was; I couldn't afford to outgrow any of them.

"Haven't eaten since a protein bar after lifting at five this morning."

"Okay, let me rephrase—I don't want to do what you do to get that metabolism." I reached over and carved a bite from Squash's pie, which he carefully protected like a mother shielding her young. "When does the lease end and the property revert?"

"Two days."

"WHAT?" I glanced around at the dark windows outside Squash's kitchen windows—the houses were close here. One light popped on. I modulated. "What?"

"Your father wouldn't let me tell you."

Now in full panic-eating mode, I looked over the pie and carefully chose the perfect bite. Squash understood from the look on my face the danger of getting between me and his pie. He wisely offered me unrestricted access. "And what do you propose we do?" Sarcasm lurked in my nonchalance.

"Just keep digging, I guess. But frankly, I'm out of ideas." For the first time ever, I heard defeat in Squash's voice.

"Oh ye of little faith. You are thinking inside the box."

"I'm a lawyer; there are certain constraints."

"Not that I've seen. But if you've gone all by-the-book on me, then it's a bit of luck that I don't operate that way." I shot him a sideways glance. He looked a bit spooked. "These guys do something to you I need to know about?"

The expected denial didn't come. "Just a bit out of my league, to be honest. Vegas reprobates are one thing—Chinese enforcers another altogether."

"Totally get it. I felt the same way when I first crossed paths with the Chinese tough guys. One put a bullet in my father's chest." And still might get away with murder if Father didn't rally. The thought sucked the life out of me. "I don't know this particular tough guy, but I know a dozen like him. Not once ever have they been limited by the sides of a box. Especially in the world in which Johnny Wu made his riches, a bit badass is how you cement your place in the pecking order."

"Sounds like the Mob." Squash brightened. The Mob we both could deal with. "We just have to find his vulnerabilities."

"One of them, a large one perhaps, is if he has any hope of throwing his weight around Vegas, he better have kept his nose clean." The game was afoot, for sure. Reveling in the opportunities for skullduggery, I resisted rubbing my hands together in glee. That'd be overplaying it for sure.

"You're sure he hasn't? Kept his nose clean, I mean."

"I was just in Macau not too long ago. A den of iniquity where the most vicious dog gets to eat. This, my good Watson, is a simple case of digging up dirt."

"Okay. Dirt I can do." Squash put his fork down and gave me his full attention. "Most normal people are locked out of any information in China. How are you going to play it?"

"I need an inside man," I said with a smile that had to be easy to read, even in the darkness.

"And you've got one."

My smug dimmed a few amps. "Yes, but I'm having a bit of trouble tracking him down." I'd left three messages, each one going into more and more detail as to what I needed. Not sure why I went to the trouble—I could've been talking to a ghost.

"You'll find him." Squash sounded confident. Of course, we really didn't have a choice, so the power of positive thinking and all of that.

Nothing like having my life in the hands of a possibly dead financier who fancied himself a pirate and who couldn't be trusted to seek shelter in the rain.

I so needed a different life.

Jean-Charles dangled one.

"Can I pour you a drink?" Squash, his hunger sated and his

pie, or what was left of it, rescued, and apparently, his obligations offloaded onto my shoulders, he remembered his manners.

I had no idea what the invitation included. Part of me wanted a roll in the hay, the ultimate de-stressor. However, momentarily conjuring the grown-up I aspired to become, I knew the calm would be short-lived. Sex always came with complications. And sleeping with someone I worked with seemed to be all kinds of stupid.

"Thanks. I've got a hotel full of gunpowder and about three thousand souls all dying to light a match. Better go grab a firehose and join my staff." As excuses went, it sounded legit. I suspected it was born out of my overblown sense of self-importance, though. Hire good staff, get out of their way, and let them do their job—that's what bosses do. Apparently, I'd done that—my phone was ego-crushingly silent as if I'd made myself irrelevant. The thought terrified me. If I wasn't relevant here, where would I find a sustaining purpose?

I shelved that bit of overreactive whining until I had time to crack that nut and examine all the meat inside—unless a squirrel had hollowed it out before I got to it. As I'd said, change was in the air. I didn't like it, but there wasn't much I could do about it. Like a train, it would run me over if I stood in the way.

I felt his eyes on me as I sauntered down the sidewalk. I resisted turning to verify—that would so spoil the play. The day would come when I couldn't turn a head, but for now, I took a little bit of fun in it. Most of the heads I turned belonged to men I would release if I inadvertently caught them. That's sort of how my life rolled these days.

Catch and release—the Lucky O'Toole theory of dating.

Clearly, I was putting the wrong signals out into the Universe. If I had any idea what they were, I would rewrite that script in a heartbeat. Maybe that whole kissing a ton of frogs to find my prince had validity. Or maybe I just needed to get laid.

Only problem there was, I wasn't into no-strings nookie. Emotional connection—the tie that binds—had to come first.

Hence that itch I couldn't scratch.

The Ferrari growled to life, angry at being idle. Mrs. Buell peeked through her curtains, which made me smile. Every now and then ruffling feathers felt good.

In no real hurry and with no obligations to tend to, I took the back roads winding my way to hotel. I never knew that being the boss made one feel irrelevant. My staff could handle the hotel hilarity. The cops had a lid on the dead guys. The city had come alive in the darkness, and there wasn't any more mischief I could do tonight.

Unless…I felt just like crashing a party.

CHAPTER ELEVEN

THE ELEVATOR doors opened on Babel in peak party mode, thumping me with the bass of male bravado and the treble of women's laughter. Since this was a private party, we'd kept the music as an afterthought and not as the main show so people could talk. Novel concept, I know. I stepped out of the elevator, took a few steps, then paused to drink it all in. Heat lamps dotted the expanse keeping the cool night at bay. The bistro lights over the pool lent an air of casual comfort. The subtle lighting from below, fractured by the ripples in the water, danced like glowing diamonds across the crush of people encircling the pool. The tall palms swayed in an invisible caress of breeze. The DJ spun from a platform off to the left. Food tables formed a horseshoe at the far end, leaving the whole right side from which to drink in the view of the heart of the Strip.

The same view as my father's.

I wondered if he was staring out at his town right now in the same way I was. As a child I used to play a similar game when lying on my back drinking in the stars and wondering who was looking at them as well. How far away were they? How close? The shared view eliminated the distance and the differences making me feel so close to my fellow stargazers I didn't know and couldn't see. If only it were that easy to bridge the gaps between all of us.

Could Jean-Charles see this same sky from Paris?

What would he be thinking as he stared skyward? Across the pond, morning would be lightening the sky and chasing away the darkness. I missed him. I missed his touch. He challenged me, but in a good way. Oddly, I missed that, too. But he came at a price. A price I didn't have the currency to pay. No, I could if I wanted. But I didn't want to. My life, my place, my purpose here, sustained me. To sacrifice that? Nobody was worth that. And the right somebody wouldn't ask me to.

The car, with its necklace of crime scene tape perched in the middle of the festivities, a stark reminder of the less frivolous side of life. Doc had wanted us to cancel the party as we couldn't find anyone to get his crime scene off the roof. We'd compromised. The access ramps to the platform had been removed and guards stood at attention, presumably to discourage anyone who might decide swimming out to the Bugatti seemed like a good plan. Given the time that had passed, Doc most likely had finished with the thorough going-over but wanted to preserve the final resting place of Freddy Morales. The way my staff had set it up made the car look like part of the party, not that anyone cared. With libations flowing and food beckoning—I could smell the tantalizing aromas from here—the cogs of social interaction were well-oiled and operating smoothly from what I could tell.

But I'd never look at a Bugatti the same way again.

I'd liked Freddy. Okay, not true. I'd understood his single sprocket on the cogwheel of life. Like a mosquito, he was reviled but provided an essential service. Vegas had a love/hate relationship with reality. Freddy and his fake documents provided an alternative. Not entirely cricket, but sometimes medicinal. A fairly benign bit of legal sleight of hand to give folks a free pass to a better life, if even for a weekend. Okay, maybe I was feeling a bit more magnanimous than I usually felt toward the grifters. I wasn't stupid enough not to see the bad side of giving someone a new identity. However, seeing someone in pieces does shake up one's priorities.

And then there was the dead guy with the fake ID. Who and what had he been running from? The answer had died with Freddy, assuming he had known. But, considering the dead bodies littering my little corner of the Vegas fantasy world, how could he have not known? Guys like Freddy made a living on that particular information highway. And that's most likely what killed him.

I scanned the crowd. Who else knew? Whose kneecaps could I break to get what I needed? Yep, at the core I was a Rothstein. Most days that bothered me. Not today. I squinted at the crowd as if that would help to bring my quest for answers into focus. All it did was give me eye strain.

A drink! That would help. A theory I'd lived by successfully up to this point. I saw no need to abandon it now. I turned right and fought my way through the partiers three-deep, finally arriving at the bar. "Beertender, I need a beverage."

Our head bartender, Sean, smiled, glanced my way, then returned to his mixology magic. Somewhere in his dance, he snagged a tumbler, filled it full of Wild Turkey 101, then slid it down the bar top. It slipped to halt right in front of me. While Champagne was bottled happiness, Wild Turkey 101 was liquid lightning. Sean had taken one look and read my state perfectly. He knew my poisons of choice and had chosen wisely.

The men clearly were beating me at my own game. First Teddie and his perfect sashay in heels, and his bead on...well...

me. Now Sean and his bartender bravado and his therapist's instincts. I needed my own bit of flair or at least competence. But what would that be? I could break a man's nose with my elbow and he'd never see it coming. A bit of badass that made me proud, but it wasn't quite the positive I was searching for. Each time I found myself cataloging my limited virtues, I found myself rather appalled at my limitations and confused as to what to do about it.

Yes, the drink would help, if only to soothe my damaged self-esteem. But that mattered, right? I nodded my thanks to Sean, who waved, then I grabbed my glass and waded back through the throng. Dodging and weaving through scantily clad women and towering young men in suits so new they practically crinkled, I finally came up for air in a small clearing on the far end of the pool near the food.

"Ah, Ms. O'Toole, isn't it?"

I looked up into the soft features of Rudy's special rookie. "Hey, Pearl. Call me Lucky, will you?"

"Seriously?" He looked like I was pulling a fast one or something. "Does everybody call you that?"

"Everybody who likes me and is happy with me." I took another sip of my joy juice, savoring the burn all the way to my stomach where it exploded in a burst of warmth. "My mother's idea of a joke, but not mine."

He cocked his head and thought about that a moment. "Funny how sometimes folks got plans for you and no matter how much they push in that direction, it never seems to take, you know what I mean?"

I thought the comment a bit odd. "How so?"

"Well, your mother named you Lucky. Not sure what she had in mind for you, but it sounds like a name with a purpose."

"Yeah, it could work for a stripper or a gangster. Not sure exactly what my mother had in mind. Never really wanted to know." I actually did know. She considered herself lucky to have me. But that was my heart story and not to be shared with the world.

Pearl laughed. "Yeah, my mom wanted me to be a violinist. That's why she named me Pearl, after Itzhak Perlman."

I was so not expecting that. "Not a bad namesake. Is she musical?"

"Man, no. She didn't have the time. Five kids, two jobs."

"Why did she want you to be a violinist then?"

"She thought people would look up to me. It'd be classy and I could make decent money. She cleaned a violinist's apartment in New York. He was good to her."

"You play?"

He looked embarrassed. "I'm okay, but all of me just got too big, you know? A violin is a delicate thing."

"Well, your mother got the aspirations right but the career path wrong. And classy doesn't come with the job; it goes with the person."

"My mother's the classiest lady I know. She worked herself half to death for all of us. Still does. She and the two still at home live in a dump apartment in Jersey with a bunch of rats and roaches. That's why I'm pushing Rudy to finalize my deal so I can get some green to buy her a new place. Something clean and bright like the rooms here, you know? It doesn't have to be fancy—she's not into fancy. Just comfortable and safe. A good place for her and my two youngest brothers, so she doesn't have to be afraid anymore. And so she can quit working and put her feet up."

"After you pay for that car." I lifted my chin toward the Bugatti.

He followed my gaze. "That? No way. I'm not the type either. Besides my wife would kill me…if there was anything left of me after my mother got through. Our family doesn't do show. My mother says it's an offense to rub others' noses in your good luck."

"I like your mother." I motioned to the bottle of Topo Chico he clutched. "You want a beer or something?"

"I'm only twenty—my height makes me look older." He dug his toe in the ground. That and the fact he had a layer of muscle most fully-grown men would die for.

"I remember now, sorry. Happy birthday." His shoes caught my eye. Red and white with a thin black stripe. "Cool kicks."

"You like them?" I nodded. "My company said I could start showing them off, but just me. They've been super-secret, a limited run for my rookie signing and all. Until I put these on just now, they were totally off the grid."

"I've never seen them," I fudged. I'd seen one other pair. "Not that that means anything. I'm not tapped into that market."

"They kept the lid on so tight there haven't even been any photos of these things, no prototypes, no nothing. I just got these and a few other pair yesterday."

"Worth a ton on the black market for the shoe collectors." People had been shot over a rare pair of Jordans. I couldn't imagine the frenzy these would cause.

"I guess. I don't pay much attention to that stuff."

"Are there any more pairs floating around?" I tried to sound casually inquisitive and not accusatory. Not sure I pulled it off.

Pearl got sort of nervous, glancing around, seeing who might be paying attention to our conversation. He leaned in and lowered his voice. "I need your help, but on the down-low, okay? I can score you some sweet seats or something…anything you want."

I worked to keep my calm and cool. "I'm your gal." I'd already proven my trustworthiness, so I chose not to oversell my qualifications.

"My company, the one that's making the shoes, they gave me

a few pair, four to be exact." He hiked his pant leg. "These are one."

"And the other three?"

He looked like he might be sick. "It was part of my contract that I keep them close, couldn't give them to anybody until this coming week when they make the big announcement."

"But you gave them to somebody."

"There's this guy, an equipment manager with the team. Older guy, works like a slave and some of the guys treat him as such. I didn't like it. When other guys, just because they could and just because Finn was white, they..." He paused and regrouped. "You know, my mother always asked me, 'Are you part of the solution or part of the problem?'"

"And they became part of the problem," I said.

"Yeah. I don't care how you been treated; you gotta be better."

This kid, with his skill and his platform, would change the world. "Finn?"

"Yeah, Finn Murphy. Nice guy, not super exceptional, if you know what I mean. But, man, he loved basketball. We talked all the time about the old days, as he called them. Boy, did he have stories."

"I bet." Finn Murphy. Now we had a name for our dead guy. A little bit of defeat gathered around my heart. Why did the good guys die, leaving the rest of us to fend for ourselves against the bullies? I didn't understand it. I didn't like it. But I was powerless to do anything against it.

Except take up the sword.

"You said you had four pairs. One is on your feet. Did you give the other three to Finn?"

"Yeah." Pearl smiled at the memory. "The dude danced around in those kicks, which were at least two sizes too big like I'd done something incredible. Then he got all worried and such. He asked me if he could have the other pairs. Said he needed a big favor and I'd thank him later."

"You gave them to him." Not really a question, but he took it as such.

"Yeah, my mother…" he continued.

"I get the picture. You did good." We both smiled. "Okay, back to the car. Any idea why the owner of the car company might think that car was delivered to you?"

"There's a lot of stuff about Vegas I don't understand. People send things to players all the time. Rudy said me and him needed a long conversation about the state of the world I'm going into. After the earful he gave me about the ladies yesterday, I'm not looking forward to it." He looked sheepish and more than a little embarrassed. "I swear I had nothing to do with that. My mother always said to be nice and to use my manners."

"I don't think she was considering somebody trying to mess with her boy."

He laughed at that. "Man, had she been here, feathers woulda been flying."

What I would have given to see that. And with Flash right in the middle. I didn't know Mrs. Coleman, but I knew Flash could be scrappy in a fight. I would've laid the odds at better than even in her favor. Regardless, the dustup would've been worth it. "You listen to Rudy. This new world is a whole different ball game than you're used to. Lots of money, lots of people willing to do all kinds of stuff to get it. You can get caught with your pants down faster than you can throw down a slam dunk."

"Yes, ma'am, I'm beginning to see that."

Just to Pearl's left, a man carrying a tray piled high with sliders caught my eye. The mound of meat hid his face, but I'd know that ass anywhere.

Jean-Charles. It couldn't be. My heart leaped at the possibility. My stomach fell. I wasn't ready to face him. Still as confused as ever, what would I say?

"Pearl, excuse me, would you? I've got to see a man about a burger."

"Sure thing." He didn't seem to think that unusual at all. "I'll follow you in a minute. Pretty hungry now that you mention it, but these folks have been waiting for a bit of my time." He turned to join a crowd of worshipers who had been patiently waiting for us to finish, perhaps out of deference to the old lady he'd been talking with. If I'd started young, I could've been his mother, so I guess that made me if not old, at least approaching it.

That thought rolled around in my spinning head as I moved to follow the man with the platter. Old. Time to grow up, choose my path and get on with it. Easier said than done when immaturity was one's go-to.

Trailing after the man with the burgers like a cur dog scrounging for scraps, I had almost reached him when he swung the tray from his shoulder with a practiced flourish, then darn near dropped it when his eyes met mine.

Jean-Charles.

Words fled, and his effect hit me like a sledgehammer. So much still sizzled between us. So much of it I wanted. So much of him I didn't.

Damn. Here I'd been hoping distance would give perspective, but all it did was prove the old adage about making hearts grow fonder. My mother had always told me in the remembering, the pain diminished until only the joy remained.

So not helping.

It also didn't help that he was still as stunning as before with those robin's-egg blue eyes, the pouty oh-so-kissable lips, and the happiness that lit his eyes when he saw me. His light brown hair still curled softly at his collar. The rest of him was cloaked in his chef's whites, but I knew every delectable square inch.

"Lucky! What are you doing here?" He opened his mouth again, then clamped it shut. "That's not what I intended to say when I saw you again," he said when he started over.

Really hoping to avoid chewing on my foot, I steered clear of the emotional territory, staying firmly planted in the safe zone. "Let me help you," I said, throwing myself into the help mode. Down to the last couple of sliders, the tray on the table had to be his target. I moved it out of the way. I stepped aside, giving him unrestricted access. "I'm wondering why you are here also. I sort of have an excuse—I own the place. But you? How is your father?" Have I said how bad I am at self-restraint, even when emotional immolation is a probability? I have a knee-jerk reaction to get the bad news out on the table where I can start to deal with it. More pain, but shorter duration. But here, there were so many questions, so many possible emotional pitfalls, I quit while I was only semi-stammering, and my exposure still manageable.

Jean-Charles replaced the tray I'd removed with the new one piled all fresh and hot. Drawn by the aromas, the hungry crowd closed in around us. Once he had things arranged just so and he'd grabbed trash and minor decorations that appeared less than perfect, Jean-Charles took me by the elbow and pulled me to the side. "Thank you." He dropped the trash in the can next to the table and then took my hands in his. The sizzle turned to heat where our flesh met. With him, it had always been that way. I didn't know whether that was good or bad, whether the fire would burn out quickly as many warned or settle into a sustainable smolder. "I am so happy to see you. I want nothing more than to take you to a private place and hold you, but right now this is not possible. I have more food I must prepare. I want to talk with you. I have much to say. Can you come with me?"

"Do you have room in the kitchen?" Not exactly a private venue, but there we'd be among friends, so I guess that counted as a safe zone. I didn't really want to talk so much as be near him for a bit.

He smiled and led me through a double swinging door to the back of the house. Here the energy was just as high as out front, but much less refined. The mouthwatering aromas of food cooking made me salivate. I swallowed hard. When had I eaten my last meal? Did cheese and crackers with the Big Boss and Mona count? Oh wait, I'd snarfed an embarrassing number of sliders followed by an equally horrifying mound of fries with Romeo in Neb's. And there was the whole embarrassing-myself-with-pie thing. No wonder my stomach wasn't responding with the same fire alarm as my mouth.

Pleasure would always be my undoing.

We dodged and darted through the dance of waitstaff as they rushed to keep the crowd happy and the tables full of fresh delectables. I trailed Jean-Charles, trying to stay as close as possible and not step on his feet. "How are you here? Your father?" I managed to half shout over his shoulder.

"My father is stable for the moment. I contracted to work this event last year. It is a big one for me and with the restaurant not open right now, I couldn't afford to back out." Not that he would have. Not unless his father was on death's doorstep.

I hadn't had a chance to take a look at the damage in JC Prime, Jean-Charles's five-star eatery in my own boutique hotel, Cielo. Come to think of it, I hadn't had a chance to survey my own holdings. A wine reviewer, thinking Jean-Charles had done him a very public, very awful wrong, had expressed his anger, which by all accounts had been epic, in JC Prime. As often happens when we make complete and total asses out of ourselves, he'd been wrong—Jean-Charles had nothing to do with the rather epic misunderstanding. But the damage had closed the restaurant—Jean-Charles would accept nothing less than perfection. Another bit of his personality I worried would someday be turned in my direction. Perfection was way beyond my reach.

In an attempt to keep me from messing up the kitchen choreography, Jean-Charles motioned me to a stool off to the side. He manned his head chef's position where he could oversee the prep work on one side and the staging and delivery on the other.

"Miss Lucky!" The booming voice of Rinaldo, Jean-Charles's Mr. Everything.

I turned just in time to brace for his bear hug. A big man with floppy black curls and a wide grin, Rinaldo was the good cop to Jean-Charles's petulant, often fiery, bad cop. My zeal matched his and I let him engulf me in exuberance.

I caught Jean-Charles's wink over Rinaldo's shoulder. "He has missed you."

"I'll say!" With a hand on each of my shoulders, Rinaldo leaned me back. "Here, let me get a look at you." He held me immobile as he took a good long look. I knew better than to squirm in the vise-grip of his hands. "So glad none of those Frenchies perforated your hide."

"You and me both."

"You and JC need to stay here from now on." Neither Jean-Charles nor I disabused him of the several assumptions that comment rested on.

"Where it's soooo much safer" My humor bounced right off his good mood.

He released me. I rubbed my arms to return the blood flow. "I gotta get back to work. My boss is a taskmaster."

"Pretty bossy for sure."

Jean-Charles shot me a look. Both of us smiled but in a pained sort of way.

So many issues remained between us, tempering my initial joy at finding him in my own playground. "Christophe? Is he with you?" Jean-Charles's son was the only male member of the

Bouclet family that I felt comfortable hugging at the moment. And God knew I was in desperate need of a safe, no-real-strings-attached, male hug. Of course, with children I'd learned there were always heartstrings attached—something primal, Mona had told me.

"*Non*, I left him with my mother." He pointed a finger at a hapless acolyte. "You, the meat is cooking too long!" He shifted his attention to another. "And you! *Vite! Vite!* We cannot have the food getting cold." He segued back to me. "I have much to do here and the boy needed stability, as well as some time with my parents." He caught my gaze and held it. "We never know how much time we have, do we?"

I had no words, so a shrug had to suffice. My father. His father. Responsibilities drawing us apart, his in Paris with the family business, mine here with the same.

The modern world with modern issues and old-fashioned hearts caught in the middle.

"What are your plans?"

He dropped his gesticulating and shrugged. "I don't know. Everything, it is in a mess."

No truer words were ever spoken.

I hopped off my stool and smoothed my slacks. Still, oddly, my phone remained silent, no one summoning me to the nearest disaster. I felt untethered, unneeded, not good. "I've got to go."

He looked like he understood. "Problems which need solving, I understand."

I didn't disabuse him of that notion. Quite frankly, I had no idea what to make of it. Besides, he was right, in a way. There were problems to be solved. I just either wasn't required in the solution or didn't have any answers.

I took my leave, not that anyone noticed. Jean-Charles and Rinaldo were consumed with the task at hand. I envied them. After the ride down, I took a quick turn through the lobby. The energy radiated from the crowd, but I couldn't find a tone off-key, or a strident note—all under control.

Oddly unsettled, I should've been happy.

On my way down and out of the hotel, I texted Romeo the name of our dead guy.

He didn't respond. I hoped he was asleep.

Maybe a walk home would adjust my attitude. I'd had enough joy juice, but that hadn't done the trick. Once past the valet stand where young men ran for cars and others pulled up disgorging revelers, the night enveloped me in its quiet, cool softness. The bright lights receded leaving only the glow of frivolity like a whisper of fun as the party wound down.

More and more I enjoyed the quiet between the chaos.

Forrest manned his post as I pushed through the doors of the Presidio. Home. The concept was still new. The last place I'd thought of as home had actually been Jean-Charles's. There with him, among his child and his niece, I'd been happy.

The lobby hadn't changed. With chrome and leather furniture, marble floors, high ceilings with crystal chandeliers, it had a dated look, supposedly high-end, but you couldn't prove it by me. A snapshot from a different time. Comfort was more what I went for...and the view. I'd bought the place because of the view. And Teddie, I guessed. But that harkened back to a different time, a different me as well.

A time traveler caught between my old life and the new me.

Yay. Could life get any more uncomfortable?

Forrest nodded but, reading my pensive mood, he didn't say anything. The elevator ride seemed short—never enough time to get my thoughts in order before being deposited into a new space. Ah well, it didn't matter, it was home. The more time I spent there, the more it would feel like it.

I strode through the foyer, angling to the right as I shucked my clothes. A nice long soak would set me to right. I'd kicked off my shoes, dropped my sweater, and had my shirt half-unbuttoned when I stopped short.

A man lounged in my bed.

Sinjin Smythe-Gordon! He was alive!

"How did you get in here?" I spluttered.

Long dark hair, aquiline features, a sardonic smile,—at least he was still clothed…well, that is if you considered his half-open shirt to qualify. So, let me rephrase, at least he had pants on. And, in deference to my sensibilities, he'd taken off his shoes before curling up on my new duvet. "Teddie let me in." He lifted a flute. "Nice Champagne. Join me?"

"Out of my bed, sailor. Even you know better than to land where you're not invited."

Join him? Was he crazy? On the bed or with a flute of my own? I didn't know which he wanted, but he'd get neither. I stalked around the bed, grabbed the bottle by the neck then made my exit, heading toward the relative safety of my living room.

Sinjin kept me waiting. In fact, by the time he sauntered in, I was pretty sure he was going to win this game of calling my bluff.

Despite trying to hide it, even in his saunter, he favored his right leg. He held out his flute. "Please, sir, may I have some more?"

His Oliver Twist impersonation could use work, but he had the right accent, that educated Brit with a hint of something more, in his case, something exotic. I filled his flute from the bottle I'd thought about swinging at his head. He looked different than when I'd last seen him. Not diminished per se, but weary, without his typical bravado. And there was the limp. I knew where he'd been since I saw him last, but I didn't know what he'd been through. And I didn't want to let my overactive imagination play with what it had been like to make nice with some pissed-off honchos in the Chinese Mob.

"Are you okay?"

He dropped his guard. Sinking into the chair by the window, he rubbed his knee. "Been a ride."

"I'm glad to see you. And it's nice to know the new iPhones have a Bat-Phone capability."

He sipped at his Champagne. At least he was cultured enough to know one should savor the good stuff. "I'm not following."

"I shine a light and you appear."

"Came at a good time." He chuckled at something hidden that I was sure I didn't want to know.

"Regardless, thank you for coming." Not wanting to let him suck down all the good stuff, I poured myself a flute. Well, that was my justification anyway. "Forewarned being forearmed and all of that, are some knee-breakers on your tail? If so, how far behind are they?"

"No, I think we're square. They got their wine and punished me a bit. Everybody saved face at my expense so I should be good to go."

I hadn't missed the "should be." "For now." I gave him a smirk as I perused the selections in the wine fridge. What to open next. "Until you double-cross the wrong guy or gal again." I gave him a look over the door of the fridge so he would know I considered myself equal to the task of at least hurting his other knee if he did me wrong. And Forrest could easily rebuff an assault, or at least the first wave. For now, we were safe in my tower.

"I have sushi coming."

"What?"

"I'm hungry. I tried to anticipate your desires, so I've ordered sushi and Thai. Should be here presently. I offer that in the humblest way and in deference to the next choice of wine."

The guy had a way of making me laugh. "Good to know."

I chose a Cloudy Bay Sauvignon Blanc that I knew could

stand up to anything and would be a nice bite in contrast to the heat of the food. I stuffed the bottle into some ice. "Seriously, you're okay?"

"Better than you. From your messages I gather you're in quite a pickle."

I took my flute then perched on the ottoman at his feet. The chair was a lone island.

He half-rose. "Here, sit here."

I waved him away. "My ass has expanded three times its normal size with all the sitting I've been doing as I hurtled home. I'm fine. Thank you."

My phone startled us both. I listened for a minute to the voice on the other end. "Fine. Thank you. Would you mind ever so much sending it up?" I disconnected and returned to Sinjin. "Forrest at the front desk. The food has arrived."

I watched the elevator monitor click off the floors as I waited for Forrest to arrive. As the doors opened, he jumped back, startled at me standing there. "Sorry, Miss Lucky. I'm not used to someone being here."

The fact that he should've been forewarned leaped to mind, but I didn't say it.

"Man, this stuff smells to die for." He held aloft several plastic bags in each of his upraised hands, surrounding me with the smells he savored.

"Not exactly the words I'd choose, but yes, mouth-watering." Sinjin jumped to take one hand's worth, leaving the rest for me as he turned and disappeared into the kitchen.

Forrest's eyebrows lowered into a frown. "Who is that?" Clearly, he was either in the Teddie camp or the Jean-Charles camp and an interloper didn't sit well.

"A colleague helping me with a problem."

He scowled at me for a moment. I guess he thought I'd break or something and give him the skinny. Frankly, the fact that I gave him any information at all should have been more than enough considering he was overstepping a bit. But he had always been protective of me, so I cut him some slack. "Thank you, Forrest." I pressed a twenty into his palm as I relieved him of the remaining bags. He started to object. "Please."

He dipped his head. "Thank you." He pressed the button and the elevator doors closed leaving me alone with Sinjin Smythe-Gordon, which I had mixed emotions about. I knew I couldn't trust him, but could I trust myself? Not that I had any choice. But sometimes my own weakness astounded and appalled me.

I so hoped this wasn't one of those times.

CHAPTER TWELVE

SINJIN ACTED as if we were on a date. I was enjoying it while life teetered in the balance. I needed to get a grip.

Disarming was the best adjective I could think of to describe Sinjin Smythe-Gordon, cunning was a close second. And out-for-himself, a blanket accusation that applied in spades. Tired and scared as I was, I needed to be on my best game, to watch for my moments of weakness and crush them. None of it easy; all of it, I suspected to be out of my reach.

Only thing to do was eat.

Sinjin had his head buried in a bag when I added my load to the others that littered the kitchen table. While I watched and sipped from my flute that I hadn't yet let go of and which was now getting alarmingly low, Sinjin extracted each container, arranging them in some sort of presumably logical order. "Sushi over here." He motioned to the right side of the table. "Thai over here." He pointed to the left side. "How about some flatware and crockery?"

Of course. Flatware and crockery. How could I have been so remiss? None of the cabinets had "crockery" stenciled on the outside, so I started with the one nearest to me. I'd only opened three doors before I found it. The flatware was easier.

Sinjin paused in his arranging to watch me with a grin. "Cook much?"

"Not much. I spend most of my time helping men who are far too impressed with themselves and far too stupid about who they try to cheat stay alive." I balanced bowls on plates in a precarious tower that amazingly didn't end in a crockery cascade. Curiously I had enough bowls, plates and utensils for all of it.

"And they are grateful for it." He sounded sincere.

Did I mention he was disarmingly charming? Before this, I'd thought the French had a lock on that. Now I wasn't so sure. Of course, he'd have to put me in the middle of the crosshairs now, when I was more than vulnerable and needing his help in the worst way. Such a challenge couldn't come at a worse time. Then, top it off with the whole he-didn't-want-anything-from-me thing.

Except everything that meant anything.

That virtual face slap sobered me right up and sent my libido into exile. That thing had gotten me into so much trouble as it was. Would I never learn? At least tonight I put the skids on before stupidity led me down the rose-covered path one more time.

Besides, I had no one to blame but myself. I had summoned him, after all.

Obi-Wan, you're our only hope. What male could resist?

Keeping the table between us, I handed him a bowl, plate and flatware. We circled the table while loading our plates—a metaphor for our entire relationship. At least we weren't loading weapons…at the moment.

I guessed that had made me smile as Sinjin asked, "What?"

"This place. You being here. It's all a bit surreal."

"This is your home, no?"

"Sort of." Unwilling yet to delve into more unpleasant things, I regaled him with the story of the renovation of the apartment.

Once arranged at the dining table in a corner of the living room angled to drink in the view, me on one side, Sinjin on the other, we both perused the options we'd chosen. In a typically male fashion, Sinjin held his chopsticks high ready to spear the perfect selection. I'd grabbed the Cloudy Bay from its ice bath and some appropriate glasses. I poured us each a healthy dose.

"Your friends love you," he said through a mouthful of what looked to be some kind of green curry and rice. "It is a special gift to inspire such strong emotion."

Embarrassed and working really hard to raise my shields against such an onslaught of suspect kindness, I focused on the food. "Do you know what any of this is?"

"Not really. Thai food is different here than in Bangkok. And the sushi is more Americanized."

"The sushi I'm familiar with." All kinds of interesting meats in sauces drenched the mound of rice on my plate. "There's a place here in town called Nittaya's Secret Kitchen. Nittaya actually cooks what I think are her grandmother's Thai recipes. It's amazing."

"We'll have to try it," Sinjin said as he forked in another bite.

His *we* was open to many interpretations. I let it ride. The odds that he would spend a dime entertaining me were infinitesimal. Not really recognizing any food on my plate, I sampled small bites of all of it. After a few tastes, I dove for the wine. "Jesus," I gasped between slurps.

Sinjin shoveled it in undeterred. "Mmm, just as it should be. I didn't know what they meant when they asked if I wanted it Thai spicy, so I said yes. A good choice."

He seemed unfazed. "I can't feel my lips."

He laughed, like a real belly, natural relaxed laugh. I'd not heard that before from him. It was nice. We fell silent as mostly Sinjin fed his appetite and I nibbled and watched. An enigma for sure, but what man wasn't? Half Brit, half Chinese, all trouble. And he was here. In my home. I wasn't at all sure I should, but I liked it. We'd crossed swords, tested each other. I liked that too. Of course, I'd won, which made the whole thing far more fun in the remembering.

But could he be trusted with everything I held dear—everything that made me who I am?

Some kind of serious trust for a gal with trust issues.

Not that I had a ton of options.

"Do you know this Johnny Wu?"

Sinjin took a moment to finish his bite, then washed it down with a long swig of wine before he sat back. Steepling his fingers and pressing them lightly to his lips, he locked me with a serious gaze. "How good are you, really?" He let his hands fall to the arms of his chair where he clutched the lion's-head knobs. The whites of his knuckles belied his outward calm.

"Hard to say." My appetite fled. I pushed my plate away but clutched the wine glass like a drowning woman clinging to a bit of flotsam in stormy seas. I met his gaze and held it. "I've not been tested, not really."

"True. The sparring we have done has been light jousting compared to the games these men play. They are ruthless, calculating and will let no one get in their way."

"Who are *they*, exactly?" I lifted my glass to my lips, steadying my shaking hand with the other one. Even being a Vegas girl, I had none of the hard edges of the Mob-toughened folks. No, I was corporate through and through.

"Hard to say. They stay in the shadows, don't seek the spotlight. But they have a goon squad that is...enthusiastic." He absentmindedly rubbed his leg.

I watched him massage the spot that obviously caused him pain and I could only imagine what they'd done to him. That he still walked and talked was perhaps a minor miracle. "So, wealthy men? I assume they operate across industries to give them more power and more money-laundering capabilities."

"Yes, heavy into gaming, as you might suspect. Also liquor, trucking, and lots of industries no one would suspect. They have their tentacles in everything. Even the politicians' pockets."

A cold chill raced through me. "Even diplomats?" The words came out in a choked whisper.

"They facilitate the movement of money. Why?"

"My father had a run-in with a Chinese diplomat recently. His son died. Someone put a bullet in my father's chest, which may kill him eventually."

"A name?" Sinjin had gone all still.

"Cho."

He rolled his eyes. "That's like saying his name is Jones."

"I know. But he was some sort of diplomat. I'll dig into it." We both fell silent, thoughts racing. "Do you think this could be a revenge play?"

Sinjin shook his head with a shrug. "Could be anything."

"The motivation matters. It shows us what's important and what's less so. We do have a few things working for us."

"Really? And what might they be?" He looked skeptical. These guys clearly had his attention. He didn't look scared, just more focused. Of course, if someone had given me a limp, I'd be focused too. But, in actuality, if Cho was hooked up with this group, they'd done me far worse.

"We have what they want." He started to say something. I shut him down with a raised finger. "And they are playing on my turf."

"Agreed, but that doesn't even come close to leveling the playing field." Sinjin looked tired. I wasn't sure exactly whether he was really tired or perhaps tired of the game. He'd been playing high-stakes games for as long as I could tell, and that would wear you out…if it didn't get you killed.

"Best I can do." I gave him a long look. "You didn't travel half the world on my account. You were close. Following..." I thought back to everything I knew about Sinjin Smythe-Gordon, every thrust and parry (not to put such a fine innuendo on it). "No, you know where your bad guys are heading. They're coming here. And they are part of this game."

"You are a worthy Pancho."

"Please, no sidekick for this gal. But they are coming here, right?"

"Yes, I know your Johnny Wu, as I've said." He absentmindedly rubbed his thigh. "And your Mr. Cho. Remember, we crossed swords with him in Macau. I did my due diligence."

"You got a bit too close."

"The same or worse is waiting for your first misstep. Are you willing to play for those stakes?"

"I'm all in. I've nothing to lose," I said without hesitation. I had no choice.

"You make a dangerous adversary then. You said they want the Babylon. Do you have anything else we could offer them in trade?"

"For the Babylon?" I scoffed and blew my bangs off my forehead. "There's no equal."

"For your purposes. But what about theirs?" He'd gone all enigmatic on me.

"I don't know their end game."

"Precisely. But something else might suit them; we don't know."

I thought for a minute. I only had one other property. My hotel. The fruition of the dream I'd harbored my entire adult life. *"Cielo,"* I whispered. And I told him about it, as bravely as I could. Being the head dog in my father's hotels wasn't quite the same as being the head dog of my own.

"It's important to you." He reached across and squeezed my hand, quickly, warmly, the sensation intense. "I will try to be wise to that."

"You're going to talk with them on my family's behalf?"

He sidestepped the question. "Negotiations are but a subtle dance."

"And sometimes not so subtle." I thought about his limp, the pain he tried to hide. "Where are you staying?"

He ran a hand through his hair and let his full-blown fatigue sneak through his bravado. He wasn't tired; he was bone-weary. "I don't know. I hear there are some nice hotels around here." He tried for a smile and half made it.

"I have a guest room. Two in fact, I think." I rose and went to him, grabbing his elbow. "Come on." I looked around, momentarily at a loss. The walls had moved. I thought about it, then got my bearings. "This way."

He let me lead him to the room next to mine. "You have to be quiet. I'm a light sleeper."

"Good to know." He matched my attempt at lighthearted banter.

"Do you have any things?"

He sagged onto the bed. "My duffel is in the front hall closet."

"I have a hall closet? Who knew?" He shook his head as I left to retrieve it.

When I returned, the sight of him brought me up short. He'd doffed his shirt and pants, and now sat on the bed in a pair of black boxer briefs. Bruises covered his torso—purple, red, a few fading to yellow with a hint of green. Multiple turns of gauze circled his ribs. And his leg! His leg was purple with a large bandage covering the worst of it. "Sinjin!" I gasped.

"Sorry, I don't mean to alarm." Pain drew in the hollows of his cheeks. Still, he looked stunning. The thought horrified me. The fact that I could actually have such a thought at a time like this horrified me even more. "I could use your help with all of this." He motioned to his bandages. "Would you be ever so kind?

I will warn you; the dressing on my leg needs changing and it's not pretty."

I knelt in front of him. "Who did this to you?"

He cocked his head and gave a slight shrug. "Your Johnny Wu or Mr. Cho, or any of their ilk. They are all the same. Sharks feeding with no guilt, no remorse. All of them are representative of the blight I was trying to send back to the rocks they crawled out from under when we first met. I thought if I could hit them where it hurts, in their wallets, I could…I don't know."

"Claw a little back from the fat cats back for the people?" Yes, his being a modern-day Robin Hood had kept me from killing him multiple times.

If you did bad things for good reasons, did that make you bad or good?

I had found myself on the bad side of that equation, which gave me perspective if not a get-out-of-jail-free card.

"We can't fight them, Lucky." He sucked in air between his teeth as I tugged at the corners of the dressing.

"How long since this has been changed?" I asked. The look on his face told me all I needed to know. "Hang on." In the bathroom, I wet a washcloth with scalding water then partially wrung it out. When I returned, I pressed it to the dressing, moving it until it had dampened and heated most of it. Through all of it, he didn't flinch, didn't say a word. I glanced up at him. His face was tight, but his eyes clear and bright. "You okay?"

He pinched his lips together and nodded.

"Here we go." Not having a clue as to what I'd find underneath, I picked at the edges, peeling the cotton back until I met resistance, then switching to another corner to tackle. It took some time, and some rewetting. Through it all, Sinjin didn't move. Where my hand rested on his thigh above the wound, his skin was warm, smooth. So unlike the men I knew, yet so alike in other aspects. I talked to distract him. "You think we can't fight the Johnny Wu-s of the world?"

"I've not succeeded so far." A hint of self-deprecation lurked in there, making me smile.

"No." I tugged at a balky bit.

"Damn," Sinjin hissed.

"You're going about it the wrong way." I shook my head. Men could be so stubborn and stupid. For a moment I thanked the Goddess that I too did not suffer from the Curse of the Y-Chromosome. "You should've taken care of this the minute you hit town." I sounded like my mother. I wasn't sure how I felt about that. And why were men who brought out the maternal in me so damned attractive? *That* needed to stop right now.

"I intended to. I stopped at your hotel. How do you mean the wrong way?"

"Cielo?" Surprised, I paused in my ministrations, giving us both a break.

He nodded. "Nice place. Says so much about you that you don't want other people to know."

What was it with everybody thinking they knew me so well? As I looked around me, I realized some of them did, but I wouldn't count Sinjin Smythe-Gordon among them. Although, as everyone loved to point out, I'd been wrong so many times before it was practically my go-to.

"Glad you like it. Why didn't you get a room and take care of yourself?"

"I tried." He motioned for me to keep going on the dressing. "I was looking for you. Told them I was a friend of yours. They didn't buy it."

"Little wonder. You look like a Disney character." The prince from somewhere! That was it. I couldn't remember. But the long flowing black hair, the open billowing shirt, the flared tight black pants, the body, the exotic look, together they screamed Disney.

"My proper clothes aren't proper anymore." He glanced at his leg.

"Well, you're here now. I'll do my best, but I'm thinking a doctor might be a good idea. We have one on call at the Babylon. I can summon him if you'd like."

"Let's see what you think first." He was looking a little pale. "So, you think I'm fighting the wrong way?"

"You need to learn to fight like a girl." I bent to my task. In a moment I had the dressing free and revealed the wound. "Damn!" I sat back on my heels.

An ugly gash split the unmarred skin from mid-thigh to the top of his knee. Some of the wound had pulled together but there were still gaps where pink fluid leaked out. The skin around the wound wasn't red or hot. Perhaps not infection, but it looked bad.

"What do you mean fight like a girl?" He sounded offended.

"You could use some stitches."

"Probably but getting a bit late now for that."

I had to agree. His body had already set to work repairing the damage. It would heal, but it would be ugly. He didn't seem worried by that. "In a fight with a man, an overpowering opponent, women are often physically outmanned. So, to attack head-on, to play his game, would end in almost certain defeat. At a minimum the damage would be great." I perused his wounds, so he got my drift.

"I should be more clever then?" I could see his manly manliness still rebelled, but he was warming to the logic.

"Attack not his strength, but his weakness."

He gave me a bit of side-eye. "Won't you be ex-communicated or something from some female brotherhood for giving away secrets?"

I laughed, but I heard his warning. He was not the kind of man to show your soft underbelly to, or who could be trusted with your secrets…not in war, for sure. Not sure about love. Weren't the rules the same, or often compared? "How'd this happen?" I asked, shifting talk away from future battles to the scars of past ones.

"It's not easy getting through razor wire."

That stuff would shred any one of the rest of us. "Perhaps a tetanus shot?"

"Please, I spend my life tangling with mongrels. I keep my shots up to date."

"You are who your friends are. You need new friends." I didn't wait for him to answer. Instead I went looking for a first-aid kit. I'd had one before. It had been in the uppermost cabinet to the right of my vanity. I opened the door and there it was. Not the same one, but a first-aid kit, nonetheless.

Teddie had always been a grand gesture guy. Perhaps he was learning love lived in the details. I wasn't going to risk my heart on it, but if he had, he had a chance at a brilliant relationship—with someone else.

I dropped back to my knees in front of Sinjin. He'd propped himself on his elbows and was trying not to look at his thigh but sneaking peeks. "Bad, eh?"

"I've seen worse," I lied. But I didn't see any infection, which was a miracle. I rooted through my supplies. Some antibiotic cream and butterfly closures would do the trick. In a jiffy I had the wound treated and dressed once again. "Now let's see about those ribs."

I moved in closer, an awkward position in between his legs. But I didn't see any other angle with as good an access. This close, I could smell him. The musky scent of male, a sweet tinge of fear, and sandalwood—just a hint—adding to his exotic aura, which so didn't need adding to. I corralled my wandering thoughts and focused on the task at hand.

The bruises along his torso were a deep purple. These had not begun to fade. Before I'd even brushed his skin, he flinched as I reached for the bandage.

"Are you sure these ribs aren't broken?"

He kept his fists clenched by his side. "No. But what if they were?"

He had a point—not much to do but bind them and live through it. I found the end of the gauze and started unwinding. Each pass took me closer, then farther away. He didn't touch me. My fingers only occasionally brushed his skin. Way sexier than foreplay.

Wasn't there a movie once with Charles Grodin and Cybil Shepherd? He was on his honeymoon and interested in cheating on his new bride. Ms. Shepherd was the dalliance he had his eye on, but she was way out of his league. She'd made him play a game like this one. Had everyone in the audience ready to strip down right then and there.

But this wasn't a game.

I could lose everything.

The man in front of me could help me get it back...or take it all.

Being a grown-up totally sucked. Being the ONLY grown-up in my family sucked lemons.

And letting myself feast on the nearly naked man in front of me would make it oh so much worse. Finally, I had him unwound. Nothing in my little first aid kit would solve the rib issue. "I don't know what to use to tie you up."

I didn't even notice my bit of innuendo until one corner of his mouth curved up and he said, "A silk scarf would do nicely, or so I've heard."

My eyes opened wide but the tiny bit of grown-up in me refused to engage. I sat back on my heels then pushed upright. "Be right back."

My closet dwarfed my meager wardrobe. It had taken me the better part of my adult life to amass the collection of vintage designer clothes that had been reduced to ashes in the fire. It would probably take the rest of my life to build out another acceptable wardrobe. But what I had was primo—I'd been in

Paris recently after all. My possessions huddled in one corner of the vast mirrored, carpeted expanse. Three Hermès scarves rested, folded nicely, in a drawer. I chose the one with the horses galloping across it. Don't know why...it just seemed appropriate somehow.

Sinjin didn't say a word when I returned, flourishing the silk. The scarf folded nicely into a thin band that just circled his torso leaving me enough cloth to tie it off. I sat back and admired my handiwork. *"Et voilà!"*

Sinjin moved and twisted slightly. No grimace. "Better. Thanks." He reached for my hand. His skin felt warm, inviting. "Come, let me hold you."

My need for physical contact, for connection, worked against logic. "Sinjin, no. This is a bad idea. I don't trust you."

He seemed taken aback. "But I assure you I have always acted consistent with my stated goals."

"Yes, but when said goals are to leave me the scapegoat..."

His voice deepened, taking on a husky urgency. "Goals can change."

He hadn't assured me he was an honorable man which gave me hope that he just might be one. Have you ever noticed that the odds of someone being something decreased proportionally with the vehemence with which they asserted they were exactly that?

Tell me who you are, and I'll remain skeptical. But show me? I'm all in.

"As you wish."

I stepped away leaving him room to stand, round the bed then ease slowly between the covers.

"Thank you for letting me stay. I don't mean to be presumptuous or forward. But I won't deny that you attract me in a way no other has. But you make the rules."

Did I say he was charming?

Not one to mince words, I forged ahead into the breach. "I bested you. I'm sure that is intriguing in its own way."

"Ah, ego. I am interested in results not ego. It is a false master and often leads one astray from what is truly important." He laid his head back on the pillow. He closed his eyes. I thought he'd fallen asleep, so it surprised me when he said, "No. Others have bested me. I am not so much clever as determined. But you, you are like me. We must work always together."

So, he did want something from me after all.

But first, my turn. "Sinjin, I need your help and I have a plan."

WITH THE APARTMENT NOW TO MYSELF, SORT OF, I TOOK THE luxury of drawing a bath and adding bubbles because they were there. I even lit some candles just for me, even though I knew that wasn't Teddie's intent when he'd put them there. And I knew he'd put them there. Only he knew these were my favorite.

After testing the water with one toe, I slid into its steaming embrace, then pushed the button for the jets to fire. Yes, I knew bubbles and a jetted tub were often not recommended together, but I took the risk. The initial thick froth of bubbles alarmed me and tickled my nose, but they settled down to a fun bit of silliness, which I so needed right now.

Man, talk about jumping from the frying pan right into the flames. My reentry into Vegas was quickly reaching terminal velocity. I laid my head back and closed my eyes. For a moment I wondered how Teddie had let Sinjin into my apartment. Hadn't he said there was only one other key besides mine? Hadn't he pushed it across the kitchen counter when we'd been in the kitchen? Hadn't I left it there? Wasn't I always slow on the uptake when it came to subterfuge? Then I realized it didn't matter. My apartment had always been a place where misfits were welcome, and I'd have it no other way.

Complicated, but comforting.

"Hey, I thought you'd still be awake."

I didn't even jump at the voice. Nor did I even flinch. Somehow, I guess I'd been prepared.

"Teddie, go away." I want to revise my assertion about my apartment being a home for broken toys.

While it was complicated, right now it was most assuredly not comforting.

"I knew you'd be up jet-lag whacked and all." He'd taken a seat on the edge of the tub. His voice gave away distance and proximity...uncomfortable proximity.

"You are being far too presumptuous. Go away." I didn't open my eyes. If I didn't see him, he wouldn't be real, right?

"I just came to check on our boy."

Our boy. What he really came for was to make sure I wasn't writhing around on the floor in heated passion with *our boy.* That would've been awkward. "If you ever come in here unannounced or uninvited again, you will be shot on sight. That's not how it works. This is my *home.* And as such, it provides me with an expectation of privacy and some control over when and where people are given access. We are not going back to the way we were. I'm a grown-up now and I demand more respect. Give it to me or get out of my life. Your choice. But for now, get the hell out of my bathroom." Amazingly, I hadn't opened my eyes, and more impossible, I hadn't even raised my voice. If I wished some semblance of a private life, I needed to be able to control access—especially to my most intimate spaces.

"I get it. Sorry. I liked the before."

I did, too. We both ruined it; well, he had pushed it, and I'd caved. A lesson in there for sure. "We're not the same people, Teddie."

He heard the hint of lethal, and perhaps the resignation of

reality, and vacated posthaste. The swishing of his garments, and his heavy sigh, followed by the cool space of his absence, told me I was once again alone, as I'd wished. However, now a bit of pissed-off boiled just beneath the surface.

All the better to think with.

If I could get the memory of *our boy*, the feel of his skin, the warmth of his smile, to stop teasing my libido and derailing logical thought altogether. A big if, given my weakened state and all. I allowed myself a moment of warm wallowing and what-ifs, then shut it down. Far more pressing things needed my attention. And solutions to problems never lay between the sheets.

That led me to Jean-Charles. Between the sheets had been amazing. I longed for his touch. I longed for life to be like it used to be when he was here and life seemed doable. But his family needed him. If he abandoned them, he'd never forgive himself. I knew. I sat in the same saddle half a world away. And somehow, at this point in life, romance via Skype wouldn't cut it.

With my right foot, I opened the drain, letting out about six inches of water. Then I turned on the tap to scalding for a warmup. Once again settled, I took a few deep breaths—I'd been told they were calming, but you couldn't prove it by me. Then I took myself back in time.

What did I know?

Precious little, it turned out. I had a dead guy under a truck in the Babylon's delivery bays. Now I knew he was an equipment guy for the NBA franchise Pearl Coleman would soon be a part of. Finn Murphy, an Irish name that bestowed no luck. He'd hidden a fake ID in his shoe…well, he'd done it, or the killer had. I pondered that for a few nanoseconds. An interesting theory but I'm not sure where it got me. I filed it away. The only guy I knew who would help me with the fake ID had been found in pieces in the very small trunk of the car delivered in the truck under which we found our dead John Doe, one Finn Murphy.

This was making my head explode.

The car, a very expensive car, had been airlifted to my roof. The owner of the dealership asserted the car was for Pearl Coleman, future NBA star extraordinaire, who had his own problems. But the car wasn't one of them, or so he'd said. Somebody had been trying to set him up, perhaps for blackmail. And the guy with all the answers? The car salesman? He'd disappeared.

We as yet had no helicopter pilot who could shed light on how that car had gotten onto my roof and, more important, who had paid for it.

And the air traffic controller who might have had some insight on the helicopter used was found with his head bashed in, just like Finn Murphy, who was running scared. Otherwise, why would he have a fake ID in his shoe?

And...to make matters worse, my father expected me to kill some Asian fellow who had been smart enough to buy the lease that my father had been stupid enough to sign, giving the Babylon to the owner of the lease when it expired...which was now thirty-six hours away.

And that was just the big stuff.

Well, other than my father in seriously failing health. An imminent death of convenience, I'd say. I'd never wanted to squeeze the life out of him, but I was warming quickly to the idea.

What was it with men and their ego-induced blackouts of good sense? The Powers That Be gave women the ability to carry life and the primal directive to protect it at all costs. And a good thing! If men were in charge, our offspring would be chips bartered in a game of who had the biggest dick.

The Romans had it right. They thought that penis size and intelligence varied in opposite proportion. My life so far was proof of that theory. Although I wasn't privy to that kind of info about my father, thankfully. But I'd have to ask my mother. Not that she would tell the truth. To her, he was perfection personified.

But my father couldn't die on me now. Not now. That would be too easy...for him. My job description covered a vast array of potential problems to solve, but protecting someone from his stupidity? In some cases that could apply, but I decided right here, right now, that I would no longer do that. Not no way; not no how. Seriously, if he did die now, somehow, I'd find him and make his afterlife a living Hell.

And then there were the minor irritations of my mother (to be honest I'd never considered life could get so complicated that I would consider Mona to be a *minor* irritation) and the men intent on disappointing me.

And the worst part? I had no idea how to fix any of it.

I'd been taught to start at the beginning, but I had no idea where that might be. I'd just have to go with Squash to see Mrs. Morales in the morning. If she let me live, maybe I could find a string to pull that could help unravel this tortured tangle.

Another person, sensed but not heard, paused at the doorway to the bathroom.

"Glad to see you're not decent."

Flash! I was so glad to see her, but I'd never tell her. "I know; don't tell me. Teddie let you in."

"He did. I wasn't able to talk him out of that nice little tennis outfit he was sporting." Once her words landed on her consciousness, she started backpedaling. "Not like that. I didn't mean it like that. I just wanted the outfit for myself. The outfit."

I lifted my head and looked at her. "Your tastes run to much younger men. Besides, if you can turn his head, go for it."

"That'd be just wrong." Flash had changed clothes as I'd hoped, but the improvement was infinitesimal. The lady loved Lycra, neon-colored if she could find it, which in this town was pretty easy. Just head to the porn stores. Lycra and her voluptuous body were an odd combination made in somebody's heaven, just not mine.

I thought about tossing her a robe, but that would mean movement on my part, which had no appeal. "Sit. Tell me your sordid tale."

"You got any hooch?"

"Help yourself."

She left me in blissful quiet for a moment, during which I tried not to think about anything. Too soon she returned, plopping her broad beam on Teddie's tiny perch. I risked another glance. She'd helped herself to my bubbles. "And to what do I owe the gift of your company...in my bathroom...at some unreasonable hour?"

My snark didn't faze her. She crossed her leg giving me an unrestricted view. No underwear. Great. She'd been on the prowl. "I've been canvasing the players," she began, then took a sip from her delicate flute.

I didn't need a thesaurus to know what she meant. "The players, as you call them, are just kids. Almost half your age. Canvassing, as you call it, could leave a scar."

Flash gave me a wry grin and raised her flute. "The lights were off. He won't be traumatized. But damn, do you remember what it was like to have sex with a twenty-year-old pecker?"

I let my thoughts drift back. Before I could answer, she answered for me. "Oh yeah, I remember. Always the grownup, you never were twenty."

"And I never had sex with a pecker. The sex I had and still have...from time to time...involves the man who operates the pecker."

Of course, that didn't mean that I couldn't have sex with a twenty-year-old, but I was the keeper of those flames, thank you very much. Sharing them would only extinguish their power.

"You were always a stickler for..."

"Connection?" This conversation was getting me nowhere,

especially considering that, despite all the men in my life, sex was not on the immediate agenda. Clearly, I was doing something wrong, just not exactly sure what. But, thoughts for another day. I gave Flash a less-than-welcoming look. "As you can see, I'm taking a bath, a normally solitary endeavor. Why are you here? If it's to tell me something, I haven't heard it. If it's to make me feel better, you suck at it and need to leave."

Nothing ever fazed Flash. She brushed down her Lycra and brushed off my attitude. "Like I said, I've been canvassing the players."

"You're using protection, right?"

She ignored me. "And Miss P was right; something *is* going down."

I scooched myself up to the limit of decency, keeping the bubble cover. "Really. What?"

"Not sure, but some of the guys are finding pot in their duffels when they get them off the team plane. Money shows up in their accounts and when they try to trace it, the accounts it was sent from have been closed. And like yesterday, girls being sent to their rooms, with photographers lying in wait. It's weird."

"Sounds like blackmail."

"That's exactly what I thought. But even though someone has the goods on these kids—they've been set up royally—"

"Nobody ever contacts them."

"Right! How'd you know?" Flash seemed genuinely surprised by my deductions. Given that we've known each other for decades, I was a bit miffed.

"It's an old Vegas game. Collect a marker, even though this is a bit bass-ackwards from the old game, and then you've got something to hold over that person. Right now, the biggest question I have is why?"

Flash shook her head making all her now platinum curls tumble. I missed her natural red. "I don't know."

"Nobody will until somebody shows their hand."

She caught the tone of my voice. "And you're going to do that?"

"I'll keep pushing and chasing until somebody bolts and runs scared."

Flash pushed herself off the edge of my tub and rearranged the tube that sheathed her to cover at least the essentials so she could avoid attracting the attention of the police. "Not much of a plan."

I hid my smile. "When you come up with a better plan, let me know. You going to tell me how you and your cameraman snuck into not only the hotel but the Kasbah?"

She shifted nervously. "I was going to wait until all this was over. Don't want to add to your burden, you know."

"Big of you." I shot her a smile, which she returned.

"You got a pipeline of girls running through the delivery bays. One of the bellmen takes the orders from guests and the girls are ushered in the back way so as not to arouse suspicion."

"Yay. You got names?"

"Working on the bellman, but Jeff, the head dog down there is filling his pockets." She winced when she looked at me. "I got proof."

"I'll need it...when this murder thing is over. I don't want to shake anything up in the delivery bays until I figure out how deep this goes. Got it?"

"Yep."

"Thanks."

"It's what friends do."

She was so right. "One more question. I caught your interviews from the car show preview party."

"The one Thursday evening?"

"Yeah, what time was it?"

"From four until nine but it went later."

"It's not your normal gig. What are you chasing?"

"This blackmail thing. I was looking for a salesman. He wasn't there. Not due in until the next morning, but I wanted to stick my nose in everybody's business anyway."

"Walker Preston?"

"Yeah."

"What about his boss?"

"Carson Rivers? Total sleaze-bag, a player with no backing. Got roving hands, too."

"Great. Anything else you discover?"

"Not really."

"Keep digging. I'll do the same. Thanks for the update. Oh, and on your way out, tell Teddie to stop letting people in here."

"He's really sorta cute, don't you think?" She sashayed out, leaving me once again in a very delicate peace.

I'd just done another release of water and refill routine and was settling back for another soak when my phone rang. I heard it, but I couldn't see it and I had no idea where I'd left it as I'd shed my clothes. Clutching a towel to my chest, I went in search. The damn thing stopped ringing just as I closed in. I kicked at a few piles of dropped clothing and found it nestled under my sweater piled on the floor of the bedroom.

"Damn." I scowled at the thing. Who the hell had called? It was late, and now I was cold; it had better be important. I scowled at the caller ID.

Mona.

I pressed her speed dial, but she beat me to it. The phone rang out again. I swiped to answer. As I held the phone to my ear, I tried not to shiver. I couldn't tell whether I was cold or afraid. "Mother? What's wrong?"

"Oh, Lucky, it's your father…" She trailed off and my heart stopped.

"What?" I couldn't speak my biggest fear.

"He's gone."

"Gone?" I think my heart stopped beating as blood rushed

from my head and the world went on a Tilt-A-Whirl ride. Grabbing the nearest counter, I held on while the world righted. "You mean he died?" There, I said it. It had a hollow, impossible ring to it.

"Of course not," Mona said, exasperated.

"No?" After vocalizing the worst, I struggled to climb back up to the tolerable.

"He left. He disappeared. He's *gone!*"

CHAPTER THIRTEEN

"*W*HAT DO you mean he's *gone?*" I stood trembling in Mother's great room, having just been deposited there by their private elevator. How I'd gotten here was a bit murky. I did remember being on the verge of apoplexy as I pushed through the doors of the Babylon after having hurled my body through the air, covering ground faster than I ever remember. I don't think my feet touched the ground. My heart pounded. I may have broken my sprint record, but I don't think I violated any decency laws. I patted my legs to make sure I'd remembered pants. *Whew*.

"What is that you're wearing?" Mona, in her unruffled perfection, gave me a haughty glance. She seemed unfazed by this new development. Gaslighting, Mona's best skill. And maybe her only real coping mechanism.

"Wearing?" I so didn't expect that question, but I should have. "This is my middle-of-the-night-oh-my-God-screw-the-bubble-bath attire. Mother, what the hell?"

Her expression softened. She reached toward my face. I flinched. Her eyes widened. "Your wardrobe is a talk for another day." With two fingers she swiped behind my left ear.

Bubbles.

"Were you alone?"

"Mother!" Her calm pissed me off.

"If not, I'm so sorry." She grabbed my elbow with both hands and pulled me in tight as she maneuvered me toward my father's couch against the window.

"Mother, this is serious. Quit acting like we're a couple of girls dishing. Where did Father go?"

As we passed the bar, I disengaged. I poured myself some bubbly from an open bottle. On second thought, I poured one for my mother. This had to be hell on her, too. Knowing something was wrong. Knowing her husband might not fight to make it through. And unable to affect any of it.

Absolute hell. Certainly, my version of it.

She took one end of the couch. I handed her drink to her, then put some distance between us as I pressed into the far corner, fortifying myself behind a low wall of pillows. "Tell me what happened." As she opened her mouth, I silenced her with an upraised finger. "First, take a deep breath, then a few deep drinks. We'll find him, the damn fool." We both knew the exertion of wandering on his own was probably enough to kill him. Neither of us mentioned it.

Mona did as I said, then visibly worked to keep her features arranged in a mask of calm. "After you left, he seemed less agitated than he has been."

Yeah, asking me to eradicate his problem would bring some sense of calm, I guessed. Better me than him and all of that. Before my mother summoned me tonight, I'd been trying to deal with that thrown-under-the-bus thing. Was I really that expendable to my father?

And now he'd gone, taking it upon himself presumably. I wasn't all that keen with this result either, but perhaps he held me in slightly higher regard than I'd been led to believe. Why did I care when life as we knew it hung on the edge of extinction?

Imagining the worst-case scenario made me focus on what really mattered. And that was family. Perhaps my father had ambled down the same pathway.

I didn't say any of this as I leveled what I hoped was an interested, go-on, cattle prod of a look at my mother.

She pulled on her bubbles, then let her mask of calm fall away. Raw fear ran red and hot underneath. "I'd ordered some more food." When she looked at me, tears glazed her eyes. "The cheese wasn't enough. He needed more protein to get his strength back. The food came quickly, and I made him a plate. Just as I was going to join him, one of the girls cried out. They've been having baby nightmares, or teething pain, or whatever babies do." Absentmindedly, she patted at her hair.

So that's where I'd gotten it. That arranging the outside trying to bring order to the inside. In my experience, it never worked although sometimes it felt good. Her hand trembled as she folded it on top of the other hand that held her glass, clutching it like a lifeline.

"Once one baby is awake, the other one isn't far behind." Mona looked tired and for the first time I could see the years, not that there were really that many—she'd been fifteen when she'd had me. But they had started to soften her jawline and had drawn down her face. "I left your father here on the couch with his plate while I tended to them. I wasn't that long. Fifteen minutes, no more."

"And he wasn't here when you got back?" I ignored the bubbles as I stared out at my city. *Where have you gone, you old fool?* But the city didn't answer back.

Mona shook her head. "He hadn't eaten a bite." Clearly that thought bothered her. "While I was with the girls, I thought I heard his phone ring."

I leaned forward. "That's good. What else did you hear? Who called? What was it about?"

A tear broke free and traced a wobbly path down her cheek. She didn't bother swiping at it. "I don't know. I didn't think anything of it. He gets calls at all hours all the time." She clutched the tissue I held out to her and dabbed at her nose. "You know this business."

Know it? I could wax poetic about the perils but now was not the time. "I guess he took his phone with him?" She nodded. "Would you have access to his account?"

"His phone account?"

"Mmm." My mind spooled up. "Was his phone a hotel phone?" If so, Miss P could find out at least the number of the person who had called. Hope flared.

"No, it was his personal one. He always told me he didn't want anyone poking into his business."

Hope dashed.

"But he did leave this." Mona plucked at a scrap of paper on the coffee table.

"He left a note?" Once again, I wondered whether Mona did this sort of thing on purpose to bleed out the drama. Or was she really clueless? Or on max overload? I'd probably never know. Like the rest of us, she was who she was, which most of the time was infuriating. At least she was consistent. Eventually we were going to come to loggerheads, and it was anybody's guess as to whose blood would flow. And there still was that whole picket-ing-our-own-hotel thing. A justification for, if not homicide, at least serious bodily harm if there ever was one.

But not tonight.

Mona read from the bit of paper in her hand. "Tell Lucky I've gone to see a weasel."

I waited for her to continue, but apparently, she was through. "That was it?"

"Do you know what it means?" She laid it on the table with

the care due the Rosetta Stone as if such a scrap could offer the key to understanding.

"Haven't a clue." Somewhere deep inside my fuzzy brain a bell started clanging for my attention. "Wait. He went to see a weasel. Those are the exact words?"

"Yes." She squinted as she read the note again. "Tell Lucky I've gone to see a weasel."

I bolted down my bubbles and stood so quickly my mother started. "You know where he went?" She looked up at me with her doe eyes all glossy and expectant.

"I do."

WILLIE THE WEASEL.

The Powers That Be certainly had a brutal sense of humor.

I bolted out of the elevator before the doors were fully open, charging into the lobby and nearly taking out a couple who clung to each other in an effort to remain standing as it was. Before we all toppled, I managed to find my footing and grab them. "Sorry."

The man leered at me and dodged around a bit trying to focus on my face. "Care to join us? You'd make a nice third." The whiskey on his breath blew me back. His "second" looked like she could go either way.

"Thanks. Not tonight." I stopped myself before I said something about needing a hazmat suit and a body sheath of latex. They reminded me why we'd taken the luggage racks out of the rooms (don't ask) and also why the entire housekeeping staff needed a raise.

I slipped past them and raced through the lobby, turning the heads of the few stragglers not otherwise already engaged in something more fun than trolling a near-empty lobby. I swung by my office and donned the extra outfit I kept stashed there. At least I'd be semi-decent. I didn't even stop to check my appearance.

The Weasel didn't deserve that kind of concern.

After pushing through the front doors, I skidded to a stop.

A valet, jolted from a light, standing nap, rushed to greet me. "May I help you?"

The look on his face told me he knew me but wasn't sure from where. "I'm with the hotel. Are all the limos engaged?"

"Yes, miss. Do you need a taxi?"

No taxi driver would take me where I needed to go. "No, thanks."

"Do you have a car I can pull around for you?" The kid was clutching at straws and unwittingly leading me down a path to…well, theft was such a strong term. Perhaps unauthorized usage? Yes, that had a better ring to it.

And this was really like in the movies, racing to stop a good person from doing something awful…like homicide.

The fact remained—I didn't have a car. But I really needed one. The Ferrari dealership had long closed and my sweet little ride was still basking in adulation at the Concours. I eyed the youngster waiting expectantly. "Yes, bring me my car, please."

"I'm sorry, miss. I'm a new hire. I know you're with the hotel, but I don't know which car is yours."

Oh, lucky day! Well, for me anyway. I glanced at the fancy iron the valets had opted not to sequester out of sight in the garage, instead preferring to keep them close for show and because the owners probably knew here in Vegas an up-front tip and a polite request will get you primo parking. The purple Lambo Huracán looked like fun. "That one."

"Yes, miss." The kid didn't even bat an eyelash. Mental note to self—more training on the valet line. Of course, I played a corporate card most didn't have; but still, he was going to give me a two-hundred-and-fifty-thousand-dollar car, no questions asked.

I stuck out my hand. "Give me the keys. I'll take it from here."

I put two twenties in his palm as he dropped the keys into mine. They wouldn't compensate for the shit show that would hit if the real owner wanted his ride before I got back. After a nanosecond of thought, I also gave him one of my business cards I pulled from a sleeve in the case around my phone. "You may need this."

"Why?"

His question trailed me as I ran to the car, jumped in, and fired it up. Putting my foot to the accelerator, I wasn't quite prepared for the acceleration. I fishtailed it down the driveway but regained control as I gunned it up the Strip heading north.

Willie the Weasel lived in a part of town befitting a weasel.

You see, Willie and I went way back. I'd stopped counting the number of times I'd broken his nose. The last time, I'd found him holed up in an estate in one of the toffier-nosed neighbor-hoods in town—a double-gated community huddled around a very nice golf course. Of course, the house wasn't his—he was just squatting for a bit. Then, like now, my beef with Willie had been over a helicopter.

Yes, Willie was a helicopter pilot, and a very good one at that. One of his two skills. The other was finding trouble. For that, he was a total birddog. If finding trouble was part of a job description, he'd be rich beyond the dreams of avarice. Life—nothing but a timing issue between opportunities and aptitudes. Some are left standing with their hand out. Willie was one of them, and, to be honest, he got what he deserved.

This car heist thing and depositing it on the top of the hotel was just the sort of mischief Willie the Weasel would be smack in the middle of. And his piloting skills were more than sufficient.

Yep, he was my guy. And I'd get answers out of him if I had to break his nose another time—if my father left anything of him to break. I punched on the accelerator, time being of the essence and all. With nothing to lose, my father was a loose cannon—no telling what he'd do.

I had to get there before he'd passed the point of no return.

Of course, I could kill him myself. That would solve a few problems. I prayed he didn't tempt me. What was he thinking?

Problem was, I knew exactly what he was thinking.

He'd go out in a blaze of glory righting the wrongs he'd inflicted—a Butch and Sundance kind of moment. So like my father.

As I slowed to thread my way through the neighborhoods north of downtown, still waiting for the gentrification wave to come to them, I realized the Lambo might have been a poor choice. I might as well have painted a target on my side. Thankfully, at this time of night, only a few diehards gathered in packs on the corners, their boom boxes blaring. They measured each car that passed, not that there were many. One rangy guy who looked like he had a railroad up one arm, so skinny his pants hung off one hip, didn't hide his lust as I accelerated by.

Like coyotes, these young men traveled in packs and for the same reason. One of them would be easy prey, but all of them working in concert, they could take down a bear.

And I was smart enough to know I was no bear. But I had horsepower on my side.

However, right now the stupidity of my decision that I was above carrying my Glock came home to roost in the pit of my stomach, gnawing away. What about Romeo?

Too far away and too tied up in rules.

The neighborhoods dwindled, each one a lesser imitation of the one before, until the houses turned into trailers. Even here, graffiti decorated most that had the bad luck to find themselves permanent in a transient neighborhood where everyone was hoping to stop just for a moment on their way up.

Willie's trailer hunkered at the back of the lot, separated from the desert beyond by a wire fence topped with three rows of razor wire. What was left of the original color had been faded by the sun to a chalky white, then covered with bright paint in the street art style of the moment. Time and sun had yellowed and desiccated the snaggletoothed plastic overhang above the door.

Decorative bars protected the windows, but they were only for show. The sheet metal siding was so thin I could probably put my foot through it. Hopefully, I wouldn't find out if I was right or wrong. However, all my previous interactions with the Weasel had gotten messy.

Before easing toward Willie's, on the whisper of a prayer that I might find my father here, I had made a turn around the block but hadn't seen any cars that looked out of place. Of course, I had no idea what kind of car my father would be in—I couldn't quite picture him sliding into this neighborhood in his behemoth of a Rolls, ragtop and all, but that was the only car he owned.

After my reconnoitering, I'd coasted the Lambo in, not wanting to arouse interest. No rats or, more specifically, no weasels skittered in the darkness. So far so good.

A pale, yellow light leaked through the thin cloth hung over one window. Willie was home, or at least somebody was. Cardboard covered the other window, held in place by multiple strips of thick black tape. Two steps led up to the solid metal door—no peephole, no windows. A frontal attack seemed the way to go.

I eased out of the low-slung car, letting the door shut with only a muffled click. I pocketed the keys, then stalked up the walkway—slabs of concrete tilted at all angles like ice buckling under pressure. In the half-light of a weak bulb on a pole at the far end of Willie's trailer, I managed to stay on my feet and only stubbed my toe once. With my mood in tatters, and my pissed-off on overload, I arrived in front of the door and gave it a once over.

A strip of light peeked through where the door hadn't quite met the frame.

The door was open.

Okay, trick or treat? Was I walking into a trap, or lucky beyond belief? Did it matter? I braced myself. Raising one foot, I rammed my heel into the door, then threw myself through the opening. I came up hard against a wall.

Willie bolted up from a chair. He'd been sitting at a small table, his hand wrapped in a dirty cloth. The surprise on his face left as quickly as it had come, replaced by resignation. "Oh, it's you. I should've known one Rothstein in an evening wasn't enough. Pull up a chair." He returned to slump over the table, propped on elbows and holding his bound hand. He lifted milky eyes to mine. "Wanna beer? There's some in the fridge."

"My father's been here?" I stayed where I was. The place was tiny, but, surprisingly, he kept it neat. The kitchen behind him had a few dishes resting on a towel to dry. Posters of NBA players adorned the walls. Some of them, carefully framed, went back a few decades. Who knew? Willie the Weasel was an NBA fan.

Pain pinched Willie's cheeks. A pallor lightened his already pasty skin. His hair had thinned some since I'd last seen him and he'd lost some weight, a good deal of weight. Drugs or illness? With him it could be anything. Neither would do much for his flying. The place seemed neat enough, but it was the smell that hit me. Not bad, just alarming. I tried to place it. Ammonia. Alcohol. Fear. Like the hospital.

Slowly he unwrapped his hand. His pinky was red and swollen. Knowing my father, that finger had been recently bent at an unnatural angle.

"You put that back yourself?"

Willie shrugged. "Not as much pain as some other things."

I reached into the fridge and grabbed his last beer. Popping the tab, for a moment I let him think I would guzzle it, then I put it in front of him. "You need this more than I do." I didn't sit down, and there was little room to pace. Could I be the good cop to my father's bad cop? That'd be a switch.

"What did my father want?"

Willie glanced up at me, sizing me up. A sly little grin that I was desperate to smack off his face lifted one corner of his mouth. "Same as you. Information."

"Slow to catch on as I am, I'd made it that far. About what?"

"Weed. He wanted to know about weed."

That curveball arced out of left field.

Weed.

That had been the one odd constant in this whole mess. So far, most places I looked I either found some or somebody was asking me about it. I leveled a stare at Willie and rubbed my elbow—a not-so-subtle reminder as to what happens when I aim that particular joint at his nose. *Think, Lucky. Think.* "You been flying under the radar some lately?"

"Not much legit work for a guy with my history."

His rap sheet alone would have been justification enough for the FAA to pull his ticket. "That was a pretty slick bit of flying to lift that car and put it on that platform without dropping it in the pool."

He gave me a bit of side-eye as he tipped back his head and took a pull on the beer. He wiped his mouth with the back of his hand. "You're smarter than your father."

In so many ways, Willie. So many ways. At this moment I didn't begrudge any male the suffering of the Curse of the Y Chromosome. What a burden that must be. "It's all about that car, isn't it?"

Willie gave me his impersonation of a Cheshire cat, which was rather horrifying, but telling.

"Tell me about that car, Willie." I stepped to the side of the table opposite him. Placing my palms on the table, I leaned in until I could smell his sickness.

"You ask. I'll answer."

I let him think he was making the rules. "What are you dying of, Willie?"

His turn for a head slap out of left field. This time he took a longer pull on his beer. "How'd you know?"

"Been around death a lot lately." I stepped back my in-his-face and took the chair across from him.

"My liver. Stage four. You never think…" He trailed off. The haunting of regrets flashed across his face.

The more years I had under my belt, the more I realized that the goal of a good life well lived was dying with the fewest number of regrets. I wasn't sure how many regrets Willie harbored, but enough that I could see them in the hollowness behind his eyes. Life could be damn hard, and sometimes the hardest part was the fact that what you started with sometimes limited where you got.

Not fair. Not even nice. But real. As a girl, I was never going to get to play in the NFL. A limitation, but not one I'd carry with me. No, the ones that hit you when you'd reached the end of your bean row seemed to be the ones that you could have busted through, if only…

Yeah, the if-onlys were hell.

I reached across the table and touched his hand. His skin was cold, dry, like a reptile's. "This flight. This car. It doesn't fit your MO."

His eyes shifted from mine.

I followed my gut on this one. "This one was a favor. It wasn't about you at all, was it?" I glanced under the table. Yep, another pair of Pearl Colemans.

The fire returned to his eyes. He sat up straighter. I could see the effort it cost him. "About me? Hell yeah it was about me. For once I got to do something that was good, that was right. Fat lotta good it did me."

"Why don't you tell me what the three of you cooked up?"

"The guy who got me into this whole thing, he came nosing around the airport asking if anybody knew a flyboy who could fly that fancy Bell his boss leased. He didn't much care about currency. He just cared about keeping it on the down-low, if you know what I mean."

"What's his name?"

"Don't know it. We kept it that way. He paid me in cash, so none's the wiser. I just called him The Salesman."

"He wanted you to call him that?"

"No. He just had that way."

"Describe him."

Willie gave me a perfect description of Walker Preston. "Okay, and everything was going okay until the third guy, the guy with the shoes, showed up."

Willie pulled his feet back.

"I know about the shoes. Tell me about the third guy. You know *his* name?"

"Yeah, Finn something-or-other. Cool dude. Totally into hoops. Apparently, he got hold of The Salesman quite by accident—he was down in the bays checking on the car we were to deliver to Pearl. Bent his ear for a long time. Upshot was…The Salesman called me, told me what was going down, how his boss and some Chinese dude were setting up these kids to get some leverage. We weren't going to stand for that, you know."

Everyone had their line in the sand. Willie had finally found his. I was happy for him in an odd sort of way.

"You believe me, Ms. O'Toole, don't you? Please tell me you believe me."

The hurt, the regret, poured out of him. "I believe you." Odd thing was, I actually did. I might regret it, but for now it seemed the right play. "Why did you three want to lift that car onto the roof of the Babylon?"

He pressed his lips together and managed a serious case of serious, which he leveled at me. "Evidence," he said, his voice low, his tone conspiratorial.

"Of what?"

"The thing is loaded with pot. Pot from northern California they can't sell there on account of the taxes and stuff make the legit stuff way more expensive than the street stuff."

Boy I needed to get a debrief from Doc. Of course, he probably thought the weed was inconsequential after finding Freddy Morales. "They were going to dump it here?" I knew the answer, but I wanted to see if Willie would give it to me.

"No, they weren't selling it." He looked at me from under his eyebrows. "They were using it."

"Blackmail." I didn't realize I'd said it until I saw Willie nodding like I was his prize pupil. "Okay, but for what?"

Willie deflated. "That's where I lose the thread. I don't know. What do they want these kids for? Why would anyone want to get them in trouble? We, me and my buddy, we didn't know the end game."

"Do you know who killed your friend?"

His eyes snapped open wide. "What?" he whispered.

"Finn. Somebody bashed his head in."

"Man, he was a good dude. He didn't deserve that. But that explains something."

"What?"

"Finn was supposed to meet me and The Salesman in the bays at 8:30. He didn't show. We couldn't wait, so we lifted the car then disappeared."

"Who offloaded the car in Babel?"

"The Salesman." He paused then continued. "If you find the guy who offed Finn, I'll kill him myself. Do you a favor. Don't have nothing to lose. Know what I mean?"

"Like my father." I let that lie there, just to see what Willie would do.

He snorted a bit as if laughing at some personal joke. "Yeah, he plays the game different than you, but I get him, too. He's got some axes to grind. Some unfinished business, he said." Willie looked at me, his eyes empty. "Is it important, this unfinished business?"

I thought for a moment. "To be honest, I don't really know. Is there a lot of money at stake? For sure. But is it important?" I pursed my lips and tilted my head. "My father made a mistake—a stupid mistake. He wants to fix it before he dies, which could be any day now. You saw him."

Willie nodded. "He's in bad shape."

Not what I wanted confirmed, but a reality I had to accept. "What did you tell him?"

"I sorta gave him the shrug-off, know what I mean?" Willie looked a little sad but a lot proud. "Glad I did, too. He's not the man to find my friend's killer and stop this." He took another slug of his beer, tilting the can and opening his mouth for the last drop. Then he fixed me with a look of resolve, which was a bit terrifying. "But you are."

"Me?" I'm not sure a compliment from Willie the Weasel held much water, but I was touched.

"Yeah. The perfect man for the job. You get stuff. People. You always made me pay when I stepped outside the lines, but I knew what those lines were, and you gave me some rope. I always appreciated that."

Funny how life delivers lessons from the oddest sources. I expected to be breaking Willie's nose and here he was teaching me a bit about life.

"So, on what wild-goose chase did you send my father?"

Willie grimaced and flinched a bit. "Not so much a wild-goose chase exactly. And I may have sent him into a bad bit of shit; I don't know. But I sent him after the owner of the dealership."

"Carson Rivers?"

"That's the guy."

"Slimy dude."

Willie grinned. "Totally. He's up to his ass in this, just not sure he knows it."

"How does that work?" I was pretty sure it would be hard to throw the book at the guy if he didn't have criminal intent. Maybe we could get him on an accessory charge, which would be okay considering we had two deaths already. Remembering that delivered a cattle-prod jolt. "Can you give it to me short and sweet? There's a future homicide or two I need to thwart."

"He's the emperor who has no clothes on."

Guilt by stupidity? I wasn't buying it. The guy had shark written all over him. Maybe Willie felt he owed the guy a favor. After all, I'd bet all I had that Carson Rivers had been the one keeping Willie flying recently, under the radar as it were. No matter what was going on with his health, Willie the Weasel always hedged his bets.

"You think there's somebody else involved in this?"

"Yeah. Can't prove it though. Just got that old feeling, and it's kept me alive so far."

"Okay, what's my next step?"

"You tell me. You already know."

"The Salesman. Walker Preston."

Willie drained the rest of his beer. "Yeah, he's pulling the strings and he's running scared. You find him, you'll get a lot of what you're looking for."

I rose to go. "I've got three murders that are a part of this. You're on the list of potentials."

"They'd be doing me a favor." He speared me with a look. "I got my boys watching. They give me the heads-up on anybody heading this way. I knew your father was heading this way, and

I knew when you pulled up. But you, you watch your back. Like I said, there's somebody else. Don't know who. Don't want to know. But there's bad stuff there."

The shiver of truth chased down my spine. Somebody else. But who?

"If you need anything…" I paused with my hand on the doorknob.

Willie raised his empty can. "I'll let you know. Where are you going?"

"To shake some info out of a dead man."

CHAPTER FOURTEEN

UNLIGHT PAINTED the sky when I climbed back in the Lambo. This time I cranked it and let it growl. The sound of an incredible machine gearing up for its intended purpose always settled me right down. And speed focused me. I whipped out of the neighborhood, then hit the 95. I'd take the longer, faster way. Squash didn't live far.

I ignored the texts and messages littering my phone's home screen, but I did catch a glimpse. Something about a missing car. Yes, the shit had hit the fan. I tried not to think about the misery of incarceration as I scrolled through my recent calls.

Squash answered on the first ring. "Trenton." He sounded all bright-eyed and bushy-tailed.

Now there was a visual. I must be more sleep deprived than I thought. I shook the alarming image away. "Hey, we need to go see Mrs. Morales now."

"I haven't had my coffee."

"Sugar hangover? I haven't been to bed. I'll be there in five." I hung up. I had no time to argue and no patience to cajole. I floored it through the mousetrap onto the 15, then braked sharply, taking the next exit as fast as I dared.

Squash was waiting out front in his go-to-court suit, pink tie, and holding a briefcase in one hand and two mugs of steaming brew in the other. Still pink from a shower, his hair wet and slicked back, he looked sorta sexy, not that I would ever play in that sandbox. Lawyers were best as allies; and keeping lovers as friends wasn't a tool I had in my limited toolbox. However, it seemed I was more the issue than the other way around. Anyway, too much to think about, and too important to risk.

He set his briefcase down, then handed me a mug through the open door. "You sounded like you might need this." He retrieved his briefcase, then folded himself into the racing seat.

"You are a prince among men." I took my first java jolt and felt a bit of function return.

"Don't let it get around." He whistled softly as he ran his finger across the stitching on the dash. "New ride."

"I stole it."

Even with my eyes on the road, I caught his wide-eyed look. "No shit?"

"No shit." I tossed him my phone. "Can you give me the gist? Where are we going, by the way? Home or office?"

"Office. Mrs. Morales gets an early start. I'm assuming someone has told her about Freddie?"

"Haven't a clue, so be prepared for anything." Dear God, the woman was homicidal on a good day. Being the messenger bringing the worst of all news didn't bode well.

Squash focused on my phone while I navigated the still-deserted streets. Light peeked through windows in some of the houses, but not many. I glanced at him, trying to gauge if a BOLO had been issued or not. His lips moved as he read. Sorta cute. I needed to either get over myself or get laid or the male population within my grasp would be in serious danger.

Getting over myself seemed the safer course of action—I'd work on that.

"Man, you lit a fire."

"I didn't have a car. My father is off on a wild-goose chase that will probably get him killed. I need to find a car salesman." I wound down. While true, the litany sounded like whining. "How bad?"

"Upshot is Romeo and Miss P covered your ass. They put the owner in one of the bungalows and told him the sky's the limit." When he looked at me, a smile broke wide across his face. "You're paying for it all, by the way. Even if you have to take out a loan."

I shot him some slitty-eye, then almost blew through a stop sign. I slammed on the brakes at the last moment. Not that I would have imperiled anyone—the streets were deserted. Somehow, we sacrificed nary a drop of coffee in the process.

Both hands gripping the wheel, the car at a dead stop, I took a deep breath. "I can live with that." At least nobody mentioned a lawsuit or serious bodily harm. Most likely that would hold up as long as I brought the car back soon and in one piece. I looked both ways before proceeding more cautiously.

Squash was right—the lights burned brightly through the glass front of Freddy Morales's office. His partner, a sketchy guy who called himself Eddie V, floated bail bonds. Freddy pretended to be legit; he made bank on selling fake IDs, passports, driver's licenses, Social Security cards—all the paper one needed to work in Vegas or anywhere else. If the evidence we collected at our hotels was proof, he also did a land-office business providing visitors with alternate lives for their stay. Part of the fantasy I didn't have too much trouble with as long as they didn't use the ruse to try to stiff legit businesses. I didn't think Freddy got into fake credit cards. If he had, whoever killed him would've had to beat me to it, euphemistically speaking. And actually, that old saw wasn't so funny, not anymore.

We both sat in the car for a moment, gathering courage in my case. Probably the same for Squash though I didn't ask. Even the tough guys wilted when confronted with Mrs. Morales in full sail.

"Why do we need to see her now?" Squash threw back the last of his coffee, then clutched his briefcase on his lap with both hands. A good shield but probably not sufficient. I didn't grace him with my opinion—it wouldn't help.

"I need a bead on a car salesman who is running scared. I believe he told Freddy some info that got him killed. I'd like to figure out what that was if I could. He's the key to the car on top of my hotel and I'm sure a few tidbits that could break this thing wide open."

"He put the car where nobody could miss it." Squash nodded. "You think he carved Freddy up as well?"

"That's for Romeo to figure out. I chase possible perps; he can string them up. Frankly, I'm losing my stomach for all of this. I need a nice place with lots of Champagne and no people, that's what I need. Right now, what I really want to know is who are they running from?"

"Weren't you just in Paris?"

"What?"

"Don't people go there to get away?"

"I need no people. Paris is packed cheek-to-jowl."

"Well, you couldn't talk to them, so I thought that might work." I didn't even want to mention my French body count. "What's the connection with Freddy, other than the obvious? We wouldn't be here if you weren't looking for something."

"The dead guy is the one I told you about who had a fake ID in his shoe." I pulled up a photo of it on my phone, then gave Squash a gander.

"Impressive work. For sure could be Freddy's."

"That's what I'm counting on because right now I got a murderer out there cleaning up his messes, two dead guys, another on the run, and bupkis in the way of leads."

Squash griped the door handle. "Let's go find what you're looking for."

I followed his lead. "Now's as good a time as any." Nothing like wasting time trading inanities.

A bell chimed as we opened the door. Squash made a chivalrous show of letting me go first. I wasn't fooled. He wanted me to take the first bullet, that was all.

I stopped dead one step inside. Squash rode up my heels. "Whoa," we both said.

The office décor was what you'd expect: beat-up furniture purchased from a liquidator. However, today it was a bit messier than usual. Files littered the floor. Desk drawers lay overturned, their contents strewn about. Pictures that had lent a bit of ambiance had been torn from their frames, then the frames broken. Shards of glass caught the light. They'd even ripped Mrs. Morales's plants from their pots and the tendrils from the walls. Yes, the plants liked Mrs. Morales, but that was more a testament to the plants and their lack of judgment than Mrs. Morales's redeeming qualities, which I had yet to be introduced to.

At the sound of the chime, Mrs. Morales popped up from behind the far desk—Freddie's desk. Pain and anger molded her features into a mask of emotion I'd never seen before and never wanted to see again. She knew.

A mother should never have to bury her son. Of all the things wrong with the world, that had to be the worst. Even though I wasn't myself a parent, I lost my breath to the sucker punch of her pain.

"You!" She pointed a witch's talon at me. "This is your fault!"

Damn, absorbing her pain, I'd wasted precious seconds that I could've used to run like hell. A head start could be the difference between life and death. Too late now. I stood my ground. "I'm very sorry about Freddy."

Squash actually stepped in front of me, not protecting me

entirely, but deflecting Mrs. Morales's total desolation. "We both are." He swept the room with his arm. "What happened here?"

I thought it painfully obvious, but since he was willing to take the lead, I let him run.

Mrs. Morales ran a hand through her hair, which didn't help. As if her energy and pain shot through each tendril, her black curls resisted any effort to tame them. Tears streaked down her cheeks unabated. She gulped her words. "They came in the back. Freddy never was much on big locks and security, even in this neighborhood. He figured most of the folks who live around here were clients, so he had a point. We never had any trouble before."

"This is the first time someone has broken in here?" That had to be a record.

"Yeah." She kicked at a file. "Guess it doesn't matter now." She swallowed a sob, then pressed a hand to her chest.

"Well, I'm not sure that's the case."

She gave me an evil eye. "How do you mean?"

I was so going to need to be smudged or find some magic juju or something to ward off the spells she cast my direction. Was it possible to smudge a person? My mother always tried to feng shui my wardrobe, so why not? Worth a shot. Better than dying in all the miserable ways a person like Mrs. Morales could dream up. I felt my knees go a bit weak, but I resisted touching anything, even pulling up the nearest chair. "You want to catch Freddy's killer, right?"

"Only if you catch him, then hand me a knife and leave me alone in a locked room with him for five minutes."

"Done," I said, with the force of an auctioneer pounding the gavel. Squash shot me a wide-eyed glance, which I ignored. They both stayed riveted, so I damned the torpedoes, although I did still sort of hunker a bit behind the Squash. "You said you've never been broken into before, right?" Mrs. Morales nodded.

"So, I'm thinking it would be too much of a coincidence not to have this break-in and Freddy's death not be related." A ton of negatives strung together, but they seemed to follow.

"The murderer did this?"

"Or someone who can lead us to him. Either way, we get what we want." If, and this was a big if—*if* they didn't get what they wanted. If that bit of evidence were gone, we'd never know what it was. Of course, I wasn't going to throw water on this fire just yet, so I didn't say any of that. Instead, I asked, "Where did Freddie keep the things he didn't want anyone to find?" I was guessing. But, if he'd heard about the dead guy at the hotel, he'd have been running scared…assuming we were right and the dead guy had been a client—which was the one card this whole flimsy House of Hope was built on.

"Over here. Under his desk." She motioned Squash forward, then disappeared as she once again squatted.

I stayed by the door—not sure why other than self-preserva-tion. Also, perhaps my well-honed need to keep my surround-ings in view rooted me where I stood. Squash disappeared behind the desk, leaving me room to do a three-sixty of our environs. Someone had wanted something badly enough to break in and trash the place. If they hadn't found what they were looking for, they'd be back. Back when someone could help them, someone who could point out the hidden places.

A chill raised the hairs on the back of my neck. With the door jamb as a bit of cover, I made a slow study of the one hundred and eighty degrees I could see through the glass front. The neighborhood—a mix of old houses falling in on them-selves, a few that still clung to hope of better days, and some that had been converted to small businesses. The neighborhood market, the liquor store, ubiquitous in places like these where misery pummeled hope, leaving escape as the only means of survival, a few bail bondsmen, the windows all dark behind a lattice of bars. All except Freddy's. Just around the corner, a bookstore, a donut shop, a record store selling vinyls from better days long past, and a hamburger stand, all brought hope close, but just out of reach.

Not much movement yet, not even cars. A five-story building to the east kept the streets in shadow as the sun perched barely above the horizon. I crossed my arms, rubbing my upper arms against the chill. A morning brush of sunlight would do wonders. Squinting, I probed into the deepest shadows. The sense of someone watching, chased down my back.

On my first pass, I missed him. Maybe he shifted, maybe he pushed himself off the wall, but something drew my attention to the alley at the far end of the building across the street. No more than thirty yards, if that. I waited.

Yes, he'd moved. I could see him better now. Shortish, gray hoodie obscuring his face, hands tucked in the front pocket, jeans, one knee torn, red and white kicks. Fancy. Clean. Too clean. He hugged the wall as he inched his head out, giving him a clear view of Freddy's place.

The door hadn't closed behind us. It stood wide, an open invitation.

I took shallow breaths, willing myself to stillness. Behind me Squash and Mrs. Morales talked in hushed tones. I couldn't make out what they were saying.

The man in the alley showed himself. He stepped onto the sidewalk and surveyed the street. Satisfied, he jammed his hands further into the front pouch, ducked his head and strode my direction. He limped slightly, favoring the leg with the rip in his jeans.

I sucked in a breath. Just a little closer... Look up! I needed a glimpse of his face.

Behind me, Squash shouted, "Lucky, this is interesting. Come see."

Damn!

The man stopped. Startled, he looked up.

Walker Preston!

I bolted through the door. Head down, arms pumping, I ran as fast as I could. As I said, a head start could be the difference between success and failure. Younger than me, and probably stronger than me, Walker Preston had the advantage, but I had surprise. A rabbit in front of a hungry coyote, he froze.

Twenty feet. My ragged gasps burned my throat. My heart, unused to this sort of exertion, strained against my ribcage.

Fifteen feet.

I reached. He turned, ducked away, then ran. My fingers brushed fabric.

Damn!

God he was quick. I lowered my head, reached deep, and kept charging as fast and furiously as my body would allow. My longer legs ate up bigger chunks of the ten-foot-wide canyon between us, but his youth and apparently his fitness kept him well out of reach.

Sucking in air, I felt my energy flagging, my legs refusing to churn with the same cadence. I had to stay close; I had to! I couldn't lose him! Not like last time. I might never have another chance.

Willie had said he was the key to everything. The thought crossed my oxygen-starved gray matter that Willie could've been shining me on. I refused to believe it. Dying men generally were reticent to sin afresh with their Maker hovering close. Yes, of course, history provided many examples of exceptions to my rule. Still, Willie was only a mild opportunist, not even in the same category much less the same league as…. Jesus, I was so losing it.

Focus!

I kept the distance between us—at least it wasn't growing. But time was not on my side.

Breaking out the other end of the alley, he bolted into the sunlight. He threw an arm up to shield against the glare. A horn honked. Walker Preston leaped. The hood of a car as it screeched to a halt brushed his legs from under him. He rolled off the hood. Dazed, he landed on his feet, then staggered once as he gathered himself.

With one hand on the hood, I vaulted around the car, then hit the ground and launched myself. I hit him flush in the middle of the back, then landed on him as we hit the ground. The air rushed out of him. I lay on top of him, using my bulk to hold him. With as much force as I could muster, I yanked one arm, folding it behind him.

He yowled in protest. With one hand under the elbow, I gained leverage, pushing his arm higher, tighter.

He pounded the concrete of the street with an open palm. "Stop!"

"Lady, you're hurting him." A male voice behind me. Must be the driver.

"He's wanted for murder," I lied, maybe…but I sounded sincere, and that's all that counted.

"Murder?" Walker Preston squeaked. He had a high voice, nasal and weak.

A car eased by us. We needed to move, but I knew if I let up, I'd lose my advantage.

Feet pounded behind us, coming closer. "Lucky?"

"Squash! Thank God."

Soon he bent over me, hands on his knees, a smiling playing with his lips as he sucked in air. "You can't stay out of trouble, can you? I let you alone for a minute. What do you have there?" His breath came as loud and as fast as mine. His face flushed a beet red.

I felt better. "I found the man we're looking for."

CHAPTER FIFTEEN

*W*ITH SQUASH'S help, I escorted Mr. Preston back to the office and secured him to a chair using several pairs of handcuffs Mrs. Morales provided. The idea of that woman with handcuffs was enough to have me running for the hills, but the need to find my father before he unleashed all manner of bad shit overrode self-preservation.

Now, if she just had a whip to keep our fugitive in line, I'd be in hog heaven. Alas, my fantasy didn't make it so.

Preston glared at me through tiny eyes set too close together in an unremarkable face. A mere facsimile of the photo I'd pulled up for Romeo from the dealership website. "And you've been working out."

"CrossFit."

Changing his appearance, and now looking for some help from Freddy. My bet was the guy had been planning on running for a while. "Nice shoes." I kicked at Preston's feet.

"A gift. Not a crime." That voice roughed up every last nerve I had.

I reached for my phone and searched for the picture of the

dead guy under the truck. Once I found it, I turned the device so the kid had a close up.

He flinched back. "Damn!"

"Recognize him?"

The kid shook his head but stared at the photo.

"Look closer." I found a picture that showed the guys shoes. "How about now?"

His eyes widened as he tucked his feet under the chair.

"Too late to hide. I know about those shoes. Not even out yet but purported to be *the* must-have sneaker. A Pearl Coleman limited edition to celebrate his signing and all. Only a couple of pairs exist."

"So?" His skin was now a pasty white and dotted with sweat, he looked truly shaken.

"I know about the guy in the photo, Finn Murphy. I know about Willie and the flights from California. What I don't know is why are you here?"

Walker licked his lips as his eyes darted around the room—a caged animal, scared and in over his head. "I heard the guy here could give me a fake ID so I could start over somewhere else."

"Why?"

He snorted. "You got all the answers."

"Some, but I bet there're some holes. Why don't you start from the beginning? Tell me about the car, you, Willie and Finn."

"Who?"

I held up my phone.

This time he managed to mute his flinch. "That guy. I know him...knew him. Not well, but we had...words recently." He licked his lips again and tried to meet my eye.

"I'm all ears."

Squash had parked a butt cheek on one of the desks that hadn't been overturned. He pulled a notebook out of an inside pocket, then searched another pocket for a pen.

He took a deep breath. The truth didn't seem to leap to his lips.

"Coming clean is your best bet," Squash said. He didn't tell the kid he was a lawyer. Suited up as he was, he looked the part, but I'm sure he didn't want any client requests interfering with our fact-finding mission. Gotta love a man willing to skirt issues to get to the core of the matter.

"My boss—"

I jumped in, "Carson Rivers?"

"Yeah. He makes a show of being one of the big dogs, but it's all a sham, built on other people's money. His car business is a shell to move…inventory…mainly to and from China. The winery is something rich people do to impress their friends. It's a hell of a business and hard to make much money."

"Especially when you're trying to fund a lavish front," I said.

"Worse, he went into pot with everything he had, borrowed money from friends, the few he had, and a bunch from some dude in China."

The whole China thing was getting very interesting. "You know his name?"

"That was a need-to-know kind of thing. But recently, maybe a couple of months ago, things really escalated—more cars flowing in, more sales, not that I was complaining. As a salesman, I got my piece. But I wondered about it all."

The cars were just a variation on the money laundering thing I'd picked up on in Macau not too long ago. The Chinese buy luxury goods, ship them overseas and sell them, then the money is out of China and not under the limitations imposed by the government. That would give the Chinese some running money, here in the States, Canada, wherever they chose to sell whatever it was they'd bought. "How many cars would you say you sold in the last year or so?"

"Tens of millions of dollars worth."

Squash let out a low whistle as he made notes.

Tens of millions still wasn't enough to buy out the lease of the land under the Babylon. There was something else there, something I could almost reach, but I didn't have it yet. "What about the pot?"

Walker Preston went still. I could see the pulse of his blood just under the skin below his ear. "What do you mean?"

So far, the kid hadn't admitted to participating in anything illegal. We'd come to the fork in that road. "The car? The Bugatti on the roof of my hotel?"

"Yeah?" He swallowed hard.

"It was one of yours."

"Yeah."

"Where and when did you have...words...with Finn Murphy?"

"Who?" I held up my phone so he could see the photo again. "Thursday afternoon, just after lunch."

"What did you talk about?"

"He confronted me about the car."

"Why?"

"He said his rookie wouldn't order such a thing and he smelled a rat. I let him talk. The more he talked, the more I got what he was saying. He'd been nosing around and said something odd was going on with mostly the rookies."

"Money showing up in their bank accounts? Fancy cars full of pot being delivered to them across state lines, which reeks of them being involved in transporting a controlled substance for the purpose of selling it? Those sorts of odd kinds of things?"

"How'd you know?"

"Cat's out of that bag. If you want to preserve your chance at not only staying alive but also perhaps staying out of prison, you'd better give us the whole skinny, right now." My mind was spinning. Walker Preston could be just as guilty as his boss, or more so. I couldn't tell. The possibility existed that his boss didn't know anything about what his employee was doing. Men playing the big shot often made great targets, caught up as they were in keeping their image alive.

"Look, all I did was help Mr. Rivers move some inventory."

"You mean weed?" He nodded. "To greener pastures?" I couldn't resist.

"Yeah, we'd stuff it in the cars, move them by private plane. Nobody got wind of it."

"Until Finn Murphy got his back up."

Walker Preston deflated. "I was okay with the pot operation. We moved it to where it was legal, but the tax structure was more amenable to making some profit. I know if the Feds got wind of it, we'd be slapped back. But I didn't see any real harm."

Riding the line of acceptable justification, but I didn't quibble. "What changed?"

"Mr. Rivers started pushing me to take the weed thing a bit further, mess with the players, set them up." He finally met my eyes and didn't waver. "None of us were okay with that."

"You agreed to help Finn?"

He showed me his feet. "That's why he gave me these kicks."

"You didn't kill him?"

The question hit him like a thousand volts. "God, no! Why would I do that?"

"He was going to rat you out whether you helped him or not."

He cocked his head and thought about that. "I guess. It's not like I was getting a cut or anything, so I didn't feel too bad about it. Mr. Rivers is an ass. And I could always get another job. I'm a good salesman."

That's what I was afraid of. "Don't try to sell me. If you do, you are on your own and I'll do everything in my power to see you in a very bad prison with a lot of prisoners looking for company."

That provided any incentive that was lacking. "Me and Finn decided we needed to get the car out of reach. It was the only evidence we had. I had the shipment paperwork, and then we had the car. At least maybe that was enough that someone would listen to us. I figured I wasn't too deep yet, and if I gave up the operation, maybe I could get a deal."

"So, you called Willie, who'd been flying some pot under the radar for your boss. And you convinced him to help?"

"Yeah, all it took was the last pair of these shoes. He's a big basketball fan. That helped. And I got the sense he had some emotional stake in the game, just not sure what."

Going out on an uptick, but that was Willie's story and his alone.

"So you didn't know there was something else in the trunk of that Bugatti, using the term loosely."

"No, what?" He didn't seem concerned, only curious. Either he was a complete psycho or he was telling the truth.

"A friend of mine—well, somebody I knew and did business with." I tried to handle this delicately as his mother was standing too close for comfort.

"How'd they stuff somebody in that tiny place?" The kid reeled back as his imagination answered his own question. "Oh, jeez!"

Mrs. Morales sprang to life with a feral growl. Squash stayed put. I stepped out of the way. She hit him in the chest, and they both wet ass-over-teakettle. For the second time in the past half hour Walker Preston's breath rushed from him in a whoosh.

"You killed my baby!" I'd never heard the plaintive, devastated, wail before, and I never wanted to again.

I let her have a couple of turns at the kid—she deserved at least that much—but, before too much blood went flying, both Squash and I gently lifted Mrs. Morales off the kid. Squash took an elbow to the gut before she calmed. Once I ensured Squash's safety, I bent down and tugged the kid's chair back upright.

His nose was a bit off-center. Blood flowed down his chin from both his nose and a split in his lip. "You let her do this." he lisped through his thickening lip, spraying blood, which I side-stepped.

"Gosh, sorry. She's faster than me. What can I say?" I leveled him with my best killer look. "The young man in the trunk of that car was her son. By my way of thinking, she deserved a few swings at you."

"But I didn't kill him!" The kid's eyes widened like a trapped rabbit's. "You have to believe me!"

"If you didn't kill him, who did?"

"I don't know!" The whole thing had the kid totally spooked. Weed was one thing., murder altogether different.

"How long have you been in town?" My version of the "Where were you on the night of…" question.

"Thursday around noon. Right before the Concours opened for set up. I can give you my plane info and all of that."

"You can give it to the police."

That didn't seem to shake him. Maybe he was telling the truth. "What was the plan?"

"Mr. Rivers told me he'd have the car in the delivery bays at the Babylon. All I had to do was offload it and make a big show of delivering it to the kid."

"Nice man, your boss. Where's he staying?"

"He was okay until the Chinese showed up waving money and making promises. He had money issues. Everybody knows it. He caved and life went in the crapper."

"Is the Chinese guy in town?"

"No, he's not due to fly in until later today."

That was a bit of an unexpected windfall. "You got a name?"

"Wu. Johnny Wu. He's got a bunch of muscle, but he scares me the most."

"Why?"

"He's quiet and deadly, like a shark."

We'd gotten his story, such as it was. I didn't have the complete picture, but I'd gotten a few answers. And a few pieces of a plan. "Can you call Romeo?" I asked Squash. "Probably ought to give him a shot at the kid. And it just might keep him safe and out of trouble while we clean this up."

"Sure." Squash retrieved his pad and pen where he'd dropped them to corral Mrs. Morales. "I take it you're not going to wait around."

"Hell, no. If the owner of that Lambo filed charges, that would put Romeo in a very awkward position. I need to return the car before things get really ugly."

As I wheeled up the driveway to the Babylon, I was happy to see there weren't any cop cars with lights strobing. I took that as a good sign. The same valet I convinced to pinch the car for me opened my door—this time without a smile.

I beat him to the punch as I levered myself out of the car. "I'm really very sorry. I had no other choice." I started to explain, then thought better of it. "Quite unlike me to commit a felony. Well, quite unlike me to convince someone else to do so on my behalf unknowingly."

"I learned a good lesson," he grumbled.

"Don't trust anyone? Not even your boss?"

"No, Detective Romeo told me that there are times that good people do bad things but for all the right reasons." He extended his hand for the keys.

I dropped them in his palm. Romeo had done such a fine job dusting-up my reputation that I wasn't going to risk sullying it once more by asking what grievous wrong Romeo had claimed I had charged off to right. "I wouldn't say those were normal kinds of things though. The vast majority of the time, wrongs can be corrected without flouting the law."

"Yes, miss."

"There will be a sizable thrown-under-the-bus bonus in

your next paycheck." I gathered the shreds of my dignity and pretended I was as good as Romeo had made me out to be as I pushed through the doors and headed toward my office.

Where had my father gone? Maybe I was closer to catching a murderer after my little gallivant on the other side of the line, but I was no closer to finding a wayward father...who, could be a future murderer if I didn't get him in my grasp by this afternoon.

Yes, Mr. Johnny Wu would be arriving to claim his spoils.

That problem still needed solving, too. But I was close. I could feel it.

How did one buy out a very expensive lease and potentially gain an NBA franchise without a passport and without billions?

Nobody stopped me as I shucked and jived my way through the gathered throng, which warmed my heart. At least some things were operating as desired. The better part of valor had me running and hiding in the stairs—I still didn't put it past Romeo to send some officers after me, just to mess with me. I took the stairs two at a time and then strode down the hall on the mezzanine, shoulders back, prepared for lambasting.

Nothing like guilt to fire the imagination.

I burst through the office door, surprising everyone waiting for me in the vestibule. More than I hoped, but not any I wished weren't there. I pointed to Miss P, who still looked swoonish, and to the Beautiful Jeremy Whitlock, who most definitely was swoon-worthy. "You two. My office." I didn't give anybody time to stop me, although the DEA agent tried. I glued him to his seat with a finger pointed at him. "You're next." I softened it with a "Please."

He seemed mollified. Well, at least he didn't break out the handcuffs or anything. Did DEA agents carry handcuffs? A random thought that got me to my office and sagging into my desk chair. "Okay, bring me up to speed." I gave the floor to Miss P.

"Well, you've made quite the splash the last few hours." She lowered her head and looked at me over the top of her cheaters. "Do you have any idea what a Lamborghini Huracan, which I had never heard of before, actually costs?" She silenced me with a finger. "They start at over two hundred and sixty thousand dollars."

"Go big or go home." The hulking mass of the desk sat between us, so I was feeling rather glib in its protection.

"You are not taking this seriously?"

"And this is a surprise, how?" I matched her smile for glare until I caved. "Look, I'm sorry. I had no choice. Do you really think I would call a cab to go off chasing my father? Or better yet, an Uber or Lyft driver? What if they'd gotten shot or something?"

"Better you than them for sure," she answered dryly. "I guess I understand, but damn the owner was livid."

"I'm sure. I'm sorry." I tried to act contrite, but I just didn't have any more fake-sincere in me.

"Wait, you were chasing your father? The man with a bullet in his chest?"

"Yep, am I Lucky or what?" I could say that without recrimination, since, well, only I would take offense.

A laugh, now a guffaw, burst out of Jeremy. "You are most assuredly the luckiest person I know."

I leveled some slitty-eye at him. "I'm assuming you have recovered from your snit?"

"My what?" He wiped at the tears of mirth that squeezed out of the corners of his eyes.

"You know, that male bonding ritual where men go to bemoan their fate of being married to a kick-ass woman? Then they wise up and realize life will be exponentially easier and never boring. That snit." That quieted him down. "I'm glad to see true love prevails because, if it didn't, I couldn't go on. So, what do you have for me?" I smiled; fake and forced it was the best I could do.

My father was still out there chasing a killer and an interloper, and God knew what he would do if he found either one. That murderer was in my sights, too; but damn, I didn't know where to find my father or Mr. Carson Rivers, my Number One Suspect. With all that had gone down since I saw him, I didn't think he'd be flashing his pearly whites at the Concours. I'd called the valet just to be sure. He hadn't seen him.

"I got nothing," Jeremy said, then leaned back. "I've been in a snit, you know. Hard to get anything accomplished in a snit."

I wasn't surprised considering I hadn't yet asked anything of him. "Indeed. I'm glad to see you've recovered. I do have something I need from you."

They both looked at me, his surprise evident. "Really?" Miss P asked, none too pleased. Based on our prior conversation, I knew she had plans at home for her husband.

"What do you need?" Jeremy didn't sound all that eager, but amenable—or at least willing to hear me out. He was that kind of guy.

"Dane."

"What?" they both said in unison.

"Look, I've got a friend in Dallas, Brinda Rose. Do you remember her? Here with the football fiasco recently?" They both just stared at me, so I forged ahead. "Anyway, I heard she's in a bit of a pickle—something about a dead husband, not that she's too broken up about it. But it seems she's a suspect. I need Dane to go down there and help her. Being from Lubbock or Midland or somewhere like that, he knows the Texas ropes. Last time I checked, he worked for you, Jeremy."

"Well, loosely."

"So, you'll be fine if I steal him and send him off to rescue a damsel in distress?"

"You sure she's innocent?" Jeremy arched an eyebrow at me.

I couldn't tell if he was worried about his friend or jerking my American bias. "Dane's a big boy."

"Are you sending him off as punishment or to see if he can earn his way back in?" Jeremy dug straight to the heart of the matter.

"I'm not sure. I have this trust issue, you see." Miss P snorted. I fixed her with a stare. "I'm working on it; let's leave it at that."

"You can have him." Jeremy sounded so magnanimous I almost laughed.

"Thanks. I think. He's been that much trouble?" I raised a hand. "Rhetorical." I turned to Miss P. "Anything I really need to know?"

"I've got everything handled. Jerry and Chastity are waiting for you in Security."

"Chastity?" Jeremy stifled a grin. "In this town? Do I want to know?"

"Yes, yes you do. But your wife can tell you. Will you two send in the DEA dude?"

Agent Simon took the chair Jeremy had vacated. He crossed one leg, resting his ankle on the opposite knee, then held his shin with both hands, as if erecting a barrier between the two of us. Personally, the desk was sufficient for me. He'd cleaned up a little—his hair looked shiny and he'd shaved. The clothes still looked like he could rub some dirt into them and not stand out in Freddy Morales's neighborhood. And he'd replaced his scowl with something akin to a complicit attitude, but I might be reading him wrong. But how much to tell him now? DEA agents wandering into my murder investigation would blow the whole thing to hell...and perhaps get my father killed.

We stared at each other over our barriers, both tangible and intangible. With the press of time weighing on me—the more I dawdled here, the more tenuous a thread held my father to this world—I broke the impasse. "Oddly enough, I do have some info for you." His expression didn't change. "But I need your agreement not to act on it until tomorrow." God, trust a Fed! What bargains with the devil I made! First Sinjin, now the DEA. Who next?

"Can you guarantee we won't miss our window to shut down the pipeline? I assume it's a pipeline?"

"Yes and yes." Making promises I wasn't sure I could keep— once out on the slippery slope of subterfuge, it seemed there was no stopping me. Rather alarming, considering how far I could fall.

He gave me a quick nod. "My word."

I leaned forward. "Okay, here's the deal as I know it." I gave him most of it: Willie (but no last name), Walker Preston, and how all of it tied in with Finn Murphy with his head bashed in in my delivery bay as well as the air traffic controller. I kept Carson Rivers to myself. According to Willie, I needed him to find my father. Not that Willie was reliable, but I didn't see any reason for him to lie—not here, not now, not about that. Either way his gig as a pot-runner was up.

When I wound down, I leaned back, giving the agent room to process.

By the time he answered, steam should've been coming out his ears. "You can give me all this, airtight?"

"My job was to give you info. Your job is to lock it up. But I've got a well-placed songbird ready to sing for a deal. Give me twenty-four hours. Let Metro catch a killer, then you can have your way with the potheads. Murder trumps a little drug-running, doesn't it?"

"Good point. I could pull my Federal privilege and take over the investigation."

This guy was working hard to evaporate my last drop of patience...the very last one. Anger sizzled just below the surface. I'd slap him if it weren't a felony...and if I wasn't desperate for what he came to tell me. "We both know that's overreaching. You better have come here with a quid for my pro quo."

He pulled the baggie I'd given him from his pocket. "Primo stuff—this came from an operation in northern California owned by Carson Rivers. I should take him in."

Amazingly, I kept my expression flat to hide my lie-by-omission, not that I felt bad about it or anything. "Not yet. My source told me about flying the weed. He didn't give up anyone else. Not yet."

"You didn't give me enough info to find your source." He dropped his foot to the floor and stood. "You got twenty-four hours, then I'll be back."

I stood and shook his hand. "Deal." As I watched him go, I thought that was a bit too easy. Somebody to watch my back might be helpful.

As I breezed by Miss P, who had taken up her old spot at the desk out front, with Jeremy propping himself on the corner as he used to do, I barked. "You two, get a room. But first, get me a car, have it waiting out front. Then call Jerry and tell him and Chastity I'm on my way. I've got questions, and they better have some answers." I pulled open the door, then stopped, and graced them with a smile. "Please?"

CHAPTER SIXTEEN

*W*E KEPT Security hidden away on the mezzanine in the far back corner behind an unmarked door, not that the simple subterfuge fooled those intent on finding it. But it kept the curiosity seekers, the overserved, and the sore losers at bay. My keycard provided the open sesame. Once inside, I stopped, overcome by a near Stygian darkness. Blinking rapidly, not that that ever helped, I willed my eyes to adjust.

A large room opened up in front of me; the wall straight ahead and the wall to my right were dotted with floor to ceiling monitors flashing ever-changing camera shots. The ones to my right captured the cameras above the gaming tables. The front wall, various sections of the property, each monitor with a nameplate defining which one. Behind each wall, large servers collected the video feeds and stored them. Each feed would rewrite after a set time frame generally defined by our Legal Department.

Security personnel sat in front of the monitors they had responsibility for. In the middle of the room, keeping an eye on all of it, Jerry wandered, hands on his hips, chewing on a cigar.

"That take the place of the cigarettes?" I said as I stepped in beside him. He'd been trying to ditch the cancer sticks for I don't know how long. At one point, after one of his many failures—I think it had been the hypnosis adventure—I'd been sure his wife was going to kill him.

The colored lights from the screens painted his bald pate. Today as he did every other day, except for the very few days that called for a suit, he wore khakis, loafers, a button-down and his ubiquitous gold Rolex. That watch meant something to him. Somehow the right time to ask exactly what had never presented itself, so I remained unknowing, which actually was fine. I didn't need to know. In fact, there were a lot of things in life I didn't need to know. In my job, I'd seen way more of the human condition than any well-adjusted person could handle.

He shifted the cigar to the other side of his mouth, then spoke to me out of the side closest. A bit disconcerting. "Yeah, Claire's given me an ultimatum."

"Again? That woman long ago earned her passage into Heaven."

"I know. She's much too good for me, but I'm not about to run her off. I know a great thing when I have it."

"Hence, the cigar."

Jerry motioned to one of the kids studying the monitors in front of us. As she rose, a colleague assumed her seat.

With the lights behind her, I couldn't see her face until she stood in front of us.

"Chastity. You look amazing." Dressed in a Babylon uniform that complemented her figure rather than exposing it, and with all the overdone makeup gone, her face fresh-scrubbed, her natural beauty stunned me. Of course, she looked like jailbait as well.

"Is she old enough to be on the payroll?" I asked Jerry.

"Eighteen last month," Chastity answered, still smiling despite my bad manners.

Legal by our official standards, at least to work in Security and places not serving alcohol.

"Let's powwow in my office, okay?" Jerry led us to his glass-enclosed cubicle in the back corner. From there he could monitor everything, and no one could eavesdrop.

We chose our spots—Jerry perched on his desk, Chastity by the door, and me with my back to both of them as I looked through the glass and the changing kaleidoscope of snapshots of our hotel…my home. "Chastity, do you mind starting?"

"No, ma'am."

I started with something easy. Something I thought I knew. "Who sent you to the basketball player's room?"

I almost mouthed *Walker Preston,* but I didn't want to lead the witness. "I don't know. I got a call. I didn't recognize the voice."

"Not Walker Preston?"

"I don't know him exactly." She didn't fidget or act nervous. Instead she held my gaze when I turned and speared her with it.

"But you had his card?"

"Finn gave it to me. He told me if there was any trouble to give it to the authorities."

"He told you to hide it in your purse?"

"Yeah. Said something bad was going down and not to trust anybody. I haven't seen him around to know what he found out."

Jerry shot me a glance. Thankfully the girl missed it. "Where did you see Finn?"

"In the lobby. He walked with me to the delivery bays."

"This was Thursday, right?"

"Yeah."

"What time?"

"Just after four or so. That was the best time to catch the guys sitting and eating, and I could get my payment and not get in the way. It's pretty crazy down there."

"The payment for the birthday prank?"

"Yeah, I grabbed that, but Jeff owed me a bunch for some other…" she glanced at Jerry, "…things."

"You got it all?"

"Yeah, I got rent to pay."

"Don't we all. What about the pot? Who gave it to you? Walker?"

"No! Jeff was passing it around. Others had to pay, but he gave me mine for free."

I bet he did. "How'd you know Finn?"

"Aw, Finn comes around all the time. He loves Rebel basketball. He's really nice. Was sorta appalled when he learned my age. He's been looking out for me anytime he's around ever since."

"How'd you meet?"

"We met in the bathroom. A couple of years ago." She stopped, then tossed an embarrassed look at Jerry who said nothing.

"Got it. And then what happened? Did he walk all the way to the delivery bays with you?"

"Yeah, he told me he was going to get some help to move somebody's car. He sort of chuckled about it. Said he wanted to put it on the roof; that way, nobody could miss it. I thought it was a great joke."

"Yep, a good one."

"I was looking for my payment," she continued. "Finn hung around. Said he was meeting somebody and he didn't want me involved."

"Did you see who he meant?" I turned to look at her. "Was it Walker Preston? The guy whose card you have?"

Now she started getting fidgety, shifting from one foot to the other. "No. I don't know him."

"But before, In Pearl Coleman's room, you said Walker

Preston told you the car was on the roof. Finn was looking for him in the delivery bays, wasn't he?"

She fidgeted and looked everywhere but at me.

Truth came hard when you've been hiding it your whole life.

"Want to tell me about you and Walker? You do know the police have taken him. He's wanted for questioning in the murder of your Finn Murphy and a friend of mine." Brutal, but a sledgehammer to break up the layer of bullshit and expose the truth.

Her knees buckled. Jerry jumped to grab her. I stayed where I was. As the bad cop, chivalry wasn't my gig. Kneeling beside her, he held her, as much as would be considered appropriate.

I let her war with her allegiances for a moment.

She looked up at me with teary eyes in a movie moment. "Finn is dead?"

"Yes, I'm sorry. I don't think he ever made it out of that delivery bay." I didn't tell her about the head bashed in and all the blood. Bad cop wasn't my go-to and I had my limits.

"And he was all ready for a great weekend. So excited about going out incognito, he called it."

That pinged a few brain cells. "What do you mean?"

"He was so cute, had me get him a fake ID. Said he didn't want anything he might do to get back to the team."

"And you got him one?"

"Yeah, one of the guys in the bays put me onto Freddy. Super sweet guy."

I didn't have it in my heart to tell her what happened to him. "And Finn?"

"He was alive when we left him."

"We who?"

She sighed. "Me and Walker. Finn got all up in his grill about something, I couldn't hear. But they got it all sorted out. It was about moving the car, like I said."

"Walker walked back with you?"

"Yeah, he left Finn waiting for the guy who was going to help move the car."

Willie.

"They had to plan it out, Walker said. It was a finesse job."

"Where'd you go after that?"

"Me and Walker went to the bar. He bought a very expensive bottle of Champagne. He was amped. He told me about the car and how he and some other dudes were going to win this game. I thought he'd already been drinking."

Maybe he had. Hell, if I'd been working to undermine a semi-bad dude who was in tight with a seriously bad Chinese dude, I'd need some liquid fortification myself. "What time was this?"

"I don't know, maybe around five? I'm sure you can check the tapes; we weren't trying to hide. We stayed for a couple of hours. Walker bought dinner; then I had to go change for the birthday thing."

"Did Walker know about that?" I circled back.

"Yeah. I told him."

"You sure he wasn't the one who suggested it?"

"Look, I'd made some deliveries and stuff for him before. I told Walker I had to go deliver a singing telegram. I did that for a lot of people—not the singing, but the delivering. A guy at the bell desk would hook me up. I know this hotel inside and out."

I made a mental note to get his name when this was all over. There was a good chance he was Jeff's partner. But that was a problem for another day.

She had our security down pat. I almost broke my arm patting myself on the back for thinking to hire her. Keep your enemies close… And I didn't need to ask her about her relationship with Mr. Walker Preston. I could see it in her eyes. The look of love…at least I wasn't the only woman I knew with bad taste in men. Although she was eighteen, so little consolation.

"Is that how you and Walker met, through the guy at the bell desk?"

"Yeah." She finally met my eyes. "I don't want Walker to know about the…other stuff."

"Your call. But just because you had to make a hard choice about making a living doesn't mean you don't deserve a good guy."

"You think?"

"I know." If she could see half the bad decisions I'd made… And someday, when I decided to talk with my mother again, I'd introduce the two of them. If Mona had any talent at all besides making my life complicated it was helping girls who'd been on the streets. "Okay, back to Finn. Where was he when you last saw him?"

She gulped down a sob and swiped at her eyes. I could've told her being a big girl totally sucked, but I figured she knew that way better than I. "I don't know exactly, but there was one truck parked way down at the end. He went that way."

I raised an eyebrow at Jerry. "Bay seven." He nodded.

"Have you looked at the tapes? Of the truck in that far away bay?" I didn't know if Jerry had gotten her take on the man in the gray sweatshirt.

"Yes. I couldn't see anything familiar about that man."

A thought hit. "Jer, did you take a look at the guy's feet?"

"His feet?" He popped off his desk and straddled the chair in front of his private monitor. "I've got the tape cued up here. We were looking at it before you came."

We gathered around. He ran the loop. As Chastity had said, nothing identifying. The shoes were unremarkable, boots of some sort. And a hoodie and jeans—seemed to be quite the popular fashion choice these days.

Time was wasting and I figured I'd squeezed about as much as I could out of this lemon. I separated myself and headed for the door. "Thank you, guys."

I still wasn't any closer to a killer or my father.

But somewhere deep inside, something niggled, telling me I was.

~

I'D ALMOST MADE A CLEAN ESCAPE FROM THE HOTEL WHEN A TEXT from Miss P caught me in the lobby.

Detour if you can to the Hanging Gardens.

Important? I replied.

Your mother.

On it.

The Hanging Gardens had sprung from the Big Boss's imagination—a modern take on the mythical gardens in Babylon that were one of the Seven Wonders of the Ancient World. Although I certainly maintained a good bit of bias, the gardens beat the ancient ones all to hell. The humidity hit me as I burst through the doors. Yes, the Big Boss had created the only tropical climate in the middle of the Mojave. Yells of kids enjoying the family pool buoyed my spirits a tad.

I still hadn't found my father. I felt responsible yet not. Age and infirmity didn't obviate personal determination, although we tended to act as if it did. Maybe, on some level, I wasn't willing to make my father wither away in some state of horrible infirmity. He would prefer going out in a blaze of glory. I got that. Losing him would be my loss. How could I make him pay for my comfort with his dignity?

He wouldn't be too pleased if I killed his wife either. I took a breath.

This place always settled me. Perhaps it was the water vapor that restored the desiccated parts of my brain…and my face. Humans were like eighty-percent water, so it made sense. The plants also made me happy. Most of the natural plants around here were prickly and fighting for their few square inches and tiny bit of our four inches of annual rainfall. I identified with them, but that didn't make me feel good. Here plants thrived, trailing from the balconies that ringed and defined the large atrium. Most of the plants flowered exuberantly. No matter the season outside, the Big Boss made sure it was always Spring in the Hanging Gardens.

Above me, a rope bridge connected our treehouse bar with the main property. In front of me, ringed by almost impenetrable jungle, flowed a lazy river most likely filled with inner-tubed guests—I couldn't see through the foliage. The river connected two pools: a family pool and an adult-only pool where swimwear was less heavily policed.

The much more exuberant than normal screams of the kids clued me in to the location of the problem I was so desperately needed to solve. How could my mother be the source of children's screams of delight yet fire homicidal tendencies in me?

It was her special gift.

The path led me through the foliage. Not wanting to know what awaited me, and because this was my hotel, I stopped a couple of times to retrieve trash and toss it into the bin. After some dawdling, I stepped into a clearing.

Pandemonium reigned in front of me.

Children dashed and darted, avoiding their parents' lunges as they giggled out of reach.

At the far end of the pool, the picketers presumably from the other night had arranged themselves in a semicircle. They held signs of all manner of disgusting animal mutilation. A woman, their leader, paced in front of them. I was in time to see her raise her bullhorn to her lips and start in on some rabble-rousing diatribe about animal cruelty.

My mother.

A proud moment.

I needed one of those tranquilizer guns they used to drop the rhinos in Africa. One shot and that woman would be out of my hair for at least a week. That thing was going on my Christmas list.

And what was that in the pool?

Animals. Lots of furred, thin, medium-length critters.

Oh, I knew who was behind that. A lust for murder flared as I scanned the underbrush. I caught him on the second pass—hunched over, skulking out of harm's way. In three strides, I had him. I grabbed him by the scruff of his neck and lifted him into view.

His little ferret face. His pansy-assed MO of letting all hell loose then leaving others to face the consequences. People would applaud if I dispatched him. However, an easy death would be too good for him.

"Well, hello, Mr. Ballantine. Excuse my lack of surprise at seeing you here." Such was my anger and his diminutive frame, I could hold him in the air like a small child itching for a scolding.

Any fight he had left him when he saw my face. "You!" was all he could manage.

"Your Lucky day." That one I particularly enjoyed.

I should've thrown him out of the hotel when Miss P told me he had registered. The whole murder thing, then the losing the Babylon thing derailed me. For some reason I felt sure he was on our forever blacklist; in fact, I was pretty positive. So how had he gotten in here in the first place?

My mother.

Family had override powers around here. Mother just forfeited hers.

With his feet barely skimming the ground, I marched Mr. Ballantine back to the main group. Mother's eyes widened in fear, but her back stiffened in protest. At least she could be counted on for a good fight—and since nothing else seemed to be going my way, a fight was just the thing to blow off some steam.

I held up my captive in front of Mona's face. "This a friend of yours?"

I could see the lie that sprang to mind. However, with her co-sign-wielding zealots behind her, she settled on the truth. She stuck out her chin. "Yes. He's one of us."

"Fine." I shoved him to the side. He teetered on the edge of the pool for a moment, then landed with a splash.

"Lucky!" Mona pressed a hand over her mouth.

"His animals. His job to gather them." The poor creatures scattered at Mr. Ballantine's ungainly half gainer, and now thrashed about wildly. The high sides of the pool kept them corralled. "I hope they bite."

Mr. Ballantine spluttered to the surface. I pointed a finger at him. "You get those weasels out of my pool right now! Put them back in their cages and leave the property." I motioned over a security team watching from the perimeter.

"My things?" he whined.

"Are here illegally. This is a by-invitation-only hotel, and you know as well as I your invitation was revoked the last time you pulled a stunt like this. We will send them to the address on your registration form." I whirled and grabbed Mona by the arm and tugged her away from the crowd as I raised my voice to address them. "Party's over. You all know as well as I that protest on this property is prohibited. You all may consider your invitations to stay here, gather here, drink here, gamble here, are all revoked. Security will see you out." At the resulting grumbling, I added, "You all are lucky I don't have you arrested." With that, I turned on my heel, dragging Mona with me. She struggled to keep up as I stalked toward the doors to the lobby. I didn't care, preferring to hold her arm tight by my side.

Her fingers pried at my grip with no luck. "Lucky, I needed a platform."

"No, Mother, what you need is a swift kick in the ass for starters. Followed by solitary confinement, well, as defined by you being the only adult left alone with two very small scream-eat-and-poop machines."

Terror lit behind her eyes. "You wouldn't!"

"I will." I opened one of the doors to the lobby and pushed her though ahead of me.

Once out of the view of her cohorts, she whirled on me, a finger jabbing me in the chest. "You can't do that."

"I can and I will. I run this hotel. And you are a menace to its operation." I had her by five inches, so I stepped close and loomed over her. "Let me remind you that you have made a public spectacle of yourself picketing your own hotel, damaging our reputation in the process. You have directly flouted company rules and overridden a blacklist designation, and, as a direct result, I now have children screaming, parents panicked, and weasels doing the backstroke in my pool!" I paused to draw in a breath before I fainted.

"They're stoats," she said, her voice strong.

"What?" The lethal in my voice trumped her strength.

"Stoats." This time a whisper.

"We're not in the UK, Mona. They are short-tailed weasels, I believe. And when someone decides to make a coat out of them, they use the term 'ermine'. I mean, who wants a weasel coat, right?"

"You're angry."

I grabbed her arm again and propelled her toward her private elevator. "And you're trying to impress me with your brilliant powers of deduction. You go to your room and you stay there until I've decided what to do with you."

"Your father won't like this." As I half dragged her through the lobby, she tried to muster as many of the shards of her dignity as she could.

"Ah, yes, my father. I have yet to find him. And for the record, no he won't like this; he'll love it." I pulled her to a stop in front of the elevator, flashed my card, and punched the button. "Tell me about a man you used to know named Carson Rivers."

Mona went slack-jawed, and still. "Who?" The word rode out in a quaver.

"You heard me." I let go of her arm. "Who was he?"

Mona plucked at her sweater, closing it tightly around her. "Just somebody I used to know. How did you come across the name?"

Her feigned nonchalance didn't fool me. "I met him. He told me you were friends. He didn't seem to carry the same fondness for Father."

"Yes, well," she patted at her hair, "they were competitors. This was a small town back then. Everybody had to fight for their share of the pie." She pasted on a shaky half-smile. "Where'd you meet him?"

"We bonded over fast cars. But right now, I need to find him, and I don't know where to start. You knew him. Did he have any good friends back in the day? Somebody who might help me?"

"Gosh, that was a long time ago." The elevator dinged its arrival. Mona leaped through the doors before they'd fully opened. "Find your father, Lucky. He's sick. He should be in the hospital. You know he's only doing this for you."

The doors shut.

Leave it to Mona to leave me with more questions, no vindication, and staggering under a shitload of her guilt—yes, her parting shot had been about her. She'd let him go.

I'd always thought inheriting most of my DNA from my father was a gift of fate. Now I wasn't so sure—Mona had impressive skills that could suit me well. Ah, well, next lifetime.

And he was doing whatever he was doing for himself. I knew that, too.

Stymied for the moment, I took a turn underneath the cloud

of blown-glass hummingbirds and butterflies. The whirl of happiness always helped with whatever ailed me.

"Did you kill her?" Romeo asked.

He appeared in my periphery as I kept turning and focusing above. "Closest I've come. Recently, she'd shown signs of maturity, or at least some insight that comes with experience. I had high hopes."

"She means well." A laugh added a burble to his words.

"When she can *do* well, that's when I'll be happy. Right now, I'm thinking a one-way ticket to Siberia."

"She deserves that."

"You're a true friend." I stopped my avoidance tactics and faced him.

"True friends help you bury the bodies."

"I hope you brought a shovel." My head whirled a bit. I put a hand on his shoulder to stop the turning.

"No." He pulled his pad from his inside pocket and flipped it open. "I've been with Doc. He's got times of death for both our hotel stiffs."

I bristled a bit at the term "stiffs," but I knew that dehumanizing the dead was one of Romeo's coping mechanisms. And he meant no disrespect. "Okay."

He read from his notes. "Finn Murphy died between five and six p.m. Thursday."

"I can't believe nobody found the body."

"Well, here's the deal. Doc said that Finn's body had been stuffed up in the undercarriage of that trailer." He looked up. "And here's the kicker...while it had been in motion."

"The truck was moved after five on Thursday and then brought back?"

"Yeah, none of the guys I've questioned so far who were working in the bays during that time noticed it coming and going. Apparently, that's a super-busy time down there, trucks moving in and out all over the place."

"Have you talked with any of the overnight shift?"

"Rounding them up now. None of them would give up your man and his alleged girlie ring, so I'm not sure that we can expect too much out of them about anything."

"The union guys always had an us-against-them attitude, so I'm not surprised. What about Freddy?"

"That's where it gets weird."

"Really? I thought it got weird a long time ago."

Romeo smiled. He'd set me up on purpose, and I hadn't disappointed. A bright spot in a dark day. "Freddy was killed a little later, Thursday evening. And, weirder still, that car was stuffed full of pot."

"The pot I knew about." I thought about the rest for a moment. "Okay, so the killer took out Freddy. We don't know where or how the killer…dismembered him. But the killer came here to get that truck and take it to where he could stuff Freddy in the trunk of the car."

Romeo picked up when I took a breath. "Finn confronted him. He killed Finn and stuffed him up under the rig before he took it to go get Freddy."

"At that point, his plan was unravelling." I could see the plan; I just couldn't see the who. "So, he panicked and whacked the air traffic controller."

"Yes, but who is he? Who is our killer?" Romeo shrugged. "As far as I can tell we got several suspects. The salesman, Walker Preston, his boss—"

"Carson Rivers," I said when I saw him go for his notes.

"Yeah. Hell, even Willie could've done it I guess."

I shook my head. "I don't know. Willie doesn't seem to have it in him. I guess you could go rough him up about it a bit. Wouldn't hurt." I gave him the address and he pocketed it. "You get anything out of our salesman?"

"Same story he gave you, or so he said. Timeline matches up.

But he could've driven that truck to pick up Freddy and then brought it back."

"No, he was at the hotel. In Delilah's. Have Jerry check the tapes to confirm Preston's whereabouts and ask him to look for Rivers on property around the time Finn was killed. We've got to place him at the scene."

"Okay, so we got jack." Romeo sounded as dejected as I felt. I told him about my father. "You can't find him?"

"If I could get a bead on my father, I could find our Carson Rivers, who has gone AWOL from the Concours."

"You think they're together?"

"Wille put Father on the scent. I'd be willing to bet he told him about the Chinese connection—I'm chasing another thing down for my father with the same Chinese connection. Both are coming together—my father is smart enough to see the connection. That's what Sinjin is helping with. My father knew Carson Rivers back in the day. I bet he had an old friend to ask for help. That'd be how my father would do it. Unfortunately, I don't have those connections." I did have one, but I wasn't going to send Romeo to shake down my mother, even though I knew she was stonewalling me. And I had no idea why she would do that. Father's life hung in the balance. What could be more important?

What didn't she want me to know about Carson Rivers?

"Oh!" Why hadn't I seen it before? My world righted. I squeezed Romeo's shoulder before I let him go. "You go find Willie and see what you can get out of him. Use thumbscrews if you need to."

"Where are you going?"

"To talk to an old family friend."

CHAPTER SEVENTEEN

SINJIN MET me coming in as I was going out. "I've got some news."

"Great. Come with me. You can tell me about it on the way." I motioned to the valet...the same kid. Not sure how that happened. This time he brought me the right car.

Sinjin didn't bat an eye as he slipped into the passenger seat of the Ferrari. "I don't know what your father did to piss off the Triad, but he's done a bang-up job." He buckled his belt and knew me well enough to reach up and grab the handhold.

Five hundred horses never disappointed. Careful going down the drive, I put my foot into it as I made the turn onto the Strip. This time I was ready for the power—I knew this car much better than the Lambo.

Sinjin leaned forward, drinking in the lights as I weaved in and out of looky-loos. "This place is amazing," he said with a chuckle.

"Coming from a guy from Hong Kong, well...we must be doing something right." As we passed, the fountains at the Bellagio fired the first salvo. I didn't slow, even though Sinjin had his nose pressed to the side window. "First time?"

"Yeah."

"Sorry we couldn't have rolled out the welcome mat." At Tropicana, I hung a right. "So, this is a revenge play?"

"I'm not sure. Motivations can be well-hidden."

No shit, Sherlock!

He caught me glancing at him and smiled as if he could read my mind. "Don't doubt what you know here." He touched his chest.

I couldn't decide whether he was for real or not. However, I'd called him, hadn't I? *Misery acquaints a man with strange bedfellows.* Yes, going highbrow. It was a Shakespeare kind of day...in every way. Well, except I'd managed not to kill my mother. I took that as a good sign. "Can you fill me in quickly? We're almost there."

He peppered me with the highlights. He'd made more headway in a few hours than I'd done in as many days. He'd found Wu's suits that had worked Squash over, figuratively speaking. Negotiations were open, the first salvos fired. "We need something stronger to make them give up the Babylon."

"I'm working on it. Should we go meet the Chinese contingent when they arrive?"

"Wu keeps his plans secret. Even his staff doesn't know where he'll arrive, or when." He laughed. "I've done battle with these guys before. When I told them I was your family's emissary, I thought heads would explode."

"Glad someone is having fun."

"Not a lot. Not yet. Their boss is motivated, and they're spooked."

"Sounds like a great guy to work for. We'll get what we need. We're close; I can almost taste it."

The French Quarter loomed in front of us. Built in an overblown New Orleans motif, the casino/hotel had faux latticework and French doors opening to small balconies with wrought-iron railings. At least that's the presentation for the street-side customers. The other three sides were industrial Vegas casino, which exemplified all that I loved and loathed about this city and its movie-set personality. I whipped under the covered drive and left the car growling for the valet. He palmed the keys. I added a twenty. "Keep it close. We won't be long."

"Should I tell Ms. Delacroix you're coming up?"

Hard to sneak in when you're one of the family. I wasn't, not really, but Darlin' thought so. "No, I'll surprise her." I grabbed Sinjin's arm. "I brought her a present."

I ushered Sinjin away before he could blow my story. At the front doors, I paused. "Look, my aunt likes two things—cheap gin and handsome young men. I'm all out of cheap gin." I pushed open the door and tugged for him to follow. "So, you're the grease."

"Is bodily affront involved?"

"No," I lied. "Well, perhaps a bit of humiliation, but nothing more."

"That I am exceptional at. This woman we are visiting is your aunt?"

"Not really. No blood relation. When you meet her, you'll realize why I think that's an amazing gift. She is my mother's best friend—has been forever. The dirt they know about each other would keep them both behind bars for the rest of their lives."

"You're exaggerating." He looked a bit shocked.

I imagined his mother was all straitlaced British…stiff upper lip and all of that. Or maybe that was his father. I couldn't remember. "Not much." I pulled him inside and headed toward the elevators.

Tonight, like almost every night, the crowd pushed together, forming an almost impenetrable mass of humanity. Several gondolas hung above us from a rail that wound its way through the entire casino. Once again, my timing was impeccable.

Trumpets sounded the lead-in to a lively jazz piece. Girls appeared in the gondolas—scantily clad in appropriate Vegas attire of sparkle bra. I couldn't see their bottom halves, but I would bet a G-string and Lucite heels finished off the ensembles. Beads draped from their arms. As the crowd below preened—some women knew the drill and showed their boobs —beads rained down on the worthy, or at least the good sports.

Sinjin kept close, leaning in and raising his voice to be heard above the noise. "Is this place always like this?"

"Only at night and only on the half-hour."

"Damn." A girl came out of nowhere, threw her arms around him, and planted a long, slow, wet one.

I didn't slow down. The man was going to have to learn some Vegas coping skills, or he'd be molested everywhere he went, especially after a liberal happy hour.

Wiping his mouth with the back of his hand, he arrived next to me just as the elevator doors slid open. "Sorry."

"Not to worry. I'm sure her shots are up to date."

That knocked him off-center. "I can't tell when you're teasing or when you're serious." He brushed back his long black hair.

I'm sure he had no idea how sexy that was. The cynical side of me thought he knew exactly. As usual, fighting with myself. If I lost, then I won—so a stalemate? Too confusing. Going to see my aunt always short-circuited any hope of logic. "Assume teasing unless I make it obvious." I pressed the button for the penthouse. My handy-dandy Do Not Pass Go card that got me into my parents' place also worked here as well. "You've ten seconds to give it up about Johnny Wu. I get the feeling that, as a nod to my delicate sensibilities, you've been soft selling our adversary. I need the straight skinny."

He took a deep breath and let the words out in one stream. "Your Johnny Wu wants to play with the big boys."

"NBA." It wasn't a question. Things in my head had gone far

enough to begin coming full circle.

His puffed chest lost a bit of puff. "Yeah. They're playing hardball. They've got an American helping them."

"Carson Rivers."

More deflation. "You know all this."

"Yes, but what I'd really like you to tell me is what they paid for the lease under the Babylon." I stared at his reflection in the polished metal of the elevator doors. Just as enigmatic. Was he a good witch or a bad witch?

"I didn't get a look at it, but the scuttlebutt from the guy doing the negotiating is it's a sweet deal for the bad guys."

"Very little money down. Maybe a share of the profits down the line?" We all knew about Hollywood creative accounting that eliminated residuals with a stroke of the pencil. No reason they couldn't, or wouldn't, do that here as well.

"How'd you know?"

"Guys in the Jesus business usually are easy marks given their reliance on the Golden Rule. And second, it'd take decades to move the billions it should take to buy that lease out of China and clean it here. Especially if you're doing it one Bugatti at a time."

The doors opened disgorging us in a long hallway papered in toile. Thick carpet bordering on shag muffled our footsteps.

I pulled him around to face me. "Tell me the one thing I need to know."

Sinjin leveled his gaze. "Johnny Wu—take him out if you have the chance. You won't get but one."

He was serious, dead serious. "Got it."

"This way." I motioned to my right. Tonight, the kitchen entrance appealed. "So Johnny Wu wants the Babylon with our arena that seats just a tick under thirty thousand as the home base for his NBA franchise." It was a good plan as far as it went. But how was a shifty dude with strong ties to the Triad going to get an NBA franchise, and a coveted one at that? Vegas was a huge sports town, and we all were salivating for a franchise. Football was here, the stadium almost complete. Hockey, too. Why not basketball?

A thought stopped me in my tracks. I grabbed Sinjin and jerked him to a stop as well. "Now it makes sense." I shook my head as I rolled that thought around like a squirrel with a prime nut. "Total sense."

"What?" My weekend pirate looked confused.

"The blackmail."

"Who's being blackmailed?"

I waffled. "Well, not really blackmailed as no one has called in the markers; no one has threatened them."

"Who?" Sinjin was clearly losing his patience, but he needed to let me play this out.

"The basketball players. Not all of them mind you, just the ones that mean huge bottom-line returns to the owners." At his confused look, I continued. "They aren't blackmailing the *players*. They're blackmailing the *owners*."

"What?"

"To get a franchise here in Vegas, you've got to have the goods, but you also need the stroke. Johnny Wu has neither, so he thinks he can muscle in here and push everybody around."

"Like back home." Sinjin's scowl deepened.

"Right. If he tells the owners that he has their biggest-draw players in compromising positions that might get them a long suspension or even banned, well, that sure buys him their ear, by his way of thinking. It's actually brilliant, in an awful sort of way. Nobody should mess with sports. Not ever." Sinjin nodded, picking up on my vehemence. "You haven't understood a thing I've said, have you?"

"I don't know basketball, nor how the league works. But I do get a power play when there's serious money on the line and innocents being used. What are you going to do?"

"Try to get my aunt to help me find Carson Rivers."

~

AS I SAID, MY AUNT, DARLIN' DELACROIX, REALLY WASN'T MY aunt. She, along with my mother, were a matching set of book-ends of my personal pain. To be honest, while Mona tried my patience, I had a grudging respect for Darlin'. Raised in a mining town in the middle of nowhere in upstate Nevada, she moved to Vegas as a young woman, reinvented herself, and had become the first female owner of an important casino. While the French Quarter wasn't on the Strip, it pulled in big numbers and earned high praise as the best "local" casino in town. Hard not to admire that. But admiring and putting up with were two different things altogether.

We snuck through the kitchen and entered Darlin's lair through one of the doors next to her throne. I called it that; nobody else had the nerve. But that's what it was, a high-backed chair on a raised platform, with unctuous young men at her feet to do her bidding. I didn't even try to prepare Sinjin for what was coming—I had no words and he had no reference.

An eerie quiet greeted us when we stepped inside the inner sanctum. The ever-present soundtrack of Vegas Rat Pack era songs had gone silent. The scantily-clad men—which I'd always been appalled by but secretly enjoyed—were nowhere to be found. Darlin' wasn't in her chair. Instead she'd pulled back a curtain and stood like a cat in the arrow of light, light that was normally absent. She blocked it at all costs. When I was young, I'd harbored the belief that there was a good probability that my Aunt Matilda (yes, that was her real name, known only to a few who kept silent in fear for their lives) was a vampire. Mother had always told me that Darlin'/Matilda insisted she be seen only in flattering light. As I grew older, I'd come to understand what that meant.

"Your mother told me to expect you." Darlin' turned from the window and graced me with a smile.

Somewhere from the casino floor to here, I had entered an alternate universe.

Gone was the garish makeup, the long blonde wig, the short mini, the fishnet hose, and the leather jacket with Elvis pieced on the back. She wore slacks, a sweater ensemble, and comfortable shoes. She looked like anybody's kindly grandmother—mine even. Her hair was short and silver, her face lined. She looked like the eighty-year-old, give or take, that she was. "You've brought a friend," she said without even a hint of a leer.

Dumbstruck, I waited for the Darlin' I knew and feared to appear. When I didn't step in with some manners, Sinjin took the lead. He extended his hand. "Sinjin Smythe-Gordon. A pleasure to meet you."

She took his hand and held his eye. "You'll see to it Lucky comes out of this okay." It wasn't a question.

"Yes, ma'am."

And I knew that he would…if he could.

"Where are my manners?" Darlin' shook herself away from Sinjin. "Come. Sit. We have much to talk about and not much time."

I didn't like the sound of that, but I did as she said, taking a seat on the couch she indicated with Sinjin next to me. Darlin' pulled around a chair. When she looked at me, she seemed at a loss.

I wasn't sure. I'd never seen her unsure before. "Mother called?" I asked. It seemed a good place to start. She nodded. "About Carson Rivers?" Another nod, this one more pained. "Who is he?"

Darlin' warred with herself. She twisted a hankie she'd pulled out of the pocket in her slacks until I thought it might produce juice.

"You're making me crazy. Who is he?"

Darlin' took a deep breath. "He could possibly be your father."

Sinjin rose and went to the bar tucked in the far corner of the room.

I leaned back into the embrace of the couch.

"Lucky, I'm so very sorry. I didn't want you to find out this way. Your mother wanted to tell you..." At my disbelieving look, she pulled back that lie. "Okay, she wanted me to tell you, but she feels really bad about it."

I sat back up and took the tumbler of amber liquid Sinjin handed to me. "Okay, so my mother, who was all of fifteen, hedged her bets by sleeping with several, well, at least two of the up-and-comers, so to speak, back in the day."

"Oh, I told your mother you'd take it badly." Darlin' turned to Sinjin, who looked like a man caught in a fight he didn't start. "Would you be a dear and get me one of those?" She pointed at my drink. He darted away like a rabbit loosed from a snare, his limp working to complete the simile.

"She screwed everything in sight; then, when she found herself in an awkward position, she took the first guy stupid enough to throw his life away on her."

"That's not how it was. You know that!"

"I wasn't there. I assume Mr. Rivers suspects he's in the running?" I threw back my drink in one gulp, then blinked away the tears as the liquid burned a path all the way down.

"You want another?" Sinjin looked desperate to stave off the explosion he thought imminent.

I smiled sweetly. "No, thank you. Any more will loosen my restraint and I might actually kill my mother. She's not worth it."

"She told me you have her under house arrest." Darlin' bit back a smile.

"Yes, and there she'll stay until we have a come-to-Jesus moment. Stop changing the subject. Mr. Rivers?" I arched an eyebrow at my aunt.

"Yes, he knows. He can count. You know, he's not a bad sort. He's just gotten in over his head."

Understatement of the century. I resisted taking a swing at the boys-will-be-boys bit of bullshit hidden in her assessment. "So, Carson Rivers has been here?"

"We're old friends."

I knew where Mother had perfected her dance with the truth.

I handed my now-empty glass to Sinjin and hit Darlin' with a bit of evil eye. "Where is he?"

She shifted to look out the window, through the sliver of opening in the curtains. "Your father was here, and I'll tell you what I told him."

"WE NEED TO DIVIDE AND CONQUER," SINJIN SAID, NOT AT ALL out of breath as we raced to the elevators. "You go after that Rivers person and your father. I'll take the airport and the arrival of Johnny Wu."

"No." I bent over, hands on my knees as I pressed the button to summon a ride to the lobby.

"You need more exercise," Sinjin scolded, not boasting even a sheen of sweat.

"Why is it that all men know the exact moment to say the wrong thing...then they say it?" I punched him in the stomach. Not a big punch. Not a full-weight-behind-it punch. Just a little, more-than-slightly-irritated punch. I knew it would catch him off guard, and I had no intention of duplicating the punch that killed Houdini. I don't know why, but that had haunted me ever since I'd learned of it. But it taught me that being the greatest isn't an escape from the mundane.

He doubled over with a whoosh of air.

Would I be in time to save my father? Would I be in time to

save the Babylon? One death would affect few, another many. Did that make one more important than the other? Who knew? Not that it would matter. I'd save what I could, then retire to the Ritz on Place Vendôme in Paris. Jordan had promised me a long stay there. He might try to feign ignorance, but I remembered, and I had witnesses.

"You might lose your hotel," Sinjin said when he'd regained his breath, enjoying heaping misery on the unknowing.

And here I'd thought I liked him. Hormones, they lead you astray every time. "I know."

"Not the Babylon. *Your* hotel. If I can get one more thing to make my position stronger…"

I stood and looked at him as the elevator dinged its arrival. "You have it. I just gave it to you."

"What?"

I held the door for him. "The ticking blackmail bomb? Wu is up to his wu tang in that." I felt sure Walker could connect those dots.

"But you said it wasn't illegal." He looked confused.

Here I'd thought him a man of nuance. "Not yet. Here, there are different rules for different people. There's the law, and there's the rules of the NBA. Setting folks up but not pulling the trigger might be okay, technically, under the law. I don't know, but to me, and I'm no lawyer, it reeks of extortion. But it wouldn't rise to that until Wu pressed home his point with the owners. We might cut him off before that."

"I can still use it." Sinjin showed a spark of life.

"Nothing like negotiation based on a future felony." I shook my head. Yeah, this whole thing had long passed weird. "But the NBA and the owners would take a dim view."

"Such a fair and equitable democracy."

I snorted. "We're supposed to be a republic. But politics for another day that includes lots of righteous bubbles, your treat."

The elevator arrived just as my phone dinged.

Willie's gone.

Romeo.

I checked at the hotel. Bugatti is missing, too.

Did Doc release it? He'd had it buttoned up tight as an ongoing crime scene last time I'd checked.

Not that I heard.

Call ATC. See if anybody there has an unidentified helicopter, flying low. Maybe disappeared altogether.

I'm on it. Where are you?

French Quarter. Leaving. Going to meet the Chinese contingent. Keep me posted.

Ditto.

As I stuck an arm out to hold the doors, I looked at Sinjin. "Let's hit the airport. You ready to face Johnny Wu and his muscle?"

"But that's not where your aunt said to go. Didn't she give you an address south of town?" Sinjin looked confused.

Now was not the time to educate him in the fine art of female obfuscation. "Darlin' is a man's woman. Knowing my father, he told her to give us the shake." I held up a hand. "I have a lifetime of reading between the lines with both my parents. The question is, if according to Darlin' that's where he wanted us to go, where is it he doesn't want us to show up?"

"The airport. In his mind, this is his fight and his alone." Sinjin caught on quickly. "Which airport? You have three."

One in three. Not the best odds. I could narrow it down. It wouldn't be McCarran, much too public. Too many people to record comings and goings, among other things people like Johnny Wu wouldn't want memorialized. That left North Town and Henderson. Henderson's tower wasn't manned at this time of night. "Henderson."

"You're sure?"

"Mostly."

CHAPTER EIGHTEEN

"YOU'RE FLYING on a wing and a prayer, aren't you?" Sinjin asked me as I turned off of St. Rose Parkway heading down to the single runway surrounded by new housing developments. Henderson Executive Airport held a place in the list of a dying breed. A general aviation airport that had been far from town, Henderson now found itself surrounded by rather fancy new developments, the residents of which would soon, if they hadn't already, start filing complaints about the noise—even though they'd bought homes knowing the airport was there. Eventually, the airport would be squeezed out, another one of the perks of Vegas lost to modern life and unappreciative sensibilities. People often navigated by small plane from Southern California or Phoenix and its environs to partake of the wonders in my hometown. Henderson gave them an easy place to land and an approach that didn't interfere with the commercial traffic and the military traffic farther north. Safer for all, but soon a memory, I feared.

"A wing and a prayer? My life is a bit more calculated than that." I wheeled into the parking lot of the single FBO on site.

"There's my father's car." The Rolls hunkered in the far corner of the lot, hidden from the light but not from sight.

Inwardly, I breathed a sigh of relief. Outwardly, I acted as if I'd known it all along. "What kind of plane will the Chinese contingent arrive in?" I should've asked this before. A transpacific beast wouldn't be able to land on the length of runway here. "Somebody said they'd be arriving from L.A.?"

"Last I saw them, that's where they were. And the lawyers indicated they were still there."

"Hmmm. What kind of flying beast would they use? Something short-distance and unobtrusive yet keeping with their power position." I hit him on the arm. "Let's go take a tour of the tarmac, unofficially, of course."

Sinjin pressed a hand to his chest. "I'm the very soul of discretion." Today he'd dressed a bit more mainstream, but still he had that exotic flair that didn't fit with his assertion of being a team player.

A wild card. Despite his show of wanting to help, I couldn't shake the feeling he had his own horse in this race. Revenge? Understandable. Financial gain? Would be disappointing. Watching my back became imperative.

We sauntered into the FBO as if we didn't have a care. The guy behind the desk recognized me. Normally not a good thing, but today I'd take it. I leaned on one elbow in front of him. "Any interesting equipment land today?" I lifted my chin to indicate Sinjin. "I'm showing my friend around. He shares my love of flying." I didn't want to ask if my father had been there—too suspicious and too desperate. Besides I felt my father would have used his stroke to get in the private gate and enter unobserved.

The attendant, Bert according to the name stitched on his chest, immediately perked up. "He want some lessons?"

"For sure. But for now, I'd like to take him on a tour of the stuff parked out back. Show him what he'd be flying, that sort of thing. Okay with you?"

"Sure, Ms. O'Toole. I know you. You're not going to hurt anything."

Anything? No. Anybody? Jury was still out on that one.

"I don't know how interested you are in helicopters, but a top-of-the-line Sikorsky just came in from SoCal. They put down on the other side of that hangar down the way." He pointed to the far end of the row of buildings on the same side of the runway and extending south.

"Really?" I didn't have to feign interest. "Not every day you get to see one of those. Mind if we go have a look?"

"Stay out of the way. You know the drill." Bert buzzed us out the door. "And those guys are being sort of private, so if they don't want you around…"

"Got it. Thanks, Bert. You're a dear." I grabbed Sinjin by the elbow and propelled him through the doors and around the corner where Bert couldn't keep his eagle eye on us.

He surveyed the small single-engine planes dotting the tarmac, some tied down for the night, a couple getting topped off as the pilots prepared to launch back to wherever they came from. "Johnny Wu wouldn't be caught dead in any of these."

"I agree. The Sikorsky is our best bet." We wound our way through the various planes, some of them quite nice, as we ambled south.

The night chill crept down my neck and I pulled my sweater tighter. Needless to say, I hadn't dressed for confronting bad guys at the airport. Silly me. I knew better. My job should require full combat gear every day. Of course, that might worry some of the guests. There was that.

Life always required some kind of trade-off. That fact alone drove me to drink. Literally. How did you draw the line between compromise and standing pat? How was it I usually knew who to shoot but not who to love? Why was I thinking about this now?

Focus, Lucky. Today I just needed to know who to shoot— and I was pretty clear on that so far.

Thankfully, nobody I knew called to us as we wandered south trying not to draw attention. After what seemed like half a lifetime but was probably no more than ten minutes, we reached the hangar Bert had pointed out. "Let's go around the back," I said as I veered to my right, staying close to the corrugated metal wall.

"Why don't I go around the other side?" Sinjin asked as he touched me on the arm, stopping me.

"Because I don't trust you." God, I felt like Jim Carrey in that movie where he had to speak the truth all the time. So much for subtlety.

"I know. You are wrong, but I will prove it to you." Without waiting for my permission, or at least my complicity, he turned left, heading toward the front of the building and perhaps an open hangar door.

A bit too exposed for my taste, but what did I know?

I wanted to tell him that one grand gesture wouldn't be enough of a base for trust, not that that would change anything, but he'd moved out of earshot. At the corner of the building, he paused to stick his head out to get a view of the front of the building. He pulled back, then with a wave and a smile, he slipped from sight.

I didn't think he had a gun—I hadn't thought to ask—but if he did, I hoped to hell he knew how to aim. My father was in there. And in his condition, he couldn't move fast, if at all. I'd worked my way all the way around to the south side of the building when I heard excited voices. Chinese voices. And none sounded too happy.

Sinjin had made his splash.

No longer worried about being spotted or stopped, I hurried

now, keeping close to the building. I stopped, as Sinjin had done on the other side, and peered around the front.

I reeled back. A guard with some sort of automatic weapon held across his body stood at the ready not ten feet away. The voices inside escalated, drawing his attention. I might not understand the words, but I sure got the sentiment.

My chance.

I brushed down my sweater and slacks and arranged myself into a less aggressive form of me if that was possible. The sleeve on my right arm slipped easily higher, exposing my elbow. The guard flinched at my tap on his shoulder. "Excuse me?"

He whirled.

I coiled and then unleashed my elbow. It connected with his jaw in a solid thunk that reverberated up my arm. "Damn!" I whispered as I rubbed my elbow until the pain became a throb.

The guard stared at me stupidly. Wobbling, like a tree with a fatal cut, he staggered.

Wincing against the pain to come, I let loose another round-house elbow. This one caught him on the nose. Blood spurted. His hands cupped his smashed proboscis that now rested oddly against his right cheek. Curiously, he'd made no sound. His eyes widened, then rolled back in his head. To break the sound of his fall, I took the weight of his body, which felled us both. His dead weight unmovable, I scrambled from underneath him. With his belt, I quickly, bound his wrists to each other, then to his feet. He'd have to stay where he fell. I hoped the night would hide him and he'd be out long enough not to give warning of my presence. As an afterthought, I took off his shoes, peeled off his socks and stuck them in his mouth.

No, I didn't feel bad about it.

His boss wanted my hotel. And, most importantly, my father was in there. All bets were off, the rules of fair play out the window. Win or be out of the game. Okay, I was done with the clichés, but they made me feel better.

I pulled my sleeve down, brushed the dirt from my slacks as best I could, grabbed the guy's automatic weapon and studied it, making sure the mode was fully automatic, then strode around the corner and into the hangar.

Nobody noticed me at first, which gave me time for a quick survey.

Halogen lights spit overhead, lighting the place like midday. The Sikorsky squatted in the middle of the hangar. A bright yellow, it looked like a bird ready to unfold its wings and leap into the air.

Two men took turns with Sinjin. Blood flew.

I couldn't see my father.

One portly Chinese man wearing Italian silk and loafers with no socks stood off to one side, aloof to the brutality yet responsible for it.

One chance, Sinjin had said.

I raised the gun and stroked the trigger. With hardly any kick, it spit a flurry of bullets. Several took out the portly dude's knees. I'd been aiming for one, but, well, an automatic weapon is a bit short on nuance.

With a scream, he crumpled.

The two thugs, one holding Sinjin up by his shirt front, the other with fist at the ready, stopped in mid-pummeling.

"Hello," I said.

They remained like statues.

I motioned with the gun. They got my drift. Once released, Sinjin fell on all fours. Keeping the gun trained on them, I sidled over to their boss who lay writhing on the ground. Honestly, I'd only wanted to get his attention. But I didn't feel bad about taking him out either.

Like I'd said, I'd been itching for a fight.

A bit one-sided this one, but I didn't have the time or patience to let the boys play, too.

"You shot me!" The Chinese gentleman spoke in perfect

English.

Ready for his turn as an NBA owner and a big-shot hotelier, I presumed. Why did so many spend so much time and effort into trying to walk in through the back door when the front door was open? Can you imagine what the world would be like if all the bad guys devoted their time and talent to good?

"A small punishment for all the damage you've wrought, Mr. Wu."

"I've broken no laws." He clutched at his knees, but the blood still leaked through his fingers. He'd dropped a pistol when he'd fallen. I hadn't seen it, but I was glad it was there. Justifiable, Romeo had requested, and the Fates had delivered.

Curiously, I was grateful, but I really didn't care. Sometimes you do what you have to do to protect your own. That Rothstein blood ran hot in my veins.

I kicked the gun out of his reach, not that he was going very far. It skittered underneath the helicopter—a good place for it.

"My father?"

"Who?" Oh, the man had so not done his homework.

I love it when that happens, which, with men, was all the time. Almost like shooting fish in a barrel. "Albert Rothstein?"

"He's your father?" He asked, giving me a bit more attention if not appreciation.

I thought about my mother's little stink bomb regarding my paternity. "Yes. He's my father. Where is he? So help me, if you've done anything to him…"

The man raised his hands, a totally inadequate yet reflexive protection move. "We were waiting for him."

"And beating the shit out of my friend to alleviate the boredom."

"The boys were just having some fun. They've crossed swords before." He pulled his bloodied hands away from his knees. "I need some help."

Still on his hands and knees, with a growl Sinjin launched

himself up and into one guy, while he swung one leg, taking the other guy down. Then he focused on the first guy, driving up and into him, propelling him back until the man jolted up against the helicopter. The man grabbed his shirt with both hands. With a smile, Sinjin grabbed one of the man's hands, prying it from his shirt. With a quick flick, he brought the arm around and snapped it at the elbow.

The man screamed and dropped. Sinjin grabbed the man's hair then slammed his head against the concrete floor. Lights out. He whirled to face the other man, who was just getting to his feet. Crouching low, he charged Sinjin.

"Make them stop," the man at my feet implored.

"The boys are just having some fun," I said with a smile.

A gunshot rang out.

The charging man threw up his hands, then fell forward.

Sinjin scrambled for cover.

I did the same, dragging Johnny Wu with me. "Did that come from outside?" I shouted across to Sinjin.

"Yeah. Got him in the back."

I knew who it had to be. Carson Rivers and my father. They'd been expected. I wondered who held the rifle and had fired the shot. I'd bet Rivers. My father was in no condition to have gained the upper hand. "Here." I slid my weapon to Sinjin. "Hold down the fort. You might want to call the paramedics. Mr. Wu is bleeding pretty badly. There's a pistol under the helicopter. Leave it there, but don't let him get it. Got it?"

"Yeah. Where are you going?"

"To get my father." I kept to the inside of the hangar using the large frame of the opening as cover. A doorway opening to the side would give me egress without exposure. I peered through the dirty window trying to figure out some way to get to Rivers without getting perforated. On the wide expanse of the runway, I'd be a sitting duck. Right now, the runway lights were off, but the moonlight was bright.

About twenty feet north of the hangar, someone had parked a tow. I squinted into the darkness at the berm that bordered the far side of the runway, providing noise protection to the neighborhoods beyond. They had to be up there. The slight elevation provided the perfect view into the hangar and the perfect place from which to sight on a target.

"Stay down," I hissed to Sinjin, then opened the door and slipped outside. Bent at the waist, I crab-walked to the tow. This was secured property and the machine was there for anyone to use to push or pull their plane wherever they wanted to put it, so I hoped the keys were in it. They were. I slipped into the driver's seat. Taking a deep breath, I turned the key.

The engine purred. Electric. Oh, happy day!

I crouched down, using my hand on the accelerator, risking a look to check where I was going only briefly and infrequently. Not much I could hit out here. The tow bar had been folded up and back and stuck up above me like a mast waiting for a sail. Setting my sights on where the shot had to have come from, I purred across the open tarmac, then took a high-speed off-ramp onto the runway. Under the cover of darkness, and hiding from the moon, I'd made it almost to the other side when the runway lights clicked on and night turned into day.

Damn!

I glanced up the runway into the sky. A bright light bounced in the night sky. A plane on final approach had clicked on the lights.

The first shot pinged off the metal casing up front.

Now I was sure it was Rivers stroking the trigger. My father was a whites-of-their-eyes kind of guy. I squatted lower but kept motoring. Speed would be nice, but the tow was strictly for power. A burst of gunfire from the hangar behind me. Sinjin and the automatic. The weapon probably didn't have the reach, but it still commanded attention.

The second shot hit the windscreen, shattering it.

Another burst from the hangar.

I'd seen enough to know exactly where the gunman had set up. My tow motored up the berm.

The third shot hit the tow bar, pinging into the darkness.

At the top of the berm, the tow almost high-centered. I stood as much as I dared, throwing my weight forward. It rocked forward slightly, then balanced, the tow bar fell forward. A man yelled. The tow hung for a breath suspended on the peak of earth. Then it rocked forward, then over, and barreled down the other side.

A man, gun in hand, jumped to the side. I leaped.

Landing on him, I forced him down. He landed hard underneath me. I grabbed the rifle. Ripping it from his grasp, I hurled it into the darkness. I worked my knee into the back of his neck. "Don't move. Not one muscle. I can break your neck without thinking about it."

I couldn't see, but his cologne gave him away. I'd gotten my man. Carson Rivers. He didn't move.

"Dad?" I shouted. "Dad?"

Silence answered.

I pressed harder into the crook of Rivers's neck. "Where is he, you bastard?"

If I killed him the world would be a better place. He groaned as I pressed harder. "Please," he wheezed. I pressed harder.

"Lucky!" A weak voice from the darkness. "I'm here. It's okay."

My father! He was alive.

CHAPTER NINETEEN

*M*OTHER MET me at the hospital, and we hovered in the waiting room.

They'd rushed my father back into surgery. When I'd found him, his pulse had been thready, his skin clammy. And he'd been so weak he couldn't stand. Fortitude must've gotten him that far —the docs didn't know why he wasn't dead. Sobering yet comforting at the same time.

"Do you think he'll make it?" Mona whispered as she clutched my hand. She looked disheveled, far from her normal put-together self. She had traded her caftan for a sweater set, matching flats and a pair of pants—normally a bit beyond my capabilities. In a world on tilt, I was happy to see some things stayed the same, or at least close to it.

She knew good and well I didn't have a clue. But she needed reassurance. "Touch and go. I think it'll depend upon how much he wants to make it. His will got him this far."

She took a deep breath and squeezed my hand until I couldn't feel my fingers. "He'll come through. He has two daughters who need him."

Three, but who was I to quibble? I patted her hand and

rescued my own before amputation became a possibility. "It'll be hours yet. I need to check on the hotel, make sure things are okay. I'll be back."

"When?" She looked lost, but so was I.

Adrift in all the horrible possibilities, I had nothing left to give her. She stopped me with a hand on my arm as I turned to go. "Lucky, I'm sorry about…"

"I know. The hotel is the hand that feeds you, Mother. Best to heed the old warning."

She waffled a bit.

"Choose another platform. And next time you even think of talking with Mr. Ballantine, so help me God…"

"I try so hard…" The idea of one more failure crushed her.

"Stop thinking." At her look, I took my waffling turn. "You know what I mean. Stop trying so hard. Big shows don't get the job done. Oh, they keep your name in the paper, but despite the idea that any publicity is good publicity, you need to reassess. Especially since you are trying to gain respect, not laughs."

She didn't bristle as I'd expected. "You're right."

"Wait. What?" Not having to feign surprise, I leaned in closer. "I didn't hear. Say again."

"Lucky, don't make me grovel." She dug her toe into the linoleum.

I didn't have the heart to tell her that wasn't going to fix anything. "Why not? You do it to me all the time, and in public, *and* often I make the morning edition…*above the fold.*"

"I know I can be a pain. I just want to help, to be a part of something bigger than me."

The woman knew just how to play me. I let her. "I know. We'll work on that, okay?"

"And about the paternity thing…" She ground to a halt.

I didn't know how to weigh in on that one either. "Does it really matter? A bit of DNA doesn't make a father."

That boosted her a bit. "And he left it all to you regardless."

"All of what?"

"The hotel, everything."

"But what about you, the girls?" I was genuinely shocked. Of course, I hadn't spent one erg of energy thinking about any of that.

"He said you'd know what to do when the time came."

Wow. Okay. My pea brain refused to expand around that idea.

I was tired, so very tired. Tired of all of it. Of the craziness and the chaos, of the not knowing and the expectation of superhuman competence. Of course, those expectations were my own...and now my father's. But that had always been the end game.

Be it until you become it.

I hadn't heard from Sinjin since he'd texted the major points of the deal he'd brokered.

Cielo was the lynchpin holding the deal together. It gave Johnny Wu a foothold. Not the one he'd wanted, but one sufficient to curry favor with the locals and perhaps with the Gaming Commission. Although I doubted that part. Wiseguys of any color, creed, or stripe weren't wanted anymore. In fact, if identified, they'd be escorted to the border and told never to darken our corner of the universe again.

My autonomy had been bartered away, and I'd be consumed whole by the family business. Not that it hadn't been doing a pretty good job of that already. The Babylon was our shining star, Cielo but a pipe dream. No contest really, but it still hurt. Dreams die hard and they leave a hole.

Mother stopped me as I turned to go. "Thank you. We'd all be lost without you."

With no appropriate words, I gave her a hug.

"Can I get you a car, miss?" The valet at the front entrance to the hospital fixed me with a smile.

I'd played this game before. This time I thought better of it. "Would you mind calling me a cab?"

Cielo perched on the far southern end of respectability on the Strip. I'd wanted it that way. With no gaming but a world-renowned spa, the hotel had been designed as a respite from the constant amp of energy on the rest of the Strip. Here one could take a deep breath, enjoy quiet and solitude, be pampered, kneaded, exfoliated, and reenergized to sin some more.

The moment I walked in the door the lobby exerted its influence. With soft music, warm wood, plants and subtle lighting, the place shouted calm—okay, it whispered calm—like a spa without everyone in bathrobes and those slimy rubber shoes. My staff greeted me with smiles but left me alone. I guessed they'd heard. Or maybe I'd just trained them well. I hoped that was the case. I should be the one to break the news. The details of the deal had yet to be hammered out. I'd make sure they all were taken care of or reassigned to the Babylon. Family is family whether blood or chosen. My reflection stared back at me from the polished surface of the elevator doors. Even though the world had shifted, I still recognized myself. A good thing, since not much else had kept the same form. My magic card gave me the green light for all floors. The buttons offered so many choices. Decision time.

Jean-Charles's flagship restaurant perched on the top floor.

As I said, dreams die hard. I needed to revisit this one. I pressed the button for JC Prime. For some reason I'd chosen the public route rather than the service elevator. Perhaps I just wanted to experience the magic we'd created. Perhaps I wanted to experience the place as a patron, not the owner. Even though much had yet to be decided, in my heart I'd let it go already. Somehow, from the start, I had known this is where I'd end up.

So I listened to the whir of the motor pulling me skyward. The burnished wood paneling was cool to the touch yet lent an air of inviting warmth. The budget had spared no expense. The music soothed. Calm filtered into my soul. Yes, the perfect experience when being lifted to partake in an exceptional dining experience.

That's all Vegas was really...an experience.

And of all the things I knew how to do, that was my very best thing—creating the magic.

The elevator opened into an opulent vestibule. The Van Gogh hanging behind the hostess stand made me smile. Jean-Charles and I had had an exuberant fight over it. I'd borrowed it from the Big Boss's private museum. Jean-Charles thought I'd been heavy-handed foisting it on him. Only a Frenchman could get all huffy when offered a Van Gogh.

The painting still hung there in all of its brilliant execution as a testament to who had won that round. I'd lost many, capitulated others, and had compromised many. We made a volatile team, JC and me, but we did good work.

But drama didn't make me feel loved. The French tended to live their lives at the top of their lungs. Not my style.

The hostess stand stood empty. I ducked around it. The restaurant, even with its scars from the recent chaos that had led to its then-temporary closing, still captivated. Subtle and warm, the focus remained on the curved walls of windows that captured all of Vegas in its glory, from the lights of the Strip to the stark desert, with the comforting hulk of the mountains on all horizons.

They say once you've lived in Vegas, you can never leave for long. The city, the desert, the raw wonder of the place keeps drawing you back. That pull lived in my soul, so I knew it to be true.

The tables still occupied their appointed spots. Chairs clustered around them. White tablecloths had been set with stemware and silver as if expecting the guests to arrive soon. Comforting greens on the walls and warm wood flooring lent an air of welcoming casualness. The sort that said come, relax, stay awhile. Most folks ran restaurants as if table turn-rate was the most important. Not here. And not Jean-Charles. I loved that about him, that genuine interest in people and in providing them a spectacular experience. And, for him, it was the same whether in his burger place or here in his five-star eatery. I loved that about him, too.

That's why we went into business together. I closed my eyes and breathed deep. His cologne lingered in the air, or I imagined it did. We'd crossed the boundary from business to personal—it had been a conscious choice. Looking back, I'd make the same choice.

But now the future looked muddy.

"Hey." His voice came from the direction of the kitchen.

Funny, I never imagined he'd be here, but somehow, I'd known he would.

He smiled an uncertain smile then gave me one of his Gallic shrugs I both loved and loathed, depending. Tonight, I found it charming and a bit sad. "Hey."

As delicious as always, he looked almost as tired as I felt. Worry had etched the laugh lines a bit deeper. Somewhere in the last week or two, he'd lost weight, which didn't look good on him. Who trusts a skinny chef anyway? The chef's whites had given way to a pair of well-worn jeans that fit in the French tradition, seductive without being salacious, topped by a sweatshirt. His hair drifted over his collar, his eyes were bright, but his smile a bit tremulous.

I knew that feeling. A minefield stretched between us. So much to say, so many challenges that perhaps had no solution. All of it rooted us each to our spots, mired in uncertainty.

This was one of the few times I didn't have to peel his son from around my legs before moving to greet him properly. That, too, tugged my heartstrings. "How bad is it?" I forced myself to move, to close the distance between us.

He veered toward the bar. "Come. Sit. I have some fabulous wine."

I took a stool in front of the bar, while he stepped behind it, putting the wooden barrier between us. In the past, my insecurities would've tried to read something into that. Tonight, I accepted the possibility he simply wanted to share some wine with me. One thing I'd learned in Paris is that the French believe that all important discussions should occur over a bottle of very good wine.

My alcohol consumption had become a source of concern, but tonight those worries fell away. Steeped in wine from a young age, Jean-Charles rarely agonized over choosing a bottle. Tonight, he made his choice quickly, as if he'd thought it through beforehand, then dispatched the cork with effortless ease. "This wine should breathe for a bit," he said as he poured a larger-than-restaurant portion into a bulbous glass. He poured some for himself, then handed my glass to me.

His skin touched mine. Heat, even in such a casual, quick brush, exploded.

Our eyes met.

"This will always be, I think." He felt it, too. That made me sad. This night was quickly taking on a theme. Jean-Charles forced a smile. "The wine, it will be better when it has a chance to open."

Watching him take the first sip of anything always made me work to appreciate the subtleties as he did. Not just of wine, but of everything. My life usually required more of a sledgehammer approach, so I struggled with the stillness, the nuance. But I knew I needed it. For the heart, as Jean-Charles used to tell me.

When he'd finished and the wine passed muster, he nodded for me to try it. I lifted my glass. "For the heart," I said. The wine didn't disappoint. Neither did Jean-Charles, actually. How could I expect him to live up to my expectations? His life was his to define, as was his place in it. Mine was the same. If in our choices, we fit together, if we made each other better in being together, if our lives ever met in a common zip code at least most of the year, then we fit. If not, we could be friends. But that sizzle thing was going to be a huge problem.

Circling back to my question, Jean-Charles looked around. "The restaurant, she is fixed, but the heart is missing."

"Perhaps we will find it again."

He seemed sad.

This all left a hole of uncertainty and regret in me as well. Not the kind of regret I could do anything about. More the regret that life hadn't synchronized for us. At least not yet. "This is the first time I remember being with you without Christophe. I know we have had some time alone, but not much." My cheeks burned at the memory of hot, hurried sex in the shower at Jean-Charles's house with the theme from *Thomas the Tank Engine* covering any noise so Christophe, as well as Chantal, Jean-Charles's niece, couldn't hear.

A smile played with his lips. Those plump, kissable lips. One of my favorite parts, among many. "This is my fault," he said. "A woman should have her own time. I did not make you feel special."

And there it was—the thing that bothered me that I couldn't put a finger on.

Yes, I was a cog in the engine of his life, but just a cog—like a box to be checked, a slot to fill, so to speak. Surely, love went deeper than that. I wanted more. I wanted to be loved for being me, not for what I could provide. Was that even possible? My parents seemed to find that balance. I mean, seriously, the only thing to love my mother for was herself. The only things she provided were headaches and occasional laughs.

"No, no, you didn't." My words surprised me. Since when had I become that honest? It felt good. What had my father said? If you don't ask for it, how can you expect to get it?

Yep, that was it. My heart hitched. Would I ever have the

chance again to absorb his wisdom, the lessons of his life? Out of my control. I'd done my worrying; now I waited.

"For this I am very sorry. There are so many things about you I love. This I need you to know." Sincerity filled every word.

Words were easy. Love lived in the details, the smallest of actions. The making of a life around each other, not fitting each other in. I was guilty of it myself.

"Life is not giving us time to show each other these things." I took another sip of wine as I catalogued what my heart knew. "Perhaps there never will be the time. We both are driven people with much responsibility for others, not just ourselves. Each of our families needs us right now. Our fathers may die. Certainly, eventually. When they do, they will leave a vacuum that will suck us in. For how long? We don't know. But, for the foreseeable future, a continent and an ocean will lie between us. And somehow I don't think either of us wants a FaceTime relationship."

"I did not want to hear these words." But he accepted their truth.

"I did not want to say them, but we both know them to be true." I slipped off my stool. If I stayed longer, I was afraid I'd never leave. We'd try again and both end up resenting each other. The time wasn't right for us. "Thank you for the wine. Perhaps it is best if I go now. My father is in surgery. I need to get back. I just came to say goodbye."

"To me?" The idea weighed heavy on him.

"Of course not. I didn't think you would be here." I reached for the wine glass and polished off the last bit. "I came to say goodbye to this hotel. I've lost it, you see." My voice hitched. I so wanted to stand on my own. Yes, I could make the Big Boss's dreams hum, but I wanted a shot at seeing if I could do that for my own. But, well, life offered a trade I couldn't refuse.

Jean-Charles's brows crinkled together in confusion. "Why did you not tell me you needed money?"

"Oh, I didn't need money. The hotel is doing fine. It's just, well, there was this problem I had to solve. Not mine, per se, but one that affected, well, everything. This hotel was part of the solution. I'm sorry. You'll have a different landlord. However, I will exclude your lease in the sale, if you'd like. You'll be free to relocate."

"Perhaps the Babylon has a good location?" He looked hopeful.

"For you, always. We can talk." Neither of us knew if he'd have the bandwidth to keep a five-star eatery going half a world away from home.

I resisted the urge to hold him, the need to be held by him. Giving in would make all this so much more difficult. My gut told me I'd put our relationship back on solid ground, where it would have the time and the room to be what it was meant to be. That felt good, but damn I needed a hug.

I'd made it halfway to the door.

Jean-Charles grabbed my hand, stopping me. I didn't turn.

"We can't have this as our last memory...at least for now." He didn't force me. His skin was so warm where it touched mine.

The connection sizzled through me. A moment, no more, then I turned and threw myself into his arms. My head against his shoulder, I let him hold me, drawing strength from our bond. The strength to let go.

Then I worked my arms around his waist. Pulling him tight against me, I leaned back, drinking him in—the sadness, the resolve, the love...and hope, hope for a future we both wanted but might never have.

He touched my face, his fingers leaving a warm trail as he memorized. His thumb brushed my lips, then he dipped his head for a kiss.

I met him in the middle, my fire to his, and our passion exploded. I drank it in, let it seep into all the dark places inside for when I'd need to feel him, to remember this, for when the loneliness closed around me.

And it would.

Our connection sizzled through every nerve. Working both hands to his chest, I pushed myself back, away from what I craved. When I turned to go, he didn't stop me.

I didn't run. I didn't need to. If time had a place for us, we would find it.

As I left, I l took a long last look at the Van Gogh. It looked perfect there. I'd have to send a security detail—the thing was wired to set off alarms from here to London if touched—to get it off the wall. No way was Johnny Wu getting this little bonus.

Now was the time to return it, time to settle those accounts.

Life going forward followed a different path.

"THE BABYLON, PLEASE," I SAID TO THE CABBIE, THEN SETTLED back and tried to process the last few hours. "Why don't you take Paradise, okay?" So like me, giving instructions. But the Strip would be slowing with its usual gridlock about now. I glanced at my phone. Still no word from Sinjin. I never should've let him go off with the Chinese suits to work on the final deal. And throwing Squash in with that crowd didn't have me feeling too great either. Here in Vegas he could handle himself. With those guys, he'd never see it coming.

Damn.

On the plus side, Romeo had his killer. Carson Rivers. But I couldn't shake the feeling that we had a minor player in this drama. The one really responsible was still out there.

With thoughts pinging and refusing to coalesce, I diverted myself by watching the scenery roll by. The traffic wasn't exactly flying, but at least we made progress heading north. Up ahead loomed the grand entrance to the Golf Club of Las Vegas, festooned with signs promoting the Concours. Cars. I'd forgotten all about them except for one. My little rather useless but wonderful Roadster had shone among all the swoopy iron. That made me happy for some odd reason. Classy always held its own.

A thought jabbed me upright. The Concours! Oh for the love of all that I held dear!

At the time Freddy was killed, Rivers had been stalking Jordan at the Concours pre-party. When Finn was killed… despite our best efforts to place Rivers at the hotel, we'd come up empty. Most likely because he'd never been there. That was my father's turf. And with what was between them, probably not a great place to show up unannounced.

And the truck.

The only identifiable prints in the cab were Jeff's.

He'd said he'd been trying to move it.

Double damn!

I dialed Willie, the only loose end. Romeo had said he wasn't home. He hadn't been at the airport. And the Bugatti was gone. "Come on, answer the phone." But it rang and rang. I disconnected and rang Jerry. Thankfully, he answered. "Is Chastity with you?"

"Just leaving."

"Keep her there, in Security. She's in danger. Don't let her out of your sight. Got it?"

"Will do."

I pocketed my phone then leaned forward and tapped the cabbie on the shoulder. "Turn around, please."

To his credit, he didn't jump. "Where to?"

"There's someplace. It's new. You can go there and spend time beating up cars and stuff. Do you know it?"

"I do." He shot me a look in the rearview. "Got some frustrations that need tending to?"

"You have no idea."

CHAPTER TWENTY

*W*HEN THE cabbie pulled into the parking lot of the Beat Up Bistro, the sign shouted open, but the place looked closed, the lights off, the parking lot empty but for the lone hulk of some sort of mammoth helicopter. Talk about a provocative name and one that totally got me going.

I'd found Willie.

And most likely the Bugatti.

Time would tell what other nasties would crawl out of the night.

The cabbie angled the car just off the road, but the flying machine kept him from going any farther. "Never seen that before." He stared at it like it was a creature from outer space.

In the weak light of a few streetlights, it did look sort of otherworldly, and definitely out of place. But I was actually overjoyed at seeing it.

The building beyond hunkered in the darkness. If there were any outside lights, they'd been extinguished. What I could see didn't fill me with optimism. The term *bistro* testified to the owner's overreaching. Made of cinder blocks with two windows bracketing the solid metal front door and no other amenities, the place looked more like a morgue than anything else. Certainly, they had spent nothing on making it look welcoming, but perhaps my murderous mood painted the whole place in darkness.

The cabbie leaned forward to stare out the front window. "You sure this is the place?"

"This is the only place in town like this, right?" Of course, the helicopter told me I was in the right place.

"Yes, ma'am. But I don't like leaving a lady here all by herself after dark. Doesn't seem right."

"This is the place, then. And I appreciate your concern. I'll be fine." I sounded way more confident than I felt. The man inside had already dismembered a friend and bashed in two heads that I knew about.

And Willie was a wild card.

Was he flying on the side of good or evil? How would I know? Just once, couldn't I go in with a plan instead of just winging it?

As I sat there arguing with myself, a car eased in next to us. Romeo! Relief flooded through me. "You don't have to struggle with your conscience," I said to the cabbie, my confidence returning. "I appreciate your concern, but here's my help. He's with Metro."

The cabbie seemed relieved. The Bash Brothers creep factor had me all jittery too. I paid him, then traded my back seat in the cab for the front passenger seat in Romeo's rig. "Thanks for getting here so quickly."

"Knowing your lack of ability to wait for backup, I broke several land-speed records. And I think I blew something important in the engine. Anybody could've followed our smoke trail. Chief is not going to be happy." He nodded toward the helicopter. "Looks like your hunch was right. I have absolutely no idea how you got here."

I hooked my thumb at the now departing car. "Cab."

"You know what I mean."

"It was something Jeff said, and lots of little things, but more later. Let's go see if I'm right. I got a Bugatti you can have but it might not be in the best shape." I glanced toward the building.

"Not exactly the unassuming ride for a humble public servant. Can you imagine the complaints?" Romeo and I peered at the building. "You think the car is here?"

"Yep. And most likely Willie, hopefully without his head bashed in."

"But I've got Rivers." Romeo looked at me, his eyes wide.

"And what song is he singing?" I knew, but I asked anyway, buying time to formulate a plan, not that it would do any good.

"He said he didn't kill anyone. Said he was shooting at the Chinese guy because he double-crossed him. Set him up good and proper."

I smiled. "I bet he did. A small-time wine guy trying to pretend he's more is no competition for the likes of Johnny Wu."

"Rivers isn't our killer, is he?"

"No. We have no video evidence to place him at the hotel when Finn was killed. And he was on TV stalking Jordan when Freddy was killed. Hardly the time to dismember someone."

"Who, then?"

"Jeff."

"He's a skank, but I never got a hint of the cold-blooded."

"You had him on your suspect list from the beginning, remember? I was the one who poo-pooed that."

"Makes me feel better, but you will tell me later how you stayed on track and I didn't?"

"You did. I just got a bit more info than you did." I cranked the handle and let myself out. "Let's go rescue Wille and perhaps save a car." After closing my door, I looked at the young detective over the top of his car. "Your job, should you decide to accept it, is to keep me from killing a future former employee."

"Save your bacon, eh?" He pursed his lips then nodded. "I'm up to the task."

Even though the windows were dark, both of us clearly felt the need to at least not be overt in our approach. Doubling over, we skittered to the side of the building where a fence met the cinder blocks but left a gap. We both skinnied through. I let Romeo take the lead. He pulled a gun and held it up near his chest at the ready. He looked at me and I shrugged. My Glock was somewhere, but not with me. Since my entire life had been renovated while I was gone, I had little surety where anything I owned might be.

The no-window thing helped us work our way around the side of the building. A weak glow came from the rear, lighting a fire of murderous optimism. Whatever was going down was still in process. One car angled across several parking spaces. Somebody was here. And I'd bet my future on who.

At the back of the building, Romeo motioned me to stop. He snaked his head around the corner. He pulled back, pressing against the wall. "Jeff, one other. Willie. He doesn't look good. He's been at him already." He grabbed me as I moved to step around him, spurred by anger and a need to stop this.

"I'll kill him."

Romeo held onto my arm. "I know. Just make it justifiable, okay?"

"At this point, it's all justifiable."

He let go. "I know."

"Lead on. I'll follow."

He snorted. "Right." After one last look, he disappeared around the corner.

I didn't even try to hide. Romeo stayed to the shadows. I didn't bother. With a quick look, I found half of a cinder block and grabbed it. A quick coil and I hurled it. It sailed through the back window and I followed right behind, ignoring the shards of glass hanging in the frame. One tore at my shoulder as I rushed through.

Jeff, a heavy wrench raised in his hand, paused, his shock registering. Willie was his target.

Talk about being in the nick of time.

"Get Willie," I shouted at Romeo. Willie slumped in a chair, a rope circling his chest, his hands bound behind him, his feet secured to the legs of the chair. He didn't move. I grabbed a sledgehammer as Jeff disappeared through a doorway. I paused for a second, no more, pulling in air, trying to summon logic.

Calm, Lucky. Be smart here. He's not going anywhere. We are all loose ends, the ends he's intent on tying up. Cat and mouse. Be a clever mouse.

With both hands cheating down the handle of the sledge-hammer so I could swing the weight easily, I inched forward. One foot at a time, I approached the doorway, stopped and listened, then eased myself through. Pausing for a moment to let my eyes adjust to the darkness, I used my other senses to try to picture where I was. A room, yes. Not too large. But that was all I had. With no light, I was flying blind.

Jeff clearly had an advantage. He knew the layout.

"I know you're in here," I said, throwing a dart in the darkness. "You may kill me, but you won't kill all of us. You're done. What I want to know is why."

"You make a deal with the devil, it eats you alive, you know." His voice still held fight, yet also a hint of the inevitable.

"I get that. Which devil? Rivers?"

He laughed. "That guy? Hell no. What a no-load. I saw the writing. The Chinese guy, he's the horse in this race."

He'd gotten that part right. "And you thought by eliminating some of his problems you might get his attention?"

"I was helping him get what he wanted. I figured he'd throw a crumb my way. That's all I'll need. I can work my way through the ranks from there."

"No doubt. You killed a lot of people."

"Yeah. Deadbeats. Who's going to miss them?" I thought about Mrs. Morales. And I was thinking of the promise I'd made to her, the one about giving her a knife and five minutes alone with her son's killer, and I thought I'd really like to make good on that.

"Who's going to miss you?" I did my best to follow him.

"I got my friends, but ain't nobody going to have to cry at my funeral." He sounded overconfident and why not? He'd gotten away with murder so far.

"Bought and paid for." I left my spot in the doorway, working my way around the wall toward the source of his voice. The hammer weighed more and more with each step until the muscles in my arms burned with effort. "Just like you. We bought and paid for you and look where it got us."

"That's just it, I don't want to be your people. You were born Vegas royalty; you wouldn't understand."

"And female. Both made my path all the more difficult." Did I really have to explain to a white male what incredible advantages he had been born with? Probably, but I didn't try. He knew it and still looked for an excuse. My words wouldn't change his mind. My foot brushed a piece of metal that squealed across the concrete floor.

"Don't try it. You stay where you are." Jeff sounded a bit less confident now, a crazy edge to his voice.

Did he think a bit of bravado would scare me off? "Sure. Sure." I stepped over the metal, finding the floor with my front foot, then bringing the other to rest beside it. I smelled oil, and raw metal, and fear—yes, for sure the acrid hint of fear. My heart pounded, which I hoped only I could hear. Other than that, calmness comforted me, it cleared my mind, focusing me. I'd get one shot. And it'd be a wild swing. I couldn't see my nose in front of my face. Closing my eyes, I tapped into my other senses: hearing, smell, sound.

I heard it. A whisper of cloth rubbing. Air moving. A whoosh. I ducked. Instinct. A piece of metal ricocheted off the wall not two feet from my head.

"Missed, asshole. I'm coming for you, Jeff. And I'll get you. Be assured of that." I could sense him nearby. The smell of fear and the acrid stench of body odor was stronger now.

Another missile. This one closer. It nicked my cheek and I felt the warm rush of blood. "Nice try. Missed again." I moved forward, this time a bit more quickly. "Bet you were shocked as hell when Finn's body fell out from under the truck for the whole world to see."

"Might've gotten away with it but for that."

I keyed on his voice, measuring distance. "Doubtful." My foot kicked another bit of metal.

Jeff honed in on the sound.

I skittered forward, ducking as I did so. The missile clanged off the wall just over my head.

"Still here, asshole. I would've gotten you regardless."

He laughed. Big mistake.

I took two giant steps then swung the hammer with all my might.

The hammer hit something soft. A meaty thunk in the darkness. Then silence.

I tucked back against the wall, finding comfort in its cool solidness. Silence fell over the room. No sound of breathing or movement. Even my heartbeat subsided.

A light flashed on. I flinched against the assault.

"Lucky, you having fun in here?" Romeo.

"No!" I dropped to all fours, propelling myself forward, sure Jeff would take aim at Romeo.

I needn't have bothered. My hands found a body, warm, soft. My eyes adjusted to the light and I flinched. Blood. Lots of blood. And brains. Jeff had gotten what was coming to him.

I fell back on my ass. "Shit."

Romeo, bouncing over car parts and around others, arrived at my side. "Shit."

We both stared at Jeff, his head bashed in, his eyes locked in a dead stare.

~

I DIDN'T START SHAKING UNTIL THE POLICE HAD ARRIVED, THE coroner had commandeered the scene, and the danger was over. All that happened in quick order, but it seemed to take forever to me. Once the shaking started, nothing seemed to make a dent in it.

Romeo stayed close. "Are you okay?"

"I don't know." After the first glimpse of Jeff, I couldn't look at him anymore. I had done that. Yes, it was for Freddy. For Finn. For Chastity who he had used instead of helping. But I had done that. I had split his head open. Judge, jury, and executioner. Although it seemed right, it didn't seem appropriate. One person shouldn't have that power, should they?

My life shattered inside me.

I'd put the pieces back together, but probably not in the same order...some of them wouldn't fit anymore, of that I was sure.

On some gut level, I knew life had changed.

I had changed.

"It's going to be okay. I'm really, really sorry. I didn't know what to do. Turn on the light. Don't turn it on. Finally, I did it, hoping to make myself a target and draw his attention away from you." Clearly, he was a little shock-ish as well, but continued as he wound down, "I'm really sorry you were the one to have to do that."

Better me than him, I thought. The idea of anybody I cared about swinging something heavy, then feeling the contact, hearing the bone crunching.... I shuddered at the thought. No one should have to carry those sounds, that reality. And I'd never joke about homicidal tendencies again. Mona may inspire them, but they no longer seemed funny. "How's Willie?"

"EMTs are patching him up. He's scared shitless and pledging fealty to you ever more."

"Until he gets a better offer." I guessed it was one thing to say you're dying and another to do it. Most of us cling to life with strength we didn't know we had. Willie was no different. His battle with liver cancer would be torment. He might even wish he'd died tonight. But I was glad he didn't die quickly on my watch. Every battle, no matter the odds, no matter the pain, had a chance of being won. "Could he shed any light?" I asked.

"Jeff called him. Said Rivers wanted his car back and that Doc had released it."

"None of which was true."

"Not that I can tell. Just Jeff luring in another loose end."

"Willie never suspected him." I thought about how easily we are fooled. How much we default to believing something is good. A good thing, I thought, but it'd kill some of us.

"The guy had all of us chasing our tails. You going to put all the pieces together for me?" Romeo asked as he sat next to me, sidling close as he looped an arm around my shoulders. "You did the right thing. It's going to be okay."

We'd been through all this before—dead bad guys—his and mine. But tonight, the load felt heavier. "I know." He waited for me to gather myself. "When we got to the delivery bays the first time, Jeff greeted us. What was he wearing? What did he say?"

Romeo reached for his notebook.

I put my hand on his, stopping him. "Think back."

He closed his eyes. When he opened them, he said, "Babylon uniform. He said he'd been getting dirty doing inspections." He must've peeked and seen my smile.

"Yep, but before that. As he walked up to us, he shucked off a gray sweatshirt, which I bet was a hoodie, and he said he'd been at his new place where folks pay him to work out their frustrations on old equipment."

Romeo looked like the class scholar who'd missed an answer. "He did, didn't he? And the sweatshirt, you didn't happen to get it, did you?"

"Wasn't smart enough at the time. I had no reason to suspect him. He's been with us for a long time."

"And taking advantage of his situation." Romeo was kind enough not to rub my nose in it.

He'd been running girls out of the back of *my* house. That alone would've been sufficient to knock the stuffing out of him and then some.

"You think the trash is still there?" Romeo asked with a hint of perk. "We could get the stuff he tossed?"

"No. Dumpster's emptied daily, but that doesn't matter, does it?" I glanced over to where somebody had covered what was left of Jeff with a tarp. "Not now anyway." A shiver chased down my spine, making the teeth chattering thing worse. Romeo hugged me tighter. "I don't want to do this anymore." I scooched down so my head rested on his shoulder. Awkward but somehow it felt really good.

"Me either. After this, I'm out of Metro. Eating me alive, you know."

"Do I ever. Anyway, here's what I got. Walker Preston was the flunky Carson Rivers used to set up the pot smuggling. He knew Willie through that. Willie told me Preston had asked around at the airport looking for a pilot willing to skirt the law."

Romeo scoffed. "He found his guy."

"And then some. Who knew Willie had a conscience? Anyway, I'm not sure how, but they had to rope Jeff in on all of it."

"Maybe Walker partook of his prostitution ring at some point?"

"Sure could have. And that would explain his current chumminess with Chastity."

"The girl sent to set up Pearl that you hired?"

"Yeah, despite her protestations, I'm sure she was a hooker at some point, most likely with Jeff's ring." A thought hit me. "Hey, if that's true, that gets me off the hook."

"What hook?"

"When I hired her, I promised Chastity I'd take care of her pimp."

"That would be good. I don't think you're in the position to take care of anybody."

"Not at the moment, I'll grant you that. But I'll regroup. To continue, Jeff provided access to the hotel. He gave some pot to one of my staff. The DEA tied it back to the stuff Carson Rivers grows. That makes a tidy little pot smuggling case against Walker, Willie, and Rivers."

"You going to go to bat for Willie?"

"Yeah, yeah, I will."

"Softie."

I was comfortable with that assessment. "The players trusted Finn; they came to him with their worries about all the money showing up, girls, weed, all that. They wanted help. Basketball is their passion and for some…most probably…a way to better the financial situation of their families. They're not about to risk that. Finn confronted Preston over the Bugatti. Little did poor Finn know he'd stuck a stick in a beehive. Jeff overheard." Damn, the whole thing made me sick.

"What about Freddy?"

"Finn asked Chastity if there was somebody who could fix him up with a fake ID. Made it sound like he wanted one for the weekend, and he didn't want anything he might do to get back to his employers."

"And she asked Jeff."

"Might as well have. One of the guys in the bays. You've already established how they all rally behind their leader."

"Not one gave him up, not even a hint. But how could Jeff overhear Finn and Preston? His shift didn't start until midnight and they powwowed around five in the afternoon?"

"Once again Chastity to the rescue. She placed him in the bays around five."

"And Rivers?"

"He's a pompous ass trying to keep his reputation polished and his winery functional. He agreed to help Johnny Wu launder money, presumably for a percentage of the take. But Wu didn't keep his side of the bargain. Instead he used the proceeds to buy the lease for the ground under the Babylon and set up the threat of a sting so the NBA owners would grant him the highly lucrative Vegas market for an expansion team."

"That's pretty much the song Rivers is singing. Says he wasn't anywhere near any of the murders."

"He's right, far as I can tell."

Romeo ran a hand through his hair. "And Jeff put Freddy in the Bugatti to point the finger at Rivers?"

"Or to give him the finger. Either way he made his point." I shivered again. The teeth chattering was getting better; the horror was not.

"What gets me is, though he's behind all of this, Wu is going to walk."

"Maybe. Maybe not. I'll leave Squash Trenton to chase those rats. For now, Rivers can point the finger, but Wu paid for the cars, not pot, at least that's how he'll spin it. They'll need a lot more to trap Wu. He's much too seasoned to be caught so easily."

"Wait. The Babylon was mixed up in this?"

I gave him the down and dirty. My father had so stepped in it as a young hothead. I thought maybe there might be a veiled lesson in there, so I didn't even try to spin his stupidity.

"Man. He's lucky to have you. You fixed it all."

"With Sinjin's help. Apparently, he strong-armed the suits representing Mr. Wu. Got them to take a different deal."

"And saved you from a lifetime behind bars," Romeo half-joked. He'd seen what I was capable of when pushed. "You think about him a lot, don't you?"

"Who?"

"Sinjin. When I see you guys together it's like he's the yang to your yin."

I gave him as much stink-eye as I could from my position. "Don't go there. I so do not need another man in my life."

Romeo just giggled. Yes, he actually giggled. "Sounds like he helped save your bacon."

"He did. If there is anything Sinjin Smythe-Gordon is good at, it's sealing the deal." I didn't tell Romeo about Cielo. Nobody needed to know. My contribution to the greater good and all of that.

"I can't shake the idea that Walker Preston was more a part of all of this." That guy had wedged himself firmly in the young detective's craw.

"He didn't kill anybody. You can chase the rest if you'd like. One of our new hires in Security, Chastity, placed him with her at the time of Finn's death, and he didn't arrive in town until Friday morning. That's according to him. You'll need to follow up on that with credit card receipts or someone who places him somewhere else. For now, I'm willing to believe him."

"Jeff panicked and started tying up loose ends."

I thought about my father, and I wondered why he didn't kill Rivers when he found him. Maybe someday he'd tell me. "Yeah. Don't ask me why. Maybe it has to do with my slippery slope theory—once you take that first step, it's all downhill."

"Man, I missed a lot of this."

"Don't beat yourself up. Really, it was talking with Chastity just a few hours ago that brought things into focus. Besides, you're the wide-eyed cop; I'm the cynical, grizzled veteran of foul play. I sorta like it that way." My energy leaked out of me so fast that I thought maybe I might faint or throw up. Fifty-fifty. "I'd be willing to bet this is the murder scene you've been looking for."

He looked around with renewed interest. "Freddy was killed here, you think?"

"A good bet. There are heavy tools everywhere. I'm betting the murder weapon is in here as well. Might take Doc some time to find it, though."

"He's a birddog when it comes to that." Romeo sounded relieved. "We got our murderer."

"We did indeed."

I looked up into the relieved expression of my friend.

My teeth chattered, my energy flamed out, I wasn't sure I could stand, but I managed a few more words. "My father?"

"Still in surgery." He read my look. "I'll take you there. Let me help you."

CHAPTER TWENTY-ONE

*R*OMEO GOT me as far as the door at my condo building. Forrest took me from there. "I got you, Miss Lucky." His arm felt steady, strong, all the things I wasn't.

We'd never made it to the hospital. En route, Mona had called. My father was out of surgery and holding his own, but they would keep him under for a while. An induced coma they called it. Something about helping him heal. Mother was on her way home to see after the twins.

I decided to do the same. Home that is. Thank God there were no twins awaiting me.

"Mr. Teddie is making you some dinner," Forrest said as he helped me to the elevator. "I hope you don't mind."

No twins, but Teddie. I wasn't sure which was worse.

"Dinner? What time is it?" Murder muddles everything. I wasn't even sure what day it was, much less the time. Running from one crisis to another could do that. It had to stop...or I would.

"Well past, but he thought you might want something warm."

That sounded more ominous than Forrest realized as he

happily grinned at me and pushed the button summoning the private elevator. "You want me to take you to the top?"

"Almost the top," I corrected. Somehow, I summoned enough energy to pull myself upright and steady my legs beneath me. If I had to face down Teddie, I'd do it from a position of strength…or as much of one as I could fake. "Thanks. I'll take it from here."

The ride up gave me precious little time to pull myself together. Oddly, I looked like I'd killed someone. Maybe that was my imagination, but I for sure didn't look myself. Rolling around in the dirt with Carson Rivers hadn't done much for my outfit—my hair either. Then the whole Jeff thing. Even though I loved these clothes, I was burning them. But what's a girl to do? As the elevator slowed, I pasted on a smile.

Teddie met me in the foyer with a glass of wine, a big smile and oozing everything I loved about him. So not fair. Once he took a good look at me, his smile fled, the blue of his eyes turned dark, and his expression adopted concern.

I used to think he faked it. I didn't think that anymore, but I had no idea what to do with it.

"Forget the wine," he said, making a quick assessment. "A tumbler of Wild Turkey coming right up." He gently touched my elbow. When I didn't bite, he grabbed it more firmly. "Where would you like to land?"

Bed sprang to mind, but only after a long soak in a hot bath —neither of which would include Teddie. "I don't know my way around enough to choose."

He steered me to the couch in the main room. Just like my father's, it boasted a stellar view of Vegas. Grateful, and losing the ability to stand, I sank into the plush pillows and fell back. "Damn."

"You look—"

I held up a hand. "Ain't no biggie. I feel worse."

He looked at the throw on the back of the couch, then

thought better of it. I hid a smile. Tucking me in would only piss me off. While he busied himself at the bar, I pulled the blanket over me. My teeth still chattered, but I could control them better now.

"Do you need food?" Teddie appeared back in front of me, a very full tumbler in one hand, the bottle of Wild Turkey in the other. "Medicinal rations."

With no pride or subterfuge left, I grabbed both and held on. "Thanks." I lifted the bottle. "You joining me?"

"I'm already one ahead of you. Drinking is part of cooking."

"I had no idea. Perhaps I should've tried it." I stared past him through the window at the dazzling rainbow of neon. Funny how the lights painted over the ugly. Somehow, I felt better. The Wild Turkey went a long way toward reviving me.

Not a proud moment.

But my life required high-octane fuel, just perhaps not quite as much as I'd been pouring in the tank recently. As I said, things were going to change. That meant me, too. I glanced at my phone. Still no Sinjin. After the airport, I'd rushed off with my father. I hadn't seen Sinjin again, which piqued my worry—about my hotel, yes, but also about him.

Then there was the Jeff thing. I fought the bile rising in my throat.

"Who are you worried about? I can tell you've been through it today. You don't have to tell me. I wouldn't want you to have to wade through whatever it was again. Anything I can do? Anyone I can check on?"

"No. My father's out of surgery. He's hanging in. They have him in some medically induced coma. Said it could be a day or two."

"So, it's your houseguest you're worried about." It wasn't a question, even though I saw a whole string of them lining up behind the statement.

The insight he had into my deepest, darkest corners unnerved me a bit, a violation I wasn't sure I'd invited or wanted. "He's playing a dangerous game on foreign soil. Part of it, a very large part of it, has to do with me. I feel responsible." I wasn't about to mention to Teddie that I cared. So odd this male friend/former lover thing. Tidbits I'd share with a girlfriend were totally wrong to hit him with. At some point we'd have to stop straddling the fence. Would we be friends with hope for more? Just friends? Or lovers?

Right now, all I wanted was a bath.

"Teddie..."

"Now's not the time for that talk."

"Which talk?"

"The one I hear in your voice." He didn't try to hide his fear that I'd shut him down and lock him out. "We'll try to start over. I miss you. I miss the laughter. I miss Rogers and Hammerstein movie nights. I miss us, whatever we were." He lowered himself to sit next to me and fussed with the blanket. But he resisted tucking it in.

We both smiled.

People who knew you, really knew you...and maybe who even knew you when...provided the glue to hold together life's worst moments. I couldn't tell whether I'd lived through one or it was yet to come, but I knew Teddie made me feel better. I raised my glass. "Friends."

Teddie, with no glass of his own, made a fist and bumped my glass. "Friends. I abandoned a plate for you in the kitchen, if you want it. Comfort food. Pasta with that Alfredo sauce you swoon over. And a plate of my mother's oatmeal coconut cookies." That part made me groan, which made him smile. "You look a bit better than when you walked in. Eat something. Take that bath I can see you're craving. Then get some shut-eye. Perhaps life will make more sense in the morning."

With that, he left. I didn't turn to watch him go. When the

elevator doors shut, I abandoned my Wild Turkey and went in search of those cookies.

Somehow, I'd managed to make it unmolested through my bath and was just toweling off when my phone rang. A number I didn't recognize. "Lucky O'Toole." I held the phone against my ear with my shoulder as I toweled dry.

"Ms. O'Toole. I have a package for you."

THE MAN HAD GIVEN ME INSTRUCTIONS TO A REMOTE SPOT JUST south of Beatty—not a short drive. I'd borrowed Teddie's car. At first, he'd been adamant about coming with me. Somehow, he'd capitulated even though my argument of wanting to be alone with the Aston Martin held zero water.

The solitude kept me company and the car boosted my spirits during the hour-and-a-half trek. The guy hadn't sounded menacing. Maybe I was stupid to go by myself. My Glock, which I'd found in one of the nightstands, nestled in my jacket pocket up against my stomach.

No sleep and little food, despite Teddie's best efforts, had me amped on sugar and little else, which had me wired but approaching nonfunctional. Not the best time to facedown the bad guys. But somehow, this just didn't feel like that. Their jig was up, and they were smart enough to know when to retreat and lick their wounds. They'd be back, of that I was sure of. But not now, not tonight.

The sun, still below the horizon, painted the sky next to the Earth in pinks and deep purples as I turned off the highway, using the term loosely, onto a dirt road. The hulk of a sand dune rose ahead of me. Three miles in, the sign on my right told me I'd reached my goal. Jetson's Stables.

To be honest, I'd half-believed it wouldn't exist, that somebody was taking me on a wild, wild-goose chase. But there it was, a ramshackle wooden structure providing shelter to the horses, who munched hay and ignored my arrival. A lone light in the trailer beyond beckoned me.

A man sat in a chair by a makeshift wood-burning stove, drinking from a mug of something steaming. "You must be Lucky."

"Opinions differ."

He pulled his lips back in what must've been a grin, showing me several gaps where teeth should've been.

"You have a package for me. What kind of package?"

He thought for a moment, his face scrunched with the effort, then he flashed that gap-toothed grin again. "Delicate."

"That's it?"

"They paid me a lotta green to get you out here and send you off. I'm doing what I promised. They made it clear if I varied from the terms…"

"I get it." This had Johnny Wu stink all over it. He wouldn't kill me; that much I was sure of. But there was a bit of gray area between where I stood and dead.

"Want some coffee before you head out?"

I nodded and accepted a mug of steaming brew of my own. I wrapped my hands around it, absorbing the warmth. Truth of it was I was dog-tired, not making good decisions, and clearly not processing well. "Where am I going?"

"About three miles northwest."

"Toward the sand dune? Not in my Aston Martin. The sand must be at least ten inches deep all the way."

He nodded and took a sip of his java. "True."

My stomach fell. I glanced behind me at the shelter I couldn't see but knew was there. "Oh no. I'm not going on horseback. Don't you have a four-wheeler with tundra tires?"

"All are spoken for as soon as the sun comes up."

Not in this weather—colder than a witch's tit. A lie, bold and brazen, but nothing I could do about it.

"I got your horse saddled. Got a pack on it with some supplies you might need."

I put up one last fight. "You said you had a package for me."

"I do. They left it out there. I have strict instructions that you have to retrieve it yourself. And, trust me, you're going to want to get there by sunup. The things turkey vultures can do…"

"I can pay you more."

"Lady, it's not about that. Trust me." The fear in his eyes convinced me to let that one lie.

My rodeo. I'd be the one to hit the deck if it came to that. "Which steed is mine?"

I'd wished I'd brought another sweater as I got used to having a horse underneath me again. Pahrump, my childhood home, boasted precious little in the way of entertainment. As kids we'd found horses to be infinitely amusing and a way to get around without parental supervision. My pony was blind in one eye and mean as a snake, on a good day. The horse I rode now was a vast improvement. He seemed to know where he was going. I'd pointed him northwest and let him ramble.

If anybody wanted to take a shot at me, they'd have a clean shot. Out on the sand flat, I had no place to hide. My Glock would be useless out here. Nobody would get close enough to be in range for my little popper. So, I enjoyed the hot coffee from the mug my horse master had provided and watched the sun below the horizon prepare the sky for its entrance.

The desert just before dawn held an expectant hush. I breathed in the calm, the cool, as my horse plodded on his path. With slight pressure from my legs, I kept him on course. Funny how forgotten abilities came roaring back when needed.

After I'd passed my fifteenth birthday and discovered boys could be good for rides to wherever I wanted to go, I thought I'd never be on the back of a horse again. Then riding a horse equated with youth in a negative way. Now, it just felt good.

Getting off of the treadmill and out of the chaos.

Maybe that's what I'd needed more of. As adults, we know this but rarely take the time. And that creates all manner of problems.

The sun just peeked over the horizon, painting the desert pink. It took my breath. Most people never see this. It lasts for a moment, no more. But you remember it forever.

Up ahead a rocky outcropping jutted from the sand. Per my rather loose directions, this was my destination. As I approached, I sensed movement on the highest rocks. Yes, a man unfolded himself from the shelter of a small crevasse where two large slabs of sandstone met.

"Can you help me?" He raised a hand to shield his eyes as he stared in my direction.

I shook my head.

Sinjin.

Somehow, I'd known it all along. In answer, I goosed the horse to a faster pace toward him. He leaped from his perch, landing on the rocks below, then launched himself to another, landing with a grunt. Then he worked his way down more carefully.

Focused as he was, he didn't look up until we both had arrived at approximately the same position maybe twenty feet apart, he on his feet…and totally naked.

"Well, now, this is an interesting turn of events," I remarked, drawing his attention.

His hands flew to cover his privates, which made me laugh. He clutched some papers which he used to ensure full coverage.

"I hardly think you're in the position to entertain such sensibilities." I took a sip from my thermos.

"Is that coffee?" His whole body shivered.

"Hot, too," I said, enjoying the whole thing way more than I should. The guy had set me up, not once but twice, to take the fall and fight it out with the bad guys. He deserved to suffer, not that he hadn't already. In the soft light, his bruises still looked dark and ugly; my dressing still covered the gash in his thigh. The bruises purpled a large portion of his body. Blood crusted his nose and one eye was swollen shut and would be purple in an hour or two. I think one lip had split, but it was hard to see details.

Despite his best effort to convince me otherwise, the man looked cold, tired, hurt, and just wanting a hot bath and a comfortable bed. Having been there myself oh-so recently, I knew just how he felt. "How'd the negotiations go?" I asked, my hands crossed on the pommel.

"Now? You want to have that discussion now?" He shivered again in the cool morning air. He had to be hovering on the brink of shock.

"How long have you been out here?"

"Long enough that I can't feel important parts."

"That is a concern. So, how'd the negotiations go?" He couldn't really complain. He'd taught me when and how to press my advantage.

"I've got the Babylon ground lease in exchange for Cielo, free and clear. That's what you wanted, right?"

"Not really, but it'll do. I'm assuming you have that in writing?"

He raised the papers, then pressed them back to their original purpose. "Yes."

"You're using the key to my family's survival as a makeshift codpiece."

He shrugged. "Vanity."

"Come on. Let's get you back to civilization and hot coffee and warm clothes." I dug in the pockets of the saddlebags behind me: one scruffy blanket and an extra thermos. I extended a hand.

He took it and boosted himself to sit behind me.

I exchanged the blanket and coffee for the papers which I

tucked in next to my Glock. "Louis, this is the beginning of a beautiful friendship."

"What does this mean?" he asked in my ear, his arms encircling my waist.

"It's a line from a famous movie." Only the most famous movie of all time, *Casablanca.* How did anyone not know that? Of course, he'd been raised on the other side of the world, so there was that.

"But we are more than friends, don't you think?" He tightened his hold on my waist, pressing close, more for warmth than anything, but his question had me guessing.

A naked man sitting behind me on a horse, in the middle of nowhere, his body beaten and battered, and he wants to make a play for me? Gotta give him an A for effort.

"Adversaries?" I asked, not willing to give even a millimeter. Trust, as I'd said, it's an issue.

"But I just risked everything for you."

And he had, well, as far as I knew at this point. If he had an angle, I'd missed it. "Why?"

"Because I love you."

CHAPTER TWENTY-TWO

*T*HREE DAYS passed with my world pretty much in limbo. I hadn't responded to Sinjin's protestation of love. The man had been half-delirious after all. And, while I'd been nursing him back to health in my guest room, he hadn't pushed me, for which I was grateful.

Love. He didn't even know me, and he certainly only had a glimpse of me in my natural habitat. And I of him in his. What happened to falling in love slowly? A dying art.

In the past, so in need of…someone…and the validation that came with him, I'd been too ready to leap myself. Too trusting, which now struck me as funny for a gal with lifelong trust issues.

But now I did trust someone. Me. And that sounded like a good foundation on which to assess and handle life going forward, including love. For now, that was enough.

My phone did a little dance on the counter—yes, I was in the kitchen doing battle with the toaster oven—a new model—and I was losing. Such a badass, I couldn't even manage a couple of pieces of toast.

Mona.

Thankful for the break from the fight, and for news of my father who still remained in an induced coma, I answered. "What's up?"

"They brought your father out of the coma. He's awake and is asking for us."

I glanced down at my PJs, nice silk but hardly suitable for public consumption. "Let me change. I'll be out front to pick you up in twenty."

"Give me thirty. The girls just woke up."

My father was indeed awake and smiled a big smile when Mother and I walked into the room. It had taken some convincing to get Mother to leave the girls home. My father still resided in ICU, and infants weren't allowed, but my mother had a bit of that rules-don't-apply-to-me attitude that made me want to wipe the smug off her face. She rushed to her husband's side. Her love wasn't an act, that much anyone could see. And all that bullshit about Carson Rivers, none of it mattered. She'd been a kid scrounging for crumbs in a vicious grown-up world.

Never a good idea to judge someone ever, but especially not using modern sensibilities as a metric for long-ago behavior.

Letting them have their moment, I held back, appreciating family. As big a pain as both of them were, I wouldn't trade with anybody.

After a bit of canoodling with his wife, my father spied me and motioned me over. He grabbed my hand. His skin was warm. "Lucky." The one word stuffed full of emotion.

I bent and laid a kiss on his cheek, which was also warm. I wouldn't say he looked his vibrant self, but I saw hints. "You do know how to get attention. We'll talk about what a damn fool you were when you get well, but don't expect me to pull any punches."

"I would expect nothing less. And I'll most likely agree with you."

I fussed with his blanket but found myself at a loss. Finally, I found the words in my heart. "The hotel wasn't that important. Not so much to risk losing you."

"I had that thought, but from a different perspective. Your mother, you, the girls, even without the hotel I had everything a man could want."

"Is that why you didn't kill Carson Rivers?"

He nodded. "Up until I realized he was shooting at you; then I would've killed him if I could. But you got there in time, as you always do." He glanced at his wife, who gave him a nod.

Oh God, they'd been cooking up some scheme. When had they had the time? He'd been in a coma for Chrissake.

"We're moving to the ranch." They had a huge spread outside of Reno with easy access to Lake Tahoe.

"What?"

"It'll be a good place to raise the girls." He sounded happy. "Your mother always said the country was good for you."

I'd hardly call a whorehouse in Pahrump 'the country', but I let her keep her fantasy. Truth of it was, it had been good, in an odd sort of way.

"With my health deteriorating while you were overseas, I signed all the papers. The hotel is yours if there's anything left. If not, you have Cielo, which proved your ideas are better than mine." He'd scoffed at my no-casino idea. Yes, I'd been validated. That made me feel like I belonged; I could contribute in a larger way other than just effectuating my father's plans.

I'd started to insist I wasn't ready, but maybe I was. "Are you sure?"

"Never been more sure of anything. Your mother and I deserve our time. And I need some rest."

"Okay, the hotel is safe with me."

He smiled as if he'd known it all along.

EPILOGUE

I'D SETTLED in for a quiet night fighting with the television remote when a voice called from the vestibule.

"May I come in?" Teddie.

The guy must have bugged my apartment or paid the staff to spy for him. No matter day or night, once I got myself settled, he'd show up. But I thought back—he'd left me in peace the last few days.

"Sure." I punched buttons, but nothing convinced the television to do my bidding. "The appliances are conspiring against me."

"I can help." He appeared in front of me holding a large bowl in one hand, a plate mounded with cookies in the other. "I noticed you were out of cookies."

"Cookies are never safe around here, especially during a crisis. You look like one of the three wise men."

"Better than one of the Three Stooges. It's Tuesday," he said, his expression telling me I'd missed something. "Movie night?"

I patted the couch beside me. "Is that popcorn in the bowl?"

"Movie night traditions are sacred." He moved the table

closer then arranged the food within reach. "I invited Sinjin. He's healing nicely. A brutal beating. Damn."

He'd taken the beating for me.

The papers had all been in order—Squash vetted everything. No angle appeared. He'd done it for me. In a way he'd owed me. But he hadn't played that card either.

For now, I decided to sit pat and let the games play out.

"What movie do you have on tap?" I relinquished the remote.

Teddie pointed it at the television which burst to life. "I had your favorite ready to go."

"*South Pacific?*"

"Of course. But Sinjin asked if it would be all right if we watched *Casablanca*."

I snagged a cookie and leaned back. "Perfect."

THE END OF
A WONDERFUL ADVENTURE

Thank you so much for going on a Lucky adventure with me. I hope you enjoyed the ride.

As you may know, reviews are SUPER helpful. They not only help potential readers make a choice, but they also help me win coveted spots on various advertising platforms.

So, if you would please, do me the favor of leaving a review at the outlet of your choice.

Read a short excerpt below

CHAPTER ONE

Two years ago, I'd married for love.

Little had I known I was marrying into a threesome.

Now my wannabe ex was dead, and everybody thought I'd done it.

Oh, they didn't come right out and say it. Please, this is *Dallas*, more Southern than Atlanta, where one would never consider saying such a thing *out loud*.

Apparently social decorum didn't extend to the newspaper. There I was, front and center in the Party Central section where gossip regularly did a hit-and-run on the truth. Today was no exception. I wadded the offending section and tossed it toward the can. It glanced off the rim.

As with everything in life lately, my aim was slightly off.

And now I was a *Making of a Murderer* story waiting to be told.

Hell, even the NFL thought I'd done it.

The letter arrived by courier this morning, the NFL logo prominent in the upper left-hand corner, my name typed out in bold, accusatory letters: Mrs. Austin Terry. They got that wrong. That Mrs. thing always irked me, as if upon marriage a woman disappeared, relegated to appendage status. I was born Brinda Rose, and that's who I'd always be—husband or no.

And husbands couldn't be counted on. Mine was cooling in a drawer at the medical examiner's office—not that he didn't deserve it.

But I'll get to that.

Apparently anger and loathing are considered unbecoming in a freshly minted widow.

Still reeling from the sea-change of the last twenty-four hours, I'd yet to open the letter. In fact, I'd yet to do anything. Paralyzed by my public fall from grace, I'd parked myself at the kitchen table and hadn't moved.

Besides, I knew what the NFL wanted. They wanted me out...bad. They'd have to stand in line.

As a lawyer, I'd told my husband a million times that he needed a will. But, at thirty and blinded by his own self-impor-tance, what husband listens to his wife?

So, with my husband's death, the huge Lone Oak Valley mansion, the fancy cars, the investments, the cash, and, worst of all, the majority interest in the North Texas Roughriders, the most storied NFL franchise and the darling of the football-crazed Dallas denizens—and an irritant to our crosstown rivals, the Cowboys—were all mine. Well, at least until they hauled me away in shackles, doomed to wear orange for the rest of my life.

As an investment advisor to the rich and famous, I knew what to do with the wealth. As a gal from New Jersey, I had no idea what to do with a football team.

This being Texas, where football was the dominant religion, the locals might look the other way when it came to most felonies. But mess with their *team?* Well, you better start running and not look back.

I'd love to run—in reality this place was proof of the fact versus fiction thing. That TV show set here back in the '80s that everyone thought was so over the top? Well, it didn't even scratch the surface. Problem was, until this little matter of a dead husband was cleared up, I'd been forbidden to go anywhere. So running was out.

Only one thing to do at this point...drink.

My former husband always kept several bottles of Dom Perignon properly chilled. Several bottles just might be enough.

Halfway through the first bottle, I felt the alcohol breeze snapping the flag of my courage. I stared down at the envelope resting against the vase of roses on the coffee table in front of the couch.

The game room was my favorite room—casual, warm, with a large fireplace that lit with the push of a button and ringed with windows that captured the backyard in all its manicured lushness. I'd wanted to add sparkling lights in the trees. My husband had suggested I kill the Jersey Girl part of me that thought tacky was a good idea. Such a great guy. The irony was he had been one in the beginning.

New Jersey and Manhattan were synonymous in Texas, lumped together in the term *Northerners,* which was always said with a sneer. Raised in one, educated in the other, I was doomed before I'd arrived.

There was a lot about the South I hadn't known. The biggest thing? When I married, I had disappeared.

For someone invisible, I sure was getting a lot of attention.

I took another slug of Champagne and stared at the letter. What was I going to do with a football team?

In a fit of courage, I grabbed the envelope, tore off one end, then shook out the single sheet inside. The careful wording showed the crafting of a lawyer. Nothing to sue them with, but everything to piss me off.

The gist of it: as a twenty-eight-year-old female, I didn't have the chops to hold my own in the cut-throat world of professional football.

Who were they kidding? I might not know football—unlike the other female owners, I hadn't lived and breathed football for decades at the elbow of my husband. But I had picked up some tips being the right-hand-man for Nolan Ponder, owner of the San Antonio, now Las Vegas Marauders.

And, as a Jersey girl to the core, I knew how to get down and dirty.

They'd given me ninety days to prove I could run the team, or I'd have to sell. Big of them. Could they do that? I hadn't a clue. One thing I did know: they'd gone fishing for tuna and hooked a Great White.

I tossed the letter in the fire then poured myself another flute of the good stuff. I raised my glass in a toast. "Game on, boys."

End of Sample
To continue reading, be sure to pick up 90 Days to Score at your favorite retailer.

The Kate Sawyer Medical Thriller Series

After Me (Book 1)

Deadfall (Book 2)

Other Novels

Deep Water (romantic suspense)

Crushed (women's fiction)

ABOUT THE AUTHOR

Deborah Coonts swears she was switched at birth. Coming from a family of homebodies, Deborah is the odd woman out, happiest with a passport, a high-limit credit card, her computer, and changing scenery outside her window. Goaded by an insatiable curiosity, she flies airplanes, rides motorcycles, travels the world, and pretends to be more of a badass than she probably is. Deborah is the author of the Lucky O'Toole Vegas Adventure series, a romantic mystery romp through Sin City. *Wanna Get Lucky?*, the first in the series, was a *New York Times* Notable Crime Novel and a double RITA™ Award Finalist. She has also penned the Kate Sawyer Medical Thriller series, the Brinda Rose Humorous Mystery series, as well as a couple of stand-alones. Although often on an adventure, you can always track her down at:

www.deborahcoonts.com
deborah@deborahcoonts.com

facebook.com/deborahcoonts
twitter.com/DeborahCoonts
instagram.com/deborahcoonts
pinterest.com/debcoonts
bookbub.com/authors/deborah-coonts
amazon.com/author/debcoonts
goodreads.com/DeborahCoonts

Manufactured by Amazon.ca
Bolton, ON

36987272R00199